AN INCARNATION OF SHADOW AND LIGHT

S.A. CHRISTIANSON

Character illustrations by Hester van Leusen
Cover design by S.A. Christianson
Font purchased from Adobe Stock

First Edition: November 2022

For Rutendo, who was there from the very beginning. Victoria, who kept me going, and Helen, who helped me realize what this book was supposed to be all along.

PART ONE
VERCHIÉL

Protect us, holy shadow and light

1

GABRIEL

Gabriel was a terrible liar.

Not in the sense that people immediately saw right through him. Rather, because he was unapologetically a repeat offender.

"Seven!"

People shouted as money changed hands. The dealer, much to Gabriel's delight, had announced his number. The heat of too many bodies crammed into one basement room was stifling. The air was a murky haze from musky perfumes mixed with thick clouds of tobacco. He inhaled a deep lungful of it, relishing the heaviness it left in his chest, a grin spreading across his face as he adjusted the well-worn mask over his eyes.

Given the Crimson Bat's reputation, many patrons wore masks at the betting tables, though some wore them simply for fashion. As a "living saint," Gabriel was one of the lucky few who got to care about both. His own mask was much like any other. It had once been a rich black but was now faded and grey, its soft velvet worn away in patches. Neither beautiful nor remarkable, save for the fact that the slits that normally revealed a person's eyes had been covered in thin layers of black organza.

Gabriel's opponent was a man who'd given a name so clearly fabricated on the spot that Gabriel hadn't bothered to remember it. Under his mask his pale skin was offset by the bright red in his cheeks from the wine.

Gabriel's heart sank when the city's clock tower rang out, the Grand Cathedral announcing the arrival of midnight. He knew well enough that he'd been absent for too long and Zoe would have started searching for him by now. He begrudgingly gathered his remaining coins.

A young woman with tawny skin in a bright silver dress looked between Gabriel and the man and rolled her eyes. "Is that it, Silvio?"

The man, who was apparently named Silvio, grinned. "I don't know, what does our friend have to say?"

A flimsy excuse was forming in his mind, but he pushed it away. It had been half a year since their former Incarnate had been lowered into the ground, and yet hardly a day went by when Gabriel wasn't surrounded by grim faces and funeral banners. The winter solstice celebrations tonight served only as a reminder of their absence. Gabriel could barely comprehend Verchiél's extravagant and drawn-out mourning practices. Citizens still dressed in partial black as if they had known them personally. It was ridiculous. If nobody else in this place was going to bother to let loose and move on with their lives, then he might as well pick up their slack.

Gabriel weighed the heavy pouch of coins in his hand, before he tossed the entire thing onto the table. Bursting with silver and gold, it drew the attention of more than one patron. He called out loud enough for the entire room to hear, "Last game. Triple or nothing."

The woman weighed the pouch, her many silver bracelets clinking softly with the motion, before grinning. "Deal him back in."

People crowded in closer, the air humming with renewed energy as the dealer shuffled the cards, hands moving in a blur. Malizia was as much a game of skill as it was of luck. Popular among both working class and nobility alike, a game could last anywhere from minutes to hours and was notorious for the many ways to win by cheating—if one was clever or inventive enough.

Gabriel picked up his playing piece, a jet-black horse's head, and set it upon the scarlet velvet of the table. He flipped three cards over from his pile, revealing a golden sun, a silver-clad knight atop a grey horse, and haloed Morven, Verchiél's Saint of Death, standing atop a mound of skulls.

People whistled or groaned as they placed their own bets along the sidelines. His opponent was flummoxed for the moment, but Gabriel only shrugged and picked up his glass of wine. "Your move."

Silvio sorted his cards with care. Gabriel grinned, and with a practised flick of his wrist, a figure appeared behind Silvio, timed discreetly enough with the jostling movements and noise of the crowd that nobody gave a second glance. Though if someone had, one might have noticed that they looked exactly like Gabriel—down to each individual freckle. The figure peered over the man's shoulder, observing which cards were clutched in his hand. Its eyes glinted darkly beneath its own mask.

By the secret glimpse through his magical double's eyes, Gabriel noted that he'd chosen blunt offence, playing with increasing fervour and drawing his most important cards first—including some he'd snuck into his hand. Silvio placed a spare quickly upon the table with an increasingly pleased expression. Likely trying to end the game early before Gabriel could gain any advantage.

But it was particularly difficult to trick a trickster.

Gabriel clapped his hands together as if deeply considering the cards before him, and in the crowd the illusion faded away like smoke. He concentrated on his useless hand of cards, the familiar sensation of his magic rose to his fingertips like frigid shadows, and as he shuffled through them with his long fingers, each of his old suits magically shifted into the ones he needed to gain the upperhand. Gabriel flicked his new card onto the table and Silvio's previously smug face fell as he watched the game suddenly turn back into Gabriel's favour. He laughed but Gabriel noticed the edge it carried. "A wise move…"

Gabriel shrugged, moving his next playing pieces—a silver gondola and a charcoal greyhound—to the centre of the table. "Must be luck."

The dealer shuffled the cards, and waited for the two men to pick their final draw. Silvio snatched his up first and flipped it over swiftly, revealing the baying hound, chained with a golden collar.

"Six," he called to the room with a smirk.

Gabriel looked at the card he'd drawn—a four— and he kept his face carefully blank as he concentrated on the shadowed magic at the centre of his being and the weeping saint turned into a silver half moon. Pleased with his impromptu improvement, Gabriel flipped it gracefully between his fingers. "Seven."

The roar from the crowd was deafening. The man slammed his fist on the table, and the meticulously stacked piles of playing pieces shook, threatening to topple over.

"You're cheating!"

The fake card fluttered from Gabriel's grip as he raised his hands in a gesture of innocence. Even as his blood hummed at the prospect of a good show.

"I'm terribly sorry, kind sir, but I assure you, I've done

nothing of the sort."

Silvio shoved Gabriel and pain shot through his side as he collided with the corner of the table. This drew the attention of most of the room. Normally Gabriel would never sink so low as to fist fight— that was far too much effort. Usually he would have shrugged it off, given a laugh and bought everyone another drink as a balm to whatever personal slight they claimed against him.

Now he shoved him back so that he stumbled.

Silvio spat back at Gabriel, his words slurred, "You want to know what I think?"

"Not particularly. But I'm sure I'm about to find out—"

A large fist smashed into Gabriel's face. He reeled backward, the air knocked from his lungs as he clawed at the table to steady himself.

Gabriel squeezed his eyes shut, irked. Bringing a hand to his face, he felt his jaw was tender— though through some miracle, not broken. It would be bruised, but he didn't care about any of that. The mask was still in place, and that was all that mattered.

He got shakily to his feet. More people had gathered now, hungry for a fight. The establishment owners eyed him darkly from across the room. The business that happened under their roof didn't concern them unless their steady flow of money was directly involved, and as one of the bouncers made his way across the crowd, their intent was clear. Gabriel was impressed. Most patrons managed to get more than one punch in before they were tossed out.

Silvio snarled at Gabriel, "I should choke the life out of you!"

"Funny"—Gabriel grinned—"that's exactly what your father said to me last night."

Gabriel expected another punch. Or for something to be

thrown at him. Instead Silvio lurched forward and seized him by his coat's collar, lifting him off the ground entirely. He moved to wrap a large hand around his throat.

He didn't get that far.

The point of Gabriel's knife was at the man's throat. Silvio froze, though he didn't release Gabriel. The entire room was now holding its breath.

"Would you be so kind as to release me?" Gabriel asked.

Silvio's frown deepened. "You wouldn't."

Gabriel pressed the blade's edge against his skin until it threatened to break. "If we both continue this way, at least one of us will regret it when he sobers up."

The bouncer pushed his way through the crowd, voice booming in a command, "That's it! Put him down and get out."

Gabriel beamed triumphantly, though his feet were still a good few inches from the ground. "Ha! See? I told you—"

"You too."

Gabriel was about to object when Silvio tightened his grip and left him wheezing for air. Gabriel coughed. "You heard him, put me down." Silvio's grip slackened but he didn't let him go, staring closely at his face. "Clearly, thinking isn't your strong suit," Gabriel said. "Why don't I order you another drink and we'll part ways as unlikely friends?"

"Your face, I've seen you somewhere before."

A flicker of irritation swept through Gabriel. The biggest problem with acting around others was that other people might not react in the ways which he'd been intending.

Gabriel laughed, feigning disinterest. "Why, of course you have! You've been gazing all night at my beautiful countenance. Many say I've been blessed with the godlike figure of a marble statue with a voice like the soothing tones of an ensemble of night-ingales—"

"No." He tightened his grip. "I've seen you before. I know I have."

Silvio ripped the mask away before Gabriel could stop him. When he caught sight of Gabriel's face he froze. The fabric slipped uselessly from Silvio's fingers and Gabriel snatched it away before it could reach the wine-soaked floor. But the damage had already been done. The ruddy complexion of Silvio's face blanched, his jaw gaped, and he struggled for words, opening and closing his mouth like a gasping fish. He released Gabriel as if he had been scorched, dropping his gaze to the floor as he spoke in a tone far too close to reverence for Gabriel's liking.

"Son of the Moon."

Normally Gabriel relished attention. It was certainly one of his highest priorities. But this was different. Unwanted, though not entirely unwarranted, as Gabriel knew what they all saw.

An Incarnate.

One of the few people in the world gifted with magic. Or rather, magic allotted for a certain time. It was passed entirely ran-domly from one stranger to another upon the death of the previous Incarnate. It went to the old and the young, the healthy and the sick, the good and the bad. There was no way of telling who might be chosen next. To some it was the highest blessing, to others a curse. But there was no control over who received it.

The bouncer quietly backed away, fearful that Gabriel might strike him down on the spot. Silvio still hadn't looked back at Gabriel. He appeared ridiculous with his head bowed, his large frame towering over Gabriel. He could have crushed Gabriel into dust if he'd had half a mind to. But there he stood, trying to make himself appear smaller. Gabriel wanted to throttle him. For ripping his disguise away certainly— but even more so for believing that he was worth an ounce of anyone's piety.

"I apologise, I never would have—"

Gabriel waved a hand as if this were a simple misunderstanding. He spoke in a polite tone, though his voice sounded clipped and on edge. The voice he hated but found himself using more and more. "No. It's fine. After all, it was my fault."

He sheathed the dagger and stuffed the mask into his coat pocket in hurried motions. If it were the day, his appearance wouldn't have mattered—at least not so much. They might have still recognized him, but not like this. At night it was a different matter entirely. When the sky was still black, so were his eyes.

Entirely ink black, the dim light from the room reflected in sharp crescents like sickles across them, mirroring the current phase of the moon of the fading night outside. "Like beautiful moons" as so many had told him before, trying for flattery, praising themselves for this clever comparison to his title. Acting as if he hadn't heard the exact same thing for years on end. Until now the only response he gave was to nod, smile placidly and let their words pass over him. "Like a reaper's scythes—the eyes of death itself," a drunk noble had told him once. Gabriel had to give him credit for being so bold, but he knew the true reason for any compliments wasn't from any appreciation or admiration of beauty. Instead it was because he was entirely different from what everyone else was, and people found him endlessly fascinating as much as they feared him.

Trying his best to put everyone at ease, he offered the same smile he'd used countless times before. Only now it felt strained and unnatural, pulled taut to the point of breaking.

He dusted himself off, and headed for the front doors, as he should have done hours ago. People parted around Gabriel, the voices and music which had previously made the area deafening were now reduced to nothing more than the rustling of clothes and exchanged whispers. His footsteps were magnified as they echoed across the room.

He thought he was going to escape without another incident when an anxious voice called out behind him, "Son of the Moon?"

He managed a tight-lipped smile as he turned toward the source of the voice. "Yes?"

The dealer stood with arms full of the coin pouches which Gabriel had so carelessly tossed upon the game tables all night. "Your winnings."

Gabriel shrugged. "The gentleman may have them. I was cheating after all."

The dealer shook his head and went as if to press the pouches back into Gabriel's grasp, but he shoved his hands into his pockets before he could. "I appreciate your generosity. However, I have no need for it."

"But—"

Gabriel spun on his heel and continued toward the stairs before they could try to persuade him, calling over his shoulder, "Split it among yourselves. Think of it as a gift."

Gabriel made his way through the front doors; the night was still young and he was grateful for it. After all, the end of the night also meant the loss of his magic until the sun set again, and after that unfortunate display he was determined to find some sort of indulgent fun someplace else to make up for the loss.

He looked at the obsidian and golden spires of the palace in the near distance. Zoe was expecting him. He should return.

Should being the operative word.

His gaze was drawn back to the crowded streets overflowing with celebrations. The people were beautiful and the alcohol was plenty; who was to say that he couldn't have a bit more fun before getting back to business as usual? It was the winter solstice after all, a night totally dedicated to him, so to not enjoy himself would be a travesty—no, a crime, in and of itself.

He readjusted his mask, dusted off his jacket and plunged back into the crowded streets, intending to soak up every bit of pleasure he could get his hands on before the night was over.

2
ZOE

Zoe shifted uncomfortably in the rigid formalwear of an Incarnate Sun—a gaudy tunic made of stiff black and golden silk. It clung to her curves in a way that drove her mad, though she managed nothing less than the most gracious of smiles as she made insufferable small talk with the endless groups of visiting ambassadors. The ascension of Verchiél Incarnate was a momentous occasion and as such people had come from across the Isles and beyond to wish her and Gabriel good fortune and establish alliances.

Or at least that was what they were supposed to be doing.

"Verchiél thanks you for your generosity," Zoe said, the words feeling like a meaningless routine after repeating them all night. "From both the Sun and Moon."

The silver throne sat glaringly empty beside her, as it had for several hours now, throughout all of the alliance negotiations she and Gabriel had been supposed to go through together, and here she still was doing all the work, like usual.

Both of the Sakai delegates nodded, a man and a woman both dressed in black silks not unlike her own, though where hers was covered in a tacky amount of gold, theirs were subtly embroidered with elegant patterns of cranes or blossoms.

Zoe passed their gift with careful hands to Alfio, who put it with the rest of the night's offerings. It was a beautiful bouquet of crystal flowers. If only they were real instead; she'd kill to be in Sakai during a flower-viewing ceremony in the springtime.

Dabria, who had little patience for such formal events, now faced the delegates and spoke bluntly. "Thanks for coming."

The delegates exchanged a bewildered look before formal politeness won out and they took their leave to join the rest of the celebrations.

Zoe cringed. "Dabria…"

"The sooner we get through the political niceties, the better," Dabria said. "All we have left is Bjordal, right?"

"We don't have any Bjordal guests," Zoe said.

Bjordal. The third and northernmost country in the Isles. It was a land of ice and snow and unmoving ideals, and contact went about as well as shoving a note into a bottle and tossing it into the raging ocean.

King Asbjorn had always been a stubborn man, but after the disappearance of his only son, Niklas, he'd all but cut himself off from the rest of the Isles entirely. He had already held nothing short of a hatred for Incarnate, but since Enzo and Aria had passed a tension had only grown between the nations. A bright red envelope stamped with the sigil of a bear and birch trees had appeared within the palace shortly after the death of the Verchiél royal family, containing a brief and formal message of condolences and thinly veiled threats about Zoe's and Gabriel's legitimacy to take any seat of power.

"We don't even have one Bjordal ally?" Dabria asked. "But they're the biggest country in the Isles."

"Don't remind me," Zoe said, rubbing her temples.

Alfio leaned forward and spoke only loud enough for them to hear. "You're doing wonderfully, Daughter of the Sun. I'm sure our former Incarnate, heavens rest their souls, would be proud of you."

She didn't tell him that she didn't want any of this, but somebody needed to properly organise Verchiél. It would be embarrassing to shirk these duties when she knew she was perfectly capable of rising to the task. After all, who else would do it if she didn't? Enzo and Aria were gone, and heavens knew Gabriel was as chaotic as he was unreliable. Meanwhile the city officials were too overjoyed at the ascension of new Incarnate to consider whether or not it was even a position they wanted to begin with. Everything was a grand mess, she considered, but at least there was plenty of champagne.

"Who do we have left?" Zoe asked.

Alfio checked his clipboard, which was overflowing with papers and notes. "According to schedule, just the Heathland councillors now, ma'am."

Zoe's stomach sank. Gabriel had promised that he was going to deal with them. Not only did he have the most knowledge of the country, but he had been born and raised there before arriving in Verchiél.

After all, she'd already met the delegates from Uzoma, a wealthy nation just south of Verchiél; they shared her same deep brown skin rather than the bronze tan of the Verchiél. She'd never set foot in the country—her grandfather immigrated to Verchiél many decades ago—but she still spoke the language and they'd treated her as their countrywoman as much as anyone else.

Zoe watched a grey-clad man approach and repressed a groan. Councillor Royle. Why couldn't it have been one of the other councillors? He was constantly in a miserable mood, which would make this all the more difficult. She managed a smile that was, if anything, welcoming, and spoke in rusty Heathall. "Welkom en goedae groeten."

She'd never cared for the briskness of the language, or the industrialization of the country. Gabriel had always been the one to translate for her.

Royle spoke in Verchiél. "Good evening, Daughter of the Sun." He looked at the empty silver throne beside her. "Where's your compatriot? I thought this night was specifically to celebrate the winter solstice?"

Undoubtedly dicking off somewhere...or someone.

Zoe's smile stretched so much that her cheeks hurt. "I'm afraid he's still preparing for the event. He does love to be fashionably late."

Royle didn't return the smile. "Perhaps it's better that I have a moment to speak privately with you."

Zoe didn't like where this was headed.

"Your compatriots' latest correspondences to Grislow's council, in particular to myself, have been...troubling to say the least," Royle began. "I don't wish to ruin the good cheer of your evening, so I'll spare you the unpleasant details. But do tell him that if he wants Verchiél to keep a safe standing with Heathland, that he should watch his steps carefully for the future." Royle lowered his voice. "He's grown bold and the council doesn't like bold."

"Bold?" Zoe asked, at a loss for graceful answers after hours of talking.

"Indeed. His correspondences have bordered from the ill-tempered rantings of an unhinged youth to outright illegal acts."

"Surely there must be some sort of misunderstanding? I'm certain he wouldn't have sent something so inappropriate to a member of the council—"

Royle brandished a letter; she recognized it as an official correspondence, as it had been stamped and sealed with the black crescent moon and golden sun of Verchiél. Zoe took the letter, reading through the eccentric, looping scrawl which she knew immediately was Gabriel's handwriting. Her heart sank with each word she read.

She met Royle's eyes. "He blackmailed you?"

"Quite," Royle replied simply.

Dabria read the letter over her shoulder. "Did you really ask your mistress to drizzle you in honey butter?"

Zoe tensed, mortified. Royle himself looked shocked, and even poor Alfio couldn't pretend that he hadn't heard her as his pale face was now tinged with bright scarlet.

Royle snatched the letter back before shoving it unceremoniously into his jacket pocket. "These are nothing but blatant lies crafted to smear my upstanding public image!"

"That's too bad," Dabria said. "I was curious to know if it was good for your skin or there was a dining element to it—"

"As the Sun of Verchiél," Zoe quickly cut across before Dabria could add anything else, "I will personally look into this matter myself in order to assure that both of our nations are being treated with the same levels of dignity and respect—" She emphasised the word, looking at Dabria, who only shrugged. "That any proper alliance requires."

Royle stood a little taller. "Let us hope that's the truth. Either way, know that Grislow, and more importantly Heathland, is keeping a very close eye on you and your compatriot."

Zoe managed a smile. "I'll let him know, Councillor Royle."

He inclined his head sharply. "Good evening, Daughter of the Sun."

"Dankt voor her komen!" Dabria called cheerfully after him.

"Not now, Dabria," Alfio whispered.

"What? I'm just thanking our guests."

Zoe drew in a deep breath, attempting to calm herself as any leader should. The entire relations of the three nations in the Isles couldn't be that bad, could it? Bjordal hated them so much that they refused to attend the gathering. Heathland, an already finicky nation to negotiate with unless profit was involved, was now openly hostile after being blackmailed. Meanwhile Verchiél was too happy with the ascension of Incarnate to care either way…

Fuck.

Maybe I should have just joined Gabriel tonight after all.

Zoe waited until Royle was far enough away before she ushered Dabria and Alfio over. "Where's Gabriel? And before you say anything I know he pays you two off."

Alfio immediately protested but Dabria only spoke in a bored voice. "He paid me."

"Why would he trust me?" Alfio asked.

"Because you don't have a backbone!" Dabria snapped.

"Where is he?" Zoe asked.

"He said he was going to the Golden Magnolia."

Zoe bit back a very un-rulerly curse word.

She was going to throttle him. The Golden Magnolia, the most famous pleasure house in the city. Personally she didn't give a damn what, or who, Gabriel did in his free time, but right now he was supposed to be here, helping her navigate the tiresome etiquette of the court, not trying to seduce any number of the staff who, unfathomably, were always delighted to see him.

"I can't be seen there tonight," Zoe whispered. "It'll start a scandal."

Dabria checked her pocket watch. "I wouldn't worry about that, he should be at the Crimson Bat by now."

Zoe wasn't able to stop her words this time.

"That little bitch!"

A pleasure house *and* an illegal gambling den? On the most important night of their new lives? Risking all of their alliances and peace talks they'd spent months organising?

Forget throttle. She was going to push him down the stairs, then set him on fire and grow a lovely garden out of his remains where she could visit him at any time and lecture him about the intricacies of responsibility and proper time management.

Zoe took the golden circlet from her curls and shoved it into Dabria's hands. "Hold this."

"Wait—" She stared after her. "Where are you going?"

"To get our man of the hour."

Even with the entire city celebrating, it was pathetically easy to find Gabriel.

In lieu of neither a pleasure house, raging party nor gambling den to be found, he'd instead opted for one of the many street front bars which had popped up specifically for the winter solstice celebrations. Sitting at a table overflowing with drinks, he was squeezed between a couple who leaned close enough to him to immediately tell Zoe that they were on more than just friendly terms.

"—well, the more the merrier!" Gabriel said cheerfully. "I

know the perfect place where we can spend the evening—"

"Gabriel?" Zoe asked. "What are you doing?"

The trio turned to her, variations of confusion quickly giving way to shock on the couple's part, and more predictably, annoyance on Gabriel's as he gave her a tight smile.

"Sorry, my dear, but we're rather busy here."

Zoe recognized the attempt to brush her off; perhaps he thought himself unrecognisable, but beneath the shoddy disguise he was dressed in the finery of an Incarnate Moon. He played the part well, he looked it too: Black hair drastically offset by ghostly pale skin. Slender to the point of being delicate. He looked like a shadow tailored to a fine edge. While she couldn't care less about vanity, he'd always possessed a tendency for preening in the looking glass.

But unlike him, she wasn't wearing a mask, and it took only a mere second for the couple to recognize her.

"Daughter of the Sun!" The man leapt out of his chair and straightened so quickly it was nearly comical, offering her a bow. "We apologise for not offering you a proper greeting immediately."

"Would you care for a seat?" the woman asked, pushing her chair toward Zoe.

"No thanks." Zoe grabbed Gabriel's arm and pulled him along with her. "I'm just here to collect him."

"Collect me?" Gabriel asked. "What am I, rubbish?"

"Do you really want me to answer that?" Zoe countered.

Gabriel strained against her grip, and in a last-ditch effort to appeal to the couple he threw a smile over his shoulder. "I'll see you both later—"

"Don't worry," Zoe reassured them. "You won't."

Gabriel watched the couple hurry down the street, still casting terrified looks back at them. "Fuck." Gabriel wrenched his arm out of her grasp. "Zoe, I was so close. I had a very specific plan laid out—" He listed off on his fingers. "Start the day drunk. End the day drunk. Preferably with somebody in my bed—and I nearly had two people back there! It would have been perfect—"

"What would have been perfect," Zoe explained what little patience she had manifested leaving her, "is if you'd actually helped me with the alliance negotiations."

"Don't be ridiculous. I wasn't even gone for that long."

"Three hours, Gabriel. *Three*. In which I had a very angry Grislow councillor on my hands after Dabria announced his sex life to the entire audience chamber."

"Did she really?" Gabriel's interest was piqued, a smile creeping across his narrow face. "Now I'm actually sorry to have missed it."

"Is all this a game to you? Blackmail? Seriously?"

"Of course not! Look, you call it blackmail, I call it my contribution in giving us more leverage with political negotiations."

Zoe wanted to finish the argument, but a considerable number of people had started to gather around them. Many watched with curious eyes at the commotion, while recognition became apparent in many of their faces.

Zoe seized Gabriel's arm and pulled him along before he could become distracted by anything else. Normally Zoe would have taken her time, but whenever she or Gabriel were recognized in the midst of the public it made for slow going. People always begged for the attention of an Incarnate, when even a glance of gold or black eyes was considered a blessing. Usually Zoe didn't mind; she craved any news of a world existing outside of the palace. Thousands of citizens all with individually messy and beautiful lives. Envy stirred in her gut at the thought of it.

As she reached the end of the street, she waved to the palace boatman she'd left at the gondola, the main mode of transportation as the old part of the city had been built upon the water. She stepped into the gondola with ease, and, as was their custom, offered Gabriel a hand, which he clung to with a death-like grip. Even these short voyages across calm waters were nearly too much for him to bear, a fear he'd possessed since they were children.

Now that she had a moment to rest and Gabriel was subdued upon the water, she began to talk in earnest. "The ambassadors were waiting for you in the alliance negotiations, that was before you decided to visit the local gambling halls and pleasure houses."

He tilted his head as if confused by her words. "Can't a man enjoy a pleasant outing to his usual haunts?"

"In a time of mourning?"

"We've been mourning for six months! As much as I adore wearing black, there needs to be a time limit to these things."

"Not to mention the exuberant allowance you were never supposed to have in the first place is cut off. No more wasteful expenses."

"But, it was necessary."

"For who?"

"For me, of course. I've been dying of boredom, and we don't need another funeral, do we?"

"Might I remind you that this evening was supposed to be for making political alliances, not celebrating until you're intoxicated?"

The atmosphere around her didn't exactly aid her argument.

Though it was the middle of the night, the entire city was packed to the point of bursting with winter solstice revellers, both citizens and visitors from across the Isles and beyond. Music drifted from street corners and through open windows while groups and couples shared the gondolas that floated lazily across the dark waters. Street carts lined every avenue, overflowing with trinkets and souvenirs made especially for the occasion: ribbons of silver and black silk, banners with phases of the moon and pastries shaped like moons and stars. Zoe had never cared for crowds, let alone parties, but she had to admit the change in atmosphere was welcome.

Gabriel waved his hand in dismissal. "Does it really matter? Once I'm king I'll be a perfectly normal person again, not an infallible 'living saint' as they so love to call us."

"So you want all the power with none of the responsibility?"

He looked at her strangely. "You're just realising this?"

"You're nearly thirty, Gabe. Aren't you getting a little old for this?"

He was aghast. "I'm twenty-six! I still have plenty of time for fun. As do you."

Though he was four years her senior, he'd always felt less like a mentor and more like a younger brother to shepherd. She knew for a fact he didn't care about ruling so much as revelry, but that didn't mean she was going to let him make her look bad by association.

"What's the matter, honeybee?"

Her childhood nickname, something she wasn't going to allow him to use to placate her.

"Other than the fact that you left me to handle all the negotiations?" she said, staring determinedly out at the water. "Or that I had to drag your ass back myself?"

"No. You're upset about something and for once it's not just me." A beat of silence passed between them before Gabriel spoke. "No Bjordal representatives I take it?"

Zoe tensed, for as selfish as he was he'd always had a particular talent for picking out exactly what was bothering her.

Zoe shrugged. "We were supposed to have some Bjordal nobility, but it turned out that someone was impersonating King Asbjorn's late son."

It was a sore point for any Bjordal citizen, and a source of juicy gossip for everyone else. The story went that Niklas had perished while hunting in the vast wilds of Bjordal, right before he was supposed to take his father's place as ruler once he reached the age of twenty, as all Bjordal monarchs did, for youthful strength was valued in a ruler. There were rumours, of course, about the convenient timing of his disappearance, but they were swiftly crushed by Asbjorn, who remained stubbornly on Bjordal's throne, though he was now nearly in his sixties.

Gabriel was unbothered. "At least it would have livened up the mood."

"Seriously?"

"Missing heirs? Family drama? It would have made for a bit of fun."

"Is all you want in life petty drama?"

Gabriel considered this."Well, there's also money, sex and power, but I'll settle for petty drama when I can get it."

"I would have thought that you'd gotten enough of all three of those tonight."

"You should know that I'm insatiable."

"Regardless," Zoe changed the subject, "King Asbjorn sent

word, and no possible alliance with Bjordal will be considered."

"They're an absolute bore anyways," Gabriel dismissed her. "Honestly, what are we gaining and what are we losing?"

An ally. One we both very much need right now, Zoe thought to herself.

The gondola had finally docked at the streets, and Gabriel hastily clambered out and Zoe followed back to the palace gates. The area was long since crowded with dozens of visitors: dignitaries, nobles and ambassadors, all who had come to witness the historic crowning to take place tonight.

Among the crowd, Zoe watched two figures in guards' uniform rush toward them.

"Dabria? Alfio—"

"Son of the Moon! Daughter of the Sun." Alfio threw himself in a bow so low he nearly fell to the ground.

Dabria scoffed. "Up, idiot! She doesn't want to see you grovelling."

"I do," Gabriel added.

Dabria narrowed her gaze on Gabriel, seizing his arm. "You were supposed to be back an hour ago."

Gabriel beamed. "I missed you too, darling."

"I can't say the same."

Among Gabriel and Dabria's bickering Alfio sidled closer to her, speaking in the same hushed tone. "Daughter of the Sun? Everyone's been waiting for the coronation. It's time."

Despite herself, nervousness stirred in her gut; this was truly a moment of no return.

Zoe exchanged a look with Gabriel, and sensing her hesitation, he gave her shoulders a reassuring squeeze. "Don't look so stressed, darling. We're going to be magnificent."

3

GABRIEL

The ballroom exploded with silver and gold confetti.

The lights had been dimmed, though the looming crystal chandelier cast the entire space with a silver glow, reflecting off the glass walls and ceiling, which allowed a view of the night sky beyond it.

People wore gowns made from material as thin as gossamer while others had replicas of armour made over their dresses. Some in black suits tailored so finely that they looked sharp enough to cut oneself against. Two individuals sat lazily upon one of the smaller chandeliers, pouring champagne upon those who held their glasses up to them, though whether that was their designated job, or they were simply guests who wanted a bird's-eye view of the festivities, was unclear to Gabriel.

Zoe observed the chaos. "Is this what you've been doing all these months instead of your paperwork?"

It was entirely different from the previous solstice celebrations. No longer rigid or formal. But that had been exactly what he'd wanted. Beautiful mayhem. At least ushering in a new era would be far easier when everyone was in good spirits and roaring drunk. He grabbed two champagne flutes from a passing tray. "I thought everybody could use some celebration after so much mourning."

Zoe looked around the room, disappointment clear across her face from what, or who, she didn't see there. "I wish Alessi were here, they'd love this."

He grinned at the mention of Alessi, her oldest friend. Gabriel hadn't seen them in many months. Zoe invited them to the party tonight, but she never heard anything back. Zoe had been devastated. She didn't talk about it much, but he still saw it in the way her face fell, and she grew quiet at the mention of them. He handed her a fresh champagne glass with a smile, relieved to see that she returned it as they clinked glasses.

"Here's to an unforgettable night for the both of us."

Gabriel threw back the drink, barely registering the bubbly taste before the empty glass was taken and a fresh one placed in his hands. A part of him knew he should pace himself but he just couldn't help it. After all, tonight was special. After the coronation no longer would he be a Verchiél Incarnate, a so-called "living saint" or prized possession to be put on display. He'd be a king. More importantly, he'd finally be properly in control of his own life. Sure there would be tedious aspects to the position as well, but it was a small price to pay for finally having what he truly deserved.

As he and Zoe walked up the stairs to the raised dais, the crowd sensed that they were about to begin speaking. Conversations died away, and everyone's eyes turned their way. He raised his hands and his voice as he addressed the room. "Tonight is a momentous occasion. Though we are all mournful, as this is our first solstice celebration without our dear Incarnate, King Enzo and Queen Aria."

He turned to Zoe as she next spoke. "It is fitting that tonight is a celebration of the return of warmth and sunlit days. Celebrate and remember them."

People nodded solemnly, raising their glasses, murmuring kind words or prayers. After an appropriate amount of time Gabriel spoke up again. "In more immediate matters, concerning the rulership of Verchiél." People hushed at that. The air thickened with tension, practically crackling like lightning with growing excitement. The corner of his lips quirked as he reined in a smile. He was rather sorry to deny them any drama. "There will be no declaration of a challenge. We have both decided to divide the responsibilities of rulership equally between us."

"We want to keep the peace to better serve Verchiél and her people," Zoe finished.

Many managed to smile and clap politely. Gabriel raised his hands to start a memorable speech just as a voice spoke up.

"Son of the Moon, Daughter of the Sun?"

Gabriel paused, his glass half raised, his gaze finding its way to the guard— neither Dabria nor Alfio—who addressed them.

"Yes?" Gabriel asked.

"There's someone who would like to meet you."

Gabriel made sure to put on a smile for the crowds who watched them closely at the sudden interruption. "We're in the middle of something."

"He won't wait," the guard said.

A flicker of irritation coursed through Gabriel. "Well, you can tell your guest that all of the Verchiél nobility were supposed to make their requests earlier than tonight for a meeting."

"He's not from Verchiél."

"Fine. Wherever he's from—"

"He's a representative from Bjordal."

Gabriel and Zoe exchanged a bewildered glance. There

weren't supposed to be any Bjordal representatives tonight.

"Very well," Gabriel agreed. "Let's meet our special guest."

People followed the guards' movements with their eyes, clearly trying to discern what exchange had just taken place. Gabriel addressed the crowd. "Apologies for the delay, we have an unexpected guest arriving."

People were intrigued, and whispers began to trickle amid the room. Gabriel spoke as soon as the guard was out of earshot. "Something's wrong."

"Weren't you the one who was complaining about a lack of excitement earlier?" Zoe whispered back, looking more hopeful than worried as he felt. "Besides, this is probably the nobility we were supposed to meet earlier."

"Or perhaps they've sent someone to murder us before we're crowned," Gabriel murmured, his fingers straying toward the hidden blade under his sleeve.

After another few moments of waiting, the crowd parted, making room for a large figure in a mask not unlike Gabriel's own, dressed in a rich silver and royal blue mantle. People hushed as their eyes fell upon him, giving a wide berth. Gabriel didn't blame them; he was easily the tallest person he'd ever seen, towering far above everybody in the room. Gabriel decided that he must be in his early thirties, with pale skin and shockingly bright auburn hair that grazed his shoulders.

The masked man stopped at the foot of the dais and bowed stiffly. "Son of the Moon. Daughter of the Sun."

Gabriel was surprised. His voice was quieter than he'd anticipated, with the roughened edge of a Bjordal accent. He expected a booming noise to come from his huge frame, but he appeared to be overly conscious of his presence, as if he were trying extremely hard to take up as little space as possible. Which wasn't working at all, as everyone's eyes were fixated upon him.

Zoe inclined her head politely, and Gabriel gave the man a beaming smile and bowed gracefully. *Intruder or not, that doesn't mean I have to lose my manners.* "It is truly a blessed occasion to be graced with the company of not only such a distinguished visitor but also such a striking individual as well."

The man took a quiet breath. He was silent for so long that Gabriel wondered if he wasn't going to answer, when he suddenly met their gaze. "My name is Niklas Osenson Askeland, first born child of Asbjorn Osenson. King of the northernmost lands, and rightful ruler of the Bjordal throne."

The entire room erupted into shocked gasps and utterances of disbelief. Zoe's hand clasped tightly over her mouth. Gabriel grinned wickedly. *Perhaps this whole ruling business is going to be a little less boring than I thought.*

Zoe raised a hand and gradually the room grew silent once more, though now it was tense and humming, like a hive of agitated bees. A thread of barely contained skepticism ran through her voice as she next spoke. "Prince Niklas?"

"You don't believe me," he said.

It was a statement, not a question. Zoe smiled kindly. "I'm sure you can understand our doubt. You've been rumoured to have been deceased for…"

"Ten years," Niklas replied.

"Exactly. And what proof have you brought with you to back such a statement?" she asked.

Niklas tossed a piece of silver toward them, and Gabriel barely caught it with fumbling fingers. It was a ring, old and worn, with a familiar crest upon it: intertwined birch trees and a bear with snarling jaws and claws raised. The crest of the Bjordal royal family. Zoe peeked over Gabriel's shoulder as she took the ring from him, scrutinising it closely.

Gabriel shrugged, feigning disinterest. "You could have gotten this anywhere."

Zoe cleared her throat and held the ring out where it was taken back to Niklas by a servant. "Prince Niklas, we appreciate the contact you've established, but wouldn't it be better if you were doing all of this in Bjordal? Surely your father wishes to hear from you."

A tremor ran through Niklas so slight that if Gabriel hadn't been watching him closely, he would have missed it. "My titles are not why I have come to call upon you."

"Then might we ask why you're here?"

"Because I'm the same as you."

Gabriel and Zoe exchanged a glance. The entire room collectively froze as Niklas untied the ribbons holding his mask in place, and as it fell away from his face, someone in the crowd screamed.

His eyes were pitch black. A sharp curving light like half moons flashed across them when he turned his face toward them. The same as an Incarnate Moon's eyes—*My eyes*, Gabriel realised.

The atmosphere within the room immediately changed. Guards had to hold people back as they began shouting among themselves. It had been years since anyone had heard of any other Incarnate. It had always been just him and Zoe. But now, there was another like them.

Like me.

Gabriel frowned. He had always been the only person called "Son of the Moon" ; he had never cared for the piety of others, but he had always loved attention. And now it had shifted; people's eyes instead went to Niklas, shouting out his title to him.

Gabriel looked at Zoe. She still hadn't moved, watching the madness play out before them in silence. Gabriel wondered how many Incarnate were left, and if there was anyone else like Zoe.

Niklas watched them calmly through the chaos. Waiting for an answer. Gabriel strode forward, raising his arms wide. "Now this is a surprise indeed."

Zoe put a hand out and stopped him before he could move any closer, her face a mask of suspicion, eyes focused only upon Niklas. She chose her words carefully, like treading over broken glass. "Moon of Bjordal, consider yourself welcome to stay as our honoured guest this evening."

Niklas laughed quietly. "I have not come for idle pleasant-ries or short visits."

Gabriel stilled, and Zoe's fingers tightened upon his sleeve. Niklas announced clearly enough for the entire room to hear,

"I have come for Verchiél's rulership."

Like fucking hell he had! Anger, swift and sudden, burned in Gabriel's gut. He hadn't dragged himself out of the filth and humiliation of his former life, hadn't spent the past thirteen years under Verchiél's former monarchs making tedious appearances at the cathedrals and leading useless sermons for someone to now take everything away from him. Niklas had no right. He was a stranger—worse, a stranger from Bjordal.

If the reaction from the crowd before had been loud, this was deafening.

People screamed, some in excitement, others full of rage as they argued among themselves or yelled indiscernible words toward the three at the centre of attention. Whichever way one looked at it, it was all chaos.

"We've already decided that no challenge will take place," Zoe called back to Niklas.

"Have you bothered to ask them what they want?" Niklas gestured to the crowd around them.

The room grew quieter as many strained to catch their words. Their eyes lingered upon Niklas, who broke off a shard from a nearby ice sculpture. "If it makes matters simpler, I will gladly allow you both to fight me, since this is so unexpected." He pointed with the jagged ice. "But walk away now and we'll have a problem. An unaddressed challenge means forfeit, does it not?"

"How do we know you're not some sort of spy that's come to start a war?" Zoe asked.

He looked at her pitifully. "And make a fool of myself in front of the entire nation?"

Not taking his eyes from them, he tossed the ice into the air. Barely had it shattered on the floor before he shot his arm upward, ice swiftly erupting from the place it hit, covering the floor in a span of seconds. People screamed and ran out of the way, some ripping their clothing in their haste to flee. Another fluid twist of his fingers and the ice shifted and reformed, swirling until it was nothing but a fine mist covering everything in a layer of frost as it drifted across the chamber.

Gabriel's breath plumed in the chilled air. Specific powers varied for each Incarnate, but having known only himself and Zoe, he'd never fully experienced its extent. He'd never been able to influence anything but shadows, illusions and tricks of the mind. Any accounts of Bjordal Incarnate were hazy at best. Though if Niklas had spent his entire life in that freezing land perhaps it wasn't such a surprise that he could influence ice.

Niklas spread his arms wide as he addressed the entire room. "I have travelled from the very heart of Bjordal at great danger to myself to reach this place. My country abandoned me and so I have abandoned it. I was in hiding for a decade because I would have been murdered if discovered." Niklas turned back to them. "And what have either of you done other than spend the palace's coin for your own fleeting pastimes?" Gabriel caught curious glimpses cast their way, and Niklas continued, encouraged by the shifting mood. "Protectors of the realm and its people? And yet you both thrive while your royal charges are buried below you." He stopped pacing and stood before them. "That's strange, isn't it?"

"That is enough," Zoe said. Her eyes burned, though not a trace of gold lingered in them this late in the night. "You come into our home and insult us?"

"Or have I spoken the truth you are determined to ignore?" Niklas countered.

She glared, taking a deep breath. Niklas smiled in return. "Not only was I raised to rule, I've had to fight for what I was given."

"If you're such a great ruler, then why are you here instead of Bjordal?" Gabriel snapped.

"You know my country's stance on our kind. My people won't accept me as a king, let alone as a citizen. Why would I let myself fade away in the snow and ice? To be maimed and killed at the hands of my father's Bjornvangar or sacrificed by cultists, when I can do so much better than either of you here?"

Gabriel had heard horrific stories of what happened to Bjordal Incarnate. About the royal family's small but elite order of Bjornvangar who purged Incarnate from the face of the earth, while hidden cults drank their blood and carved their bones in secret. But to Gabriel it had all felt like stories rather than real life, so he'd never paid much attention.

"How trustworthy are you if you turn against your own people?" Zoe spoke up.

"My people are those who would take me for their own, not those who would see me tied to a pyre before accepting the truth of what I am. And isn't Verchiél the city of the Incarnate? Isn't this where we were always welcome?"

"You are welcome here, but not to rule," she answered darkly.

"And why do you have these titles? By the will of your dead monarchs? Or your living citizens?"

"You have no right—" Gabriel hissed.

"And you do?" He raised a brow, amused, and paced before them. "Enlighten me, wise rulers, shouldn't your own people get to decide that for themselves?" Niklas addressed the crowds. "People of Verchiél, I would humbly ask for the honour of competing for the title of your ruler. As a leader I would do everything in my power to stop a war before it comes to pass, but should it arrive, know that I will fight for you. I will starve for you. I will kill and be killed for you."

Royalty and Incarnate all in one, no wonder they were awestruck. Niklas looked every bit the part in that moment: straight-backed and towering over everybody in the room, his voice hardly anything more than a calm lull. People were hypnotised as they watched his every move, clinging on to each word. He commanded the room and everyone in it. Every move and word was deliberate.

After a time, Niklas' voice trailed away. Gabriel could tell the crowd were still waiting for him to say more— he even found that he wanted to hear his voice again. The clacking of Niklas' fine leather shoes came to a halt at the centre of the room. Gabriel hadn't noticed how silent the area had grown while he'd been speaking.

Niklas raised his hands, palms upturned, hesitating only a breath before he addressed the room with one final question. "Verchiél, will you have me?"

The room was tense with silence. Nobody dared to move.

Until a single clap sounded out.

It started as a small thing, a disturbance, a ripple. Until it grew and swelled into a mighty crescendo, leaving the room thundering with the deafening roar of applause and cheers which shook the walls and foundations of the palace itself

Niklas turned back to them, and the barest hint of a smile tugged at his lips as if to say, *Your move.*

Gabriel's mind whirled furiously with their options. They could have him sent away, claim he was delusional and have him dragged right from the palace. People would talk—no doubt for years to come—but eventually things would return to a shaky normalcy. He looked around the room but noticed there weren't any guards to be found. Even Dabria was gone.

Gabriel frowned. He couldn't deny there had been a change. Even if they did somehow manage to have Niklas escorted out, that would only further prove his point. This was nothing like their duties or paperwork, he couldn't ignore this— neither of them could. They needed to meet him head-on.

Gabriel strode toward Niklas, Zoe's hand falling away from his arm. She hesitated a moment longer before following closely until they stood side by side. Zoe's hands shook slightly, though she kept her head held high, her eyes bright. She looked so small compared to Niklas, who stood well over both of their heights.

"Will the Sun and Moon accept my challenge?" Niklas asked. "Will we settle this tonight and see who has the right to rule?" His voice was courteous, calm even, his dark gaze roving over them both, and Gabriel was struck by how closely he scrutinised them, as if also seeing them both for what they were for the first time. "Or will you both forfeit your place here and give me the authority of rulership?"

"I accept."

Gabriel spoke without hesitation, barely letting him finish his sentence. Niklas appeared pleased at his eager response. They both turned their gaze to Zoe, who drew in a deep breath, as if she wanted to answer this question at a much later time— or not at all.

She looked between two different pairs of the same black eyes and spoke clearly for all to hear. "I accept your challenge."

4

ZOE

The rules of the challenge were simple. Through surrender or death, the last person left standing won. Though Zoe would be damned before she let anyone die tonight.

Zoe, Gabriel and Niklas spread out along the massive ballroom floor, circling each other until they formed a large triangle. Gabriel near the side of the room by the towering windows, Niklas—strangely enough— chose the back of the room near the wall, and Zoe stood before the open entrance. Some guests lingered unwisely along the edges of the room, but most went to the upper balconies and cheered. Zoe felt like a part of a grand show.

She chanced a quick glance toward Gabriel, who, despite his earlier foreboding, looked delighted to be a part of such an impromptu spectacle. He ran his fingers languidly through the air. Shadows danced around his fingers and arms—liquid darkness— devastatingly finicky to control, but sharp enough to cut to bone, and dense enough to smother.

He practically bounced on his feet, waving to people in the crowd and occasionally winking and throwing sultry looks to Niklas, who ignored him. Zoe wished she felt the same way as she bunched her fists tightly until her hands stopped shaking. She could feel the faintest wisp of her magic deep down, but she couldn't summon it, not until the sun returned—just as Niklas had planned.

She cast Niklas a glance; he stood rigidly in his corner of the room, determinedly avoiding everybody's eyes as he roughly unclipped his royal blue mantle and tossed it behind him, revealing a plain but sharply tailored black peacoat beneath, buttoned securely all the way to his throat. He tied his auburn hair back from his face.

A group of servants stepped forward with a city official— the one who would have given the pre-coronation ceremony for Zoe and Gabriel tonight—The group bowed respectfully to the three of them in turn before speaking.

"Verchiél's Incarnate, Zoe Okoro and Gabriel Capello will be competing together as a single team against the challenger, Niklas Osenson. What's more, as this challenge is to take place during the night it will be in the domain of the Incarnate Moons. As such, the Incarnate Sun, Miss Okoro, will be the sole participant permitted the use of a weapon in the absence of her magic."

He gestured to the group of servants, who made their way toward Zoe. Each carried a wooden case in their arms and people whispered, their attention momentarily drawn away from Niklas to watch the proceedings. The servants stopped before her and each opened the cases. She was greeted by the burnished hilt of a rapier and a shield. In the second case was a barbed whip and the third held a set of wickedly curved daggers, which sat delicately upon their silk-padded display.

Zoe extended her hand, pausing a moment as she considered her options. Gabriel's magic was based on illusions and deception. Not much on the offensive front. But Zoe figured she could pick up the slack of his attacks if he could focus on drawing the attention away from her. Her fingers brushed against the first case containing the sword.

She didn't want to harm Niklas. Perhaps they'd even be able to make some sort of an alliance if he would defect to Verchiél. She could turn this to their favour.

Satisfied that her hands were now perfectly steady, she trailed her fingers along the hilt before passing by it entirely. People were surprised as she decided not upon the sword or whip or daggers.

She chose the shield.

It was smaller but finely made and fit comfortably upon her arm. The servant raised a brow at her choice and offered her the sword along with it, but she gave only a curt shake of her head before the servants hurried back into the crowd.

The city official nodded at her choice and continued speaking. "Will the Verchiél Incarnate tell me to what end will the duel be determined? Lethal? Or non-lethal?"

"Non-lethal," Zoe quickly answered, ignoring the irritated glance Gabriel gave her. "The match winner will be determined by first surrender or incapability of further participation."

The city official's gaze moved back to Niklas. "Prince Osenson, do you accept these terms?"

There was something like surprise in Niklas' dark eyes, but he nodded in agreement.

"I do."

Zoe still wasn't entirely sure what Niklas was capable of. That trick with the ice had been devastating, and that had been only with a single shard. She eyed the vast quantity of ice sculptures around the room, hugging the shield tightly to herself, very much wishing that she'd paid more attention to what was happening before tonight. She wracked her memory for stories about Bjordal Incarnate, but nothing came to mind, only what happened to them if they were discovered. That was no good whatsoever. She needed to focus on not dying, not the other way around.

The city official nodded. "As a guest of Verchiél, Prince Niklas has the right to the first move."

Niklas was silent for a time before he called out in Bjordal, "Dur ös moyvn."

Zoe frowned, trying to remember the Bjordal lessons her old tutor had drilled into her mind all those years ago—another thing she now wished she had paid attention to.

"Er öst, du moyvn," Gabriel replied smoothly, never missing the chance to speak even if it was in a completely different language. Niklas was surprised but flashed them a grin that was a baring of teeth more than anything else.

Gabriel met her gaze and called back to her, "Our move first."

She nodded, taking a deep breath to steady herself as she took her place on the floor, trying desperately to reassure herself. They'd been trained in some combat before. More than that, they were Verchiél's Incarnate. Their city's Sun and Moon. How could a single person ever stand against them?

With a final shout from the city official, the crowd let out a tremendous cheer and the three opponents circled each other.

Barely had Niklas taken two steps when Gabriel disappeared in a sweep of shadows. The crowd let out a startled gasp and Niklas paused mid-movement. But Zoe knew this old trick. They'd practised it countless times. She held out her hand and felt a cold shift of air behind her. Gabriel reappeared for a split second and grabbed her hand in his, pulling her along with him, her vision temporarily blurred with darkness.

In a blink, they reappeared behind Niklas, and still using

the momentum they'd built up, Gabriel swung her around and she bore down on him with the shield. Niklas barely had the chance to register them before she bashed him across the face. He stumbled, clutching at his jaw. People cheered and the city official marked the first hit.

Niklas spat blood. His teeth stained a watery pink. "A fine trick."

She shifted the shield more comfortably upon her arm, and despite herself a small smile formed on her lips. "Want to see the rest?"

Before he could answer Gabriel swept her across the room once more in a swirl of shadows. It was disorientating, but they'd practised enough times over the years that she'd grown somewhat used to the unnerving sensation of being pulled in and out of thin air. They continued to press forward against Niklas, forcing him to keep moving. Swapping hands and places in between her attacks enough that it became a complex dance between them. Gabriel blinked in and out of view so quickly he looked like nothing more than a shadowed blur, forcing Niklas to move as Zoe pressed forward. She lunged at Niklas with increasing speed, but for someone so large he was unnervingly fast, and he dodged out of her way every time.

Suddenly Niklas dropped to his knees, pressing both hands flat to the floor. Zoe stumbled but didn't fall, her legs frozen to the floor from the remnants of frost which now encased her legs in thick ice. Gabriel, who had been expecting to catch her, tripped without the counterbalance, disappearing back into shadows before he could fall. Niklas stood over her, hand half raised as if deciding what to do. He curled his fingers back slowly, and she felt an icy chill growing around her, noticing the ice that encased her legs now crept swiftly along the rest of her.

Panic surged through her, and she brought the edge of the shield down with all her strength and crushed the ice at her feet. She fell backward, but before she could hit the floor a pair of arms reached out and caught her, she was pulled back into a cloud of smoky darkness. Her vision blurred around the edges and she found herself far across the room, well out of Niklas' reach.

She was met with Gabriel's lopsided smile. "Close one, huh? Wait here, I want to try something." Before she could interject, he was gone again. She shivered as he passed, the cold chilling her to her very bones.

Gabriel didn't reappear beside Niklas as Zoe had anticipated, but instead halfway to him, in the exact centre of the floor. "Gabe!" Zoe shouted after him. "What are you doing? We're supposed to fight together—"

The temperature suddenly plummeted, and Zoe watched with growing horror as Niklas subtly shifted his fingers. A shard of ice swiftly erupted from the floor where Gabriel had been previously standing, but instead of an impact, Gabriel appeared to separate into two people as two figures walked away from the attack unharmed. Niklas stopped short, his gaze flicking between both uncertainly. Gabriel revelled in the reaction. Both mirroring each other's words and actions, they paced around Niklas lazily, each step of their feet in perfect synchronisation.

"A bit confused, my dear?"

"Not possible…" Niklas' voice came out so quietly that Zoe swore she imagined his words.

With a graceful flick of Gabriel's wrist, a third voice joined the chorus. "Tell me, Prince Niklas, can you see—"

A fourth edged in on his right, causing him to take a step

back.

"—what is a lie?"

The fifth appeared behind him, trapping him between the others.

"—and what is the truth?"

Gabriel swept both his arms down with force. Niklas froze, taking in the disquieting sight of dozens of versions of Gabriel circling him. Niklas took a fraction of a step backward, and a shard of ice cracked loudly beneath his heel. In that moment each illusion rushed forward at the same time. But instead of fighting, Niklas pivoted swiftly on his heel, to meet Gabriel—the real Gabriel—head-on.

Gabriel's confident eyes grew wide. He feebly attempted to correct his miscalculation, but Niklas easily seized him by the collar, using his previous momentum to throw Gabriel over his shoulder. The illusions vanished into wisps of shadows when Gabriel hit the floor hard. Niklas simply stared at the sight of him sprawled in a heap. Now he was the one pacing around Gabriel. With a controlled twist of his hand, a sharpened shard of ice formed from the freezing air around him. "Thoughtless. You waste your energy on flash rather than function."

Gabriel rolled swiftly to the side as ice swept across the ground in sharpened shards where he'd just lain. He smiled between heaving breaths. "I could go all night."

Niklas tapped the shard against his palm, considering the smirking form of Gabriel. "Is that so? You seem to be growing slow."

Gabriel stumbled. His foot caught in a patch of frost he hadn't noticed, which froze over and wholly encased his leg in ice. He tried to pull away, but it spread from his leg to his arm. Niklas approached— "and clumsy" —bringing the point of the ice shard to rest at his cheek, tapping sharply enough to draw blood—"and weak."

With a cry and a sharp twist Gabriel broke free, completely disappearing in a swirl of shadows. But instead of landing gracefully on his feet as he usually did, he collapsed clumsily onto his side, skidding across the floor until he came to a final crash in the corner of the room, shadows rolling off him like smoke.

Niklas scoffed. "You use your magic like a crutch, you lean too heavily on it rather than using it to sharpen your own strength." Niklas stood eerily still, silent, focused. His black eyes were inscrutable. A chill descended upon the room, followed by a hollow and aching cold. A faint cracking filled her ears; all the ice sculptures were shaking and splintering.

Zoe screamed, "Gabe—"

From every direction, ice shot toward them, and Zoe dropped to the floor, covering her head with her arms, barely missing the largest shards as they whipped over her head unnervingly fast. She gritted her teeth as flecks of ice like razors grazed across her arms and back, her tunic ripping as if it were made of paper. Her ears rang long after the last of the ice clattered to the floor. The crowd above let out a hearty cheer, and Zoe threw an irritated glare their way. Did they not understand that their kingdom was at risk? Perhaps they simply thought it was all part of the party— some sort of staged show. She wished it was, that would have been more believable than what was happening.

She chanced a look around. Her heart dropped. Did Gabriel have time to get to cover? Tables and chairs were ruined, statues had toppled over, the floor was scratched to oblivion, the glass walls shattered, and her arms and shoulders stung from many cuts.

But Gabriel wasn't anywhere to be found.

She got shakily to her feet, advancing upon Niklas. "What did you—"

A single crystal ornament dropped to the floor. As they looked up, they saw Gabriel perched precariously upon the largest chandelier. He waved pleasantly with a smile. Ever the showman. He made no move to come down as he continued to observe the scene below.

Niklas' gaze moved past Gabriel's perched form to the link where the chandelier met the ceiling. Time slowed as Zoe readjusted her grip upon the shield, and rushed forward.

"No!" Zoe shouted. "Don't—"

But before she could stop Niklas, he threw a shard of ice upward with immense force, and it whipped rapidly past Gabriel's head, his hair ruffling with the movement. Gabriel looked smugly down upon him but was met only with a grin from Niklas. Gabriel barely had a moment to process what had happened before an audible crack resounded throughout the chamber. His gaze snapped up to where Niklas had thrown the ice shard. Cracks grew across the glass ceiling and the chandelier drooped with his weight.

Zoe screamed just as the ceiling shattered.

The chandelier plummeted from its hold, and Gabriel fell along with it. Glittering shards caught and reflected light from an infinite number of angles, suspended in the air for a moment in time, a dark figure caught against the shining glass. Zoe's breath hitched as she imagined his body broken and bleeding against the marble floors below. All because they'd been too slow.

She was wrenched from her thoughts when a large figure barrelled into her. The air was knocked from her lungs as they both landed at the side of the room, falling none too gently upon the marble floor. She yelped as pain shot through her shoulder, which took the brunt of the impact.

Zoe tried to shove Niklas away. "What are you doing—"

"Get down!"

Niklas threw himself over her just as the chandelier came to a final deafening crash against the floor. Crystals and broken metal rained down, scattering and bouncing across the room as heavy clouds of dust fell upon them. Niklas hissed in pain as rubble pelted him from above, but he continued to shield her.

Her gaze drifted past Niklas' shoulder, just as Gabriel disappeared completely in mid-air with a twist of shadows. Clouds of sweeping dust threatened to choke her, and grit was caught in her eyes. The distant sound of shattered glass was too loud in her ears, and she realised that she couldn't do anything more. She curled up on herself, pinching her eyes tightly shut and burying her face against her arms.

After what felt like an eternity, a hush fell upon the ballroom. The only remaining noise came from the shards of glass that fell unevenly from the ceiling, and the distant shouting of crowds on floors far above them. Zoe blinked and was met with familiar black eyes in Niklas' unfamiliar face.

She pushed herself away cautiously as if she'd suddenly found herself in the grasp of a wild animal, not sure whether to thank him for helping her or shout at him for causing all this in the first place. He appeared to be facing a similar dilemma, opening his mouth as if to speak, but thought better of it as he got to his feet with some difficulty, dusting himself off briskly. His previously fine jacket was shredded and coated in white dust and blood, his shoulders hunched as he limped away.

Zoe got shakily to her feet, mentally cursing herself. She'd

lost her shield somewhere in the fight and she felt defenceless
without either it or her magic. Zoe stopped pacing and let her gaze
settle on one of the piles of rubble. There were broken shards of
metal through the room. She could grab one before Niklas had a
chance to turn on her. She stepped back silently, keeping her eyes
upon him the entire time, but Niklas wasn't interested in attacking
her in the least. All his attention was upon the mess before them,
his eyes scanning it frantically as his jaw tightened. She reached
out and found a bent shard of metal about the size of her forearm,
which she heaved from a pile of rubble.

Niklas' dark gaze flicked toward her at the sound, but he
made no movements to confront her. She didn't fail to notice how
he shifted so that she would be in his periphery. She tightened her
grip upon the bar to steady herself as her eyes scanned the room
closely.

Where was Gabriel? He'd disappeared plenty of times before but never for so long. Her gaze was drawn back to the chandelier upon the floor. She imagined him pinned somewhere beneath it
and was ill at the thought. She checked the railings above but there
was no one there except for the guests wailing in distress or staring
down at them in shock.

Her mind hummed with jumbled thoughts, which were interrupted when a collective shout rose from the crowd above them.
She raised the metal bar defensively, expecting to see Niklas ready
to finish the fight. But he was still where he had been by the centre
of the room, his gaze upon the pile of wreckage. She followed his
line of sight and relief swept over her like a crushing wave.

Gabriel had finally reappeared beside the ruined chandelier,
breathing heavily and clutching at his side. His dark clothes were
caked in a thick layer of dust and small shards of glass fell from

his shoulders and dark hair with each movement. Though her relief was tainted by annoyance. Knowing him, he'd waited until the last possible moment for dramatic effect.

Gentle laughter filled the tense silence as Niklas strode forward. "Is this the best you can do? Parlour tricks and children's scuffles?"

Gabriel weakly shot a hand forward and a vague shadowed shape rushed toward Niklas, who waved his arm lazily as it dissipated like black smoke before it even reached him. "But since you both fought so well, I'll give you both the chance to yield."

Zoe held Niklas' gaze steady, her mind sorting through options. Should she try to fight him after he'd offered them an out? But she was already so tired. She wasn't the Daughter of the Sun right now. Right now, she was only Zoe Okoro, a frightened and all too human opponent who could be cut down with a flick of Niklas' wrist as if it were nothing more than batting a moth away. Gabriel was hardly better off, his usually cheery demeanour replaced by a terrible glower; a sheen of sweat had broken out over his clammy face. Her eyes trailed toward his injured side, which he held gingerly, but his clothes were too dark to see any wounds. Niklas' offer was truly the best choice. It was a chance to make not only an alliance, but a bond between another Incarnate. An all too rare gift.

Zoe stepped forward, making sure to speak loudly enough so the whole room could hear. "I yield."

Niklas nodded solemnly then waited on Gabriel, who made no move to respond. He was still breathing heavily, his brows drawn so deeply together that for a moment his eyes were wholly pitch black, like a raging storm at night. It was unsettling. Zoe couldn't remember ever seeing him so angry.

She called out to him, "Gabe?"

With a sharp flick of his wrist, Gabriel drew a hidden blade from the silver snake wound around his arm. Panic tore through Zoe. She knew in that moment that he wasn't going to just hurt Niklas.

He was going to kill him.

She shouted out across the room, "Gabe, no, that's not—"

He lunged forward before she could finish her words—disappearing into shadows then reappearing only inches from Niklas, who stumbled backward, but not far away enough that Gabriel couldn't wrench his head back and expose his throat to the razor-sharp blade.

Zoe wasn't entirely sure what made her do it. Whether it was the desire to stop Gabriel's dangerous actions or a need to pay back Niklas for helping her, she hurled the metal bar at Gabriel before she could think twice. It landed true and hit Gabriel's arm, and she winced as if she'd felt the blow herself. Gabriel gave a sharp cry and stumbled sideways, barely catching Niklas with the blade. A slash of crimson appeared along Niklas' jaw, missing where Gabriel had originally intended by a mere breath.

Gabriel disappeared into shadows before he could hit the floor and almost immediately reappeared beside her. He looked at her with confused eyes, clutching his arm gingerly. Zoe felt the tone of the room shift. Where people had gasped or cheered in excitement or delight now a grim heaviness lay upon the area, with harsh whispers and pointed fingers thrown their way. Niklas had paused as well. The cut under his jaw bled freely as he watched them both with interest. Zoe moved closer to Gabriel, trying to keep her voice low. Niklas' stillness, however, betrayed that he heard every word they exchanged.

"What are you doing?" she hissed to Gabriel.

"Winning," he answered simply. "It's not like anyone else would have seen the knife."

"That's exactly the problem!" she protested. "You nearly murdered a man in front of the entire country."

"So? Death is a possible outcome in a challenge."

She wasn't frightened as much as she was shocked. Though Gabriel had confided in her that he'd done things he wasn't proud of before he arrived in Verchiél, she'd always assumed it was just another dramatic tale he'd weaved for more attention. But seeing him now, wreathed in shadows with a bloodied blade in hand, she believed he was capable of every bit of violence he'd claimed.

Blood rushed in her ears and she took a shaky breath. "We're supposed to fight together—surrender together. We promised that it would be a non-lethal match."

His voice took on an edge. "I had him."

The air crackled around them and she lowered her voice so it matched his. She was startled that he still had the blade in his other hand. "Please, just put that away."

"No."

Niklas was entirely forgotten as they sized each other up. Gabriel shifted, putting more pressure against his side until his knuckles whitened, sneering and speaking in an irritated tone. "I don't need you to always be telling me what to do."

She was glad it wasn't daytime. She could already feel the heat which crept beneath her skin in her agitation. "Gabe. I'm ordering you to stand down."

His eyes grew wide before he let out a sharp laugh, which resounded across the room. "Ordering me?"

She nodded. "You've already done enough."

He was about to argue but with his next movement he

winced, and gripped the edge of the chandelier to balance himself. He gritted his teeth as he spoke through unsteady breaths. "And you haven't done nearly enough."

She noticed the blood which stained his hands when he took them away from his side. The idiot would rather bleed out than admit he was wrong; typically, he hurt himself when she couldn't use magic at all. "You can barely stand, just let me—"

"I already told you I don't need your help!"

Her face burned from anger and embarrassment in equal measure. Niklas addressed the room calmly. "Is this who you would have as your leaders? Two children who cannot even put aside their squabbles for the good of their country?"

Muttering ran throughout the room. Gabriel wiped the blade along his ruined tunic, and sheathed it in a quick motion until it was seamless, nothing more than a harmless and decorative silver snake. But the damage was already done. The city official descended slowly to the centre of the ruined room along with a large group of guards. The three duellers watched him closely, all reacting at the same time.

Niklas inclined his head slightly.

"Yes?" Zoe asked nervously.

"What?" Gabriel snapped.

The official winced at their reactions. Zoe's stomach dropped when she noticed he carried only one silver circlet with him, clearing his throat, he looked to Gabriel, who eyed the circlet in his hands with desperation.

"Deepest apologies, Son of the Moon, but you've been withdrawn from the challenge."

Gabriel's lips curled sharply until Zoe saw his canines. "What do you mean 'withdrawn'?"

The man took a step backward. "You weren't permitted either the use of lethal force or a weapon, both of which you used upon an unarmed challenger. As the rules state—"

"Hang the fucking rules. We're the ones in charge," Gabriel spat with gathering fury, and she didn't blame the poor man for cowering. Gabriel appeared more like a monster than a king, a livid expression over his usually gleeful face, shadows gathering until he was wreathed in them. Zoe had seen this happen only on occasion, when he lost control of his emotions during the night and his magic had more control over him than the other way around.

The man nodded shakily. "Neither of you have been officially crowned, and since Prince Niklas has challenged you both by Verchiél tradition within the allotted time frame…"

Niklas stepped forward, took the silver circlet from the man, and placed it atop his auburn head. "He's saying it's a pity for you both."

Gabriel bristled at the sight of Niklas wearing the circlet. The latter of whom was ragged and coated in blood and dust, but the cold silver shone regally upon his brow. Gabriel didn't bother to whisper when he spoke. "He's a stranger. He's not even Verchiél."

Niklas smiled pitifully. "Neither are you, if I recall correctly? I heard you were nothing more than a urchin they picked up off the Grislow streets—"

Gabriel snarled and lunged forward viciously, but a large guard blocked his path, staring him down. Gabriel glowered right back as Zoe pulled him away, trying to put as much space between them as possible. She frowned as she noticed the bright droplets of blood which trailed along Gabriel's side, standing out starkly against the white marble.

She grabbed his arm to keep him from rushing off again, trying to get him to hold still as she whispered next to his ear. "Stop it."

"He's not—"

"Enough. You're making everything worse."

Niklas addressed the gathered guards. "Please escort Verchiél's previous Incarnate back to their chambers."

"You think they're going to listen to you?" Gabriel laughed harshly, looking at the guards. "Escort this pretender outside."

But none of the guards reached for Niklas, they reached for Gabriel and her. "You're Verchiél guards!" Gabriel protested. "You're supposed to listen to us."

"They take orders from the ruling Incarnate only." Niklas watched them both closely. "Attend to the Moon as well, he seems to be delirious."

Just as she was wondering if the night could possibly get any worse, Gabriel twisted around on his heels, gathering her up in his arms, and the last thing she saw were his black eyes as he pulled her away with him into the shadows.

5

ZOE

Zoe's vision swam in and out of focus as she was dragged along-side Gabriel. Glimpses of the ensuing chaos flickered past her eyes as they disappeared and reappeared throughout different parts of the palace. The mobs of panicked guests and frantic servants eventually thinned in numbers.

Zoe's grasp had started to loosen, and just when she thought she couldn't hold on any longer, Gabriel finally stopped when they reached a dim room, quiet and unoccupied. He collapsed to his knees and Zoe stumbled backward, landing on a canvas-covered couch in a sudden puff of dust.

What had they done? Not only had they lost, but Gabriel had nearly killed Niklas, another Incarnate, in front of everybody. She took in their surroundings with a wary eye, as if she expected someone to jump out at any moment with weapons drawn. It was empty, but it wouldn't be long before someone found them.

"How could you do that?" Zoe asked. She held her arms around herself and shivered. "You were going to kill him."

"I was going to win," Gabriel explained, getting to his feet.

"But he's an Incarnate, like us. Does that mean nothing to you?"

His dark eyes were feverish. "I was keeping us safe."

She opened her mouth to argue but his face suddenly

bunched in pain and he hissed.

She reached forward. "Gabe, just let me see—"

"I'm fine," he replied curtly.

She didn't believe that, but it was obvious that he wasn't going to press the subject further. "If you want to run back to Niklas, go ahead. But I'm leaving. I'm not going to have my fucking life dictated by somebody else in power again."

"Leave?" Nervous laughter bubbled out of her at the absurdity of the idea. "Where else is there for us to go?"

"We can figure something out."

Zoe bit her bottom lip. "So, we have one choice left?"

As he spoke another kind of panic began to well up in her chest. She hadn't left Verchiél in, well…ever. It had always been her home, and though she'd longed to travel beyond its borders, she'd never imagined it to happen in such a way. As much as she disagreed, she still knew Gabriel. She wasn't going to stay here on the promise of Niklas, a stranger.

Well, one that made sense. Stay and be imprisoned. Or leave and try to find a way to sort everything out.

"Well?" Gabriel prodded impatiently. "Are you coming or not?"

Zoe nodded. "I'll lead the way."

Gabriel was barely conscious.

Zoe dragged him along the hallways as quietly as she could manage. Guilt surged as she urged him onward, her legs moving faster than his could, spatters of blood leaving an obvious trail on the marble floors behind them.

He was eerily quiet, so she'd kept up a steady stream of

whispers, trying to keep him awake as well as trying to keep her nerves from getting the better of her, asking him which direction to take, though she knew exactly where they were going: Verchiél's royal crypt.

When Zoe had explored the palace years ago, she had discovered a hole in the far wall of the crypt. It was a cramped mess and endlessly dark, but within it was another set of catacombs which sat underneath the main floor, far older than the one they were currently in—if such a thing could be believed in this longstanding city. It held none of the lofty grandeur which its royal counterpart possessed. She had never mentioned finding it to anyone else except Gabriel, as neither of them were allowed in the crypts without permission.

Zoe stopped at the stairway leading down to the crypt, a pair of sturdy stone doors looming imposingly high above them, carved with many celestial designs. Her eyes sought out the small wooden door set into the right panel.

Gabriel sagged in her arms again and she nearly collapsed under the sudden weight. Gritting her teeth, she heaved him upward. He'd always had a slender frame, but their height difference made travelling together far more difficult. "You know," she said, guiding them carefully down the stairs, "if you die then I'm going to dig you back up so I can kill you all over again."

He grinned weakly. "Don't worry, I'll come back to haunt you—"

"You're already haunting me."

Barely had she gotten them to the bottom of the stairs before shouts echoed toward them—far louder this time—and lights flashed from the entrance of the hallway.

"The guards must have missed us dreadfully," Gabriel said.

Zoe wasted no time. She hooked Gabriel's arm over her shoulders and strode through the small door. Gabriel hissed in pain at the sudden movements as she barred the door behind them, plunging everything into darkness. The only light came from the bright orange glow of a single torch set by the entrance, and the only sounds were the pounding of her own heart in her ears and Gabriel's mumbling, but she was unable to catch any of his words.

Her hand curled tightly around the blazing torch, plucking it from its rusted holder. She squinted ahead and jumped back as a pale hand reached out to them. She flashed the torch toward the source, her eyes adjusting to the darkness. A walkway cut a line down the middle of the colossal chamber. On either side, standing rigidly at attention, were hundreds of rows of ghostly statues. She breathed out a sigh of relief. The pale hand belonged to one of the marble statues—in the likeness of one of the Incarnate Suns and Moons stretching back generations, marble in shades of jet black or stark ivory, others made entirely of tarnished gold or silver, almost like the players of an extravagant chess board.

Gabriel slumped ungracefully against the statue of an Incarnate, who looked down upon them as if offended that the current Moon would be weak enough to pass out at their feet. He was nearly as pale as the marble. She bent down beside him, placing the torch upon the ground.

He mumbled something again, and the ghost of a smile crept across his face. She frowned, trying to catch his words. "What?"

He gave her a feeble grin. "I was saying that if I die down here at least they won't have to move me far to bury me."

She scowled, but it was a relief that he still had enough wits about him to make jokes. Her eyes drifted back to his blood-soaked hands clutching at his waist. "Let me see."

He moved slowly, as if trying to process her words, before taking away his hands. She unbuttoned his tunic, fingers shaking as her hands slipped over the glossy buttons. There was a gash across his waist. Far away enough from anything vital—not necessarily fatal—but the more blood he lost, and the longer they stumbled along in darkness, would make them an easier target.

"I'm going to try to help you with this," she said.

He nodded weakly. She placed her hands firmly against his side. He drew in a quiet breath and flinched but didn't pull away.

Zoe had done exceptionally well with mastering the healing aspects of her magic. She'd read accounts and journals of many Incarnate Suns being unable to heal so much as a scratch. She still remembered the first time she'd cooled a fever, healed a cut and set a broken bone. Most of them had been for Gabriel as he had little concern for his well-being—evidenced by where he currently was. Though it was still a finicky and delicate process, it was far easier to simply burn something away instead of trying to put it back together again—piece by insufferably tiny and fragile piece. The fact that she didn't have a shred of magic within her reach right now wasn't going to make things any easier. She didn't know the slightest thing about healing when magic wasn't involved.

Fists pounded on the door. Zoe fumbled with her hands, panic surging through her. Threads of muffled conversation drifted through the dense material; they spoke Bjordal, but Zoe didn't need to guess what they were saying to understand that they were debating how to break down the doors.

Gabriel's breath hitched again. His eyes squeezed shut tightly, and his skin was clammy this close. She focused more intensely than she ever had while healing, hours of study and lessons flashing through her mind as she desperately willed herself to be able to do something—anything to help. Her shaking hands worsened, fingers and palms sticky with blood.

Tears of frustration pricked at the corners of her eyes, but she blinked them away. Right now, she needed to concentrate. The magic was still in her, she just needed to reach it. She focused every bit of energy she could muster. But calling to it at night was like screaming into the void. It wouldn't answer her.

Fists pounded against the door again. The frame shook insistently, the block of wood underneath shifting slightly. She closed her eyes and imagined all the things that thrived in sunlight, the wild animals that she had seen during walks in the rich green forests in the summer countryside, the endless golden fields of sunflowers they passed on their trips to neighbouring towns. Zoe opened her eyes, but everything was the same. The dark tomb around them. Her hands soaked in her friend's blood.

Gabriel rasped, "It's not working…"

"Just give me a minute—"

"We don't have a minute."

She ignored him as she refocused, her hands shaking so badly she couldn't keep them still. Gabriel tried to wrench her bloodied hands away. "Stop, we have to go—"

At the contact of his hands, the room lurched and spun, but still she didn't dare let go. Warmth didn't blossom underneath her fingers as it usually did, rather a terrible cold. It seeped past her skin, feeling as if it cut down to blood and bones. Gabriel must have felt it too, as he cried out in shock. When it faded, she took her hands away carefully, afraid of what she would see. Fearful that perhaps she had accidentally made the wound worse. His breathing had evened out. Only echoes of pain remained across his features, but a quick intake of breath was his only response at the sight of his side.

The wound was healed. But rather than the usual flawlessness her magic left, there was a large and twisted scar, looking as if it were already many years old and poorly healed.

"Zoe, what did—"

The door behind them exploded into a shower of splinters, decades of dust rising along with it. Gabriel seized Zoe's hand and pulled her behind a group of statues. They huddled next to each other, Zoe trying her best to shrink herself down as she snuck glances back toward the ruined entrance. As the dust cleared, light began to grow. Nearly two dozen guards filed through the small opening, many bearing torches as they moved into an orderly file, standing rigidly at attention as a commanding voice boomed out.

"Søk etter."

At least she understood what that meant. Search.

Zoe and Gabriel locked eyes. He put a finger to his lips and she nodded silently. Better to let him go first; at least he could see. Gabriel crept forward stealthily. Zoe trailed behind him. Both crouched low and attempted to keep to the darkness in the room as dozens of lights fanned out behind them, each guard marching down the rows of graves, searching.

They managed to make it halfway across the room when a guard about twenty feet away from them suddenly shouted out.

The guard's voice died away as Zoe stretched her hands toward the torch they held, willing for the flame to bend for her.

Gabriel's panicked voice sounded out next to her. "Zoe?"

Her eyes grew dry as she refused to break eye contact with the flame, recalling the feeling from only a moment before. But that had only worked when Gabriel had grabbed her arm…

Zoe seized Gabriel's hand in hers and focused with all the concentration she could muster. "What are you doing?"

He shook off her grip and gathered her up in his arms. Just as he'd done in the throne room. "Time to go."

The room around her faded, and for a moment they were suspended in an inky blackness. Then they reappeared close to the end of the crypt. Zoe lurched as fast as her tired legs would carry her toward the hole.

Guards shouted and scrambled toward them, but she didn't dare slow or turn around. A few stray pistol shots whipped by them, burying deeply into the wall ahead of them, and a hot, searing pain erupted as a bullet grazed her arm.

They skidded to a halt as they reached the end of the crypt. Zoe's arm stung terribly and there was a stitch in her side, but when Gabriel squeezed himself down into the break in the wall, she followed as quickly as she could manage.

She nearly lost her balance from the uneven floor as her feet hit the ancient crypt. Gabriel took her hand and guided them forward. It was damp and cold. She shivered and wished she had more than her flimsy tunic for warmth. She heard the guards still behind them, the brightness gradually growing from the torches, illuminating the area. She caught glimpses of the crypt— rows upon rows of stone shelves lined with skeletons. A dry crunch resounded through the tunnel when she accidentally stepped on one.

She shook her foot free. "Gross, gross, gross."

"I don't think they much appreciated it either…" Gabriel's words trailed away and he froze in his tracks. She ran right into his back.

"Hey, why did you stop—" She grew cold when she saw what he did.

They had reached the end of the tunnel. There was no place for them to flee. There had been a collapse long ago, and the remaining part of the tunnel that would have led them further underground was completely blocked off. They tried to shift the fallen slabs of stone and rubble which littered the pathway, but the collapse had wedged the slabs of old stone firmly into place. She felt along the surfaces of the walls, noting that there were no doors or entryways, not even cracks or seals to a hidden path.

"Well, this is delightful," Gabriel said, out of breath.

Zoe's eyes adjusted as the torches grew brighter behind them, watching as the guards began to enter the tunnel in the distance, their voices echoing harshly off the stone. Her heart gave a jolt. She couldn't believe they'd come this far and were going to be captured.

She tried to take a deep breath, but she couldn't hide how shaky her voice was. "Gabe? What are our options?"

"Extremely limited, darling. I might be so bold as to say non-existent."

She groaned, backing away from the rubble. "That's not what I want to hear—"

She tripped on a loose stone, and Gabriel caught her. Her wounded arm burned with the motion, but she looked to her feet. They had spent so long searching for an opening or a crack along the walls and ceiling, they had completely neglected to search the floor.

The main entrance to the crypt had been hewn from the stone of the ground itself, but as more space was needed later as additions were built underneath, stretching out far past the bedrock of the palace, where it would nearly impossible to miss different parts of the city: old cellars, tunnels and streets, buried and long since forgotten. Which made more sense as to why this floor was so uneven— sunken in and collapsed in some parts. Honestly, it was a miracle that they were still standing right now.

"Here," she said, shifting some of the floor tiles. "We can get out this way."

Gabriel was next to her in an instant. He found a crack that had faint draft coming from it. "What we need," he decided, "is something that's great at smashing things."

Zoe nudged a slab rock toward him with the toe of her shoe. "Will this work?"

He picked up the rock and stood above the spot where they'd felt the draft, raising the stone nearly over his head.

She instinctively took a few steps away. "If you get immediately swallowed up after this, then it was lovely knowing you."

"Tell people I died as I lived."

"Doing stupid shit?"

"Exactly."

He brought down the stone with all his strength and smashed it against the floor. A loud echo rang through the tunnel and the floor cracked and shifted under her feet. Gabriel scrambled away as swiftly as he could manage just as the floor cracked and buckled beneath them. She lost her balance and lurched backwards as a large portion of the floor gave way. She squeezed her eyes shut as clouds of ancient dust rose up into the air, causing them both to cough.

Everything was deathly quiet, but as the dust settled, she was greeted by a sound that sent a chill through her. She peered down. Beneath their feet was a darkened waterway, its current rushing fast and loud. She snuck a glance at Gabriel, who hadn't moved. His usual confident grin had entirely vanished, his dark eyes wide. He pushed himself back against the wall like an animal trying to press itself in the corner of a cage. She was tempted for a single moment to simply grab him and drop down into the water together, but he'd never forgive her if she did.

She approached slowly and gave a shaky smile. "It's… not that bad." She offered her hand. "We'll jump together."

Gabriel was horrified, giving her a look as if she'd just suggested he shoot himself in the face. She grasped his hand and tugged him along with slightly more force, hoping to have him begrudgingly follow along. But when the sound of his feet sliding along the slick stone tiles echoed throughout the tunnel, she understood that he wasn't going to cooperate.

"We need to get out of here."

His eyes were glassy, his voice faraway. "We don't even know where this goes, for all we know it could lead to a dead end beneath the palace. We'd end up with no air, we'd be crushed, we'd be…" He put his head in his hands and huddled against the wall.

A shot whizzed by them. It promptly buried itself with a dull thunk into the stone next to their heads. Concentration shattered, she looked back up again; the guards were about fifty feet away now but quickly covering distance.

"We need to leave."

"No."

Another shot rang out, grazing Gabriel's shoulder. He hissed and drew himself closer to the wall.

She tried a different tactic and hardened her voice. "Either jump with me now or let them take you."

"No…" He shook his head and his voice croaked weakly, so different from what she knew.

"Gabriel." She knelt in front of him, forcing him to meet her eyes. "Either you come with me, or you go back to Niklas."

He was silent for so long she wondered if he'd heard her, but when she offered her hand this time, he took it, shaking badly. They braced themselves against the edge of the gaping chasm below.

She looked back at him. "On the count of three?"

He shook his head, though if it was in affirmation or denial, she was unsure. Zoe began counting.

"One."

He held a vice-like grip upon her and she squeezed his hand in reassurance.

"Two—"

She leapt swiftly from the edge, and he let out a shout and tightened his grip upon her hand as they plummeted into the waters below.

6

DABRIA

When Dabria had first accepted her position at the palace, she'd thought she would be adorned and decorated with the highest of honours. An elite body-guard stationed in the beating heart of Ver-chiél! Surely they had chosen her because she'd been the best and brightest. Like a heroine from one of the paperbacks she loved to read. A gleaming sword in one hand and a gorgeous woman leaning against her in the other.

But instead of gory sword fights and swooning women with ample amounts of cleavage, she spent her days and nights patrolling the palace halls where the most exciting thing that happened was making sure no handsy nobles walked off with any of the prized silverware. Boring. Dull. Repetitive. When the old Incarnate had unexpectedly kicked the bucket she'd been hopeful that things would finally get exciting for a change. But instead she was assigned to protect the pampered princeling, who, despite not having a single drop of royal blood in his anaemic veins, had picked up on the whole *"everyone else is beneath my high and mighty ass"* act real quick. She didn't know which she hated more, kleptomaniac nobles or Gabriel. Either way both made her want to gouge her eyes out with the aforementioned silverware.

"Dabria, please stop glowering at the guests."

"I'm not glowering."

"You are and it's frightening people."

Dabria crossed her arms and looked away from one of the guests who'd been making eyes at her and proceeded to glare at Alfio instead. "I wouldn't be if people weren't so stupid."

She and Alfio were standing guard around the palace. A waste of time as the "guarding" turned out to be nothing more than redirecting lost delegates, keeping drunken party members in line or shooing away newly formed couples when they decided that the prized rose gardens made an excellent place to roll around. Dabria hated them all for the fact that she couldn't partake in any of it. What she wouldn't give to be pleasantly buzzed with her hand up a noble-woman's dress.

A tipsy man was trying to get their attention. Dabria, who had been doing her damnedest to ignore everyone, was finally forced to address him when he cleared his throat for what must have been the dozenth time.

"What?" Dabria snapped.

"—would you like and how may we be of service?" Alfio quickly added.

The man looked at Dabria. "You should smile more, you'd look prettier."

Dabria stretched her face into the widest smile possible and spoke in a sickly sweet voice. "Eat glass."

Alfio laughed anxiously and redirected her away from the man. "We're just going to go patrol now."

Alfio kept his hand on her shoulder until the man was out of sight. Dabria swatted him away. "You should have let me fight him."

"You can't fight the guests, Dabria."

"Don't tell me what I can't do. I'll fight you too—"

Dabria's words were lost as an ear-splitting crash exploded across the area. They watched as the domed ceiling of the ballroom shattered and collapsed. Shouting resounded through the air. Dabria immediately bolted ahead. Alfio followed closely behind, alternating between muttering curses and prayers beneath his breath. By the time they made it up the stone steps of the palace they were out of breath from running. Sweat ran down Dabria's back. She blew another strand of hair from her eyes, and took in their surroundings.

Chaos.

People screamed and fled; it was like trying to swim up a river. All Dabria could think about was Zoe and Gabriel. What would happen if they'd been hurt? Or if they'd been killed? The thought spurred her forward as she sprinted ahead of Alfio, but when they reached the upper hallway near the ballroom, silence greeted them, the area empty.

Statues were overturned, confetti littered the floors, fine clothes had been torn and trampled and broken glass was everywhere from the shattered ceiling above. The ruined chandelier sat in a heap of crystal and twisted metal. Dabria took a step forward, her foot grazing the arm of a fallen guest. She reeled back, looking up and down the hallways, but there wasn't a single standing person left. She hadn't even seen any guards as they travelled. That bothered her more than anything else.

"Where are they?" she muttered.

Alfio called out for Zoe and Gabriel at an increasing volume which made Dabria cringe. When nothing but silence greeted him, his voice took on a nervous tone. "Oh, what if we've lost them? We'll lose our heads—"

Dabria didn't know what to make of it. Was there an attack— a bomb? Her mind whirled furiously, and through the distant echoes of screaming and Alfio's panicked muttering Dabria heard something. Small and quiet at first, but unmistakably different in nature from the chaos around them. It wasn't frightened or angry.

It was calm.

"Shut up, Alfio."

He was genuinely offended. "I only said—"

Dabria clamped her hand over his mouth and kept her eyes trained upon the doorway behind them. Alfio's eyes followed hers. He tensed rigidly as he finally heard what she did.

Footfalls, steady and rhythmic, echoed from the darkened hallway. The exact sound that fine leather shoes made when they clacked across a hard surface. The stride was too heavy to be Zoe or Gabriel. A familiar chill rose up her back— the one that said she had reason to be worried.

She let go of Alfio and slowly drew her sword. To her dismay, Alfio's breathing had become further unsteady. She glared, about to tell him off, but stepped back in shock.

His breath plumed in the air around them. His eyes followed hers and he clasped his hands over his mouth as if trying to stop something from escaping him. His wild eyes turned back to her, but Dabria's breath rose into the chilled air as well. Movement caught her eye and she watched as frost spread along the floor and walls, coating the glass so the area darkened, the moon only a pale blur in the sky beyond. She backed further into the chamber. Something was very wrong. Verchiél was never this cold, not even at night. She drew the old pistol from her belt for good measure, grateful when Alfio stuck to his sword with two hands. He'd never been a good shot, not even when he wasn't completely terrified.

The clacking noise stopped, and from the dark, she caught a flash, like the eyes of a wild animal. Dabria called out in an authoritative tone, "Show yourself."

Silence stretched out for so long that she'd thought the intruder had left without a word. Dabria took a step back as a man materialised from the darkened hallway, bringing an unearthly cold with him.

She tightened her grip upon the pistol as a towering man approached, his eyes darker than the night sky, half moons of light reflected across them. The mantle he wore was torn and ragged. He frowned as he considered them, as though surprised to still find anybody standing in this place.

"Who are you?" Alfio asked.

"Your new king," the man replied.

Alfio tensed but Dabria found herself laughing as she lowered her pistol a fraction. "Is that you, Gabriel? And here I thought people were lying when they said you were a shape-shifter."

The man didn't laugh. "Allow me to make this far simpler." His lip curled back in a manner like he was baring his teeth. "Kneel."

The shot from her pistol was Dabria's only reply.

It hit home right between his eyes. But instead of the sickening crack of bone and the sharp spray of blood she expected to be rewarded with, the bullet passed right through him as if he were made of smoke. His form dissolved into shadows.

Alfio let out a frightened shout and Dabria jumped in shock.

"Why would you do that?" Alfio cried.

"Oh, I don't know, maybe because I didn't want to be murdered?"

"But didn't you see his eyes? He's an Incarnate."

Dabria huffed and squinted around the area, trying to spot where she'd last seen the man. She didn't have the time or the patience to try to explain to Alfio that just because this stranger was an Incarnate didn't mean it was okay for him to waltz in and stage a coup on a whim. Alfio began muttering again as he searched the area with her. The trick reminded Dabria of Gabriel's illusions, the way he used them to make people look where he wanted to...

She whipped around just in time to raise her pistol as a pair of dark eyes stared her down, amused. The stranger spoke in a calm tone. "You're cleverer than most."

She lunged with her sword, but he swerved to the side unnervingly fast, and she was thrown off balance. He used the momentum to lunge for Alfio next, and wrenched him to the ground by the throat. Alfio gave a yelp as he fell hard against the marble. Dabria trained the pistol on his tall form again, though she doubted that it would do much good.

"Get away from him!" she spat.

Alfio sounded hurt as he spoke back to him. "Incarnate are supposed to protect us."

The stranger considered them. His eyes were the same as Gabriel's at night, but Gabriel didn't have a way of making his look so cold—devious at times perhaps— but this was something else entirely new to Dabria. It made her painfully aware of the fact that all she had to protect herself was a sword and an old pistol.

The man stepped forward. "What runs through me doesn't make me blessed or selfless, it makes me strong."

Dabria fired off a rapid round of shots, emptying the pistol's barrel until it was left clicking hollowly in her shaking hand. Every bullet hit him square in the chest, striking across his lungs, his heart. Killing blows. But they simply passed through him. His form dissolved like dark smoke, then reformed, whole and unhurt. Unstoppable.

The man stood before them, looking at them with something like pity. "I'm no saint."

A chill ran through her that had nothing to do with the cold. Alfio wore a look of utter betrayal, not taking his wide eyes from the looming figure before them. Dabria knew how highly Alfio always held Incarnate, how he was always tripping over himself to do the slightest things for Zoe and Gabriel. Now he finally saw what she did: a single person with far too much power in their grasp.

The man leaned forward. "Last chance."

Dabria and Alfio were silent. The man shrugged to himself as he twisted his fingers and the cold around them grew unbearable, cutting deep. Past skin and bone to a place at the centre of her being. She would do anything to make it stop. A man or even a monster she could handle. Magic was another thing entirely.

"Wait!" Dabria sank to one knee.

"Dabria, what are you doing?" Alfio's tone came out panicked, but she couldn't bring herself to say anything to him. She couldn't even meet his gaze. She pushed the thoughts of what Zoe or Gabriel would say if they saw her. All Dabria could bear to think about was surviving another day.

The man gave her an approving nod before his gaze narrowed in on Alfio, who flinched as if he'd been struck. "I'll give you one last chance as well."

Alfio's breathing was still unsteady, but there was also something Dabria had never seen in his eyes before—a determination or a resilience he'd always lacked. Maybe her betrayal had stirred something in him, or the nature of this Incarnate had opened his eyes a little.

The man tilted his head slightly to the side as he spoke, his tone almost questioning. "Kneel."

Alfio let out a shout and charged forward, drawing out his own sword. Gone was his usual nervous self. He looked every part the royal guard in that moment. Somebody stronger and more capable. The Incarnate disappeared in a swirl of shadows, almost instantly reappearing before Alfio to plunge a shard of ice through his chest. Dabria inhaled sharply as hot droplets of blood scattered across her cheek. She caught the man's voice, speaking just loudly enough for her to still hear. "Your precious Moon taught me that."

He wrenched the shard out and let go, and Alfio stood suspended. For a moment, it was almost possible to hold onto the foolish hope that he had somehow survived. But then he swayed and hit the floor hard, convulsing, then lying eerily still, his eyes glassy, blond hair stained.

Dabria couldn't bring herself to wipe away the blood from her face. She felt as if she'd never be clean again. She clutched a fist to her mouth, biting back a wave of nausea. The man let the ice fall to the floor where it dissipated into a cloud of mist, before he dusted himself off. "A shame," he called out in a clipped tone. "Come along now."

She wrenched her eyes from Alfio's crumpled body to the man who considered her worth hardly anything more than a disinterested glance. He didn't start walking ahead of her, as she half expected him to, but waited until she began walking before him. Strong and not entirely stupid. Dabria made a mental note. She was tense as she walked toward the throne room, imagining this stranger driving a knife through her back and leaving her to bleed out over the floor, but he did nothing other than keep up a steady pace at a safe distance as if he expected her to turn around and attack him in turn.

The area around them had quieted; the guests had fled. The sound of her footsteps was the only thing Dabria could hear over the blood pounding in her ears.

What have I done, what have I done, what have I done—

She balled up her fists until fingernails dug sharply into her palms. *What needed to be done for myself.* That steadied her enough to know she wouldn't spontaneously collapse or run at this stranger with a sword drawn like Alfio—oh Alfio. Her throat burned but she swallowed her queasiness back down. She couldn't afford to break down now.

They entered the throne room and the man considered the area around them. Both thrones were untouched. Decorations were strewn everywhere, several of the marble statues toppled over in large chunks, littering the floors with white dust. The fallen bodies, mostly guards, all of whom she noted hadn't been anywhere at the party earlier. Here and there did she see guests in their finery buried under rubble and dust, dulling their shining jewels and silks.

Dabria watched him. He nodded to himself as he stared up at the wide windows, his gaze momentarily swept over the gold and silver thrones but just as quickly went to survey the rest of the room. He turned in a slow circle as he crossed the area. "Impressive. It'll need some reconstruction, but it's better than I could have hoped."

"You've never been here?"

Dabria's surprised remark was out of her mouth before she could stop herself. He halted in his steps, as if he'd forgotten that she was there. She expected a reprimand, even a swift crack across the face for questioning him, but he only smiled patiently. "After my true nature was discovered my world closed considerably around me."

He continued walking, his steps echoing sharply against the empty room. Dabria scrutinised him. His accent was Bjordal and his blue mantle had been subtly embroidered, not with the red and gold of the Osenson family, but with the emblem of a silver stag. She wracked her brain for where she'd seen that symbol before.

"Who exactly are you?" she asked.

"Niklas Askeland. Though most remember the family name Osenson."

"You're lying," Dabria answered without hesitation. "The Bjordal prince died years ago."

He stopped pacing, looking back to her with something akin to pity. "What must it be like?" He spoke softly. "To believe everything you've been told?"

She didn't answer at first; his tone set her on edge. But when she couldn't stand his gaze upon her any longer, hasty words escaped her. "Okay, fine, so let's say you are the Prince of Bjordal, you must have been gone for what—five, seven years?"

"Ten."

"So, why are you here?"

He appeared to be reconsidering his decision to bring her along with him as his upper lip curled at her questioning. He drew a deep breath through his nose before answering. "My father had the idea that our unsteady relationship combined with my powers would cause me to defect to Verchiél, so I could be used as some sort of weapon against him." He grinned. "Funny, people often cause the very things they try to prevent."

He moved away from her, clearly desiring to bring their

conversation to an end. But Dabria walked closely beside him, matching his long gait step for step. "But you're royalty. Couldn't you just overthrow your father?"

"Are you aware of Bjordal's beliefs regarding people like me?"

Dabria knew that they didn't like magic up north like they did here. Something to do with it being against their religion. Personally, she'd never understood the moral arguments. Especially since Heathland had maintained a neutral stance along the lines of: *We don't give a shit unless it involves money.*

"I've heard a lot," Dabria said. "I hope half of it isn't true."

"Whatever you've heard is all true, but only half the story."

"But why would you want to rule a country you've never been to before?"

He stopped in his tracks and Dabria had to double back to stand beside him.

"When I was in Bjordal, the only thing keeping me safe was my title," Niklas said. "Even then, I faced the threat of losing it every single day." His attention focused on her and Dabria realised those points of curved light in his eyes weren't reflections at all, they were his irises. He leaned forward so closely that she could see her reflection in their pools of bottomless black. Even death did not have such eyes. They felt…old, as if they were something shaped and taken from the very heart of the world itself. But if it was all true, that this magic had been passed on for generations, hundreds if not thousands of years, how many people had shared the same eyes? How many strangers had been unknowingly connected by this magic?

She wanted to look away but found herself transfixed. His grin sharpened but her reflection only frowned in return as he spoke hardly above a whisper. "What is your name?"

"Dabria."

When she spoke, her voice had lowered to match his. He continued speaking in a calm lull. "And what is it, Dabria, that you desire above all else? What is it that you lie awake at night dreaming of, your heart's greatest and grandest desire?"

Dabria wondered if this was some sort of trick on his part, even as answers surfaced at the back of her mind. She imagined herself in the gleaming uniform of countless captains before her, the ones who shone while they paraded above the filthy streets filled with vagabonds and castoffs like she used to be. If she had such a title people would have to recognize her, instead of constantly shunting her to the side because they'd rather ignore her and her ideas.

Niklas must have seen the change written across her face, as he waited expectantly, and she found herself spilling out secrets to a stranger and enemy. "For years I've had to look after other people. Protect them," Dabria said. "Make sure they're the ones who are whole and sound at the end of the day. But that also means I'm just a nameless person in the background. I want people to see me. I want them to know what I can do."

Niklas' expression was solemn. "So, you are a protector in your line of duty and in your life, but this has kept you from moving forward?"

"I guess you could say that."

He nodded. "I have no love for bloodlust. I see no reason why a single person more must die under my rulership. And yet certain times in life call for calculated measures—measures that others might call extreme or cruel." He paused and Dabria found herself hanging on to his every word, realising the pounding of her heart was now from anticipation rather than dread. "Would you carry out those measures for me as my personal guard and right hand?"

Dabria's heart sank slightly. "I don't want to be your guard."

"You're not in the position for negotiations."

"Neither are you. How long will it take for someone to overthrow you after they've heard you've killed the Sun and the Moon?"

He was genuinely surprised by her words, his brows rising. "I didn't kill them."

"Is that so?" She crossed her arms tightly.

"Yes. It is," he replied. "Did you think I was wandering the palace for my own amusement? I've been searching everywhere but neither myself nor my guards have found them."

Dabria's stomach settled a little more now that she knew they were both still out there somewhere. Then redoubled in pain when she realised that Zoe and Gabriel were both still alive and she'd just betrayed them. "But what if they come back? What's going to happen then?" she asked.

"Then I hope we can form an alliance. The combined power of Incarnate is no small feat, not to mention that I don't see the point in thoughtlessly throwing away lives which might be spared," he answered as if it were the simplest matter in the world.

"But do you need me as a guard? You can handle yourself."

"During the night? Certainly. But the day is a different matter. I may be an Incarnate, but I am still only one man, all too capable of being captured, tortured, killed…or betrayed." He stared at her closely. "Tell me, Dabria, would you be up to the tasks I require of you without betraying me?" She was silent; he must have sensed her hesitation. "You see, as strong and capable as you are, you've already betrayed your former charges in a matter of moments. How much faster would it take for you to do so to me?"

"I won't betray you if you don't give me a reason to."

"And what would that reason be?"

"I want something from you."

The barest smile tugged at the corner of his lips. No doubt he already sensed what she was going to do. She met his dark eyes, growing lighter as the morning rose, and spoke loudly enough for her voice to carry around the ruined room. "I want to be captain of the royal guard."

He was surprised at her declaration, but his smile only widened. "If half this city had your ambition, we'd be far better off. Consider the title yours, Captain."

He moved to turn away from her, but another nagging question found its way to her. "And if you betray me?"

A peal of laughter revealed that he was immensely pleased by the question. It was an unsettling laugh, rough and barking, as if joy were something only half remembered. "If I betray you then I give you full permission to drive a knife through my heart without a single word of protest."

She scrutinised him closely, but his face was startlingly honest. She nodded. "I'll hold you to that."

"I would expect nothing less."

The first rays of morning light streamed through the windows. Dabria squinted against the sudden brightness. She was startled; in the sunlight Niklas' black eyes were entirely gone. In their place were a pair of warm amber irises.

He held a hand out to her. "Do we have a deal?"

"Yes." She grasped his large hand in hers. "We do."

7

NIKLAS

Niklas' footsteps echoed through Verchiél's royal crypt. He took in the sight of the vaulted ceilings and countless statues of gold and obsidian Incarnate which stood proudly at each cold, marble coffin. The entire wealth of the city had been poured into this place. It was a fortunate thing that Verchiél held Incarnate, alive or dead, in such high esteem, or this place would have long since been stripped of its wealth. Not that Niklas held any fear of retribution from the dead, the living had already shown him the worst life had to offer.

Apparently the Verchiél Incarnate had escaped through here. Niklas had to admire their determination. Perhaps they were more resourceful than he'd given them credit for.

Niklas paused before one obsidian statue, and with a sweep of his arm the top slid from the stone, pushed with unnatural force from the strength of the shadows around him.

Niklas considered the skeleton, anger quietly simmering in the pit of his stomach.

It was decorated from head to toe in silks, delicate silver armour and opals, and even the hollow eye sockets had been filled with jewels of obsidian, meant to recreate their magical darkness in life. Even the dead Verchiél Incarnate were better off than any living in Bjordal.

He broke off a few finger bones from their hand and pocketed them. He met their obsidian jewelled eyes, speaking coldly. "Makt'il de'öm gripen den."

Power to those who seize it. An old Bjordal proverb and a lesson he'd learned the hard way. After all, a piece of another Incarnate allowed him to form a connection to them: hair was preferable, blood in a pinch, bone at wit's end. He'd avoided her attention for as long as he could, but if he kept putting off contact, he'd only face more wrath in future visits.

He forced it out of his mind and turned to the task at hand. He reached into the pouch where he'd stored the bones, fingers brushing past them, and grabbed a familiar lock of pale blond hair between his fingers.

Verchiél believed that an Incarnate's magic was a gift from the heavens. Heathland thought that it was nothing more than a defect of the blood, something unnatural yet profitable. For Bjordal, the stories had come from something darker and much more mundane. More specifically a ritual, which cultists had done countless ages before. A select few sacrificed themselves during the day, others at the dead of night, trapping a bit of power in themselves. Creating the very first Incarnate. Something that was still passed on to this day.

Verchiél baulked at this, declaring it to be blasphemy. Surely Incarnate were something untainted by human hands. While Bjordal decried it, claiming it as the great sin which had first begun humankind's downfall from grace and inherent morality, to be bold enough to place themselves above the gods.

Niklas had never cared for the pointless debates so many philosophers, academics and religious zealots had argued over for centuries. It was only the cost that concerned him. After all, it often required a price to use.

He removed a blade from his belt, the steel tinged with a unique blue hue. He considered it for a moment before he slashed it across his palm in a single, clean motion. No blood rose to the surface, but rather a substance like black ink, his own magic, forcibly pulled from his body.

Verchiél would kill for it; Bjordal would kill because of it.

He drew his hand in the air in front of him. The power hummed in his veins and the lock of hair was scorched black and turned to ash in his hand. Shadows enveloped him; he couldn't tell which way was up or down, he simply kept walking forward. Until finally.

The shadows dissipated and he stepped down onto cobblestone streets and tried to gain his bearings in the city he did not recognize. The surrounding buildings towered in white-washed walls or earthy terracotta bricks, the area eventually blending into the lemon groves and lavender fields beyond the city. A hue of warmth which enveloped everything and only made the already unbearably balmy weather stifling.

In the distance celebrations still raged on as they would until news of the palace incident spread. Even now people rushed to and from their businesses, starting their work for the day or heading home after a night of revelry.

Niklas wandered through the dim streets, navigating the tangled mess of cobbled alleyways and shop fronts with little success. A flash of white-hot pain burst through his skull and he flinched.

She knew he was here.

He stopped at the corner of the street, his gaze drawn upward to a lavish set of apartments, his eyes focused on the only lit window, on the top floor. The pain in his head flared until he could scarcely breathe. He strode forward swiftly, keeping his eyes fixed ahead of him.

His magic was leaving him, and a dull ache was spreading throughout his body, a reminder of how weak he'd grown without it. It would only become worse as the day went on. But she'd been as resolute as an immovable block of stone, so he'd relented. After all, he knew better than to disagree with her.

The Sun of Bjordal had never been a patient person.

Niklas slowed his pace, and unease crept through him when he saw that the door to the apartment was battered and hanging off its hinges.

"Silje?" he called out.

Silence answered his call. He drew in a breath, steeling himself before he slipped inside. The apartment was ruined. Paintings crooked on their frames, furniture knocked over, pillows shredded and soft down littered everywhere. Niklas' feet tread cautiously over shattered glass and crystal ornaments. In the midst of it all, his eyes landed on a figure collapsed on the floor. Her pale skin and white-blond hair were spattered with red, limbs twisted at odd angles, a dark stain at her throat.

Niklas knelt beside her. "Silje?" Silence hung in the air, but beneath it he caught the subtle rise and fall of her breath. "If you're going to play dead," he said, "remember to hold still. I could see you giggling from across the room."

Another pause before a single eye opened, the palest blue staring up at him. She smiled. "Almost got you, didn't I?"

"No, you didn't—"

She threw her arms up and screamed.

He stumbled away, his heart racing. "Silje!" he growled.

She clapped her hands together in a fit of laughter. "You

should see your face."

"What is…" He tried to calm his racing heart. She was always doing such things; he'd never comprehended her sense of humour. "What is all this?"

"Well—" She sat up, speaking cheerfully. "You took forever to get here, so I got bored."

"Bored?"

"Yes. Bored. What else was there to do?"

His eyes went to the magnificent bookshelves whose previous tenants now lay sadly scattered across the floor. "You couldn't have just read a book?"

She gagged. "These ones are all boring. Not a single story with pirates, would you believe it?"

"This isn't funny."

She pinched her fingers together. "It's a little bit funny."

"And what will happen when the family comes home and finds their apartment ruined?"

"So? I won't be here."

"But the mess will."

"Doesn't matter because I don't have to clean it up."

He squeezed his eyes shut and drew in a deep breath, calming himself. "Why did you summon me?"

"Do I need a reason to visit my favourite brother?"

Brother. That was one word he was always relieved to hear. Though in truth they were half siblings. King Asbjorn, their father, was the thread shared between them that had bound them tightly since childhood. After all, Silje had saved him; she'd been the one who'd found him a decade ago, half starved and lost in the Bjordal wilds after he'd been exiled. If she hadn't found him, then he wouldn't have a single person left to call family. That frightened him more than anything.

"I'm your only brother," Niklas corrected her.

"With an attitude like that, you're lucky you're still my favourite."

"Silje," he said crossly. "No more games—"

She sucked in a deep breath before she stuck out her tongue.

"How…mature," Niklas said.

"Sva!" She rose to her feet, dusting herself off. "Da skalen vi vaeren seriouse." She whirled on him, her smile gone as she stared at him indifferently, her pale eyes like ice. "Duer ös senkt."

You're late.

"You might have not noticed," Niklas explained, "but a coup is a lot of work. Are you even going to be present for the coronation?"

"Can't." She waved her hand in dismissal. "I have business in Heathland next week."

"Can't you just skip it?"

"No. Sometimes a visit requires a personal touch."

"You're not visiting *her* again, are you?"

"That's none of your business."

They stared each other down. Even though he was her elder by a year, Niklas had never been one to hold up long against her willpower, and soon enough, his eyes fell to his feet.

"Where are we?" he asked.

"The port district of Verchiél. The family here was out for the night at the theatre, so I let myself in."

"And the servants?"

"I told them there was a burglar in the building and to run and hide." She gestured toward herself. "Technically, I wasn't wrong."

"Subtle."

He was rewarded with a slight grin at that. Probably the closest thing to gratitude he was going to get. He kept his face carefully blank. She was supposed to be in Bjordal. She'd changed her plans without him— again.

She didn't seem to notice his discontent as she smiled. "Look how much has changed already. You've been crowned, and without a single scratch on you." Her pale eyes flicked across him, lingering for a moment longer over the cut underneath his jaw. "Well, hardly a scratch. I trust everything went smoothly?"

Niklas was shocked by her words. There was something almost like pride in her voice. He took the silver circlet from his head and the pain around his temples instantly lessened, though there was still a dull pounding in his skull. "It depends on who you ask."

Silje's tone took on a hardened edge. "I'm not asking anybody else. I'm asking you. What happened tonight with the other Incarnate?"

There it was.

He bit the inside of his cheek, attempting to remain expressionless. But this time she was paying close attention to him, and it wasn't so easy. He chose his words carefully, his eyes still upon the circlet in his hands. "I don't know."

The confession was met with silence. A slow smile crept across her features, but it didn't put him at ease. It reminded him of a lean and hungry wolf, ready to snap something up at a moment's notice.

"What do you mean you don't know?"

Her voice was low. Her tone was a warning. Niklas' eyes

found their usual way to the floor. "They're gone. I don't know where. Nobody has found them yet."

"You were supposed to watch them, not let them slip right through your fingers!"

The top of her head barely reached his chest, but he still took a step backward. He'd learned the hard way that it was best to stand far away when her mood was off.

"They fled before I had a chance to reason with them," he countered.

"Or did you not do everything you were supposed to?"

He met her eyes then, growing brighter by the passing second. Early morning, the time of day where both had a sliver of magic in their veins. It still astounded Niklas. The chances of becoming Incarnate were slim to none, but the chances of siblings becoming Incarnate? It should have been impossible, and yet here they both were. A matching set and the bane of their father's existence. Sometimes Niklas wondered if there was a higher power at play. If so, they must have a dreadful sense of humour.

"I did everything exactly as you planned," Niklas said.

The corners of her mouth twitched savagely. "Are you certain you understood my instructions?"

"Perhaps it wasn't the instructions that were the problem so much as the person giving them."

She took a deep breath through her nose, turning away, ignoring him a little too deliberately, and neatly smoothed out the folds of her coat. Her face cleared from the previously stormy expression, and she clasped her hands before her, the image of composure once more.

"Enlighten me," he said. "If I'm so woefully incompetent, why bother sending me in the first place?"

"Not incompetent, brother, simply difficult." She walked along the shelves in the room, lingering before a cupboard of amber-coloured bottles of alcohol. She picked one up at random. "But not so unreasonable that you're entirely useless."

He watched her pour herself a glass of whiskey. "I'm delighted to know I'm still of use," he said dryly.

"As am I," she said. "Besides, you know as well as any that the night is your time to truly shine." Her voice took on a faraway tone as she looked at the glass in her hands. "I wish I could have been there. To see such a duel. It will be spoken of for years to come."

"You should have waited for the summer solstice. It would only have been another half year away."

She shook her head. "Hesitation would have cost us everything. The other two would have been long since crowned. And we'd be trapped back in Bjordal with all our hard work lost." She twitched her fingers lazily. "Honestly, someone puts a crown on your head and suddenly you're full of opinions, aren't you?"

"A crown," he mused. "Something I was supposed to be given a decade ago."

Years ago, he was going to be a king, promised by his father and mother, blessed by a royal title and beloved by a country and its people. But instead of a crown he'd been given powers that half the Isles called a curse and the other a blessing. For all Silje's faults, she was the only person who had ever accepted him for what he truly was.

The sound of glass shattering brought him back to his senses as he watched Silje toss her now-empty whiskey glass into the fire. She gestured to the circlet. "Put it back on. It suits you."

He placed the circlet back on his head, but it felt too tight.

It had been made for the Verchiél boy, so it was too small for him to wear comfortably.

She nodded in approval. "Much better. Perhaps we'll make royalty of you yet."

He sighed. "Silje."

She looked at him expectantly, a faint smile on her face, and he almost lost his nerve with what he was going to say next. "I still don't agree about capturing the other Incarnate. They're long since gone, perhaps we can just—"

The fire sparked with Silje's temper and singed the carpet by the hearth.

"What? Let them go?"

His words came tumbling from him now desperately wanting her to understand. "They can live their own lives, separate from us. They're people, not dogs to be hunted like we were. It feels wrong."

She clucked her tongue. "Your feelings are inconsequential."

"But they are like us. We've swapped places. So, in a way they are us. We can't just—"

She held a hand up. "They're an unknown variable. Having two incredibly powerful people in direct opposition to us leaves too many possibilities open. Too many chances for something—or someone to come back and haunt us." She looked at him closely, and sensing the miserable look on his face, she softened her voice, the way he so rarely heard anymore. "Think of it this way, do you want to go back to the way things were?"

His next arguments died on his lips. She spoke the truth. Things had improved for them, given Silje's uncanny talents for getting them wherever they needed to go. But that didn't change the decade of the things they'd done to survive.

Run.

Hide.

Fight.

Sensing she'd struck a nerve with him, Silje continued speaking. "We don't want to go back to Bjordal, do we?"

"No, we don't. We need control."

"Exactly. Control."

Silje was a person who divided the world into obstacles and assets.

Niklas was an asset.

He tugged at his coat, agitated, but quickly brought his hands back down to his sides. She didn't like it when he was fidgety. His gaze found its way cautiously toward her to see if she'd been watching him, but she only proceeded to address the fire before them. "It doesn't matter, they're still two of the most wanted people in the Isles, they won't stay hidden for long. After all" —her gaze pierced him— "you're going to be the one to find them, yes?"

"Yes," he responded automatically.

She scrutinised him with those pale eyes of hers, and he fought the instinct to look away. She had always made him feel as though she could see right through him.

"Once you return, you're not to leave the palace under any circumstances. Send some of your guards to find them," Silje said.

The thought of dealing with any more of them today made the pain in his temples grow. He thought of Dabria. He hoped that she would have more luck than anyone else. Silje was the last person he wanted to find the Incarnate first. "I already have someone seeking them out."

He squinted and held a hand up as the morning sun was bright past the windows. By now his magic was holding on by only the weakest thread. He grabbed one of the finger bones from his pocket and spoke before she had the chance to start asking him more questions. "I need to leave."

"Niklas, we're not finished—"

She reached out to stop him, but he had already stepped away, drawing his blade across his palm and letting the shadows envelop him. He was grateful that as far as her reach was, it wasn't infinite. Not yet.

Niklas stumbled back into the crypt in the palace, exhaustion leaching through his entire body as his magic left him. He coughed and specks of black came away with his hand. He'd strained himself too much, and he was going to pay for it today.

The skeleton of the Incarnate stared blankly at him, still clad in its deathly glory.

"Faen vok," Niklas cursed, forcing himself to his feet.

With some difficulty he managed to drag himself back to his new rooms, the previous Moon's.

Everything was decorated in black silks and silver, and the countless frivolous items such as wardrobes bursting with enough finery to clothe an entire village, and the incredibly lewd oil paintings proudly on display in their gilt golden and silver frames, told Niklas everything he needed to know about Verchiél's previous Moon: that despite sharing the same magic, they *wouldn't* get along.

With a glance in the mirror he caught the last traces of darkness leaving his eyes as the sun hit them, returning to their

usual amber hue. He collapsed into the nearest chair, too exhausted
to move. His senses slowly came back to him. Marble floors beneath his feet. Waves lapped upon the shore and echoed in his ears.
He fidgeted with the ancient finger bones before tossing them into
one of the drawers of a nearby vanity, which held another lock of
Silje's hair. He looked out the window to the old city built upon the
bright ocean waters where many gondolas bobbed with the calm
waves, the sun just starting to crest over the tallest buildings of
rust-coloured brick and sun-bleached stone in the distance.

City of the Incarnate...

It was something utterly foreign to him, to have his own
rooms— and such lavish ones at that. So strange compared to the
endless hunger of the years spent in the Bjordal wilds. For every
bit of comfort, every soft bed and warm hearth he enjoyed, he
recalled a hundred nights and days when he had been freezing,
starving or both. No matter how much he scavenged or hunted, his
bones had run sharp and jagged right against his skin. And the cold
cut deep, persisting through the endless miles of frozen waste-
lands filled with vicious beasts who held no fear of humans. In that
place you could travel for months without seeing another person.
So easily, you could lose yourself entirely. Niklas almost had, but
somehow, through all of it, he'd found Silje— or she'd found him.
He'd never been quite sure of the truth.

His gaze moved to the room behind him, taking inventory
of its contents: a plush round bed, far too large for a single person,
and decorated with too many little pillows; above the ceiling was
beautifully painted with a dark, starlit sky. There was a fireplace
carved from obsidian, but with Verchiél's warm weather, it stood
as a decoration more than anything, the hearth swept and cleared
of either wood or ash. This was where he was going to be living

now. He knew he should be grateful, that many would die to have a chance to bask in such finery. But it only left him unsettled and on edge. He felt like nothing but an intruder in a world that he didn't belong in.

The pain grew in his temples and he brushed his fingers against his head, meeting cold metal. He took it off and spun the silver hoop in his fingers.

He remembered how the other two Incarnate had looked when he'd placed it upon his head, the girl fearful and trying to hide her shaking hands, the boy looking back to him with fury in his familiar black eyes. Despite all the years of careful planning— Silje having organised everything down to the smallest detail— he'd still been curious to meet them. He was supposed to have laid low until the speeches. He didn't exactly blend in. Too tall and hair an odd shade for this far south, but he couldn't help himself. The only living person he knew with magic, other than himself, was Silje. He hadn't known what he had expected when he had arrived at the solstice, a small flame of hope seated in his chest when he'd sought out the two people Verchiél held so dearly. But after to-night, what he'd felt for them was neither admiration nor respect.

He had been disappointed.

The lavish celebrations, the adoring crowds, the food and drinks served as if it were never-ending. He hadn't seen so much extravagance since he'd been at court as a child. Even then it was always controlled, within sense and moderation; a way to show so-cial standing and respect rather than wasteful flaunting simply for the sake of it. It was obvious that both Verchiél Incarnate had been living in luxury for years on end, the only real threat to their lives being an unpleasant social afternoon. Both dressed in finery that cost a small fortune and indulged in every excess, with an entire city holding them aloft. Niklas prided himself upon his restraint and reasoning. But the jealous thought that if he'd simply been born further south then it would be him tucked safely away within a palace all his life followed him like a rabid hound snapping at his heels all night. The only thing any Incarnate in Bjordal was given when they were discovered was a royal firing squad or the edge of a cultist's knife, depending on who found them first.

He threw the circlet unceremoniously inside the vanity along with his morbid growing collection of pieces of other Incarnate, and snapped the drawer shut. He watched the sun rise higher in the sky, glad for the sight of it, even as he pictured Silje's golden eyes burning across the city.

8

GABRIEL

When the surface of the water broke Gabriel nearly opened his mouth again from the shock of cold. His hand slipped from Zoe's as they rushed forward, and in a moment of guttural panic he instinctively reached up for the surface, wanting to escape the water, but his nails only dragged along the stone ceiling of the tunnel. He wanted to scream but he still knew that he'd drown if he allowed himself a moment of something so careless.

His heart pounded so fast he thought he'd faint. Along with a wave of bitter resentment. He was back again, in that dark, unforgivable place. It had come years too late, but here he was, trapped underneath the roiling current of the water. He wished he'd stayed in the palace and just let Niklas imprison him. It would be a kinder death, wasting away in a cell, than anything the water had to offer him. He opened his eyes and immediately regretted it; the water was so dark that he couldn't see anything. This place was cursed if even his sharp eyes couldn't pierce the darkness. He squeezed his eyes shut again and desperately hoped, as the current swept him and Zoe along, that they were both still headed in the same direction.

His head was clouded. His chest was going to explode, small lights danced in the darkness of his vision, and when he thought he couldn't stand another second of it, the current miraculously released him into a calm body of water. He opened his eyes, revealing a dim light toward the surface. He wasted no time in paddling his weakening body toward it.

Gabriel gasped when he breached the surface, drawing in a heaving lungful of air, coughing from all the water he'd swallowed. His throat burned, and his eyes were blurred. He sank again as he struggled to keep himself above the water, clawing for purchase upon something—anything—that might help him but finding only cold air. He tipped his head back, drawing in as much breath as he could before sinking under.

"Gabriel!"

Arms encircled him, wrenching him above the water, helping to keep him afloat. He coughed and sputtered, his eyes stung from the salt, his muscles were sore from trying and failing to keep himself buoyant, and his limbs heavy as if they were made of lead.

Zoe spoke. "Stop moving, or you'll drown us both."

He stilled at that. He clung to Zoe as if she were his last hope in this world. She was so warm compared to the freezing water around them. He took a chance and stretched his feet, hoping to hit the bottom, but felt nothing but water. He shivered imagining what might be below them, down in the hidden places and the muck.

Zoe patted his arm, sending splashes of water against his face that made him twitch. Her voice was apologetic. "Sorry, I thought you were going to faint."

"I still might, can we get out of here?"

Taking in his surroundings, he saw that the current had let them out in the harbour. Sailing vessels large and small were docked around them, and Gabriel could see the lights of the palace in the distance.

"But where are we going to go?" Zoe asked.

The palace. That was the answer on his lips before realisation struck him. He was tossed out again. With nothing to his name. All of their planning and connections he'd made for years had amounted to nothing. Although... Maybe this time was different. Zoe was here too. She'd picked him instead of Niklas. He turned around in her grasp until they were face to face and was met with her dark brown eyes. The sun hadn't risen enough to turn them to gold.

"This was a terrible idea," he said.

"You were the one who wanted to escape."

"What were you thinking going on the count of two? Nobody goes on two."

"I thought you wouldn't jump if I waited until three."

She was right, but he didn't want to give her the satisfaction of knowing that, so he remained silent. He found his gaze drawn back to the rows of boats over her shoulder, the harbour bursting with visitors for the solstice, and for the first time during this whole ordeal did he find a small grin tugging at his lips.

"Remember that ship you've always wanted?"

She followed his gaze, understanding what he was suggesting. "You've got to be kidding."

"Got a better plan?"

She bit her lip, but he could already guess the answer she'd give him. He noticed how sluggish her movements had been growing as she paddled wearily, trying to keep them both afloat.

Between the two of them they managed to swim into the crowded harbour. Their progress was slow, partially from wanting to be discreet but mostly because Gabriel could barely swim and was struggling with staying afloat, let alone moving forward. He kept his eyes shut and imagined the marble hallways of the palace, or the stone streets or even a field in the middle of nowhere, just anywhere that wasn't water.

He'd worried at first that their soaked clothes would draw attention, but apparently half of the party had decided to spend their evening swimming and the deck was crowded with guests in soaked gowns and suits.

As they reached the deck, Zoe hurried along beside him, clinging to his arm as if fearful they'd be separated.

"There's too many people here," she hissed. "We'll be spotted."

"Where there are bigger crowds, there are more places to hide," he explained.

"Really?" Zoe asked, narrowly dodging a drunken couple who stumbled past, spilling their drinks along the deck. "Or did you conveniently pick the boat that just so happens to have an out-of-control party happening?"

"Do you really think"—he grabbed a party mask from one of the drunken guests— "that I'm so reckless as to risk our capture for a party?"

"Yes."

"Have some faith." Gabriel slipped the mask on. "We lay low and get a ride out of the city. By morning no one will know where we are. It's brilliant!"

"We could be captured a million times before that."

"Or we could find a million ways to escape," he countered, digging around in his soaked pockets before he came up with his old mask.

"You still have that ratty thing?" Zoe asked.

"It's lucky I do," he said, fitting it over Zoe's eyes. Even with the disguise they still needed to find somewhere inconspicuous to hide; the sun would be rising soon and Zoe's golden eyes would be easy to spot.

He walked along the deck, careful to avoid the large patches of lantern light, letting the chaos of the crowd conceal them.

Suddenly a loud bang echoed across the deck and an explosion of gold and silver fireworks lit up the sky. Zoe jumped in fright, clutching tighter to his arm as the crowd around them let out a happy cheer.

From the upper deck, a ghostly woman walked down the stairs, her hair and skin nearly the same pale shade. She was immaculately dressed in a midnight blue velvet suit and Gabriel found himself unable to look away.

"Gabe," Zoe whispered, trying to tug him along with her. "Let's go."

"Now hang on." He stared at the woman, awestruck. "I think we should hear what she has to say."

She captivated him in a way he couldn't quite quantify. She was beautiful, certainly, but there was something else magnetic about her, beyond her appearance that rooted him to the spot.

As if she could sense his stare, across the crowd, she met his gaze. Her eyes were cutting, as if she could part flesh and bone like a curtain and see to the very centre of him. But that was ridiculous, he was one face among hundreds, it couldn't be him that she was looking at.

Her lips curled into a smile as she addressed the crowd. "A toast, to good fortune."

Another set of fireworks went off and people cheered and drank alongside her. Gabriel clapped with the rest of the party.

Zoe tugged on his arm again, this time more insistently. "The sun's rising soon!"

His fixation was broken and indeed he noticed that the sky had begun to lighten. Zoe shifted uncomfortably beside him; though she was wearing the mask, he imagined the flecks of gold which would already be blooming in her brown eyes.

"Let's go below deck," he agreed.

Zoe wasted no further time and navigated swiftly through the crowd. Gabriel had to give her credit, for as anxious as she was, she knew how to lead when she was determined enough.

They had nearly made it to the cabin doors when a group of drunkards sprinted past, bumping into Gabriel as they laughed and popped champagne corks along the way.

"Fuck—" Gabriel struggled to reorient himself and turned, alarmed to find that Zoe was nowhere to be seen. "Zo?" He craned his neck in every direction, party goers jostling past him, drinks raised high and voices loud. It certainly wasn't the first time they'd been separated at a party. At least this time he wasn't trying to ditch her on purpose.

He circled the area carefully but he still didn't see her. So absorbed was he in his search that he didn't notice when a pale figure bumped into him.

A hand shot out and seized his arm, steadying him, and he stared into the eyes of the ghostly woman.

He managed a laugh. "My dear, please forgive my clumsy feet."

"You spilled my drink," she said simply.

Sure enough there was deep crimson wine spilt across the

deck.

"I'm terribly sorry," Gabriel apologised. "I'll happily fetch you a new drink. But first—" He bowed and offered a hand. "May I offer you a dance?"

Surely Zoe wouldn't mind if he was gone for a few more minutes. She probably wouldn't even notice.

There was an unnerving intensity to the woman's gaze, as she stared unblinkingly before she placed her empty glass on a passing tray and took his hand, sweeping them across the deck. She led, and there was a strength to her that was startling for her petite form.

"I saw you, in the audience." She tilted her pale head to the side and peered at him; it reminded Gabriel less of a gesture of curiosity and more of a bird of prey analysing a potential meal. "You kept staring at me."

"How could I possibly have eyes for anyone else other than the gorgeous company currently in my arms?"

"Honeyed tongue, do you taste as sweet as you sound?"

The music swelled and he leaned forward, voice sultry. "Perhaps you'd like to find out?"

She smiled. "Are you always so agreeable to strangers?"

"If the strangers are lovely such as you, of course."

She tightened her grip on his hand, leading them faster. "You don't know a thing about me, perhaps I'm a murderer."

He laughed. "Well, you're clearly someone with refined taste. What sort of things do you like?"

She considered the question solemnly. "A glass of wine, someone beautiful in my bed…" They slowed and she pressed closer; he caught the powdery scent of expensive perfume and oddly enough the faintest tang of ash. "An enemy at my feet."

"It sounds like we're a lot alike," Gabriel said.

"Perhaps"—her voice lowered a fraction—"you'd like to join me in my cabin for some more private affairs?"

He fought the urge to grin like an idiot. Perhaps he'd finish this night off like he'd originally intended after all.

"My dear, I'd love nothing more—"

In the morning sky, the sun rose, its first rays bright in his eyes, and his stomach dropped when he remembered—

Right. He was supposed to be looking for Zoe…

"—but I'm afraid I've lost my friend," Gabriel admitted, the elation he'd felt moments before already fading.

"She's fine," the woman assured him.

Gabriel paused. "How would you know that?"

She merely smiled in response and walked toward the cabin. He didn't hesitate as he followed, not wanting to lose sight of her.

When he passed through the doors he was greeted by the sight of a lavish cabin, a long table set with a dinner of every kind of delicacy he could imagine, bottles of blood-red wine and a platter of spiced pheasant and honey-glazed pears. Despite the large dinner, only three chairs were set around the table, and in one of them, sat Zoe.

Zoe immediately stood up.

"Gabriel! Where have you been?"

"Sorry for the delay, Zoe," the woman said. "I was offered a dance I couldn't refuse."

Gabriel looked between them. "You two know each other?"

"We've only just met," the woman explained, "but Zoe was kind enough to accept my invitation." She picked up one of the wine bottles. "Have a seat and help yourselves, I'll pour the wine."

Gabriel sat across from Zoe and picked up the platter of honey-glazed pears. He offered it to Zoe but she only shook her head adamantly. It was then that he noticed her hands were clasped tightly in her lap and her leg was tapping out an errant rhythm, one of her nervous habits.

Gabriel slowly realised that every dish on the table was either a favourite of his or Zoe's. He speared a few of the pears onto his plate, talking to their host.

"It's very kind of you to invite us to such a fine dinner, I'd like to give a proper thanks but we don't even know your name."

Two glasses of wine were placed before them and the woman smiled warmly.

"Silje."

"Silje…?" Gabriel prompted.

"Nordviken."

Gabriel met Zoe's eyes and she mouthed. *Bjordal.*

"Silje," he rolled her name over in his mouth, liking the way it felt on his tongue. "What a pleasure to have a Bjordal host."

Silje watched him carefully. "Does that bother you?"

"Of course not," Zoe answered quickly. "Forgive us, we're not used to many northerners venturing this far south."

Something flashed in Silje's eyes, so quickly Gabriel swore he imagined it—cautious, no, calculating. It vanished just as quickly and Silje's easy smile returned. "The pleasure is all mine." She raised her glass. "A toast to auspicious meetings."

The three each clinked glasses, and he took a sip of the wine. It was rich and sweet and he recognized it as one of the vintages stocked at the palace.

"You have impeccable taste, my dear," Gabriel said, noticing Zoe hadn't fully taken a sip, only wet her lips, then placed her glass back into the table.

"Of course," Silje said, watching Zoe with amusement. "It's a special occasion after all. It's not every day that I have two Incarnate aboard my ship."

Gabriel tensed, glass still raised partway to his lips. His smile strained, he spoke as calmly as he could manage. "My dear, I'm sorry but you're terribly mistaken."

Silje gestured to his mask. "I think you'd be telling a different story if you removed that."

"If you wanted that kind of show I'd be more than willing to oblige—"

Zoe elbowed him before addressing Silje. "Please, I know what this looks like, but you can't turn us in."

"My dear Sun," Silje said patiently. "I have no intentions of doing any such thing."

Gabriel frowned. "Why?"

Silje twisted her wrist in a complex motion. There was the sound of a crack like a bone being snapped, the tang of gun-metal in the air, and her pale blue eyes filled with bright gold.

They were all silent. For a moment Gabriel's memories flashed back to the solstice, to the same way he'd felt when he'd first seen Niklas' eyes and knew that he wasn't one of a kind.

Zoe clutched a hand to her mouth, and looked at Silje with an expression Gabriel couldn't quite place. "You're a…"

"An Incarnate Sun?" Silje said. "Yes. Though I must say it's an honour meeting the Sun of Verchiél."

Gabriel scrutinised her eyes, but they were the exact same gold as Zoe's.

Silje smiled at Gabriel's incredulous expression. "Did you think you're the only one who can use illusions?"

A beat of silence passed between them. The muffled sounds of the party outside raged on before Zoe spoke up, removing her own mask to reveal the same golden eyes. "I've never heard of any Incarnate who can hide their eyes."

"It's a nice trick to have, especially in Bjordal of all places." Silje rested her elbows on the table, leaning forward. "Look, let's not waste time. I know you're both in trouble and I can help you."

"What makes you think we need help?" Gabriel asked.

"Or that we're in trouble for that matter?" Zoe added.

"Oh?" Silje smiled patiently. "Was I mistaken in my assumptions that two waterlogged Incarnate who should be at their own coronation ceremony just so happen to be on my ship instead? Or do you both enjoy late-night swims in the harbour?"

"We may have run into a spot of trouble," Gabriel admitted. "What interest is it to you?"

"I like doing things that seem impossible," Silje said. "Helping you both survive is a good start."

"Survive what?" Gabriel asked.

She looked between the two of them as if this were a very stupid question. "Six months ago King Asbjorn named a new heir, Hakon Vollon, a man who hates Incarnate. And now that Asbjorn's true son, an Incarnate, has taken the Verchiél throne, why wouldn't Hakon declare war against such a threat?"

Gabriel vaguely recalled this information from various meetings in the Verchiél palace, but all of this had happened around Enzo and Aria's funeral processions so the declaration of a new Bjordal heir hadn't exactly been in his top priorities of things to worry about.

"If Bjordal marches, Heathland will aid them and Verchiél

won't last long," the woman continued. "What hope will you have of regaining your thrones? You both experienced that tonight, nowhere is safe for you anymore. And once Bjordal declares war, it will only grow worse. Even Heathland remains in Niklas' favour."

"And what do you gain from helping us?" Gabriel asked.

"Change." She held her head higher. "I don't want a country divided by false beliefs."

"There's something I don't understand," Zoe said. "If you recently travelled from Bjordal and you're also an Incarnate, shouldn't you know Niklas?"

Silje turned her golden gaze back to Zoe and smiled sweetly. "What are you talking about?"

"I mean that—" Zoe's voice faltered mid sentence, her golden eyes watching Silje as intently as Silje was her. "I don't know Niklas, that's not something you should be worrying about, is it?"

"No…" Zoe's voice was quiet. "I suppose not."

Though he couldn't see her pale irises anymore, Gabriel knew that Silje was watching him closely. A sense of unease warned him, but he couldn't put a finger on why the feeling was there in the first place. So he settled for doing what came so naturally to him. Being difficult.

"Yes." He crossed his arms tightly. "Nothing to worry about in the least."

Silje smiled and reached for his face, cupping his cheek. "Are you feeling alright, darling? You must be so tired."

Gabriel blinked, confused as whatever he'd been trying to grasp suddenly slipped away, like water through his fingers.

"Gabriel?" Zoe asked. "Is something wrong?"

"No," he said. "Nothing at all. I was just going to say that if you both think it's a good idea, then I do too."

"Heavens." Zoe felt his forehead. "You don't have a fever, do you?"

Silje spoke. "We'll need to leave immediately. Grislow in Heathland is my next destination. I'm certain you could manage an audience with the council, perhaps they'll take your side rather than Niklas'."

Silje gave Gabriel a strange feeling. But it wasn't necessarily a bad thing to him. It was something beautiful and dangerous, something he didn't understand but wanted to be closer to.

Safe with me, the voice echoed.

"We're safe with her," Gabriel said.

She was helping them, and if he played his cards right he'd make sure that things ended up his way. Though it was a cruel twist of fate, to have to go back to where he'd come from to regain his throne— his home.

If he was lucky, things were going to be far more exciting than he'd originally thought.

"Off to Heathland?" Zoe asked.

Gabriel nodded. "Off to Heathland."

PART TWO
HEATHLAND

From Venture to Industry to Fortune

9
DABRIA

There had been few times in Dabria's life when she'd felt hopeless. But the day after the coup, she'd wept until there was nothing left in her.

The afternoon sunlight made Dabria squint as it reflected sharply off the canal. She had avoided her reflection all day, ignoring her swollen eyes and sallow cheeks. She never thought that she'd betray another person but she'd been wrong. First Ada. Now Alfio. Was there no one she would stand with?

Found some trouble again, Bria? Ada's old voice echoed through her mind.

No. She was going to see this through, even though the palace was the last place she wanted to be right now.

Overnight, people had heard of the events of the coup, and both supporters and protestors of Niklas had gathered around the palace. It had started as a few bystanders, mostly drunken party goers wanting to take part in the action, but over the course of the morning dozens had arrived until a sizable mob stood heckling and arguing with not only each other but also anyone who passed by. Unfortunately, once they saw her uniform, this also included Dabria.

"Traitor!"

Dabria, who had never been inclined toward just ignoring

her problems and was too tired to care, turned toward the nearest heckler and snapped,

"Fuck off!"

The man startled before answering smugly. "Fuck me yourself."

"Luckily you're not my type."

The man glowered. "You've sold us out to Bjordal."

Dabria held his stare. "He's Incarnate, why do you care where he's from?"

The man looked at her as if she'd said something incredibly stupid. "Don't you see? This was all King Asbjorn's plan, he's using his son to infiltrate Verchiél. It'll only be a matter of time before Bjordal invades us again."

One of the counter protestors scoffed. "First ignorance and now conspiracy theories? Prince Niklas is the Son of the Moon, he's meant to be here with us—"

A punch was flung and a fight broke out. Dabria jumped back as the crowd devolved into chaos. She placed a hand on the hilt of her sword, but before she could draw it, another guard spoke quickly.

"We'll handle this, Prince Niklas wants to speak with you."

Dabria tried to refuse, but she was shoved beyond the gates and a group of guards rushed past her to pull the fighting men apart. It was odd, Dabria considered, how much could change in a night.

The state of Verchiél's palace was little better than the exterior; piles of swept rubble and shattered glass littered nearly every area. The mess was only made worse by the groups of people who lingered stubbornly in the hallways. Aristocrats arguing over who to swear fealty to, servants uncertain whether their duties had changed, while guards watched them all with wary eyes, ready to stop any fights from breaking out. There was still a divide concerning who should rule. Dabria didn't need to strain her ears to hear what people thought of their newest Incarnate.

Demon.

Saint.

Traitor.

King.

But to Dabria, Niklas just looked tired.

In the sunlight, Niklas appeared hollow. His hair was messily pulled back, his amber eyes tired and his back slouched as if something weighed heavily on his shoulders. As if trying to save face for his haggard appearance he was dressed in a sharply tailored jacket that fastened diagonally with a set of silver buttons.

He stood in the doorway of the ballroom, deep in conversation with a group of Verchiél elites—wealthy merchants upset at what effect this would have on the Verchiél economy—while the nobles fawned over an Incarnate who finally had some royal blood in him.

Niklas' voice was a soothing balm while he answered their many questions, but his hand constantly twisted a ring around his finger. The nervous action was at odds with his voice, which was easily swallowed up by a collection of many raised arguments.

"...he can't be named king until there's been a proper coronation..."

"...why would you dare question a saint..."

"... he's no saint, he's lost our Sun and Moon..."

"...you've as good as declared war with Bjordal..."

At Dabria's approaching footsteps, Niklas gave her a curt nod before he addressed the gathered group. "I would be more than happy to continue these discussions at a more appropriate time. However, my captain is here and I urgently need to speak with her."

With mutters, the group slowly dispersed. Dabria stood beside Niklas and said, "Haven't you managed to get them all kissing your ass?"

"Are you aware—" Niklas' previously civil had tone vanished, his voice exhausted. "That most kings would have you killed for speaking so disrespectfully?"

"Lucky for me you're no king."

Dabria revelled in testing boundaries, in prodding and poking to see how far they could be pushed. Her exhaustion made her more reckless than usual, and in that moment as Niklas glared down at her, she wondered if he would truly follow through with his words. But his frown turned into a small smile. "Since I've been blessed with the company of one so honest, tell me, what do you make of this afternoon's discussions?"

"Discussions? In case you haven't noticed there's a mob outside."

"I'm well aware."

"Do you really think that Verchiél wants you?"

"Verchiél doesn't want me. Verchiél wants power, and what is power to them?"

The question was asked with a casual air, but there was an earnestness behind it. He expected her to consider it seriously. Verchiél was a small country, even by the standards of the Isles. Mighty neither in military nor political influence, but they did have one thing. Dabria thought about the marble statues of Incarnate who lined the palace walkway, generations dead but still remembered. How Zoe and Gabriel had been chosen by the king and queen despite not having a single drop of royal blood between them. Why Niklas had been able to vie for Verchiél's throne in the first place.

"Magic," Dabria decided.

Niklas nodded. "They want what I am— what I can do. It doesn't matter where it comes from, all that matters is that they have it."

"Is being a useless figurehead something people need?" Dabria gestured to his eyes, entirely ordinary in the sunlight. "You're not even special right now."

"It gives them hope, more than that, they feel as if they have power."

"Feeling like they have something and actually having it are two entirely different things."

"You're right, and because of that, I need your help." He walked into the ballroom, where many tables of construction equipment lay after the mess created the previous night, and Dabria followed, using the opportunity to slip his silver ring from his finger as he walked past.

"I'm aware that there is a ceremony to take place tonight at the city's main cathedral. A winter solstice celebration, in which I am to be the main feature," Niklas said.

"Yeah, it's some old tradition, why?" Dabria asked.

"Verchiél's Moon left behind a small spy network in his absence," Niklas explained. "One who with some persuasion had no qualms about working with me instead. They've recently acquired information which suggests that some still loyal to Verchiél's Sun and Moon would be most displeased, or may even become violent due to my presence."

Dabria frowned. "You made his own informants turn on

him?"

"I didn't make them, I asked them. You as well, if I'm not mistaken?"

Dabria bit the inside of her cheek, wanting to disagree. But the space beside her where Alfio normally stood at attention was empty. A painful reminder of her choice.

Niklas stopped at one of the tables and Dabria was greeted by the sight of various weapons laid out methodically. She approached with caution. "What's all this?"

Niklas gestured freely. "A gift."

"A gift…" she repeated, reaching for the nearest sword. Alfio's face flashed across her mind and her hand paused.

What would happen if I killed Niklas now?

They were the only two people in this chamber. If she moved fast enough she could attack him before he had the chance to defend himself and leave him for dead. She would be long gone before anyone was the wiser— after all, Niklas wasn't an Incarnate during the day, he was just a regular person.

Dabria's eyes narrowed on Niklas. He was standing casually, his hands clasped behind his back. If she didn't know any better, she would have thought he was bored. But there was something else in his stance too, still tangible to her scrutiny; his jaw was clenched and there was a tension in his energy, like a tightly coiled spring.

He nodded toward the sword. "Aren't you going to pick it up?"

This was more than a gift. He was testing her— tempting her— with a possibility, but even if she did manage to kill Niklas, he'd been instated as the acting Incarnate during the solstice. There would be blood to pay if she harmed him.

Dabria managed a smile. "How generous." She caught the subtlest motion of Niklas' shoulders relaxing. *No, I won't turn on you—not yet.* A small but angry voice spoke from the back of her mind, and this time she didn't push it away. She let it linger and simmer as she turned back to her new bounty.

She pulled the sword from its sheath and gasped. Blue-tinged steel greeted her; it glinted cold and pale as ice in the afternoon light. She held it up in the air, the metal reflecting in subtle hues of pinks and purples when it caught the light at different angles. She marvelled at how weightless it was in her hands.

"Himmel stal." Dabria and Niklas spoke at the same time.

He nodded, the faintest hint of pride in his voice. "Also known as Bjordal steel. The best in the Isles. Lighter, faster and also stronger—"

He tossed up a small chunk of marble from one of the many ruined statues. Dabria instinctively tightened her grip on the handle of the sword and swung it upward. She barely felt the connection as the blade glided through the stone like water, and two halves of marble clattered to the floor on either side of her. She bent down and picked up the chunk of stone, running her thumb along the smooth surface. A perfect cut. She shook her head. "Only Bjordal soldiers are allowed to carry them. They have to earn them through—"

"'Vilen.' Our trials of willpower," Niklas finished, "and so I did."

"You're giving me your earned steel?"

"They are mine to keep or give as I please. I have no use of them other than to reminisce fondly. What use are they collecting dust when they could serve you instead?" Niklas rolled one of his sleeves up. "For all my homeland's faults, our weaponry is second to none." He flipped one of the knives over in his hand, and much to her shock, slashed it across his arm. A moment passed and rather than blood, the cut bled black, like ink.

Dabria took a step backward, repulsed. "What the fuck..."

"Himmel stal is crafted from the very heart of the world itself. Delved from the northernmost reaches of Bjordal." He flipped the knife around, offering her the hilt. "Supposedly one of the places where Incarnate first found their power."

She took the knife and out of curiosity pricked her own finger. A scarlet bead of blood welled up.

She met his eyes. "Meaning..."

"They dispel magic."

The knife and sword suddenly felt much heavier in her hands. "You're giving me something that could kill you?"

"Any blade can kill. These are different because they give you an advantage that no other weapon could."

"But if they dispel magic, couldn't you just use them to get rid of yours and take your throne back?"

He laughed, a dry and humourless sound. "Do you think that there would be any Incarnate left if such a possibility existed for my country? No. They will dispel the flow of magic and weaken an Incarnate for a short time—not banish the magic entirely—but this will give you an edge you've never had before."

A sense of confusion rose in Dabria as she looked back to Niklas.

"But why are you giving me any of this? These are weapons for fighting Incarnate."

"Yes," Niklas continued, "but I'm not the Incarnate you should worry about."

Does he mean Zoe and Gabriel? They'd never tried to hurt

her, and for as much of a twat as Gabriel was, she'd never once veiled her threats to punch him in the dick if he tried any weird magic shit on her.

"I can handle myself," Dabria said.

"I know. That's why I chose you. But as strong as you are, you're all too human." He must have sensed her anger at the comment because he added, "I mean it as a compliment, Dabria. Few could claim so much."

Her eyes flicked to the cut along his arm, to the dried spatter like ink. He noticed her stare and rolled his sleeve down. "I will pay the price when my magic returns. Nothing is without cost, even if it's delayed."

"Incredible." Dabria's voice came out a little too awestruck for her liking. She held the sword close, running her finger along the sharpened edge of the blade, her eyes roving over the assortment of other knives and weapons. "All these are mine?"

"If you wish, every last one."

She turned the blade over in her hands. "Well, if this concludes our business—"

"A moment." Niklas held his hand out expectantly.

"What's the matter?" she asked. "Do you want a goodbye hug?"

Niklas frowned. "I have no issues with you stealing, with the exception of it being from me."

"Beg your pardon?"

"Don't play stupid. You're much cleverer than that."

Begrudgingly, Dabria dug Niklas' silver ring from her pocket and placed it in his outstretched hand. "I just wanted to see it," she mumbled. "That's the Osenson family crest, but last night you introduced yourself as Niklas Askeland."

"Askeland is my mother's house. Shortly after I left home I renounced my father's name."

"But doesn't that mean you can't take the Bjordal throne?"

"I'm a heksa. I couldn't take the throne in the first place."

She frowned, turning the unfamiliar word over in her mouth. "Heksa?"

"A cursed one."

Niklas moved to leave, bringing a swift end to their conversation. But Dabria caught his arm, halting his movements.

He winced at the contact, a pained expression on his face, and she realised she had grabbed his wounded arm. "Sorry…" she said, taking a step away. "But what about the ceremony? There's already a mob outside. If are also rumours about a protest during the ceremony, then it's not going to be safe for you. So how exactly am I supposed to keep you from getting hurt if there's a riot?"

"You're the captain," Niklas said. "Figure it out."

Dabria tamped down her anger at the smug response and waited until Niklas left the room, listening as his soft footfalls faded down the hallway, before she pulled his silver ring from her pocket. Having been distracted by the pain, Niklas hadn't noticed when she'd swiped the ring from his other hand.

Dabria smiled contentedly to herself and slipped the silver ring over her thumb. She turned back to the table and reached for one of the knives. She couldn't fathom how something so ordinary could possibly have any effect over an Incarnate— over magic itself— but it sure beat having nothing at all. She would take what she could get to gain an advantage; Niklas understood that too. Perhaps they were a little more alike than she'd originally thought.

10

NIKLAS

Ten Years Ago

Niklas had always been told that he was everything a Bjordal prince wasn't supposed to be: quiet, soft and weak.

In the winter courtyard of Castle Osenson, Niklas knelt on a disk of stone worn by generations of touch, surrounded by a pool that reflected the grey winter sky. The only thing that kept him from falling into the icy water was his careful balance to level the purposely uneven stone. It was a symbol for rulership: if a king was calm, so was everything around him. Even his smallest actions would send out ripples across the water. For three days before his twentieth birthday, by order of the country's head priests, he was to fast and pray. To mentally and spiritually prepare himself for the responsibility of undertaking his country as well as his impending marriage ceremony. This was supposed to be a holy moment meant for reflection and contemplation in complete solitude.

The priests clearly hadn't taken Silje into account.

"So have you slept with your bride yet?"

Niklas shifted and a ripple broke across the smooth surface of the pool. "Of course not. That would be conduct unbecoming of me."

"Are you sure?" Silje paced lazily around the pool. Despite the ancient prayer ceremony needing to be done alone, she'd snuck in and made no signs of leaving. "She was holding your hand for so long during the engagement feast that I thought she was glued to you. Father's certainly chosen a clingy one."

Another set of ripples broke across the water. Silje had a talent for picking away at the things he most wanted to conceal, but he forced himself to be still. He needed to succeed. Though Silje was always presented as his distant cousin in public, in private Asbjorn had never made any effort to hide the favouritism between his children. Proudly claiming that even Silje, "the bastard daughter", possessed greater spirit in a single finger than Bjordal's crown prince did in his entire body.

He tried to focus past the present moment and repeat the virtues he'd been mentally reciting for hours now.

"Arner. Patyn. Stryken—"

Mistaking his silence for moroseness, Silje added helpfully, "She's cute. A little sweet for my taste, but I'm certain she'll balance out your depressive tendencies."

"I suppose," he said, desiring to bring an end to the invasive conversation, but Silje gave him a knowing look, her eyes cutting to his core.

"You're still pining after that boy in your cohort, aren't you?"

He slipped, the icy water splashing his legs as he tilted forward, but before he could fall into the frigid pool, Silje threw out a hand and steadied him.

"Sva, Silje!" he growled. "I'm supposed to do it by myself."

"I can still drop you if you'd prefer an ice bath?" She

smiled sweetly.

"No—" He grabbed her other hand, letting her help him up. Between the two of them Niklas managed to step back onto the ground of the courtyard. He stretched his back, muscles tense and constricted from sitting for so long. "Don't tell Father."

"About interrupting your prayers? Or that you've been sneaking out with your betrothed *and* your sparring partner?"

"Either," he said. "I don't need him or the priests giving me another lecture about a man's proper duties."

"I wouldn't dare." She grinned. "It's more fun this way."

Niklas met her eyes then, fully golden, forgoing the usual tricks to hide them when they were alone. He'd known about Silje's condition since the day she'd changed. Kept in check by the strictness of their father and the sigils she'd been taught to carve into her skin.

Only he and Asbjorn knew; everyone else either loved her or feared her, sometimes both at once. He'd been taught to fear what she was, but first and foremost she was his sister. He could never find it in himself to consider her any other way.

"I was thinking," Niklas began, taking advantage of their father's absence to speak freely, "there is something I want to change when I'm crowned."

"Legalise haze leaf?"

"Silje, I'm serious."

"So am I."

He drew in a breath and spoke about what he'd been meditating on for hours now. "I'll tell people the truth. That you're my sister."

For once, Silje didn't have an answer. It unsettled Niklas as much as it amused him, and he found himself talking to fill the uncharacteristic silence. "They'll have to listen, to accept you."

Silje's voice was quiet. "You mean it?"

"Of course. You'll be known as an Osenson, as you should be."

Her golden eyes blazed with a sudden intensity. "Swear it."

"I promise." He held out his hand, which she immediately shook. "Truthfully, I wish that Father would choose you as heir instead. I'm no good at any of this."

The moment of intensity passed as quickly as it had come, and Silje smiled once more. "In that case, can I marry Lady Halldorsen instead? I want to know if she tastes as sweet as she looks."

"You're horrible."

She shoved him backward into the frigid pool. Ice water enveloped him and shock coursed through his entire body. He breached the surface and drew in a shuddering gasp. "Silje!"

She laughed and watched him crawl back onto the courtyard, shivering violently.

"Th-this was the last day of prayers," he said through chattering teeth. "When I go back inside everyone will think I fell!"

"Don't worry." She offered a hand, which he reluctantly took. "Once you're crowned, it won't matter."

But Niklas was never crowned. He changed that night. Awoken from terrible nightmares of shadows and endless cold, only to find himself as frigid and confused as he'd been while dreaming. He'd woken half of the castle with his screaming and fits of paranoia.

One child as a heksa was a bad omen, but two? It was abhorrent. Asbjorn made a swift decree exiling Niklas. He was given a week's worth of supplies and cast into Bjervik, an ancient forest, for things that were meant to be lost and forgotten.

But Silje followed him. After all, he'd made her a promise and he would fulfil it. So they travelled together. The corrupted son and bastard daughter alone in the wilderness.

The city officials had told Niklas that if he wanted to stay in Verchiél, he needed to go into the city and get to know their citizens. A task seemingly simple enough in and of itself, though it was considerably more difficult with an army of fully armed guards present at his back.

Niklas walked through the crowded streets, and tried to make himself as inconspicuous as possible. A difficult feat on any day, let alone in Verchiél where his vivid red hair and height marked him as a foreigner.

The citizens clearly hadn't gotten any more used to him as he had to them. They stood at a distance, whispering among themselves as they watched the procession pass. He was grateful this entire excessive display was to take place during the night; he didn't feel as if he'd have the energy without his magic.

"This is highly unnecessary," he muttered.

"I don't give a fuck, it's tradition," Dabria said from beside him. "Just make your rounds and once we get to the cathedral, wave your hands around and do a little magic trick to make the people happy."

Niklas looked at her properly. She was haggard and pale, the dark shadows beneath her eyes more pronounced; she looked more exhausted than he felt.

"Are you alright, Captain?" he asked at a volume no one else could overhear. "You don't look well—"

"If you finish that sentence you're not going to look so

great either."

He fell silent. He had barely known her for more than a week, but already he understood that she was the sort of person who made good on her word. He changed the subject to the event at hand.

"What exactly is a moon viewing ceremony?"

"You look at the moon," Dabria replied simply.

"Then why was I required to wear such ostentatious garments?"

Niklas tried not to fidget in the ink-black and silver robes he'd been forced into. The attire had been made for Verchiél's Moon, and mercifully the palace tailors had taken it out to accommodate for his size, but it still felt too constricting, as if it would tear with the slightest movement.

Dabria shrugged. "Tradition."

"Do you have any advice for me?"

"You're asking me for my opinion?"

"Of course. Any ruler should converse closely with their captain to plan a strategic approach."

"Slow down, this isn't Bjordal, you're not going into battle, you're going to be charming people."

Niklas' heart sank. Charm had never been a requirement for any Bjordal ruler, and though he felt as if he'd given a convincing speech the night of the solstice, he'd practised that for months under Silje's critical eye to get it just right. Performing for, and charming, what was essentially an audience had never been his strong suit.

As if reading his thoughts, Dabria added, "You could start by being more likeable. Lighten up the whole brooding look."

Niklas frowned. "I do not brood."

"You do and it makes you even more unapproachable than you already are. That kind of 'big strong man' shit might work up north, but here people like leaders who are more personable."

"But a good leader should be more concerned with their actions rather than cultivating a persona."

"Look," Dabria explained. "You're overthinking this. You just do a magic trick that reminds the people why you're special. Then you're good until the next ceremony."

Niklas considered this. "And this public display of magic pleases them?"

"Are you kidding? They love it. It's like a national holiday."

It was so absurd. Using his powers at the solstice party had been one thing, but to be able to casually display magic in public without consequence and be rewarded for it? He wanted to laugh, but with so many eyes upon him, he only nodded in solemn acknowledgement of Dabria's words.

They passed through the streets, their procession marked with lanterns in cold silver flames. People watched from the sidelines or from windows above; many waved ribbons of silver and black along with bells of silver. The entire street filled with the gentle tinkling of bells and chimes.

As they neared the cathedral, Niklas paused to take in the sight before him. Places of worship in Bjordal were structures made of carved wood and moss, still partially connected to nature even in the largest cities. Verchiél's cathedral was a colossal place of polished marble and stained glass. Hundreds of figures adorned the archways, and he realised they were Incarnate, or "saints", as they were officially known after passing. There were no gods to worship here; he held what they worshipped inside of him. What an extravagant thing, to be remembered so fondly even in death.

Amid everything, Niklas caught the faint tang of smoke in the air.

He turned to Dabria. "Captain? Are there any ceremonial fires for the festivities?"

Dabria frowned. "No, it's a winter solstice, the only flames allowed are the ones in the lanterns."

That did not comfort him. He tried to sense where the scent had come from, but the wind had shifted and it was gone again. Perhaps one of the lanterns had been shattered. This was a bustling city after all, it's not like they'd just have open flames about.

The moon was full and bright tonight, casting everything in a pale light. Many thought an Incarnate's power was magnified in direct light of either the moon or sun, but Niklas had never felt anything more than an aching cold in the deepest places of his being. So he kept his eyes to the ground, and to the people around him. He approached the front of the gathered crowd, the people all looking expectantly at him as he took his place.

He drew in a deep breath before he spoke, making sure his voice carried.

"This is a sacred night for Verchiél and her people. The country of my birth and the country which I now call home have long held much strife and animosity toward one another, but it is my hope that we can forge a new path together. One which does not rely on the location of our borders, but one of rebuilt trust and respect for one another."

He snuck a look at Dabria, who nodded for him to continue.

"I realise my arrival has also marked the subsequent departure of your previous Incarnate, but rest assured it is my intention not only to build a true alliance between myself and other Incarnate, but to unite and care for all citizens of this country."

He drew in another deep breath, a hint of ash caught in his throat.

"I regret that it is only myself present at tonight's festivities. However I still wish to partake of the traditional display and offer a gift which only my magic can provide."

Silent anticipation greeted his words. He looked to Dabria for an indication of how to proceed, and she only responded with an irritated hand gesture. Which might have been telling him to continue or something far more rude, but he didn't take the time to dwell on it.

He turned to the water and stretched his hand out. Everyone held a collective breath as they watched.

Each Incarnate's magic took time to form. Though the magic existed in some binary of day or night, no two Incarnate's powers were ever quite the same. Even those sharing or learning the same abilities found their magic took shape in unique ways.

He'd never been quite sure if it was the thing inside him trying to better reflect his person, or if he had been given what he most needed at the time he'd received it. Either way he preferred not to dwell on why his magic had chosen such a form. As cold and biting as the wilds had been to him.

The familiar cold was welcome, as the water moved at his command, swiftly changing to a frigid mist which froze into ice, creating the intricate form of one of Verchiél's oldest saints—Camille, Daughter of the Sun.

The choice was twofold. First, to show his understanding of Verchiél history. Second, she had been an Incarnate Sun, a counterpart which he unfortunately lacked. A figure of ice made a poor replacement for the real thing, but he knew the subtleties wouldn't be lost on Verchiél's people.

As soon as the last feather of her extended wings was complete, he dropped his arms, exhaustion washing over him. The place where he'd cut himself with the Bjordal steel stung painfully before going numb. Luckily his magic had already returned, but the pain lingered stubbornly with it.

A silence suddenly turned to cheers and clapping while one phrase chanted in Verchiélen.

"Fis de l'aluna!"

Son of the Moon.

Niklas listened, unable to move in that moment. Was this what it was like to be an Incarnate in Verchiél? He felt confusion and elation in equal parts as he offered a short bow, which caused even more people to cheer. In the crowd, Dabria begrudgingly flashed him a thumbs-up, which somehow allowed his shoulders to relax, a small smile coming to his face despite himself. Perhaps he could do this after all.

Throughout it all, Niklas stilled, an approaching sound catching his ears. After all, it was one he knew well from his time being hunted by cultists and soldiers alike in the Bjordal wilds—

The scent of fire and the echo of angry voices.

Niklas jumped back just as a fire bomb flew past him, where it hit the newly made ice sculpture, shattering it as it burst into a sudden flame.

Niklas raised his arms to shield his face from the cloud of ice shards and sparks, looking up to see a mob approach from the city's back streets.

The acrid tang of smoke rushed past them as the mob hurled more fire bombs through shopfronts or smashed them into the street ahead of them. A few were armed with torches which lit up the night in a sudden shock of orange and gold, drowning out the silver flames of the ceremony. Many waved Verchiél flags or brandished the sigils of the Verchiél Sun and Moon.

They surrounded the cathedral square from every side. Dabria drew her sword, barking out orders to the nearest guards, who swiftly formed a protective circle under her command.

Dread coursed through him. The bystanders, he couldn't let them come to harm. Before he could second-guess the decision, Niklas swept his arms forward, the jacket tearing with the motion as power surged through him.

People screamed as the water from the canal crashed onto the street in a massive wave, sweeping across and freezing into a barrier, walling off the citizens around the cathedral so only he and the guards were left to face the protestors.

Suddenly a man broke away from the crowd of attackers, anger seething in his eyes as he barred their path.

"Out of the way!" Dabria snapped.

"He's a usurper," the man spat, glaring at Niklas.

"He fairly won a duel within Verchiél's tradition of Incarnate ascension," Dabria retorted, her tone sharp. "If you have a problem, take it up with the city officials."

The man scowled at Dabria's words, turning to address the crowd. "He may share in the same magic, but he's not our Moon. He's not our Incarnate."

Niklas was silent, listening as the whispers in the streets grew and more people crowded in.

The man stepped forward. "He's not saying anything because he knows I'm right. We all know Bjordal will come for us now, all because you were too selfish to keep out of everything." The man jabbed a finger in Niklas' direction. "Couldn't live without lounging your ass on another throne, could you? What right do you have to be our king?"

In Bjordal, a show of force would be required after such a display of disrespect. But given his country's long history of invading Verchiél, coupled with the fact that direct confrontation had never been his preference, and with Dabria's advice still fresh in his mind, Niklas stepped forward and spoke calmly.

"May I speak with you? We can address the concerns you have—"

The man looked at Niklas in disgust. "I don't want anything from you, I want you to get out of our city!"

A few voices from the crowd cheered along with the man's words. The man nodded, encouraged. "I say we should throw you out ourselves just like you did to our Sun and Moon."

The voices grew louder now, some moving forward to join the man while others shouted and waved their flags wildly.

Niklas had feared this, the people not accepting him. Silje had assured him that they would love what he was more than who he was, but he had never had the gift for swaying others as she did. There were too many people, everything was too loud—too close. He backed away as the man advanced, spurred by the growing frenzy of the crowd.

Dabria stepped in front of him, drawing her sword and preparing for a fight, but Niklas saw how quickly the man was moving, the anger in his eyes. He'd be cut down trying to reach him, and the last thing Niklas wanted was more blood to be spilled.

Niklas threw himself in front of Dabria, pushing her out of the way. His body tensed as a heavy punch collided with his jaw and the taste of copper filled his mouth.

The entire area fell silent, people hushed with wide eyes.

The man stared up at him with an expression of disbelief, his hand still held aloft, as if shocked by his own actions.

"Idiot," Dabria hissed. "Why did you do that?"

"Do what?" he asked. Watching as two guards seized the man, who began to struggle and scream.

"It's the law," Dabria explained. "Citizens can't lay a harmful hand on an Incarnate inside the city, or else—"

The guards forced the man to his knees, bowing their heads before Niklas.

"Son of the Moon, tell us, what punishment would you give to him?"

Niklas was frozen, his mind whirling as he watched the people around him.

"Punishment?"

"Blood or life?"

Dabria nudged his side, nodding toward the man. "They're waiting."

He looked up and sure enough the crowd around him was watching; some whispered among themselves, others began to wail or shout.

"Go ahead." The man looked up at Niklas without fear. "I'll die with a smile on my face knowing I stood for the good of this city."

The man was right. Despite what Silje had told him, he hadn't asked to come in so much as knocked down the door and barged inside without permission. He'd taken away what this country held most dear, their Incarnate—their faith—and imposed himself instead. He couldn't do this any longer. Incarnate or not, the people had already decided themselves.

Niklas wasn't their king.

"Release him."

Both guards looked at him with expressions of shock, but made no move to release the man.

"Release him," Niklas repeated, louder this time so his voice carried. "He's right. This is his city and he has every right to protest as he sees fit."

One of the guards objected, "But, Son of the Moon, you're—"

"You heard your Incarnate," Dabria snapped. "Let him go."

The guards, still dazed, backed away, releasing the man. The man got to his feet, dusting himself off with aggravation before his eyes snapped back to Niklas. "Fucking northern bastard, you won't last."

The crowd lingered, people agitated, still whispering and casting angry looks at Niklas. A loud clapping from Dabria sent them all into motion. "Unless you want to spend the night in a cell, get off the streets!"

The crowd slowly dispersed, deterred by Dabria's anger as well as the palace guards who stood protectively around him. They made way for himself and Dabria as she cut a path through the area with renewed energy.

Her eyes landed on Niklas and she spoke curtly. "You. With me. Now."

Niklas hesitated, looking from the still-smouldering street fronts to the bystanders still shielded behind the wall of ice. "But I—"

"The guards will clean up the mess. I'm not going to have you roasted alive because you wanted to help clean up."

Niklas wanted to object but another glare from Dabria told him that he would be foolish to do so, and he followed her in a tense silence. Only once they were back within the safe confines of the palace, black and gold gates locked behind them, did Dabria whirl to face him.

"Idiot! Do you have any idea how foolish that was?"

"Foolish?" he asked. "Stopping them from harming a citizen was foolish?"

She inhaled, her eyes narrowing. "That's a strange attitude, considering you didn't have much of a care for our citizens the night you arrived."

He fell silent; he knew exactly what she was talking about. Her friend. What had his name been? Alfio? Niklas still overheard her whispering it sometimes, as if she forgot he was no longer beside her.

"Dabria, I—"

"If you're going to live in this city you need to learn the way it works," she said, her eyes not quite meeting his. "You've just made the biggest mistake you could."

"But I'm fine," he protested. "I can take more than a punch."

In Bjordal he'd taken more— far more. He'd been starved, beaten, imprisoned, tortured and nearly murdered for being Incarnate. A single punch was nothing.

"That's exactly what I'm talking about," Dabria insisted. "I've never been one for faith, but things are different in Verchiél. You're not a monster here, you're an embodiment of their beliefs, a vessel of the heavens, a motherfucking saint. And now, for the first time, they've all seen that they can harm an Incarnate without consequence. They don't trust you. How much longer before those same people go one step further and come at you with knives and pistols rather than a raised fist?"

"Then I'd be better off in Bjordal," he muttered.

"You'd better hope you're only risking exile rather than execution"—Dabria gave him a scathing glare—"you're well acquainted with the concept, aren't you?"

Shame burned deep in his gut and he lowered his eyes, silent. He hadn't just put himself on the line, he'd put Dabria on it too. He had to be careful from now on.

Smoke rose in the night sky as fires burned in the city.

They had so much more to lose.

11

GABRIEL

There was a trick, Gabriel considered, to drowning.

It happened the moment you were powerless to do any-thing. There was a second of realisation, an epiphany where one could do nothing but wait and accept what was to come.

Every night since he'd plunged back into the water, he dreamt that he was back in that place. Dying all over again, when the filthy river water had rushed down his throat, and canvas scratched against his skin as he tried to claw his way out of his bindings. The closer Heathland approached, the more the night-mares bled into his waking moments until his mind was filled with anxiety and anger in equal measure. All he could think about as he watched the grey city line of Grislow come into view was how little it had all changed

"Zoe..." Gabriel whispered, not taking his eyes from the city. "Can you just kill me now?"

Zoe didn't look up from the ledger she'd been making notes in. Her curls pulled back into a bun as she bent over a ledger, making notes, and her brown skin shone with a golden hue in the sunlight.

"I already healed your seasickness this morning."

She had. Like clockwork they had built a routine: each morning as the sun rose and every night right before it fell, Zoe had kept the physical effects of sickness at bay. But for as much as her magic did, it couldn't stop the dread that gnawed constantly at his gut. She had told him that she couldn't fix the problem if it was in his mind rather than his body.

"No, no," Gabriel insisted, sinking to the deck. "I feel ill."

"Ill enough to miss out on chores around the ship?" Zoe flipped a page. "But well enough to play Malizia with the crew?"

"Oh, so you were the one who taught them." An amused voice spoke up. "I thought they'd picked it up from the ports." Silje approached. Her pale hair was in two plaits, and she had dressed in a sharply cut tweed suit with brown riding boots. If he hadn't been so consumed by existential dread, he would have admired her fashion sense.

"Silje"—Zoe gestured to Gabriel—"perhaps you can try something that might help?"

Silje bent down and, exactly like Zoe had done so many times before, took his face in her hands.

"You look fine to me," Silje said. "But just to be sure—" Rather than the familiar and comforting warmth of magic, pain scorched from Silje's palms.

Gabriel yelped and leapt to his feet, rubbing at his face, which was hot to the touch.

"Odd…" Silje frowned, tapping her lips. "I can't feel anything wrong with you."

"Must have fixed it…" he muttered.

"Well." Silje clapped her hands together. "Since you're up, would you mind joining our briefing before we dock?"

He was about to protest, but Silje's smile tightened. "You were supposed to be the one relaying this information to us before we docked in Grislow. You handled all the negotiations while in

Verchiél, isn't that right?"

In his week-long stupor he figured he must have agreed to it at some point.

He cleared his throat. "Right."

Silje slid onto the bench beside Zoe, resting her head against her shoulder. A flicker of jealousy sparked in his gut and he tried to stamp it out as he found his words. "Yes, well… we've got to decide who we're going to make an alliance with."

"What more is there to decide?" Zoe asked. "We're going to choose the council. They've allied with Verchiél before and should do so again." She looked down at the ledger in her hands, brimming with notes. "We'll be able to form a solid alliance if a majority of the members are willing to hear us out. In addition, you'll need to make a private apology."

"Apologise?" Gabriel asked, confused. "To whom?"

Zoe gave him a stare he was all too familiar with, mostly because she looked that way only when she was unhappy with him.

"You blackmailed a councillor, Gabriel. Or have you forgotten already?"

"I didn't forget! But if he didn't want his secrets discovered, then he should have done a better job of hiding them," Gabriel countered. "The council are nothing more than useless figureheads, a relic of a bygone era. Everyone knows that the conlords own Heathland in everything but name."

Zoe snapped the ledger shut. "Not this again."

"You're considering the conlords?" Silje smiled. "An unusual choice."

"Gabriel." Zoe rubbed her eyes tiredly. "We're not taking help from any of them. They're criminals."

"Isn't that just another word for someone of business?"

Gabriel countered. "Heathland is growing faster, and more importantly, richer than any other country in the Isles. The reason being that the conlords have been the ones who can best adapt."

"Only because they draw people in and then leave them kicking and screaming in a never-ending array of loopholes and shady contracts. We're not taking any help they offer. The council might be old-fashioned, but we know who they are and what they would offer."

"Do we?" Gabriel asked. "I'd bet my last coin that they'd sell us out to Niklas in a second flat."

"Like any conlord wouldn't?"

"We're fair game at this point, but there's plenty to choose from and I already have one in mind: Ada Vard."

Silje clutched Zoe's hand tightly. "Zoe's right. You need a connection that won't sell you out."

"Don't be ridiculous, I wouldn't suggest it if I didn't know her well enough—"

"Oh? And just how well do you know her?" Zoe asked. "I thought the council asked you to help stop her operations?"

He had, at least at first, with good intentions. But since he'd once shared a semblance of a childhood alongside Vard in Grislow, his good intentions had soon turned to a pact made underneath the table to keep her business untampered with in exchange for whatever information Gabriel required. Given that they now only corresponded through letters or messengers, Gabriel took some respite in the fact that he wasn't entirely lying to Zoe.

He spoke carefully. "I may have run into her a few times."

Zoe gave him a long, hard look and Silje spoke. "I agree with Zoe. You should choose the council." Gabriel opened his mouth, about to disagree, when Silje smiled and suddenly he felt a sense of calm wash over him, quelling his arguments.

"Don't you think so, Gabriel?"

Her golden eyes were unwavering, the calmness only growing stronger and heavier, like a blanket.

"I don't know," he said.

He thought he might have imagined it, but for a moment she appeared delighted. "Are you sure you don't know?"

The heaviness settled over him entirely, crushing whatever arguments he had been ready to partake in. "I…suppose not."

"Heavens," Zoe reached forward and placed a palm to his forehead. "You're not feeling ill, are you?"

Silje waved away Zoe's concern. "He's fine, right, Gabriel?" Silje's eyes snapped to his, flickering gold in the sunlight.

"I'm fine," he agreed.

Silje nodded, evidently satisfied before she added, "There, now that we're all settled, I've already arranged for our accommodations in the city. I can send a message as soon as we dock in Grislow."

With the unofficial meeting adjourned, Zoe tucked the ledger under her arm and rose to her feet, and Silje along with her, the pair walking arm in arm.

That same jealousy burned heavily in his chest. As if sensing his stare, Silje cast a glance back to Gabriel, whispering something to Zoe before she lagged behind. "My Moon," Silje said, "what's wrong?"

"Nothing," he replied too quickly, a bitter edge to his voice.

She took his hand and squeezed hard. "Remember? You can tell me anything."

He looked from Silje's expectant face across the waters. He could now clearly see the grey city, the buildings caked with pollution from the factories, the tangled webs of too crowded streets. Being so close to Heathland left him on edge. Though they were actively seeking aid, it didn't stop the horrible creeping feeling that he was backtracking in life. Heading right back to the bleak place where he'd started.

Silje squeezed his hand again, and he forced himself to muster a smile. Though he had a feeling that was far too strained to be considered natural. "Just a bit sore from your little trick earlier, that's all."

She managed a hollow smile of her own. "That can be easily fixed." She held out both of her hands. "May I?"

"May you what?"

"Kiss you."

"Oh—" Heat, sudden and unexpected, flared up his neck and he stumbled for words. "Er…well, I mean y-yes…" *Stupid*, he cursed himself. He had no idea how Silje managed it, but she was the only person capable of reducing him to the pitiful nervousness of a bumbling youth.

Silje laughed and rose to the tips on her toes. His skin burnt as she kissed one cheek, then the other. "Much better," Silje said. "Don't you agree?"

"Yes," he said, managing a modicum of poise. "Much."

"Now, are you going to tell me what's wrong?"

A familiar and comforting feeling rose with her words, and with it, a soothing thought.

Tell me, it said. *Trust me.*

He felt himself relax, and leaned against the railing beside her. "I think contacting the council is the wrong idea. We have new circumstances so we'll need a new plan. Zoe thinks there's something to be salvaged, but I know Heathland. If we don't have something physically tangible to offer them"—*like a throne*, Gabriel thought bitterly—"they won't consider us. The only thing we have to offer is a hefty reward for our capture from the man many have already allied with. Not to mention that it would put them in a particularly good place if they were the ones to capture us. Which is why Vard is a clear choice."

Silje looked thoughtful. "Trust me, you don't want to work with people like Vard. She's only after one thing."

"Sex?"

Silje laughed. "You're not her type. Besides, she only makes deals with money."

"A shame. One of the few cards I have to offer is off the table."

"Silje?" one of the crew called out across the deck. "We need you to look at—"

"Busy," she snapped, which sent the sailor retreating below deck.

She smiled apologetically and moved to go but Gabriel asked another question. "Does this mean you'll consider my idea?"

"Absolutely not," she said. "I just like talking to you."

The sting of her refusal softened by the prospect of more attention.

"You do?" he asked.

She nodded, eyes bright, and gestured for him to lean down. She whispered so closely to his ear that he felt her warm breath on his skin. "You amuse me."

Her golden eyes turned back to pale blue as she winked and strode across the deck. Her pale hair swished behind her as she bounded down the stairs.

Shouting caught his attention and he turned back to the

railing, the crew bustling around him as they prepared to dock. He could see the citizens among the docks. People arriving or departing, some eager to leave while others shed tears. Many of the dock-workers played cards between shifts, calling out greetings loudly, clapping each other on the back and keeping conversations. Amid all the noise, he didn't hear a single word of Verchiélin the air.

They had officially arrived in Heathland.

Heathland. The so-called "Golden Country" from the wealth they'd managed to accumulate over generations of gold mining. It had helped establish them as the centre of trade after the biggest industrial boom in the Isles, which had taken hold nearly fifty years prior and showed no signs of stopping since. Though in reality, Heathland was as drab and grey as cold stone.

The River Vernhaven cut through the centre of the capital of Grislow, dividing it into multiple districts of varying nature, though casinos lined almost every street. In addition to factory work, the economy of Grislow was heavily based on gambling. Given that casinos were illegal in Verchiél, due to supposed moral corruption, and uncommon in Bjordal, people travelled from all across the Isles to indulge, giving Grislow a monopoly on the industry.

If Verchiél was the city of the Incarnate, then Grislow was the city of organised crime. There wasn't a single business here, from industrial blocks to coffee houses, which wasn't connected to a gang or some illegal activity. Though the country touted their capital as a "model of industry, prosperity and commerce," everyone knew better. The money was as dirty as it was plentiful.

Market stalls were squeezed along the streets, people chatted loudly as they bustled about to and from their destinations.

Even the people seemed to be duller than their Verchiél counter-parts, dressed in muted hues of grey, black or brown, and every-thing had a dusting of soot and ash from the many factories in the industrial district.

Zoe was desperate to explore the city, her neck sore from how quickly she craned her head to every angle, hungry to take in every new sight and sound possible.

They waited in front of the Grislow council headquarters. Silje had pulled some strings and managed to arrange a meeting for them with the council. Zoe was equal parts nervous and excited to finally have someone in a position of authority to speak with. Though Silje had gone into the building nearly an hour ago and shown no signs of returning since.

Zoe paced impatiently, sun hat pulled low over her gold-en eyes, staring up at the massive building of grey stone. Carved above the looming doors was the motto: Fer Oondernem om Indus-trat om Valvart. *From Venture to Industry to Fortune*. Or as Gabri-el liked to say, the three things any good citizen of Grislow would happily sell their soul for.

"So are there more gods than just Heathall?" she asked, scrutinising a stone fountain carved into severe angles from dark grey stone. Coins glittered dully in the water, offerings which were collected at the end of each day, while the stern figure atop it, where Heathland had derived its namesake, glared down at her as if offended by her mortal eyes upon his likeness.

It was so odd to have a literal representation of a god in question when all she'd been raised upon in Verchiél were abstract ideals of the heavens. The closest thing Verchiél had ever had to godly figures were Incarnate, and she'd seen enough of Gabriel's hangovers to know that there was nothing remotely holy about him.

"How the fuck should I know?" Gabriel snapped, cigarette clenched tightly in his fingers, an old habit he'd picked back up with his growing stress. "It was years ago."

"I was just wondering, since you grew up here." She was careful with her choice of words. Though he'd been born in Grislow, he vehemently denied any claims to a Heathland nationality. Claiming instead that he was Verchiél blood through and through. She knew it wasn't a love for Verchiél so much as a hatred for his old home.

"Not everything here is so bad," Zoe said, trying to change the subject to something that would cheer him up. "Alessi's living here after all. We should go and see them, they're living in the Merchant District now."

"Ah, yes," Gabriel said blithely. "The only thing that could possibly make this trip better, a visit with my ex."

"They were my friend before that," Zoe said, a touch of defensiveness to her voice. "I was the one who told you two not to get involved."

"Who was I to deny the heart's wants?"

"I don't think it was your heart that was wanting."

Gabriel glowered and she leaned against the railing, trying to coax something more than misery from him. "You've got to have at least one good memory from here."

"Yes," Gabriel agreed. "Leaving."

She nudged him. "No stories of a first kiss? Or a petty crime? I'm certain you got caught for stealing at least once."

"Why do you care?"

"Because you've never told me anything about this place."

"Have you ever considered that there was a reason why I

never told you?"

"Yes, but that doesn't mean that I don't want to know—to understand."

His jaw tensed. He was silent as the sounds of the city continued past them, carriage wheels rolling against cobblestone, children laughing as they ran across the street. It felt loud in Zoe's ears.

His grey eyes held hers; there was anger there but also a weariness she was unaccustomed to seeing. She wasn't sure if it was the absence of his magic, or the way Grislow seemed to leech the colour out of everything, but he was even paler than usual, a dullness to his ink black hair.

"What could you possibly begin to understand?"

Indignation burned in the pit of her stomach. Though she couldn't deny the stark contrast of their upbringings, the fact that he had always held back so much from her was part of the problem.

She managed to hold his gaze steady. "Try me."

He pulled a long drag on the cigarette, holding the smoke in for a time before he exhaled, his voice hoarse. "My penniless good-for-nothing mother sold me to a conlord as soon as I became an Incarnate. I was eight. We're quite valuable here, and what better investment could a criminal make than in magic that is catered to illusions? He raised me, raised being a very generous term for a glorified servant and thief. The other children fucking hated my guts because they saw me as his favourite. Though I could never tell since he beat me as much as the rest of them." Now that he had begun speaking he seemed unable to stop as his words tumbled faster from his lips. "They hated me so much that when a rival boss offered them a better position in exchange to off me, they tied me in a sack and tossed me in the river. Lucky for me they didn't tie it very well since I'm still here."

Zoe was silent, unsure how to respond as she began to put together the pieces of his life she'd never understood. With a gnawing sense of guilt she recalled how many times she'd pushed him into the ocean or splashed him with water because it made him screech and her laugh. Even recently how she'd dragged him into the dark waters back at the palace, how it must have felt like death all over again.

"That's why I never cared about any fucking god," he said. "Because the only person I could ever rely on was me."

"You're not alone though," Zoe said. "I'm here."

His expression softened for a moment. He opened his mouth to say something before a bright voice interrupted them.

"There you are!"

Silje looped her arm through hers, and Zoe didn't miss how Gabriel bristled.

"Well?" Zoe pressed Silje. "How did it go?"

"You were supposed to be back an hour ago," Gabriel said, his voice unusually curt.

Silje's lips twitched, whether in amusement or irritation at Gabriel's tone, Zoe wasn't sure. "I was able to speak with a councillor about Zoe's idea to ally with Heathland…however, they weren't exactly sold on the idea."

"Why not?" Zoe asked.

"Because we don't have anything tangible to offer them," Gabriel said. "I told you both already that they won't work with anyone unless there's money up front."

"And I suppose the conlords are different?" Zoe challenged.

"They're more willing to take chances, to play a game

which the councillors have no idea or skill to engage in."

Zoe was at a loss. Surely there had to be some sort of miscommunication. Something she could sort out using just the right words to cut a deal as she had so many times before back in Verchiél.

Zoe moved toward the door. "I'm certain I could talk some sense into them if I just had a moment—"

Silje held fast to her arm, shaking her head. "They don't know either of you are here. They might be neutral for now, but walking in when they might be allying with Verchiél's new king isn't a good plan."

Zoe relented, allowing Silje to lead her away from the building.

"I've booked a carriage, it should be waiting in the Market District." Silje smiled at Gabriel. "Perhaps the Grislow boy can show us around? I've been told you know these streets well."

Zoe winced. The comment was innocent enough and normally he would have laughed it off, smiled and offered some sultry joke back in return. Now he seethed with anger and stormed away into the crowd.

"Hey," Zoe called after him. "Don't walk too far ahead."

"Oh, forget him." Silje squeezed her arm in reassurance. "The poor little man wants to pout all by himself."

Zoe fell quiet beside her, both walking in relative silence. The more she learned about Gabriel, the more it seemed to only push each other further away, in a way that Zoe couldn't quite put a finger on no matter how hard she tried.

"Zoe?"

She blinked. She hadn't realised Silje was talking to her.

"My dear"—Silje reached forward and brushed her

cheek—"you're crying."

Zoe hastily wiped at her eyes, embarrassed. "What's wrong?" Silje squeezed her arm gently. "You can tell me anything you like."

She watched the back of Gabriel's dark head far ahead in the street. "He's just so…" Silje watched her closely, her expression curious. "Difficult sometimes," Zoe admitted. "He told me something personal, but I don't think it helped."

Silje considered this. "Have I made a mess of things?"

"You didn't know," Zoe reassured her. "I'll apologise to him after he's calmed down."

"You shouldn't have to apologise for anything." Silje squeezed her arm, voice serious. "Ever."

Zoe laughed, unnerved by Silje's intense stare.

"Besides, I don't see what all the fuss is," Silje added. "I'd love more people to talk about my problems with. It's not a luxury I ever had."

"You can talk to me, if you ever need to," Zoe offered.

Silje smiled. "My dear, you are such a sweetheart."

She placed a kiss on her cheek and Zoe's face flushed with warmth. Zoe had to admit, for as awful as things had gotten…

She smiled at Silje, delighted to see she returned the gesture.

At least she wasn't alone.

As if reading her thoughts, Silje asked: "How old were you when it happened?"

Zoe didn't need her to elaborate; she knew exactly what she was talking about. When she'd become an Incarnate.

"Twelve," Zoe said. "I had a fever that lasted for days. It felt like my whole body was on fire. The only thing I remember is waking up one morning and seeing my gold eyes in the mirror."

Silje nodded. "You're special. You can burn things entirely away or heal them." She took Zoe's hand in hers, giving a gentle squeeze. "You hold life and death in your hands."

When Zoe had first been taken to the palace, there were no other Suns besides her and Aria, they'd told her, only a Moon she'd meet one day. She was one of a kind. She looked at her and Silje's linked hands.

Two of a kind.

"How about you?" Zoe asked.

"Thirteen."

Thirteen. Only a year older than she'd been. It was peculiar. Though the inheritance of magic was something that happened sporadically, there were some few instances in time when there seemed to be patterns. To occur in a similar age range or in a specific country, but then they changed once more, unpredictable, unknowable. Zoe counted. Four of them. All incredibly close in age. Though they'd once been scattered to each end of the Isles. Could there perhaps be more? It was improbable, but not impossible. There were hardly ever more than a handful at a time, but she suspected that between Bjordal's bigotry, Heathland's commodification and Verchiél's religious overtones, the true numbers were being miscounted.

"Were you lonely?" Zoe asked.

Silje laughed brightly, though there was a cheer to it that felt forced. "Loneliness is for people who aren't enough in and of themselves."

"But it must have been difficult," Zoe said, "being so young in such an unsafe situation."

Silje gave her an easy smile. "It was boring."

"Boring?" Zoe asked, surprised.

"Yes," Silje said, offering no explanation or additional conversation.

Zoe squeezed her arm, pressing the subject. "How do you feel now?"

Silje was thoughtful before she replied. "Not bored."

"Silje?" A voice interrupted them. "Klaaren om te gaan?"

Gabriel stood before them. Zoe noticed that his eyes were puffy and rimmed with red. Silje seemed to notice it too, but neither pointed it out, allowing him some modicum of privacy.

Something about them conversing in Heathall irked her. After all, he knew that she didn't speak it well.

Rude, rude, rude, a singsong voice rose in Zoe's mind. *Are you really going to let him get away with that?*

An unexpected wave of irritation rose in Zoe and she spoke boldly. "If you have something to say you can say it in front of me."

Gabriel's brows rose in surprise before he replied coolly, "Maybe if you'd learned the language, you could understand."

Ah, but it's his fault that he keeps so many secrets from you, isn't it? the eerily familiar voice continued. *Can you really rely on him?*

"Maybe if you'd taught me, I wouldn't need to ask." Zoe snapped back.

"You wouldn't understand."

"I could if you ever gave me the chance."

"Not about that, about life. Real life." A similar anger flickered in Gabriel's eyes. "You grew up eating on silver dishes while I had to scrounge for scraps. You were nothing more than a spoiled merchant's daughter."

Anger burst like fire in her gut and she clenched her fists, feeling the golden magic roar to life, sudden and angry. Gabriel flinched and patted out his coat, his shoulder singed with ash where a small flame had brushed him.

"Oops," Zoe said, not sorry in the least.

Silje snorted, a laugh escaping her. As quickly as it had come, the anger vanished, though it still left an aching sadness in its wake as she held Gabriel's cold stare.

"Gabe, I—"

"Let's just go."

Silje placed a hand on her arm, offering her a reassuring squeeze before the trio walked in mutual silence. They slowed as they approached a waiting carriage, something Silje had assured them would transport them to where they'd be staying while in the city.

"Ladies first." Silje held an arm out. "After you, Zoe."

"Thank you." She took Silje's hand, offering Gabriel a pointed look.

He gave her a sickly sweet smile before offering Silje a hand. She climbed in and seated herself beside Zoe, while Gabriel took the other seat beside Silje.

Silje banged on the ceiling of the cab and the carriage lurched into motion. She settled comfortably between the two of them.

Safe, the feeling reassured her, *you're both safe with me.*

Zoe looked over and held Gabriel's gaze steady and he glared right back. Things had changed between the two of them and she couldn't entirely put her finger on it.

13

DABRIA

Dabria paced before the doors of Niklas' study.

Though the guards had managed to quieten down the protests and stop the fires in the streets, people were still on edge and the palace gates remained locked and Niklas was still uncrowned. If this was still early days, she feared what would come next.

She drew in a breath and raised a hand to the thick oaken doors, but stopped before she could knock, unsettled by the growing volume of voices within the room.

Niklas was in a heated argument, speaking rapidly in Bjordal. Dabria had managed to pick up a few words and phrases, often with Niklas cringing at her poor attempts at an accent, but now he was speaking so fast she couldn't understand a word.

Suddenly, a woman's enraged shriek struck Dabria's ears, followed by hurled words that Dabria was certain were terrible curses. She leaned forward and pressed her ear against the door, curious to know what was going on, when suddenly the argument in the room fell silent.

The woman called out in Verchiél, "The door's unlocked."

Dabria stood up straighter and pushed the door open.

Niklas stood by the window, brows drawn together and mouth downturned. He was breathing unevenly, clearly trying to compose himself. But it wasn't Niklas who her gaze lingered upon.

Dabria drew in a breath.

The woman stood behind the polished desk. Her pale blond hair spilled over her shoulders, and a smile bordering on arrogance graced her sharp features. Though nothing disturbed Dabria so much as her eyes.

Pure gold.

The Bjordal steel knife was in Dabria's hand, and she whipped her arm back to throw it, but Niklas was immediately beside her, seizing Dabria's arm.

Dabria snarled and struggled in his grasp. "Let me go."

"What do you think you're doing?" he hissed.

"Is this some sort of magic shit? Who is she?"

The woman's voice, smooth as velvet, slipped between them. "So, this is the person my dear brother has entrusted so much responsibility to?"

Dabria bit back the devastating retort of: *That's right, bitch!* as soon as she registered what she was hearing.

"She's your sister?"

"It's a pleasure. Though I wish it were under better circumstances." The woman gestured to Niklas. "Aren't you going to properly introduce us?"

"Dabria." Niklas gave her a pleading look. "Please—"

Dabria realised how ridiculous she looked, her knife still clutched tightly in her hand, which in turn was clutched tightly in Niklas' grip.

"Fine. Just get your hands off me."

Niklas released her and she wrenched her arm away, glaring daggers. "Try that again, and you'll lose that hand."

Niklas nodded and looked between the two women nervously. "Dabria, this is Silje."

Dabria tightened her grip on the knife and kept her eyes locked on Silje, Niklas' words only increasing her suspicion. "First you expect me to believe you're a prince back from the dead, and now she's some sort of lost princess?" Dabria withdrew a second knife. "You must think I'm quite a fool."

"Would you excuse us, Niklas?" Silje asked. "I'd like to speak with Dabria alone."

Niklas frowned, an edge to his tone. "Whatever you have to say to her can be said in front of me."

The air crackled and hissed, and Dabria tasted ash in the back of her mouth. Niklas fell silent.

"Be a dear and wait outside." Silje's smile was radiant, at odds with the dangerous energy. "We're going to have a chat with just the ladies."

Niklas made no further protests, only bowed his head and left. Silje waited to speak until the sound of his footsteps faded down the hallway.

"My brother"—Silje shook her head apologetically—"has always had an inclination toward brooding." Silje's gaze snapped back to her, making Dabria wish that she was looking anywhere else. Her golden eyes weren't anything like Zoe's— as warm and familiar as a sunlit afternoon. Silje's were too bright and piercing, like staring straight into the sun.

Silje nodded at the sword in Dabria's grip. "Put that away. We're going to fight with words rather than weapons."

Dabria tightened her grip. Silje's smile remained, though her voice took on an edge. "I said put it away."

Pain scorched through Dabria's hand and she dropped the sword with a gasp.

Silje tapped her lips. "That's the second time I've had to

ask you to put a weapon down. Do that again and I won't ask nicely."

Dabria flexed her hand. "Do you honestly think I'd do anything you ask of me?"

"No, but that's why I like you." Silje walked around the desk. "Too often we lose our resilience in the face of fear, but you only cling tighter to it."

Silje observed the paintings around the room, and stopped before the portrait of Enzo and Aria. Her hand came in contact with the canvas, smouldering where her fingertips touched. "Whatever does not serve us"—she drew her hand away, revealing a single scorched hand-print in the centre of the painting—"we burn."

Dabria watched the tendrils of smoke rise from the painting. "Is that so?"

Silje approached and Dabria considered her with a wary eye. There was an effortless grace to Silje's movements, as if she expected the world to move around her rather than the other way around. Dabria very much wished that her knife was still in her hand. "Do you know why I wanted to talk with you?" Silje stopped before her, a slight bounce accompanying the movement. "The same reason my brother spared your life in the first place." She reached forward and cupped Dabria's cheek. "You're going to work for me."

Dabria stiffened. "With you?"

"Yes. For me. Doesn't that sound fun?" Her smile was all teeth. "You see, my brother has a good heart, but too often he allows his emotions to get in the way. He tends to unexpectedly pick up new additions to our plans." Dabria caught the hint immediately— she was the unexpected addition. Dabria had a strong feeling that she had been the subject of their argument she'd heard through the door.

"He's also informed me that he's made you captain of the Ravannen royal guard." Silje said. "You're clearly well suited to the role, knowing the workings of the city and its people. Have you always lived here?"

"Born in Grislow. Here by circumstance."

"Are you happy here?"

"It pays the bills."

"That's all?" Silje looked disappointed. "But don't you want more?"

Suddenly a voice rose from the back of her mind.

Tell me, it beckoned. *I can help you.*

Fear gripped Dabria, but she wasn't going to listen. She was going to play things her own way.

Dabria met Silje's golden eyes. "If you want me to tell you, ask instead of using magic."

"What magic?"

The force of it slammed against Dabria's mind and she strained against it, biting the inside of her cheek from the effort.

Listen, the voice said. *It's so much easier.*

Fuck off, Dabria thought.

So feisty, Silje said. *I like it.*

Dabria didn't move. Her eyes locked with Silje, who stood casually, dusting her coat off as if the effort of her magic cost her nothing at all, while Dabria fought to remain conscious, darkness edging at the corners of her vision.

"I could force you," Silje said sweetly, and suddenly every bit of fight faded from Dabria, her mind going eerily blank. In another strenuous moment in which Dabria was certain she'd finally faint, the intrusion of Silje's magic finally faded.

But that's no fun, Silje decided, *it's better to fight.*

Dabria gasped, catching herself against the side of the desk to keep herself from collapsing, out of breath as if she'd just sprinted.

Silje laughed and clapped her hands together, delighted. "You have much more willpower than most."

She reached forward and Dabria bristled, bracing herself, waiting for another mental assault, but none came. Silje only helped her to her feet, smiling. "I'm impressed."

Dabria stepped away, trying to maintain her composure as if she hadn't just had her very consciousness assaulted.

"Now, my darling," Silje said, "would you be so kind as to tell me what you want?"

Dabria paused and considered the question. A quiet thought rose in her mind but the voice didn't belong to Silje, it was her own. One thing she hadn't allowed herself to consider a possibility, mostly from the fear that came along every time she thought of it—of her.

"You know people, don't you?" Dabria asked. "Important people with connections?"

"I wouldn't be here unless I did."

Dabria focused on the space beside Silje, not quite able to look someone in the face as she admitted what she'd been holding back for so long.

"I knew someone in Grislow, someone important to me, but I haven't spoken to her in years. I don't even know how to contact her anymore…" Dabria's throat tightened and the rest of the words wouldn't come out. She hated the fact that she'd told a secret to this woman of all people, but she couldn't go without knowing anymore.

"So you want me to play the role of messenger?" Silje tapped her lips thoughtfully. "I'll need a name."

Dabria drew in a breath, the name she hadn't spoken aloud for years heavy on her lips. "Ada Vard."

Dabria still remembered clearer than anything her last day in Grislow. When everything had gone wrong and she'd seen all the fear and sadness—but worse than that, the hate in Ada's eyes. For being a coward and breaking their promise to have each other's backs, for leaving when she'd needed help the most.

Silje's golden eyes widened before she burst into a fit of laughter, the sound unrestrained and harsh to Dabria's ears.

"Did I say something funny?" Dabria asked.

"The Mutt of Grislow?" Silje wiped at her eyes. "How do you know her?"

"Can you send her a message or not?" Dabria snapped.

Silje smiled, though it was the furthest thing from reassuring. "Of course. Grislow is my next destination after all. But you'll have to keep your end of the bargain and aid Niklas, new dynasties don't simply rule, themselves you know."

Another worry surfaced in Dabria's mind. "But the people of Verchiél are unhappy with Niklas."

Silje's smile tightened, a small motion, but Dabria felt the burning rage behind it.

"I'll tell you a secret. Poor Niklas, he thinks that our father disinherited him because he's a heksa, but that was just a convenient excuse. He could have taught him how to hide it, as he did for me." Silje's eyes snapped to Dabria, sudden and intense. "In Bjordal, strength is everything. But even now he fights against his nature, choosing weakness. I need you to lend him the strength he so obviously lacks."

Dabria frowned. "Meaning?"

"The fastest way to rule isn't through trust, but fear." Silje's voice lowered. "Convince the people of Verchiél that Niklas Osenson is worth fearing."

"How?" Dabria asked, incredulous. "The people are already rioting, they nearly killed Niklas. I can barely keep them from knocking the gates down, let alone listening—"

Silje seized Dabria's arms, her golden eyes blazing. "You don't gain respect by sitting back and expecting it to be handed to you like a prize for playing nicely. You fight for it. You bleed for it until it can no longer be denied— until you can no longer be denied. Never ask for respect, Dabria. Demand it."

Dabria recognized it. Anger as well as desperation, is a most dangerous combination. It was something she knew well, but there was an unstable quality to Silje that unsettled Dabria, and for once in her life she was unsure of the right words to answer with. Silje seemed to remember herself and let go of Dabria, whose sleeves were still smoking slightly from where Silje had touched her.

Silje took a step back and folded her arms behind her back once more, taking a deep breath before speaking. "Tell our dear Niklas that Asbjorn will take him back as heir if he successfully takes Verchiél for Bjordal."

"Wait—is that true?" Dabria asked.

"Fuck no," Silje snorted. "Asbjorn hates him. It would actually be funny if poor Niklas wasn't so pathetically put out by it."

Dabria paused, confused. "Then why would I tell him that?"

"Because he needs to be convinced that there's a reason why he needs to rule Verchiél. This will give him one."

"But it's all a lie."

"So?" Silje shrugged, unfazed. "It doesn't matter."

"I think it does," Dabria countered.

Silje scowled. "Look, whether he rules because he snaps out of his newfound idiotic morals or because he believes that our father will accept him as his heir doesn't matter. Either way it still ends with Niklas ruling Verchiél, so say what you need to say to get the result you need."

Dabria didn't have time to unpack the layers of justification Silje was giving herself, instead she simply shook her head, worry gnawing at her gut.

"This doesn't feel right, that's pretty personal…"

"Is it?" Silje said. "In that case I suppose I don't need to worry about delivering your message to Vard since that's pretty personal too. She's probably much too busy for the likes of you anyways…"

That bitch.

"Fine," Dabria snapped before Silje could cut her off. "I'll do it."

"Wonderful!" Silje clapped her hands together. "I don't suppose you have a heartfelt letter for me to personally deliver?"

Dabria frowned. "Just let her know that I'm here, and…that I want to see her again."

Silje's eyes sparked with interest. "You two sound like you were close."

"None of your business." Dabria said, determined to not give Silje any more personal information than she already had.

Silje clucked her tongue, disappointed. "I like you better when you're not so tightly laced"—she leaned forward, voice low—"then again I like all women like that…"

Dabria considered that in another world, she might have returned the gesture. That was, if Silje wasn't such a creepy bitch.

"Just tell her," Dabria said, crossing her arms tightly. "And I'll convince Niklas."

Silje was, if anything, unperturbed and continued on as if this were all perfectly normal business. "I'm happy to hear that, I'm certain we'll make an excellent partnership."

Dabria knew the matter couldn't possibly be nearly as simple as that, but she settled for nodding.

"Oh, and Silje—"

Dabria turned back to the desk, but Silje was gone, the room empty and silent. Dabria picked up her knife from the floor, running her thumb along its edge. Her reflection frowned back at her, shadows beneath her brown eyes, her hair lank and stuck to her cheeks. She needed rest, but everything around her was spiralling out of control. She wished she had Alfio to talk to, and another pang of guilt swept through her, which left her further drained.

She was starting to miss Zoe and Gabriel. Niklas had begun to grow on her, albeit in a pernicious sort of way, but she didn't know what he wanted so she didn't trust him—and she certainly didn't trust Silje. There was a feeling about her that made her want to both grip her pistol and put as much distance between themselves as possible.

She ran a hand through her hair and sheathed the knife with her other, looking back to the room, her eyes drawn back to the scorched hand print in the middle of Enzo and Aria's portrait. She wondered what sort of trouble she'd gotten herself into now.

14

NIKLAS

Whenever Silje wanted to calm down, she burnt things. Niklas, however, preferred to make tea.

The table before him was overflowing with tea tins, which a near army of staff had delivered at the mere mention of wanting a simple cup. Apparently patience wasn't a virtue which Verchiél Incarnate required.

He picked up the neatest tin, the brightly coloured label proudly claiming to provide *"The sweetness of Verchiél"*. He tentatively sniffed a tin of tea leaves, his nose wrinkling at the overly sweet scent. Chocolate and…caramel in tea? How did one brew something that was more like a sweet shop than a drink? He missed the simple earthiness of Bjordal herbs.

He set the tin down with the dozens of others, equally monstrous, before he spoke aloud.

"If you have a question, you can knock."

Footsteps approached and Dabria spoke. "You looked like you were thinking."

He was thinking. He couldn't stop thinking, that was the problem. How was he going to let Silje know that he didn't want to help her with this facade anymore? He had tried to broach the subject about leaving Verchiél to its people, but she'd already been livid at the news of the protest. It had clearly unsettled her as her words to him were more biting and cruel than usual.

Still every bit as weak willed as you were in Bjordal. No wonder Father hates you.

Her words picked at an old wound, but her anger came from her lack of control over the growing tensions. In Silje's mind there had never been a reality in which the people hadn't loved them. To be refused as Incarnate in Verchiél? Apparently not even magic could heal the fractured divide between their nations.

"Which do you prefer?" Niklas held up two tea tins. "Cinnamon and golden sugar? Or candied peaches?"

Dabria frowned. "I prefer coffee."

"Astute," Niklas said, and put a spoonful of each into the teapot, knowing no matter which flavour he chose, he was going to hate it.

"Tell me," Niklas said, preparing the tea. "How did you and Silje get on?"

Dabria shrugged and plopped herself down in one of the chairs across from him. "No offence, but she's kind of a bitch."

"Your words, not mine, though I'm curious, what did she ask you?"

Dabria picked at her fingernails, managing an idle shrug. "She wanted to know what duties you've given me."

"Oh?" Niklas poured a cup of tea, sweetness perfuming the air. "And what did you tell her?"

"That Bjordal are more trouble than they're worth and between the two of you I've barely gotten a moment of rest."

Considering the riot still being cleared up outside, Niklas couldn't disagree. Though there was an element of forced detachment to her tone and her posture, particularly in the way she clutched her hands. He knew it well because he'd done the exact same thing countless times. To keep them from shaking.

"I see." Niklas took a sip of the tea. It required more than a little willpower not to pull a face.

"How is it?" Dabria asked.

Niklas took another sip, no better than the first.

"Vile."

"Then why are you drinking it?"

Niklas set the teacup down.

"You originally hailed from Grislow, did you not?"

"What's it to you?"

"I'm trying to gauge your understanding of Bjordal culture."

"Does it involve drinking disgusting tea?"

"Quite the opposite. We value strength, fortitude and the glory of battle, perhaps above all else. But I believe there are other virtues which would be more vital for a person to embody."

Dabria raised a brow. "Such as?"

"Kindness."

Dabria snorted. "Kindness?"

Niklas ignored her sarcasm and continued speaking. "A Bjordal ruler might be wise and have led the country in great ways for decades, but as soon as their successors reach the age of twenty, they're replaced. It's the age of adulthood, coming into maturity. We value the strength of a new adult and young blood much to the detriment of other qualities which are too often overlooked."

"What are you trying to say, Niklas?"

He gripped the teacup; it burned his palms but he only clung tighter to it. "These protests, the opposition I've faced, Silje is of a mind that they can be dealt with like any other battle. But I believe a touch of kindness would go a long way."

A note of darkness entered Dabria's voice. "Were you being kind when you killed my friend?"

A hollow pang echoed through his gut, a reminder that for as much as he was growing to trust Dabria, she had solid enough reason to despise him.

She rose to her feet. "Do you think kindness is going to solve your problems?" She gestured to the crowd still gathered in protest past the window outside. "Will kindness keep them from tearing you to shreds?"

No. At the rate things were going, they'd as soon see him gone or worse. Just like back home.

Niklas took another sip of tea, more for something to do. He resisted the urge to gag.

Dabria frowned. "You don't have to drink that shit."

"It would be impolite not to try after the trouble gone through to deliver it to me—"

Dabria knocked the teacup out of his hand and it shattered on the marble floor. "This is what I'm talking about! Do you want people to think you're some pushover?"

Silje's and Asbjorn's voices echoed through Niklas' mind.

Still as weak as you were in Bjordal—

Dabria slammed her hands down on the table, any pretences of casual conversation between them abandoned. "They're doing this because they know they can push you and you'll yield. They wouldn't dare if they knew what you're capable of."

"Such as?"

She gestured to him, incredulous. "You're a motherfucking Incarnate! You can make weird magic shit happen. You want your problems solved? I'll tell you right now, you need to be the person you were when I first met you." Dabria's stare burned. "You need to prove to them that you're worth fearing."

Niklas clasped then unclasped his hands, taking a moment to respond.

"That's not what I've decided."

"But if you just—"

"I appreciate your concern," Niklas cut across before she could argue. "But rest assured that I will handle the situation with the care it requires."

He meant the refusal as a dismissal as well, but Dabria didn't leave. She continued to stare at him, her deep brown eyes full of determination, or perhaps stubbornness, he could never really tell with her.

"Silje told me why you were disinherited," Dabria said.

Niklas tensed. "I should have thought that was rather obvious."

"She told me the real reason why."

"And what," Niklas said coldly, "would you possibly know about my father?"

"He's testing you," Dabria said.

Niklas didn't expect that.

"Testing…me?"

Dabria looked around as if worried someone might overhear her before she moved closer. "Look, Silje told me not to tell you, but I think you should know. He's been watching, and now that Verchiél is under control of Bjordal, and his son no less, why wouldn't he welcome you back with open arms?"

Niklas was unmoved. "A military and political advantage is one thing, but I know Asbjorn. The only thing he hates more than me is a heksa, which, unfortunately, I also am."

"But don't you see?" Dabria pressed. "Why does Silje get

to come and go as she pleases and you were kicked out? It doesn't make a lot of sense, does it?"

His suspicion wavered, revealing an old and painful wound he'd picked at many times. Silje had changed young, many years before he did. True she wasn't a legitimate child, so she didn't have anything to inherit in the first place. But she hadn't been exiled for it either.

"Bjordal would never allow it," Niklas said, more to himself than Dabria.

"But if you could hide it like Silje does? What then?"

Niklas was silent. As much as he wanted Asbjorn to accept him, had hoped for it, he knew it couldn't possibly be so simple.

"Why wouldn't Silje have told me this herself?"

"She thinks you're too soft to go through with fully taking Verchiél," Dabria said. "That's why she wants me watching you, so you don't back out or do something stupid."

"Sva!" Niklas cursed, rising to his feet. "She always has some little scheme she leaves me out of, and for what? So she can play power games with myself none the wiser?"

Dabria watched him pace. "But aren't you wiser for it now?"

Niklas halted. Was Asbjorn truly testing him? It wouldn't be the first time Silje had lied to him about something vital. The temptation grew stronger the more he thought of it. Bjordal. Could he finally go home? As he'd wanted to do since the moment he'd been forced to leave? He could speak his own language, return to his own culture and no longer have people scurry around him in fear of him being a northerner.

"Personally I'd vie for clearing up the protests first," Dabria said. "But I'm going to need your authority to order that."

Niklas considered the shattered fragments of porcelain in silence. He'd been trying to cultivate trust, to make people understand that he was on their side, but perhaps the answer he'd needed was one he'd been denying for so long. Trust took time to cultivate, time he didn't have, but there was something else—

Fear.

How simple and unrefined.

"Call the guard to disperse any gatherings, fully armed this time," Niklas decided. "The coronation will happen on the night of the new year, as it was originally intended."

A ghost of a smile flitted across Dabria's face, but it didn't fill Niklas with the relief he'd hoped for. Only dread as he watched her leave, his violent orders carried with her as she swiftly exited the room.

He turned to the window, and watched the protestors outside. Dealing with Silje could wait. In the meantime he has much else to worry about.

15

GABRIEL

Gabriel stood at the window of his darkened room and looked down into the streets of Grislow.

Being back was like looking through a distorted reflection. Every street corner and towering building was so painfully familiar, Heathall clear in his ears and sneaking back on his lips and in his thoughts. He had slipped back into the rhythm of the place easier than he would ever admit, but he wanted no part of it.

Three days had passed since they'd arrived, which meant three days trapped inside with no news of either the council or Verchiél. Today had been the worst day of all, the night of the conservatory gala. People had been flocking to Grislow, Heathland's capital, day and night from all across the Isles and beyond. The city was only growing in crowds and excitement. Gabriel could hear the muffled fireworks through the glass and it left him twitchier with each passing second.

Despite all the personal contacts that Silje had sent, attempting to gain an audience with the council, even with alternate identities, had proven an impossible task. On a good day, a polite refusal was sent back, but on a bad day they heard nothing at all.

No news, no aid and, worst of all, no allies.

He'd waited for three days.

He wouldn't wait any longer.

He exited the room in silence and made his way downstairs, his footsteps hushed upon plush carpets. Silje hadn't been exaggerating when she said she'd arranged suitable accommodations. Their carriage had taken a short ride from the harbour and pulled up to an impressively large estate for something to be found in the middle of Grislow. Clearly older than the industrial boom, it was a small space of greenery in the midst of the grey city, surrounded on every side by the ever-changing factories and cheap apartments that grew like weeds.

Walking down the staircase, he spotted Zoe seated in the parlour, a game of Malizia set up.

He'd anticipated this. Everyone had agreed it best to keep out of the public eye unless absolutely unnecessary. Which left everyone inside all day with just enough time on their hands to worry, but not enough to actually solve anything. The space had quickly grown stifling. Everyone was irritable and impatient, waiting for news that would never arrive.

He chanced a glance toward Zoe, but she hadn't looked up at his approach, instead analysing her hand of cards with focused interest.

She spun the card on the table. "Do you ever wonder what our lives would be like if we weren't Incarnate?"

"Considering I was born in a slum, I'd probably be dead by now. So, no, it's not something I like to dwell on."

She placed the cards down. "Gabe, if we can regain Verchiél—"

"When," he corrected her.

"I don't know if I want to go back."

Silence stretched between them. Zoe looked at him imploringly; only the faintest traces of gold remained in her deep brown eyes, fading fast as the night grew outside.

She's selfish, isn't she? a voice rose in his mind. *Never had to rough it like you. She doesn't understand what the real world's like.*

"You're the Sun of Verchiél," he said. "First you were handed everything in life and now you'd just give it up?"

"Maybe I want to make something for myself instead of just doing what everybody tells me to."

He couldn't believe what he was hearing. "What would you even do?"

Zoe fidgeted with the cards. "I don't know, take up my family's business again, travel, make a name for myself…"

He laughed. "You? Travel?"

Zoe tensed, speaking defensively. "What's so funny?"

"You're like a child, you don't know what the real world is like."

Her fists tightened. "Rich coming from someone who's not taken an ounce of responsibility since we met."

"Oh? And how do you figure that?"

She laughed, a harsh sound coming from her usually soft-spoken tone. "Everyday you found an excuse to slack off, even at the winter solstice I was the one who was doing all the work. It would have been a disaster without me."

He waved his hand in dismissal. "That's because you're better at stuff like that."

"I guess I'm better at treaty negotiations and paperwork too?" She stood up. "You were lazy then and even now you're still trying to take the easiest way out of your problems."

He bit the inside of his cheek, an anger building in his chest, and with it, the same voice from earlier resurfaced. More insistent.

Tell her, the voice cooed. *If she doesn't hear it from you, she'll find out the hard way.*

"You have no sense of your own purpose," Gabriel said. "Do you even have a life if you're not trying to gain validation from somebody else?"

Silence fell upon the area. Zoe's brows drew together, hurt flashing across her face, and for a moment he thought he'd finally taken one step too far before she spoke slowly.

"Just…just go."

Gabriel set his jaw, a part of himself wanting to continue the argument. To finally exchange more than a few spare words at a time. The endless silence drove him mad, but Zoe turned away, sitting so her back was to him, cutting him out of the conversation entirely.

He left the room in silence, and entered the front foyer. In the entrance was a spiralling staircase, which led to extra sets of rooms and a long mirror that ran across the length of the wall.

From his pocket he procured his old velvet mask. The beloved ratty thing being one of the few objects he still had left from Verchiél. He placed it over his eyes, tonight entirely black like the sky outside, tying the ribbons before flashing his reflection a smile that looked more like a grimace. If he pretended hard enough, he could still be in Verchiél, safe and comfortable. But if everything tonight went according to plan, he'd be one step closer to his throne and getting his life back, no need for playing pretend.

"I don't believe that mirror's been used so much since you arrived."

His eyes caught a movement in the reflection behind him—a person walking soundlessly down the stairs.

"Silje." He managed a smile. "You're up late."

In an ever-changing display, tonight she'd rouged her lips with bright scarlet, and wore a high-necked flowing black dress, with a short cape of metallic feathers that had been draped over her shoulders, clinking softly with each step.

She didn't return the smile, her voice sharp. "Where are you going?"

"Out." He edged toward the door. "Zoe's having a game of Malizia in the parlour, if you'd like to join her?"

"I've already decided to go out for a stroll."

"Dressed up like that?"

"I dress how I feel."

"And how are you feeling tonight?"

Her rouged lips curled into a smile. "Dangerous."

"In that case…" With one hand he opened the front door and with the other he offered it to her. "After you."

"Such a gentleman," she said, though her tone suggested otherwise. She took his hand and stepped outside.

He closed the door behind them and fell into step beside her. They walked side by side down the short drive, gravel crunching beneath their feet.

"Have you managed to contact the council yet?" He'd asked Silje the same question day after day, though she always gave him a variation of the same answer.

"Yes," Silje said. "Though I haven't received word back. It appears the celebrations have left their minds preoccupied."

Sensing his disappointment, she added, "But Zoe's come up with some truly clever plans. We'll have a solution whether they like it or not." She nudged him playfully, her voice shifting to a taunting tone. "I'm shocked she left you in charge of relations with

Heathland when she could have easily had it in the palm of her hand."

"You and Zoe sure seem to be spending a lot of time together," he said, not bothering to conceal the note of jealousy in his voice.

"I like Zoe," Silje said. "She's kind to me." They reached the end of the drive and she turned to face him. "I like you too."

He paused, knowing he was compromising his precarious position, but Silje's words were encouraging and he took the risk. "Perhaps you'd like to have a glass of wine with me after your stroll?"

"Just the wine?"

"Do you want more than wine?"

In one swift motion, she rose to the tips of her toes and brushed her lips against his. Not quite a kiss, but enough that heat rushed to his face and he was grateful for the mask.

"Tempting." She smiled. "But I'm busy tonight." She turned fluidly on her heel and walked down the street without a single look back, offering nothing more than a wave over her shoulder.

"G-good night!" he called after her, his lips still burning.

He watched her walk into the crowd, her long black dress like wisps of shadows gathered around her, the cape of metal feathers chiming softly as an ill omen.

He waited until she was out of sight before he walked in the opposite direction, away from the safety of the estate and off to find his own trouble.

Gabriel passed the bustling shop-fronts and the coffee houses until he came to the docks at the lower end of the city. The entire neighbourhood was built with wood and cloth covers overtop of the buildings, a feeble attempt to block out the pollution and ash from the growing industrial district nestled so close by.

The area grew brighter with each passing step, the faded grey brick buildings replaced by lavish colours in every conceivable hue, an attempt to liven up the scene though no amount of paint or washing could ever get rid of the grey ash that settled in every nook and crevice.

Heathland's pleasure district. Though the only people who came away with any pleasures were those who were clever enough to convince visitors to part with their wealth. It was a long and winding span of a single massive street. Toward the southern end, all manner of gambling halls, and to the north, pleasure houses, each catering to a specific manner of clientele.

Music drifted out from various establishments, and people danced in the streets, some in lavish costumes and others wearing hardly anything at all. Someone popped a bottle of champagne and the foam exploded into the street amid shouts and cheers. Despite himself, Gabriel found himself smiling, the energy infectious.

Several blocks later, the noise was some of the loudest Gabriel had heard along the streets and he knew he had found his destination.

The locale of the Hound's Teeth. Three storeys tall and painted the richest royal blue. The gang was heralded by the so-called queen of the south side: Ada Vard. Countless charges, accusations and investigations spanning years had been laid against her, but none had managed to catch her, and fewer dared to try. Because there might only be one hound, but she had many teeth and they were all sharp.

Gabriel slipped into a darkened alleyway around the side of the club. So narrow in some places he had to shift to shadows to squeeze his way through.

He emerged grime and dust smeared at the back of the building in a narrow lot, empty save for a few old barrels. He cursed when he saw that the back door had been boarded up, but looking up, he saw another opportunity: a window.

He concentrated on the location, an unfortunate three floors up, and with a painful twist of his wrist, rose up as a shadow and reappeared on the window ledge. He threw his arm out and balanced precariously. With one hand he kept himself steady, and with the other he shifted into shadows, managing to sneak underneath the window latch. A few moments of struggle and the window opened with a rusty creak. He slipped inside, feet landing soundlessly on soft carpet.

The darkness was no barrier to his sight and he took in the entirety of the office. It was a cramped but well-used space, and like the rest of the club, decorated with royal blue. A chandelier hung from the ceiling, and there were paintings along the walls of various street scenes in Grislow. Several heavy-duty safes lined the walls and a large mahogany desk took up the majority of the room.

He checked his timepiece. Right on time. He chanced another glance around the office but it was empty. Perhaps she was downstairs; it was a busy night. The muffled noise of dozens of voices and music echoed in the club beneath him. His eyes landed on the door, but before he could take a single step, a voice spoke from the darkness.

"You do realise that you could have used the front door."

A lamp flicked on and Gabriel winced at the sudden brightness. The large chair behind the desk swivelled to face him, occupied by the one person he'd come to see.

Tall and lithe, she was dressed impeccably in a waistcoat, her dirty-blond hair shorn nearly to the scalp along the sides but slicked back along the top. Save for her face, every inch of exposed skin was covered in a startling assortment of tattoos, the most prominent being the snarling canine jaws that stretched across her neck. Her two-toned eyes rested upon him—one dark brown and the other a stark green, both full of judgement.

"Vard," he said.

"Capello," she replied evenly, then nodded to the chair across from her. "Sit."

"How long were you waiting?" he asked, plopping himself down in the seat across from her. "Have you spent all night in the dark?"

"You're one for drama yourself." She tossed a note-card across the table. "Got your message."

"I thought you were supposed to be at the conservatory gala this evening," Gabriel said.

"I've decided to be fashionably late. As the guest of honour, Councillor Carrington can't start his speeches until I'm present."

"Your animosity is something to behold."

"Bastard should have thought about that before he called me a mutt."

She opened a box of cigars and offered one. He shook his head in refusal; though Ada would have nothing but the finest of everything, he was still unwilling to ingest anything she offered.

Ada clearly knew what he was thinking as she asked with amusement, "You think you're important enough for me to kill you? Let alone waste a box of perfectly good cigars?"

"Oh, darling, I think I'm important enough for many people, including you, to kill me."

Ada helped herself to one of the cigars. "You're as insufferable now as you were back then."

"Yes, well, when your old crew nearly murders you, you remember it."

Ada was unfazed as she cut and lit the cigar with deft fingers. "I never threw you in the river, Gabriel."

"You didn't try to stop them either."

"You were competition. Your absence left a bigger space for me."

"I see basic human decency is too much to ask for."

"You've been down south too long if you've started thinking like that. Gone soft." She tilted her head back and blew out a plume of smoke, her voice hoarse when she spoke. "Verchiél has always been too busy clinging to what little power they have. Bjordal has gone for their age-old tactic of fearing what they don't understand and Heathland? Well, we've done what we always do best, turn a profit."

He watched her tap ash into the tray. "And what about you? What do you want?"

"What do any of us want? At the end of the day it all comes back to power and control."

Gabriel saw his opening. It was now or never.

"I need a favour," Gabriel began.

"Don't do favours."

"Fine. I need your services—specifically financial. Between bribes and hired muscle, ousting a usurper won't be a cheap ordeal."

Ada gave him a long, hard look. "Why not ask Carrington? Since you two are on such good terms."

"He's refused my recent correspondences." Gabriel's voice darkened. "I'm looking for an ally with some backbone."

"Interesting…" Ada's expression brightened.

"Yes. I think we could really—"

"I said it was an interesting idea, not a sound one. Allying with you publicly could put me in a very precarious position. After all, you're not exactly popular right now, are you?"

Gabriel's temper flared at her words and he rose to his feet, snapping his fingers so the shadows in the room sprang to life. They crept around him, thick and viscous like tar.

"I think," he said coldly, "you'll find it in your best interest to listen to me."

As children, Ada had never feared his magic so much as been annoyed by it. Or more specifically the fact that it was something he had that she, probably, never would. Even now, she didn't flinch, let alone spare a glance at the shadows around her. She only placed the cigar neatly in the tray, considering him calmly.

"Are you threatening me?"

Her voice was rough, the growl in the back of an animal's throat. Usually Gabriel would have avoided any conflict with her of all people. But time was running short and he was desperate, watching behind his eyes as he saw Verchiél, his home and throne, slipping further away.

"Perceptive." He placed his hands on the desk, making sure he was in her space. "It's a wonder you've made it this far, mutt."

She seized his jaw, trapping his face in an ironclad grip. "This isn't Verchiél and you don't carry any weight here. You might be Incarnate, but you're in my city now—" She squeezed his jaw tightly. "You'll listen or you'll leave."

He glared, indignant. "You're giving orders to a prince."

"You *used* to be a prince," Ada corrected him. "Think very carefully. Did you come here for an ally or another enemy? Because I can guarantee I'm worse than all the rest combined."

"How? One of my enemies is an Incarnate."

"I don't need magic." Ada smiled. "Ivy? Would you be so kind as to join us?"

The door swung open and from the edge of the darkened office, a large figure moved toward Gabriel.

A woman so tall and broad-shouldered that her height rivalled that of Niklas stood behind him. Her pale hair and skin marked her as Bjordal, and she wore the royal blue and black of the club. Ice-coloured eyes rested on him, seething with anger.

"Where are my manners?" Ada lamented. "I haven't introduced Ivy yet."

"Hello, Ivy," Gabriel said quietly.

"Don't mind her. She's just here to make sure that my guests don't break anything." Ada tightened her grip and he felt the bones in his jaw click. "You're not going to break anything, are you?"

Gabriel weighed his options. He could fight them; it was night and he had the power to do so. But he didn't trust Vard not to have something terrible up her sleeve. Not to mention that it would be wasting valuable time and effort, neither of which he cared to give up without getting something better out of it.

"No." He met Ada's eyes. "I'm not going to break anything."

Ada held his gaze for a moment longer before she released him. Gabriel immediately sank back in his chair, moving his jaw to test that it wasn't broken.

"That's what we like to hear," Ada said. "Isn't that right,

Ivy?"

With all the stoicism of a rugged mountain, Ivy nodded once, but remained silent, her eyes not leaving Gabriel.

"The Hound's Teeth are more than pleased to offer viable alliances," Ada continued, all business. "However we require suitable terms to consider your request."

Gabriel leaned forward, infusing a tone of excitement into his voice. "What do you love more than money?"

"Easy. Nothing."

"Try again," Gabriel suggested.

"I don't have time for guessing games." Ada pulled out her timepiece and looked at it impatiently. "On with it."

"Why, what you've built yourself upon, of course. The secrets of others."

Ada paused, a flicker of interest evident in her expression. "Go on."

"That's it."

"Pretty shitty secret." She snapped the timepiece shut and rose to her feet, cracking her neck with the motion. "Let's go, Ivy, this one's all talk. We've still got another twenty minutes to kill before we can make our grand entrance—"

"Wait!" Gabriel stepped before Ada. Not close enough to physically stop her, but enough to block her path to the door. Ivy was across the room in an instant, looming over Gabriel, but Ada once again held up a hand calmly.

"Stay out of my way."

Ada's voice was quiet, only a whisper, but Gabriel immediately recognized the threat. He didn't dare push his luck this time as he stepped backward.

"Just think about it," he insisted. "There's a party happening just a few minutes away, imagine all the gossip, the affairs, the scandals!—An entire night of secrets I could gather. All in exchange for helping me. It's hardly any loss on your part."

"Don't do favours and I don't need you." She shoved past him, grabbing an oversized blazer from a coat rack and swinging it over her shoulders. "I already have people who find secrets. I have them all across the city."

"But you don't have any like me."

"If by 'like me' you mean spoiled little bastards? You're right. I don't. Besides, you're still promising me what you don't have."

"Isn't that what all investments are? You're a businesswoman. Surely you can see the long-term benefits."

Ada eyed him up and down. "Or, I could just save myself the trouble and turn you in now."

Ivy took a step toward him and Gabriel's mind whirled furiously. He could still flee but Ada would have the whole city up and looking for him and Zoe within the moment he did.

He drew in a breath before playing his last card. "You might not do favours, but I will. In exchange for your support, I'll do whatever favour you ask. It's not everyday that you can get such an offer from an Incarnate."

A slow smile grew across Ada's lips. "Whatever I like?"

A twinge of concern swept through Gabriel at the unhinged gleam in her eyes, but he found himself nodding. "Yes, whatever you want."

"Ivy." Ada snapped her fingers. "Papers." Reluctantly, Ivy crossed the room to one of the safes and spun the combination. Gabriel tried to peer inside but Ivy's broad back was to him and he caught only a glimpse of stacks of documents and books.

Ivy closed and re-locked the safe and handed Gabriel a long and thin canister. Curious, he moved to unscrew the lid, but Ada slapped his hand away. "Don't open it, you twat."

"Why?" He shook the canister, and a faint shifting noise sounded from within. "What's inside?"

"Documents. An identical set resides within Councillor Carrington's own safe." She nodded to the canister in his hands. "I need you to swap his papers out with these. And it needs to be done within the hour and not a second later."

"That's it?"

"That's it."

"Oh…" He weighed the canister, disappointed. "I was hoping for something a bit more… well, exciting, you know? Maybe stealing some jewels or a painting. Something fun."

Ada's lip curled. "Not all business is fun. I believe you'll find this task difficult enough to manage on your own. By the end of the night you may wish you hadn't taken it."

"Why?" he asked, curious. "What are the papers?"

"Doesn't matter. All that matters is that the original papers are in my hands by the end of the hour with our mutual friend none the wiser." She offered a hand. "Do we have a deal?"

Gabriel paused. In Heathland, a handshake meant much more than a sign of good faith, it was as serious as making a pact or a blood oath. If he took her offer, there was no backing out.

He looked at her hand. "If you're going to be at the gala tonight, why can't you do this?"

"How would it look if I were wandering the councillor's private offices? Our rivalry isn't exactly private."

"Don't pretend you couldn't remain unseen."

"Yes, but I have other things on my mind, and why

shouldn't you do it?" She gestured to the window. "You have a knack for creeping into places you don't belong."

He rolled the canister from hand to hand. "And if I don't want this job?"

Ada reached forward and cupped his cheek, speaking softly. "If you don't want to pay your debt to our alliance this way, I know of a wealthy dowager in Les Ronnes who has an obsession with the arcane." She brushed the hair away from his face, gently, almost a caress. "I'm certain she would pay me handsomely for your pretty black eyes."

He clutched the canister tighter. "Understood."

She patted his cheek before releasing him. "Delighted to hear that. Now, alliance or no?"

"What are the specifics?"

"We'll need to have a contract drawn up, of course, but in simple terms, if I deem your job complete, I'll offer aid in regaining your throne. And once you're back on said throne, you will make sure the council doesn't interfere with any of my business."

"Ally with me now," Gabriel said. "Help me take back Verchiél and I'll make sure you own Heathland. No strings attached. Run it, rule it, ruin it for all I care."

It was a risk— a huge one at that. But an ally as powerful as Ada was an opportunity he refused to pass up.

"If that's the case," Ada said, "as far as you and I are concerned, I am Heathland."

His gaze went from Ada's eyes to her outstretched hand. He didn't even want to think of what Zoe would say if she saw him now. But they needed to move forward, and if he didn't make an alliance with Ada, then somebody else would, and he would much rather be on the council's bad side than Ada's.

He took her hand, shaking it in a tight grasp. "We have a deal."

"Delighted. Now get the fuck out. " Ada cast another look at her timepiece. "I'll meet you on the conservatory roof in an hour's time."

"Just can't wait to see me again, can you?"

"You? No. The papers? Yes."

"Don't make me feel so special."

She tutted. "You're very special. You're going to get me exactly what I want."

"Speaking of wants," he said. "There's one more thing—"

"No favours."

"None," he agreed quickly. "However, I need you to make an inquiry into a woman named Silje Nordviken."

At the thought of Silje, a series of conflicting feelings rose in his mind: fascination, enamor, distrust, but stronger than them all was a small voice in the very back of his mind...

Trust her. Stay with Silje—

The one thing he did know—or felt—was that there was something...off about Silje's magic, but he couldn't put a finger on it. Every time he drew too close it slipped away from him, always out of his reach of understanding, yet it beckoned him to continue chasing. But if Silje wanted to play games, then he would reciprocate.

Starting by figuring out who she really was.

Gabriel was shocked to see a look of surprise flash across Ada's face. It looked so out of place he nearly laughed.

"How do you know that name?" Ada asked.

"So you do know her?" Gabriel asked, intrigued.

"Of her." Ada shrugged disinterestedly, the look gone again

as quickly as it had come. "If you finish your task tonight, inquiries can be made and investigated."

Gabriel wanted to ask more questions, but Ivy held the door open, which Gabriel took as his cue to leave. He moved to exit, but Ada stopped him. "Out the window."

"Why?"

"Because I said so." Ada shoved ahead of him, calling out over her shoulder, "I'd wish you luck, little Moon, but there's no such thing."

"Have fun at the party," Gabriel said glumly.

Ivy lingered only long enough to spare Gabriel one final glare, her nose wrinkling in disgust at the sight of him before she shut the door with a forceful snap.

Gabriel let out a long breath. He supposed in terms of a meeting, it could have gone a lot worse. He looked down at the canister in his hands.

One job and he'd finally have an ally strong enough to truly start taking back Verchiél. His home and his life.

One job. One night. One hour.

He could do that.

Gabriel tucked the canister safely into his inner jacket pocket, and slipped back out the window, silent as a shadow in the night.

Zoe had never known her mother. She was lost the moment she was born. Never had the chance to remember as her father had, or received the chance to get to know the world around her as others did because her father assured her it was always too dangerous, too unpredictable, too much for her. She needed to stay close, where it was safe and she wouldn't get hurt.

Even after she'd been sent to the palace, she was still kept close to someone else, for another reason though it was so similar. After all, she couldn't put herself in danger, she had an entire country depending on her well-being.

Despite these good intentions, she just wanted to prove herself. But now Zoe was beginning to wonder if they had all had a point.

Zoe was jostled about in the bustling Grislow streets, struggling not to be swept away in the erratic flow of the crowd. It was a lively night and citizens and tourists alike flooded the shops. The scent of meat pies and pastries wafted from the food carts that cluttered the streets.

Unsupervised children ran amok, whether they were just playing or up to something more criminal, Zoe had no idea, but she made sure to steer clear and avoid the urge to constantly check if her coin purse was still in her pocket.

She pulled the hood of the new emerald green coat Silje had brought her over her curls, making sure her face was hidden from any passing eyes that might recognize her as the Daughter of the Sun.

Alessi lived in the Merchant District, not far from where they'd originally docked. But now it was late and the gates were barred, though a few of the city's Grey Guard, still milled around, chatting idly and sharing a hand rolled cigarette.

"Excuse me?" Zoe approached the group. "Would you open the gates for me?"

His brow rose at her Verchiél accent. "Sorry, miss, the streets are closed."

"But it's very important that I get through," she pressed. "I have business there."

"Do you have a merchant seal?"

"A seal?" Zoe asked.

The man added in a softer tone, something close to pity, "Get home, love, you're clearly not from around here."

Her resolve intensified and she stood straighter. What had Gabriel told her? That any citizen of Grislow would happily sell their soul for?

She held up the coin purse Silje had given her and the men fell silent.

"Are you sure the gates are closed?" she asked.

The first man took the coin purse, judging the weight, which he clearly found no qualms with as he grinned.

"Well, would you look at that? I believe I've found my keys, right this way, my lady."

He snatched the coin purse up. Zoe winced. That was probably much more than a simple bribe required, but then again money seemed to be of no object for Silje; Zoe could hardly use any of the fine things she gave her fast enough.

As Zoe passed through the gate, the man leaned closer. "Bit of advice? Watch yourself in there, streets might be nicer but it's the people inside that you should worry about."

"Thanks for your concern, but I have a friend here."

The man only shook his head. "You poor thing."

Zoe opened her mouth to ask what he meant but the gates had already clanged shut behind her, leaving her on the quiet side of the street.

She turned to the Merchant District. Compared to the rest of the city, the streets were quieter and cleaner here, and the neighbourhood consisted of many halls and office buildings.

Alessi had said that they lived in the home closest to the dockyard, 1715. She strode forward, continually looking from the address in her hand to the sprawling manors before her and mentally reciting her plan.

She needed an invitation to the gala so she could have an audience with the council. After all, if Alessi was doing well enough to have earned a place in the Merchant District, then they would certainly have the kind of access she needed to reach one of Heathland's near untouchable council members.

Once she reached the last building, her feet slowed. This couldn't possibly be right. A sprawling manor greeted her, far finer than most of the places here. The last she had heard the business hadn't been doing too well. She supposed that things must have turned around. This was...well, opulent beyond anything she'd ever known before arriving at the palace.

Tentatively she walked down the drive, hesitating only a moment before she knocked with the large brass hound's head mounted on the heavy oaken doors. A moment passed before footsteps sounded from inside and a bored-looking servant woman answered the door. "Sorry, no clients during off hours—"

"Is Alessi here?" Zoe blurted out. "I need to speak with them, it's sort of an emergency."

At Zoe's tone the woman's face scrunched up in suspicion, her eyes narrowing. "And just who are you?"

"Mable?" a cheerful voice spoke from the estate interior. "Who are you talking to? You don't have any gentlemen callers after you, do you?"

"Alessi, it's me!" Zoe shouted into the foyer before Mable could usher her away.

"Zo?"

She caught a glimpse of them, deep brown skin, wide smile, dark hair that swept down their back in curls. Their face burst into a wide smile and suddenly Zoe was swept off her feet.

"Zo!"

The world swirled past her eyes, and only once she was sufficiently dizzy was she placed back down.

"Alessi!" She clung to their shoulder. "Would you warn me next time you do that?"

"Warn you? What about warning me! If I'd known you were stopping by I would have thrown a party."

"Don't say that, you're sounding like Gabriel."

At the mention of Gabriel, Alessi looked outside expectantly. Zoe's gut twisted in guilt when she recognized hope on their face.

"Sorry," Zoe added. "Gabe isn't here."

Alessi nodded but Zoe caught the flash of disappointment plain across their face. "A shame, that bastard still owes me a drink, but speaking of—" They clapped their hands together, look-ing at Mable. "Would you be so kind as to bring our guest some tea?"

"Course," she said bluntly, making her way down the hall. "I wouldn't expect your royal highness to be able to find the right side of a teapot if your life depended on it."

Once she was out of earshot Alessi turned to Zoe. "I as-sume you're not here because of Gabriel?"

"No, actually, I need your help with something."

Alessi managed a smile, though it was slightly more strained. "There's much more comfortable seating inside."

They led Zoe into a well-furnished salon, the walls papered in warm hues of red, and covered with a few scattered mirrors and a taxidermy ram's head. Alessi sat down in a large wingback chair and she on a divan so soft that she immediately sank into the cushions.

"So"—Alessi clapped their hands together, all excite-ment—"tell me everything!"

Where to even begin? Zoe thought to herself.

"Well…" she started. "I'm certain you know all about what happened during the winter solstice."

"Er, yes…I heard." A bit of Alessi's excitement trickled away. "I'm grateful that you're here and safe—not that I ever doubted you," they quickly added at her look. "It's not often we get so much news from down south, but it's all anyone wants to talk about these days. Well, that and the bloody conservatory gala…"

"Actually, that's exactly what I'm here to talk to you about," Zoe sat forward, encouraged. "I need an invitation to the gala so I can gain an audience with the council. I realise it's a lot to ask," she added quickly at Alessi's shocked expression. "But as soon as Gabriel and I are back in power, we'd make sure to compensate you for your troubles."

Alessi was silent for a long moment, tapping their fingers against the arm of their chair thoughtfully. "Of course, but…" A few more taps and their frown deepened. "If I help you, I only hope that you'd be able to return the favour."

"If it's setting up you and Gabriel that's a no. I already made that mistake once and I won't make it again."

"Not quite." Alessi smiled, though there was a strained look to it. "You see, I'm in a bit of a pickle, financially that is."

Zoe paused, looking from the silk and velvet divan she sat upon to the chandelier, which was set with gold and emeralds. "You live here, aren't you doing well?"

"I don't technically own it so much as do business here, it's just easier to live close."

"Then whose place is this?" Zoe asked.

"My boss, she's been gracious enough to let me stay here."

"Your…boss?" Zoe asked. A tension had entered the room; Alessi had trouble meeting Zoe's eyes. "I thought you were running our family's business. You wrote me a letter and said it was doing great."

"I may have exaggerated a few details," Alessi admitted.

"Such as?" Zoe pressed.

Alessi drew in a deep breath, and Zoe immediately recognized the attempt to gently find the right way to give her bad news. Something which, historically, had never worked well between them.

"Do you remember the boat?"

Zoe didn't expect that. "What boat?"

"I had a boat—a beautiful thing! Went all the way to Sakai.

I even managed to negotiate an exclusive trade deal. We had everything: silks, tea, rice wine, you name it."

"But we've never done trade outside of the Isles," Zoe countered. "We don't have any vessels large enough to make the journey to the mainland."

"Er, yes about that…" Alessi nodded, a touch of hesitation entering their voice. "I had a proper vessel commissioned. I took out a loan from a third party who was interested in investing in the voyage."

Zoe blinked. "And how were you going to pay that off?"

"It was carrying enough valuables to pay for itself several times over," Alessi said. "It took months of negotiations but the deal was supposed to be the first of many."

"Supposed to?" Zoe pressed, dreading where this was going.

Alessi's brown eyes fell to the floor, their previous spark dimming. "It…er, sank."

Zoe blinked, processing their words. "Sank?"

Now Alessi spoke faster, their words tumbling out. "Yes, well, the vessel construction ran late and by the time it was ready to sail, the storm season had just begun. I wanted to hold off until the waters cleared but the trade deal with our contact in Sakai would have fallen through. I thought it better to chance it and rush the sailing rather than coming out of it with nothing at all." A note of bitterness entered Alessi's voice. "Turns out I got less than nothing because the whole damned thing—ship, cargo, crew and all—sank to the bottom of the ocean. The *Capello* didn't survive the maiden voyage."

Zoe processed this; it wasn't unusual for a cargo or a ship to be lost in this line of work. Even crew members could be lost at sea if the conditions were bad enough. But for Alessi to have lost all three? It was so different from the way their parents had run the business. Among all this information, one detail in particular stuck out to her.

"You named the boat after Gabriel?"

"Of course," Alessi said. "It was his idea—oh, thank you, Mable!"

Mable had arrived with a tea tray in hand; Zoe watched her place it on the table and pieced together the entire timeline for this nonsense.

"When did all of this happen?" Zoe asked numbly.

"About this time last year, why?"

Exactly the time Alessi and Gabriel had broken things off. It had been something that had puzzled her. Something neither of them had ever spoken of.

"Let me understand this correctly," Zoe said. "You and Gabriel got drunk, came up with this stupid idea—"

"I thought it was quite clever," Alessi countered. "And we weren't drunk, just a little tipsy—"

"And then you decided to take out a massive and ill-advised debt."

"It was a standard-sized debt and it was only mildly discouraged."

"All because you wanted to get rich quick?"

"It's not Gabe's fault. I was the one who went ahead with the plan. He actually tried to talk me out of it the next day when we sobered up."

Zoe stared at them in disbelief. "Then why did you do it?"

They looked embarrassed. "I really thought it could work. You hear all these stories about getting a good trade deal with the mainland and making a profit."

"Lesi." Zoe rubbed her temples. "You always do this, jump in headfirst without a long-term plan. First you wanted to be a musician then a painter—"

"I did sell several of my pieces," Alessi said with some defensiveness.

"Gabriel buying them doesn't count!"

Alessi fell quiet, long fingers tapping the edge of their teacup irritably.

"I thought that I'd actually make the business my own rather than something that was just handed down to me. Maybe if you hadn't been an Incarnate, you would have been the one in my place."

Zoe had to admit she'd considered that more than once. What her life would have been like if her eyes had never turned gold. As she looked across to Alessi now, bound up in countless decisions and consequences, she wasn't entirely sure if she would have done a better job.

"So what's happening with the business now?" Zoe asked.

"I suppose there's nothing for it…" Alessi drew in a deep breath before they met her eyes. "I sold it."

Zoe baulked.

Sold it? What had been their parents' livelihoods and was meant to be theirs? Though it was a life Zoe had long since made peace with giving up, she'd still taken solace in the fact that Alessi would be running it. That a piece of their families' legacy would still live on in its own way.

"To who?" Zoe asked.

Alessi spoke carefully and it was clear to Zoe that this was a conversation they'd run through in their mind many times before this moment.

"A wealthy investor who agreed to undertake the debt in exchange for the business and its earnings in their name until I can earn out what they originally paid."

Zoe couldn't believe what she was hearing. "But you've still got the debt! At least you had the business in your name before—"

"You didn't let me finish," Alessi added, irritation evident in their tone. "Yes they technically own the business now, but they're helping me run it. I'm making far more than I was on my own, plus the interest rate is actually manageable. You'd take the deal too if you saw what the Grislow banks were offering…"

Zoe shook her head, processing the information. "It was still our business, why didn't you let me know?"

"It was time-sensitive. In all honesty I'm shocked anyone took the offer to begin with, I thought I would have been laughed out of the room."

"But"—Zoe clenched her hands in her lap—"why didn't you tell me how bad things had gotten?"

"Because you were about to be crowned! I thought you'd have enough on your plate without worrying about one failing little shipping company."

Though their words were true it had still been something that tied them together as far back as childhood; all four of their parents had partnered to make the business work. Zoe would have run it alongside Alessi, that is, if she wasn't an Incarnate.

"Lesi," Zoe said. "I could have helped."

"I thought I could handle it myself, I had done it for years on my own."

"What's that supposed to mean?"

Alessi shifted uncomfortably, choosing their words carefully. "When you left for the palace, after you became an Incarnate, you...acted like you didn't even remember me."

She recalled those first frightening days. When she'd cried herself to sleep, and had only a mind for the way things used to be. But as time passed she grew used to it, to Enzo and Aria, to Gabriel when he'd arrived a few years later. Eventually, she even grew comfortable. It wasn't the home she'd left, but it was someplace new she found herself taking solace in. And as time passed and that feeling grew, so did her distance with her old home— her old life.

She hadn't forgotten that time. Apparently Alessi hadn't either.

"Do you even realise how much I missed you?" they continued. "You used to write to me everyday, then all of a sudden it was only every week, then every month or year." They struggled for words before speaking quietly. "Whenever I was in the capital I would always walk by the palace, hoping I'd catch a glimpse of you. I thought you didn't want anything more to do with me."

"That's not true. I missed you so much. I wanted to see you again."

"Then why didn't you?"

Days had slipped into months, which in turn had slipped away into years, all of that time steeped with regret.

"Because I felt guilty," she said. "You were always talking about how you wanted to leave home and I was the one who got to."

"So you thought cutting me out of your life was a better solution?"

"No, of course not. I just didn't want to make you feel..."

"Feel what?" Their voice grew colder.

"Jealous," she admitted.

"Of course I was jealous," they snapped. "A part of me still is. To be given a gift of the heavens, and then to live in a palace? To have everything in my life taken care of? Do you have any idea what I would give to have even a scrap of what you do?"

"What good did any of it do me?" she shot back. "It's all gone now. At least you still have a life that you chose instead of having everything decided for you."

"Poor thing," they said. "Having to live in a palace. That must have been so hard on you."

"At least you still have your family," she said icily. "That's more than I can say."

Silence fell upon the room, both staring each other down.

"Listen, Zo..." Alessi pinched the bridge of their nose, speaking with some hesitance. "Things aren't the same as they once were."

"What do you mean?" Zoe asked.

They stood up. "It's easier for me to show you." Before Zoe could say anything more they reached out to the taxidermy ram's head and pulled one of the horns down, and to her shock, it moved like a lever. Suddenly, a soft noise came from within the wall, and Zoe watched as a seamless panel shifted to the side, opening to reveal an additional door.

Zoe stood in shocked silence, staring at the new door before her.

Alessi tensed, looking at her. "I suppose you want to know what's become of the old business— " They reached forward and turned the handle, and it opened, the key already in the lock. "Follow me."

Alessi disappeared into the darkened doorway and Zoe cast

one look back into the parlour before she slipped behind the hidden door.

Zoe's vision flooded with black as she entered a hallway. It was narrow and low ceilinged and she had to keep her hands along the walls to guide herself forward, the floor sloping slightly downward with each step. She spotted an open doorway ahead of her, slowing her steps as her eyes adjusted to the light, and as she entered the room, her jaw dropped.

The chamber was a tall, circular room lit by a single massive chandelier and filled with... well, it looked like everything.

Countless piles of books were lined upon the towering shelves. There were ornate cabinets of curiosities, musical instruments, old suits of armour, thick chests with rusted padlocks. She placed her hand on a globe and spun it around, her fingers trailing from the isles to the larger continents beyond.

She stopped before a Malizia board; it was far more ancient than the set she had been playing with. She picked up the pack of cards, stained by age, and noticed they'd been painted with real silver and gold. "What is this place?" she asked partially to herself.

"I deal in luxury goods and trade, and don't touch that—"

Zoe opened the lid of one particularly heavy-looking wooden chest, revealing neatly stacked piles of books which were yellowed with age.

"These have been out of print for decades!" Zoe lifted a volume with near reverence. "Getting a copy is next to—"

"Impossible." Alessi crossed the room and snapped the case shut, a plume of dust rising with the action. "I'm aware, just as I'm aware"—they delicately plucked the book out of Zoe's grasp and locked it back in the trunk—"that they're on their way to their new owner tonight who wants them in pristine condition."

"Where did you get them?" Zoe asked. "They must be worth a small fortune."

Alessi shrugged, re-organizing things. "Found them at an auction. Right place, right time. Didn't even know what I got when I bought them, thought I was getting the trunk." They tapped the toe of their shoe against the heavy chest.

"Alessi," Zoe began carefully, placing the set of cards back on the table, "what exactly do you do here?"

"Yes, well…" Alessi said. "I provide a much wider and eclectic selection than the average connoisseur. My aim is to bring a sense of wonder and intrigue to my clients that can't possibly be replicated anywhere else—"

"Lesi," Zoe spoke slowly, uncertain if she even wanted to know the answer, "are you a smuggler?"

Alessi was silent for a long time, struggling with words, starting and stopping their sentences until they spoke quickly. "Listen, I can explain everything. I'm not really a smuggler, but—"

"But you still chose to sell the business to become one," Zoe cut across, shock and anger sweeping through her in equal measure. "You know this is exactly the sort of thing our families lost so much business over?"

Alessi frowned, matching her tone. "Have you considered that's why they went broke in the first place? They failed to change and they paid the price for it. I was just the only one left standing who could pick up the pieces."

"You're a thief."

"I'm a privateer."

Zoe opened her mouth to argue but suddenly the sounds of Mable frantically shouting and running through the parlour echoed down the hall.

"Your company has arrived."

Alessi's gaze snapped back to Zoe, panicked. "You need to hide. Now."

"What, but—" Zoe dug her heels into the carpet as Alessi placed their hands on her shoulders and began pushing her back into the room toward a large wardrobe. "Why?"

"I have an important guest visiting this evening and she doesn't know you're here," they added.

"Who is she?" Zoe asked.

"Someone who'd love to turn you in for a reward if she had the chance." They opened the door of the wardrobe and motioned her inside. "Get in."

Zoe straightened, indignant. "I'm not hiding in a wardrobe." She looked around the room. "Shouldn't a secret room have a second door?"

"In the works," Alessi said, casting a look back to the darkened hall where the sound of footsteps and a pair of voices echoed loudly.

"Please, just trust me," Alessi said, pleading. "If she sees you, I won't be able to help." Alessi gave her a nervous smile, squeezing her shoulder. "I'm right out here."

Zoe stepped into the wardrobe; it was large enough that she didn't need to squeeze herself inside, instead standing at her full height among the soft velvet and fur coats.

Alessi moved to close the doors but she caught their wrist. "Wait, who is she?"

Alessi held the sides of the wardrobe with a tight grasp before they answered.

"My boss."

They closed the panels and darkness flooded Zoe's vision.

There was a crack in between the doors, just wide enough for Zoe to peer into the room. As her eyes adjusted to the sudden darkness she watched as Alessi walked back to the entrance, just in time to greet a pair of women.

One was so tall Zoe had to look up to see her face and the other was lithe with sharp-boned features, her oversized blazer resting comfortably upon her shoulders. As she surveyed the room, Zoe caught the glimpse of two-toned eyes.

Zoe sucked in a quiet breath, pressing herself further into the wardrobe. This couldn't be right, Alessi was working for—

"Ada!" Alessi blurted out, a tone of nervousness evident in their voice. "I wasn't expecting you for another"—they checked his time piece with a frown—"half an hour." They snapped the watch shut, their smile tightening. "May I offer you some tea?" They gestured to the tray behind them. "I believe I have a few biscuits to go along with—"

"Plans change," Ada dismissed. "Got it?"

"Yes." Alessi said. "Of course, it's just…" They walked back toward the trunk Zoe had been inspecting earlier and heaved it forward another few inches with a strained face. "Right here."

Ada watched closely as Alessi opened the trunk lid and showed her the books. Ada picked one up, inspecting it closely before tossing the volume back into the chest. Alessi's face spasmed, horrified.

"Ivy, darling?" Ada said, glancing at the woman over her shoulder. "Would you mind?"

Ivy stepped forward and took the trunk from Alessi, heaving it up onto her shoulder as if it weighed nothing.

"Er, yes…very good," Alessi said, eyeing Ivy dubiously and dusting themself off.

"What a lovely place you have here." Ada paced leisurely around the chamber, hands in her pockets. "You've built the collection faster than I'd anticipated." She paused at the Malizia set Zoe had been admiring earlier, shuffling the cards through her long fingers. "I'm impressed."

Alessi held themself a little taller, a note of pride in their voice. "Yes, well, collection isn't an easy business and it certainly isn't built overnight."

"Of course not." Ada continued her inspection of the room. "That's why I only work with the best."

Ada's gaze fell upon the wardrobe and Zoe froze. Though the wardrobe's panels were made of thick wood, Zoe couldn't help but feel they were nothing but air when presented with Ada's piercing stare.

"What a beautiful wardrobe." Ada crossed the room. "Post Keating?"

"Pre actually," Alessi said. "But it's very old and fragile, so I wouldn't get too close—"

"Don't fret." Ada trailed her fingers along the panels, so close that Zoe felt her warm breath through the crack in the doors. "You know I like to see everything up close—"

A crash resounded throughout the room and Ada's attention snapped back to the parlour entrance, her hand falling away from the wardrobe.

Alessi was spewing apologies as they helped one very angry Ivy gather up the books that had fallen from the chest.

"I'm terribly sorry," they lamented. "I've been so clumsy lately, and such beautiful books…"

Zoe knew they didn't need to fake the worry in their voice as they picked up the leather-bound volumes with tender care.

Like a storm, Ada swept back across the room, weaving through the cluttered objects with ease before she snatched the book from Alessi's grasp. "If I were you, I'd watch your step."

Though Zoe couldn't fully see them from her point of view, she could just imagine how they were making a show of being flustered and apologising from the tone in their voice. Ada held their gaze for another moment before she added, "You've kept your end of the bargain. The money will be in your account by the end of the night."

Zoe saw the relief in their shoulders as Alessi thanked her.

"And this." Ada procured an envelope from her suit and handed it to Alessi. "An invitation for the gala. Have a little fun for a change." Ada winked, before she walked back out the door. "Let's go, Ivy, we've got ten minutes to kill."

Ivy spared one more glare to Alessi before ducking down through the passageway, the sound of Ada's chatter fading away along with her.

A few minutes passed before Alessi threw open the wardrobe doors, the cold air hitting Zoe's flushed cheeks.

"You sold our family business to Ada fucking Vard?" Zoe asked, livid.

"Technically, yes," Alessi said, "but please, just—"

Zoe pushed her way past them. Just her luck, she looked for the proper way to do business and got caught up in yet another bad scheme.

"Zo, wait—"

Alessi pulled Zoe to the side, speaking quietly. "I know you don't want anything to do with people like Ada, but she was the only one who offered to buy the debt. If it wasn't for her I'd be destitute by now."

Zoe's original anger softened as she looked at Alessi anew. There were new lines around their face that she'd never seen before, and though they weren't yet thirty, grey hairs had begun to sneak into their dark curls. Things hadn't stopped and waited for her when she left for the palace. She shouldn't have expected Alessi to wait for her either.

She wrapped her arms around them and to her relief they returned the hug.

"I'm sorry I left," she said, her voice muffled by their shoulder.

They patted her back reassuringly. "I mean it's not exactly like you had a choice, did you?"

Zoe tightened her grasp. "I should have written to you more often, I should have fixed it all—"

"You're here now, that's all that matters." Alessi pulled away, their eyes holding hers steady. "You were trying to help me before, but we can help each other now." Alessi placed their hands on her shoulders. "Take the invitation. Talk to the council. You might still have a chance to sort things out before we lose them completely."

Zoe looked up at Alessi. There was a small smile on their face, but they were tired too. Heavens, they were both so tired.

"Alessi," Zoe said. "I'm sorry, and if you'll have me, I'd love to accompany you to the gala."

"Excellent!" Alessi clapped their hands in excitement, already in motion and striking up a steady stream of chatter. "I'm afraid I don't have anything by the way of dresses. Mable has a few pieces, but they're not exactly gala fashion. Although I have quite the collection of suits if you'd be so inclined?"

"A suit," Zoe said, "sounds perfect."

17

GABRIEL

Gabriel shifted back from the shadows, his feet landing on the roof of the conservatory, the glass panels rattling with his sudden weight.

He crouched and looked into the glowing interior of the party. The conservatory was by far the most ambitious construction project to have been taken on in Grislow since the building of the original castle itself. Years of elaborate planning and the place was a maze, only further emphasised by the grounds that were surrounded by intricate hedges and waterways. It would be open to the public soon enough, but for now nobility and the social elite celebrated its achievement in glamorous privacy.

It was beautiful and it was also packed to the point of bursting. What better time to make his own entrance?

He pulled back his sleeve to check the ink lines of the map he'd hastily traced along his forearm. Ada had left him a map, the information not exactly secret as the construction plans had shown to the public. The council's own private offices were further back, along the third floor. But he couldn't enter from the outside without breaking the glass. The windows were a part of the sealed panes that made up the rear dome of the conservatory. He needed an inside door.

He glanced at his timepiece—thirty minutes before he

needed to meet Ada, still plenty. He snapped the case shut, patting his jacket to check for the reassuring weight of the pistol and knife Ada had lent him.

He shifted back to the shadows, making his way down along the side of the building. He'd considered trying to enter from the ground with all the other guests, but between multiple security checkpoints and a near army of watchful guards, he decided it was better not to risk it and instead snuck along the roof.

It reminded him of how he'd lived the first part of his life, hiding in shadows and running along rooftops. It was fucking unfair that he needed to repeat it all over again. Although now he found himself struggling, his fingers slipping against the places where he failed to find a proper hold, his feet unsteady.

He paused to catch his breath atop the archway of the build-ing's west entrance, clutching a stone gargoyle for support. He considered that perhaps he wasn't as fit as he liked to believe. Then again, as a rule, he never made any effort to exert himself unless it was with company in bed.

He leaned over the edge of the archway, watching the crowd below him that moved like a sea of glittering finery.

He should have been invited here himself, a newly crowned prince. Welcomed with honour and applause and no shortage of gorgeous individuals just waiting to earn his favour.

The image faded quickly as he picked out the guards in their soot-grey uniforms. He wasn't a prince— not yet. But the sooner he finished this job, the closer he would be back to the life he deserved.

He squinted his eyes and measured the distance. A jump— with magic— would put him exactly where he needed to be, far enough past the final checkpoint not to be scrutinised. But there was the pesky problem that it was fifty feet away and timing was key for catching himself, lest he become as flat as a particularly magnificent pancake.

He weighed his options. At least if he was dead, Ada couldn't blame him for anything … Who was he kidding? Ada was exactly the sort of person to complain about his untimely demise inconveniencing her, or twist it to her advantage somehow.

He spread his arms and took the last step, letting himself fall. The cold wind whipped past, making his eyes water and heart race. Despite himself a smile spread across his face. But the on-coming crowd approached closer than he'd anticipated. With a painful snap of his wrist, he shifted to shadows before he hit the ground. But as soon as he reappeared on his feet, his legs buckled beneath him as if his body still carried the force of the fall.

He collapsed and people around him shrieked and pushed out of his way. Panic tore through him, as he tried to find balance so suddenly that his foot shot out and stepped right onto a trailing cape of snow-white feathers.

A loud tearing noise resounded throughout the area and he grimaced, desperately hoping he wouldn't be tossed out of the gala before he'd even walked through the doors. After all, this woman looked like a noble, with deep brown skin and close-cropped hair. Her gown caught the light as small crystals had been sown into the fabric, appearing like droplets of water. Her appearance was made all the more eye-catching as a live owl sat perched on her shoulder.

She whipped around with a shocked stare, eyes wide at the state of her dress. Gabriel jumped back as the owl spread its large wings, on the verge of taking flight before the woman tugged at the golden chain connected to her wrist. It settled begrudgingly against her shoulder.

"T-terribly sorry. Clumsy feet," he said, keeping his head low and hoping he wouldn't sound too out of breath. He eyed the owl up and down dubiously. Its head swivelled in every direction, beak snapping at anyone who got too close.

People whispered, curious glances thrown his way. The woman inhaled sharply, shooting him a withering glance. "Watch yourself," she warned, before marching into the conservatory, feathers and disgruntled hooting drifting in her wake.

Some discontent murmurs followed Gabriel, but quickly enough everyone continued along their business, needing to move forward to make room for the incoming crowd. Gabriel chanced a look at the checkpoint guards behind him, but he found nothing more in their eyes other than disinterested glances. Apparently wardrobe malfunctions were a common enough occurrence not to raise any alarms.

As soon as he passed the conservatory threshold, he lingered around the edges of the sprawling chamber. Tropical plants rose as high as the glass ceiling, giving off a scent of greenery in the bustling chamber. A massive whale skeleton was hung from the ceiling while below displays of animal skeletons lined the hallways, like some sort of grand procession long since dead.

He pretended to take in the sights with the other guests as he searched for a path to the upper floors. Past the swelling crowd, he spotted a staircase. He stepped forward just as a pair of hands seized his shoulders.

"You!"

Gabriel was met by the sight of an extremely frazzled butler. His pale skin was coated with a sheen of sweat, and his left eye bore a twitch that Gabriel had a feeling was caused by the event at large.

"May I help you?" Gabriel asked with a strained smile.

The man spluttered. "Help me? What about the help you're supposed to be giving? What do you think you're doing wandering around out here? You're supposed to be on the floor."

"On the floor…?"

It was then that he noticed among the guests there were many figures carrying silver trays, each clad in a crisp black suit eerily identical to the one he wore.

Gabriel laughed, understanding. "I'm afraid you're mistaken—"

The man unceremoniously shoved a tray full of glasses into his hands. "I don't want to hear your excuses, just get back out there. We're in over our heads with all the extra guests."

"No, really," Gabriel insisted, irritation creeping over him as he was shepherded toward a group of waitstaff. "There's been a huge misunderstanding—"

But before he could so much as blink the man had rushed onto the next servant to chastise. Gabriel shifted uncomfortably with the new weight in his arms, considering his options as he looked at the other servants surrounding him.

"Oi! You, waiter boy."

He looked up to see a pair of well-dressed women. The first who had called him now snapped her fingers briskly. Her skin was a warm brown and her dark hair swept down her back in an intricate braid. Beside her was the woman with the owl whose cape he'd just stepped on. Her eyes settled on him with distaste.

He contemplated that he could pretend he hadn't heard them over the din of the crowd and make a hasty retreat to continue with his mission, but the woman called out again.

"Hurry up! We're waiting."

Gabriel had no issues with causing a fuss, on the contrary it was one of his most favourite things to do. But if he did so now and people realised he was a rogue Incarnate masquerading as a waiter? No, better to serve the drinks for the time being. He'd find a way to recover his dignity later.

Begrudgingly he approached with a tray in hand. "Yes?" he grunted.

"My," the woman chided. "How rude the waitstaff have gotten." She examined him with a critical eye. "What's your name?"

"Hugo."

"Lovely to meet you, Hugo. You may address me as Sena, that is Tari and Thaddaeus."

"He doesn't like you," Tari said.

"I'm delighted to return the sentiment," Gabriel said, eyeing the owl with distaste. Thaddeus continued to glare, his feathers ruffled with agitation at Gabriel's presence.

Sena looped her arm through Tari's. "I'm told you were the one who ruined my lovely Tari's dress."

He gave Tari a nod in acknowledgement. "I've already apologised."

"Apologise again." Sena smiled sharply. "Louder."

"Do a bow as well," Tari added. "Something with a bit of flourish."

"I'm not—"

Thaddaeus gave a screech that drew the attention of more than one patron.

Gabriel seethed, clenching his jaw so tightly a pain began to blossom in his skull. Having to sneak into a party he would have been escorted to with honours only a few weeks ago was one thing.

Being mistaken for a kitchen boy and ordered to dance around for someone's amusement under threat of being attacked by an angry owl was quite another.

"I'm not doing that," he said.

"Oh?" Tari raised her brows. "Why not?"

Because I'm a fucking prince, he thought bitterly.

"Such displays are beneath me," he explained.

"Beneath you? You hear that, love? This one's feeling high and mighty." Sena shrugged. "Perhaps he'll remember his manners once he's spent the rest of the party outside."

Gabriel was about to argue but at the chime of the conservatory clock tower, thought better of it. He was on a time limit. If he was kicked out it would be even harder to complete his job. The sooner he gave them what they wanted, the sooner he could leave. Ego be damned.

Face burning with indignation, he obliged and bowed low, speaking in an overly sweet voice. "Please accept my humblest apologies for the ruination of your beautiful cape, which surely cost a dozen swans their lives."

He waited, wondering if perhaps he'd pushed it too far and they were about to demand his immediate removal when he heard giggling.

He looked up, irritated at the amused smiles on their faces as they leaned together and whispered, "He really does have strange eyes. Here I thought she was lying."

Instinctively, he held a hand to his mask, but it was still in place.

"Oh, don't worry," Sena reassured him. "You can't see unless you know what you're looking for."

Tari snorted. "As if she'd have any idea of what constitutes normal eyes. I swear the green one can see through the back of her head."

Understanding swept through him. "Vard sent you—"

Tari shushed him, glaring. "Voice down. Technically we shouldn't even be speaking to you."

"Just thought we'd check in and see how you're getting along," Sena added. She shoved her glass under his nose.

He frowned. "You know I'm not actually a waiter."

She smiled. "It's for the act."

He poured her a fresh glass while she spoke. "We noticed you were heading for the staircase, but if you're planning to sneak through a door all by yourself, I'd advise against it. There are locks and you need the proper combination or it will trigger a set of alarms."

He stopped pouring. "When was someone going to tell me this?"

"One of us would have gotten to you eventually." Sena looked thoughtful. "Probably."

Perfect. Now his only other entry was barred as well. Ada's words echoed in his mind.

Might wish you hadn't taken this job.

But he needed it. Needed the resources Ada could offer him so he could take back what was rightfully his. She was testing him and he'd prove himself. He'd search through this entire damned conservatory if he had to find another way to the safe.

The echoing chime of the conservatory clock sounded out and Gabriel looked up.

Twenty minutes.

"So if there's a combination," Gabriel insisted. "I just need to find someone who has it."

Sena nodded into the crowd and Gabriel froze as he saw the familiar figures of Heathland's councillors taking part in the festivities. Royle's booming laughter carried across the chamber.

"If you've been watching them then why haven't you gotten the combination already?" Gabriel asked.

"The combination changes throughout the day. By the time I told you it would be useless," Sena explained. "Besides, that's your job, isn't it?"

"But what will I—"

"What you'll do is your own problem. We have our own work to worry about."

"Other than standing around and looking pretty?" Gabriel asked.

"Jealous?" Tari asked.

"Obviously."

"I gather information," Sena said. "And she's in charge of—"

"Sabotage," Tari finished.

Gabriel gave Tari's delicate feathered dress another look, having difficulty imagining her sabotaging anything, and she winked in response, stroking Thaddeus' feathered head. "Can't predict what you don't see coming."

Sena rested her head upon Tari's shoulder, looking up at him with a grin. "Best be on your way, little Moon. We have business tonight as much as you do."

Gabriel thanked them and excused himself, unable to help himself as he cast a quick look over his shoulder. But neither Sena's nor Tari's eyes were on him; they'd already engaged in conversation with another woman, speaking intently among themselves.

Was she another person to trick? Or a member of the Hound's Teeth come to report? He didn't have the slightest idea. He cast a look around the sprawling chamber, from the people in fine silks to the waitstaff who rushed about the floor, wondering who among them shared the inky symbol of a hound's tooth.

He made his way through the crowd, dodging the requests of various guests as he marched toward the trio of councillors. His eyes flitted over Norbert and Theodora for a moment before settling on Royle.

He looked happier than he had when Gabriel had last seen him in Verchiél only a few months ago. Clothes pressed and hair combed meticulously. Speaking enthusiastically with the people around him.

Gabriel didn't know just how much information Royle had, but besides Carrington, he'd been in the council's employ the longest. Familiarity would be the best choice for garnering information.

Gabriel followed from a distance and as soon as Norbert and Theodora left, he approached Royle, holding the silver tray aloft.

"A drink, sir?"

Royle didn't spare him a passing glance, only waving a hand in dismissal as he continued to speak with various guests.

"Are you quite sure, sir? They're particularly fine this evening."

"No thank you," Royle dismissed him, a flicker of irritation in his voice.

The chime of the conservatory clock sounded out and Gabriel checked the time from the corner of his eye.

Fifteen minutes.

There was nothing for it.

Gabriel bowed low. "Of course, sir."

He moved to walk away but tripped at the last moment, knocking himself into Royle and spilling the drinks onto his suit. Glass shattered and the silver tray crashed upon the floor, and guests shouted and hastily backed away from the sudden mess.

Gabriel caught Royle's arm and helped heave himself back to his feet, holding a hand at his back to keep him steady. "I'm terribly sorry, sir. Are you all right?"

Royle's face flushed scarlet, his voice livid. "You clumsy little—" As soon Royle caught sight of him, his eyes widened. "You…"

Gabriel pressed a hidden knife to Royle's back, speaking sweetly. "Would you take a walk with me, sir? You should clean up before your suit stains, after all"—he jabbed the knife closer—"you won't get the chance once it's set," Gabriel finished with a smile.

Royle stared him down, but Gabriel knew full well he would stall only long enough to spare some fragment of his pride.

"Please excuse me, everyone," Royle addressed the group. "I need to…" He eyed Gabriel up and down with distaste. "Tidy up."

Some mutters were exchanged but the group went back to conversations among themselves, eyes passing over Gabriel with disinterest.

Gabriel guided Royle forward, keeping a hand to his back as he forced him along at a steady pace.

"How are you here?" Royle hissed. "I thought you'd died in Verchiél. You wouldn't believe how relieved I was. I drank my oldest bottle of wine in celebration."

"Delighted to know I continue to disappoint." Gabriel slowed as they reached the base of the staircase and gestured to Royle. "After you."

Royle paused at the sight of the stairs. "Where are you taking me?"

"A detour." He followed behind Royle. "I heard you know a combination."

As the heavy oaken doors of Carrington's office opened with a series of metallic clicks from the lock, Gabriel shoved Royle inside before quickly closing and re-locking the doors behind them.

Royle hadn't stopped speaking the entire time. "You can't just come back here and threaten me again. I'll have you arrested and charged for—"

"Oh, would you shut up!" Gabriel snapped. "I'm not here for you."

Royle paused mid-sentence, his eyes narrowing in suspicion. "Then why are you here?"

Gabriel nodded toward the large safe in the corner of the office. "Do you know what that is?"

Royle bristled at the question. "It's a bloody safe."

"Yes, and there's something very important inside, which I need you to retrieve for me. You have precisely"—he checked his time piece with a frown—"ten minutes?"

He shook the time-piece, tapping the glass face, but the hands ticked steadily on. He was shorter on time than he'd thought.

"But this is Carrington's office," Royle protested. "We're given the combinations for the doors, but I don't know anything about the other's safes."

"Then you'd better hope the guards get to us before I get to you." He shoved Royle toward the safe. "Get to work."

Royle looked back to him in disbelief. "But I—"

"I said," Gabriel repeated, drawing the pistol from his jacket and seating himself comfortably upon the desk, "to work."

Zoe gasped aloud when she saw the conservatory. It was a massive structure of steel and glass, towering far above the surrounding buildings like a bejewelled monarch clad in finery.

The estate paths were packed and she could barely move two steps without being jostled by another person. The excitement was infectious and she smiled alongside Alessi.

Looking around at the lavish and even eccentric fashion, Zoe was grateful that Alessi had taken the time to help them blend in by lending her one of their best suits. Zoe wore a rich burgundy, the fabric having a slight sheen to it that caught the light. Alessi was in a suit of deep green.

They approached the security checkpoint where groups of Heathland's Grey Guard inspected the authenticity of each guest's invitation. Zoe noticed a large group of people arguing with a pair of guards, none of which showed the slightest bit of sympathy at the group's absence of an invitation.

"All right," Alessi said, "let's try to enjoy ourselves, shall we?"

"We're not here for the party," Zoe reminded, eyeing the guards warily and tightening the ribbons of the mask Alessi had lent her.

"Right," Alessi said. "Zoe, come along with me—"

As they approached the entrance, an impatient guard thrust a hand out automatically. "Invitation."

"Yes, here you are," Alessi said, proudly hanging over the creamy paper, which the guard scrutinised with a passing glance before waving them along.

"Right this way."

Alessi grinned and nodded to her. "Come along, Zoe."

Zoe moved to walk inside but the guard held out his hand again, looking at her expectantly. "Invitation."

"I—I don't have one." The answer was out of her mouth before she could help herself.

The guard gave a heavy sigh. "No admittance without invitation. Come back with one or leave."

The guard motioned to the guests behind her to move forward but Alessi cut across, speaking politely. "Actually, she's with me."

The guard gave another deep sigh. Clearly this wasn't the first time this had happened tonight. "One invitation permits one guest. No plus ones. Those are the rules."

"Look, my good man," Alessi said, reaching into their jacket for their coin purse. "I realise it's a busy night for you. Why don't I give you something more sustainable for your troubles?"

The man only laughed. "Nice try." He pointed to the rioting crowd in the streets. "But if it didn't work for them it's not going to work for you."

Anxiety churned in Zoe's gut, but Alessi seemed unbothered by this. "Very well, then let her inside, she can have my invitation."

The man frowned once more, his growing displeasure palatable. "One invitation per person. No exchanges. Those are the rules."

"That's ridiculous, there's no reason why she can't—" Alessi protested, no doubt ready to haggle until this man gave in, but the crowd behind them began to grow irritable.

"You heard him, get in or leave!"

More guests tried to shove her out of the way, but Zoe didn't budge, feeling a resolve solidify in her as she addressed the guard. "I'm an invited guest of this gala, I've just misplaced my invitation."

The guard eyed her up and down. "Is that so?" He gave a wave over his shoulder and two more guards approached. "Please escort her out. She seems to think the rules don't apply to her—"

"Actually," a cool voice cut through the tension, a lithe arm sliding across Zoe's shoulders. "She's with me."

Zoe froze, frustration turning to horror as she was greeted by the sight of Ada Vard's two-toned eyes.

Ada smiled with amusement, before addressing the guards. "You haven't been giving my guest a bad time, have you?"

At the sight of Ada, the other guests fell silent and all of the guards straightened to attention so quickly it was nearly comical.

"Miss Vard!" the man said. "Apologies. I wasn't aware you had a guest tonight."

"We were separated in the crowd." Ada gave Zoe's shoulders a squeeze. "Isn't that right?"

No, we certainly weren't, Zoe wanted to say, but swallowed the words at a shake of Alessi's head. She was so close; the council was right inside— unwanted company or not— she wasn't going to back out now.

"Yes." Zoe forced herself to grit the word out. She met the guard's eyes with a cold stare. "We were."

Between the gaze of both women the guard deflated. He spared Ada's outstretched invitation the briefest of glances before stepping out of their way, giving a deep bow and many wishes to "enjoy the festivities" with the motion.

Zoe bit back a nervous smile, the small victory dampened by the arm that was still wrapped snugly around her shoulders. Typical. The one person she wanted nothing to do with, and she was literally trapped under her grasp.

Alessi walked on the other side of Ada, clearly wishing to smooth things over. "Thank you for stepping in, Ada, but we don't want to trouble you—"

"It's no trouble whatsoever," Ada replied coolly, making no move to retract her arm from Zoe's shoulder.

Alessi cleared their throat; any trace of confidence they'd shown the guard vanished in the presence of Ada. "I'm sure you have a busy night ahead of you, we'll let you get going."

"Actually…" Ada slowed her steps. "I was going to give your dear friend here a private tour of the conservatory."

"Oh, I wouldn't want to impose!" Zoe quickly said, only earning an all-too-knowing smile from Ada. "I wouldn't have suggested it if it was an imposition."

Zoe looked at Alessi imploringly, but they all knew who wielded the power, not only in this situation, but this city. Alessi couldn't do anything.

Alessi nodded. "Do be sure not to keep her all to yourself this evening,"

"Don't worry, Alessi." Ada turned away with Zoe. "You won't even know we've been gone."

Zoe looked over her shoulder, watching Alessi stare back at her with a helpless look. As they walked further into the conservatory, it became increasingly clear that everyone knew who Ada was. People parted around them in a mixture of hushed whispers or too bright smiles.

Many stopped to speak with Ada, shaking her hand and thanking her profusely. After what must have been the dozenth guest walked away with awe in their eyes, did Zoe finally ask, "Why do they keep thanking you?"

Ada gestured to the conservatory around them. "I've funded a few public projects here and there."

Surprise entered Zoe's voice. "You built the conservatory?"

"Not entirely…"

Zoe snuck a glance at Ada. She was all severe angles. A sweep of hair that rested along a sharp jaw and a nose that looked as if it had been broken and reset multiple times. Even through her suit Zoe could feel the sinewy muscles in her arm.

As influential as this woman was, she hadn't made it here from a circumstance of birth. She'd pulled herself up to the highest echelons of wealth and society because she was clever, and such people never did anything without reason.

"Why did you help me?" Zoe asked.

"I simply saw a woman in need, so I offered my assistance."

"Why give if you're not getting?"

Ada laughed, a sound that had a roughened edge to it. "Do you think I'm so heartless?"

"I think that everyone wants something," Zoe said, watching Ada closely. "But you haven't told me what you want from me."

"Many things, Daughter of the Sun."

A chill swept through Zoe at the use of her old title. Ada

only shrugged, her arm finally falling away from her shoulders. "In exchange for your admittance, I would only ask for the smallest of repayments. A jaunty little stroll around the conservatory with yours truly. Costing nothing more than a few minutes of your time."

Zoe paused. At her silence, Ada continued. "Do keep in mind you're more than welcome to refuse. But that means you'd need to leave the party. A deal isn't fair unless both parties are benefiting from the exchange, wouldn't you agree?"

Zoe didn't miss the words she was deliberately choosing. *Deal. Exchange.* Evoking a sense of nothing more than a fair bargain. No doubt Ada already knew about her merchant upbringing.

"You know who I am." Zoe lowered her voice to a whisper. "So convince me that you're not going to have someone drag me away the first chance you get."

Ada's smile softened. "Lovely, if I wanted to trick you I would have done so when you were hiding in Alessi's wardrobe."

Zoe's cheeks flushed but Ada only checked her time-piece impatiently. "You need to make your choice within the next minute though. It's a very busy night for me."

Zoe bit her lip, thinking hard. But wasn't all this a deal? They weren't doing anything illegal. Ada had an invitation and as such she was rightfully a guest. For as much as she wanted to put as much distance between herself and Ada, a few minutes of begrudging company for a chance to solve things with the council was more than a fair exchange.

Zoe met Ada's gaze. "Five minutes."

"Ten."

"Seven."

The corner of Ada's lip twitched. "Never a more astute

business woman if I've ever met one. Seven it is."

They stopped before a looming doorway. Matching sets of wooden carvings of various creatures stood guard on either side. Zoe read the large engraved plaque above the entrance:

'The Vard Hall of Natural History

"My mark is literally engraved in this place," Ada explained. "As much as the council might loathe it, every time any walk by here they remember it's because of me. I want the people of this city to know what I can give them— what I can continue to give them."

"That's...brilliant," Zoe admitted, unable to keep the genuine impressed note out of her voice.

"Glad you agree since we've been the first invited to tour the hall."

Zoe hesitated at the sight of the looming doors. Ada had shown no ill intent toward her— so far. But when the prospect of a walk had been presented, she had thought it would have been in the crowded chambers well within eyesight of countless people. She certainly didn't want to be left entirely alone with Ada Vard of all people.

Zoe searched the hall for Alessi, but caught no sight of them in the massive crowd.

"Don't worry." Ada winked. "I promise I won't bite unless you want me to."

"Seven minutes," Zoe repeated.

Ada set her time-piece. "And not a single one more."

19

GABRIEL

"Are you finished yet? I'm bored."

Gabriel held the timepiece in one hand, balancing it on his knee as he watched the moments pass by. "Tick-tock," Gabriel called out. "Nine minutes."

"Just wait, you little bastard!" Royle spat as he spun the tumblers with all the deft precision of someone awaiting a bomb to explode.

"If that's the worst insult you can think of, you're not trying hard enough." A part of him wondered whether Royle truly didn't know how to open the safe or if he was stalling long enough for someone to catch them. Either way, he didn't want to consider what would happen if he returned to Ada empty-handed. "If you don't finish within the next thirty seconds, I'm going to shoot you regardless—"

Suddenly the safe let out a series of methodical clicks as the locks spun into place. The heavy door swung open with a creak.

Royle took a deep breath of relief, dabbing sweat from his brow as he stepped back, gesturing freely to the safe.

Gabriel didn't move. "Open it."

"I already did."

"All the way. My face is much too gorgeous to waste if there are any additional surprises inside."

"Don't you have magic for things like that?"

"Yes, but I can't be bothered to spare the effort. Now move."

Royle heaved the heavy safe door entirely open, offering a mock bow in the process. "You'll hang for this, mark my words."

"Delighted to know our animosity remains mutual." Gabriel eyed the sheer volume of documents and canisters with some trepidation. Many were of the exact same make as the one he held in his hand.

"Help me look, would you?"

"I'll do no such thing," Royle said. "I've already risked my position tonight in countless ways."

Gabriel snapped his fingers and an illusion appeared. Royle eyed it warily before approaching the stacks of documents. "What am I looking for?"

"This." Gabriel pulled out the one Ada had given him from his jacket pocket.

Royle paused at the sight of the canister, his hands falling away from the safe. "Where did you get that?"

"So you know what it is?" Gabriel asked, genuinely curious. Ada might have forbidden him from opening the canister, but she'd never said he couldn't ask questions.

"Yes." Royle reached for it, but Gabriel held it out of his grasp. "I was the one who signed off on the orders myself."

"What's so important that you'd sign it?"

Royle paused, looking at Gabriel with renewed interest. "You don't know, do you?"

"Of course I know," Gabriel replied coolly. "Why else would I have them if I didn't?"

"Tell me, Mr. Capello. Why did you return to Heathland?"

"I was tired of breathing fresh air."

"Since you have an answer for everything, would you mind telling me what currently resides within the canister you hold in your hands?"

"Documents." Gabriel clutched the canister tightly. "Important ones."

Royle tapped his fingers thoughtfully against the safe. "She tricked you, didn't she?"

"Who?"

"Don't play stupid, boy. Ada Vard has half the people in this city working for her, while the other half want her dead, sometimes both at once. I'm simply interested in why she chose you for this."

"How do you know she sent me?"

"Because you like playing games. Gathering a few little secrets here and there. Pretending you have a single clue of what you're doing when you're nothing more than a spoiled princeling—"

"Smugness doesn't suit you, Royle."

"—but Vard would know that too. She doesn't choose special people, she chooses disposable ones."

Gabriel observed Royle closely. "You're awfully well informed. And just how would you, a councillor, know so much about a conlord?"

"This is Grislow. Vard is a household name."

"Those are the words of a man who knows something on a personal scale."

Royle pressed his thin lips into a severe line, falling silent.

"Not feeling particularly chatty anymore? Fine—" Gabriel turned back to the safe. "We have our own matters to attend to—"

"I'm not going to help you." Royle shook his head, backing away. "Not if it's for her."

Gabriel curled his fists, nails biting painfully into his palms as he reined in his frustrated impulse to do something violent. He was so close to getting what he needed. There was no way he was going to return to Ada with the wrong documents. He was going to do exactly what she'd told him to do.

"I suppose you're right," Gabriel said. "After all, how is it fair for you to get less than what you deserve? Would you prefer a bullet or a blade?"

Royle's face went from confusion to panic as Gabriel snapped his fingers and the illusion seized Royle from behind, pressing the knife to his throat.

"What do you think you're doing?!" Royle hissed, struggling against the grip of the illusion.

"You see…" Gabriel raised the pistol. "Shooting you would be quicker, but it's going to make such a dreadfully loud noise."

"You're not going to kill me. You need me."

"Do I? Because it occurs to me that you think I'm desperate. As such you're under the impression that you're going to be able to bully me into whatever terms you desire. I'll make things simpler—"

He curled his fingers into a fist, watching as the illusion tightened its grip on Royle, a frightening strength only magic could achieve, feeling muscle and bone threaten to snap and tear under its grasp.

"I've never been a squeamish person. I have no issues with—" Gabriel shot his hand forward and the illusion twisted Royle's arm until it threatened to break. Royle gave a short cry of pain. "Force," Gabriel finished.

"You're of Verchiél— adopted into a royal house," Royle said, his voice pained. "When people hear about this—"

"Bold of you to assume anyone will hear at all. But you said it yourself, I'm not anyone special right now. I'm just an old shadow of this city. Vard didn't choose me because I'm delusional—" He leaned into his space. "She chose me because I don't give a fuck how things get done, so long as I get what I need."

"You'll run out of time," Royle spat.

Gabriel held his gaze steady. "I have all night. The only person I'd worry about is Vard. What will she do when she finds out you've been hindering one of her operations?"

Royle's face paled.

"If you've worked with her before— and don't give me that look, Royle I know you have—she must know you so well at this point. After all, she was the one who told me all about your little secrets in the first place."

Royle's eyes blazed with anger, fear momentarily forgotten as he struggled against the illusion's grasp.

"Just think," Gabriel continued, "how much easier will it be for Vard to pluck apart the flimsy threads holding your life together. That would be far crueller than anything I could do to you tonight."

He was pulling lies from thin air by this point. But that didn't matter, it evoked exactly the response from Royle that he wanted.

"She wouldn't do that…"

"I wouldn't put it past her," Gabriel said. "We both know there's someone much cleverer than you or I making sure I succeed in this plan. If she's gotten me this far, then what's going to stop her from covering up the tragic details of your pathetic demise?"

More likely Ada would drop him at the first sign of trouble. But Royle didn't know that. Let him play up his own importance.

"So." Gabriel took the pistol away. "How are we going to do this?"

Royle let out a long breath, looking to the safe before he finally nodded. "I'll do it."

Gabriel snapped his fingers and the illusion released Royle, standing back in the corner of the room to await an order.

Royle stretched his arm stiffly before he reached inside the safe and picked up one of the canisters, offering it to Gabriel.

Gabriel held out Ada's canister and swapped it with the one from Royle's hand, tucking it safely away in his jacket pocket. He'd have more than enough time to make it to the rooftop.

"A pleasure, Royle. Rest assured you'll be seeing much more of me once I return to Verchiél—"

"She hired us once too, you know."

Gabriel paused. "Who's us?"

Royle fidgeted uncomfortably before speaking. "The council. She contacted three of us—months ago. Telling us to withhold correspondences from Councillor Carrington, while also substituting missives of her own."

Gabriel frowned, mind whirling. "What does Vard have to gain from relations in Verchiél? Her concern is Heathland."

"The information wasn't for her. It was for a client."

"What client?"

"I don't know."

"Think harder. A name."

"She never gave her name."

"Fine," Gabriel said impatiently. "Appearance. Hair, eyes, anything."

"I never saw her face. Vard dealt with her directly. I just overheard them speaking."

"And what were they speaking about?"

"I don't know—"

Gabriel's temper snapped and Royle backed away as freezing shadows flared from him. "What do you know other than the extent of your own ignorance!"

"You didn't let me finish." Royle glared, still edging away from him. "I didn't know what they were saying because they only spoke to each other in Bjordal."

Something flickered in the back of his mind, a feeling, a suspicion— no, the realisation that he was forgetting something important. Something he was close to grasping before it was immediately snuffed out again. Replaced only by a heavy calm.

Safe, it said. *You're safe.*

Gabriel shook his head, feeling a headache come on. "That makes no sense. What would a Bjordal woman want with messages between Heathland and Verchiél?"

"Couldn't say. I was just the messenger. But if I had to guess, I'd say the fact that a Bjordal client collecting Verchiél political information only months before a Bjordal prince suddenly usurped Verchiél doesn't sound coincidental."

"The usurper said that Councillor Carrington backed his claim. Not Vard."

"Either he was lying or Carrington kept that from his subjects. Until the night of the solstice we were all unaware King Asbjorn's son still lived."

"You think Vard helped stage the coup?"

"No. I think someone made a deal she couldn't refuse. She's ambitious, but she also has no interest outside of Grislow."

So someone had been tampering with Verchiél politics long before he or Zoe had been aware. All the while Vard had been aiding her. He'd give Vard an earful once he saw her. Conlord or not, something of this scale couldn't go unresolved.

So lost in his thoughts was Gabriel that he didn't notice Royle had continued incessantly blathering.

"—which is exactly why I'll warn you to reconsider your association to Vard. Nothing good will come of it."

"You're afraid," Gabriel observed, "of what will happen if I work with her. Especially now that I know what you've been up to. You do realise that treason is a punishable offence?"

Royle lunged and brandished a small marble bust from atop the desk.

Gabriel raised a brow, unimpressed. "You aren't going to try to kill me with that, are you? The least you could do is get a little more creative. Perhaps a decorative paperweight or a comically small pocket knife?"

Royle shook his head. "Vard picked the wrong person for this job."

Gabriel smiled, amused. "Is that so?"

Royle nodded. "You're a cunning bastard, but you're not very bright."

Gabriel prepared for him to hurl the statue at him. Instead Royle threw the marble bust at the window. Glass shattered and an alarm sounded.

It was a high-pitched, screeching noise that made him cover his ears, so loud it reverberated in his bones. In the instant that Gabriel was distracted, Royle lunged forward, landing a heavy punch to the side of Gabriel's face.

Gabriel gasped and fell to the floor, struggling to focus as lights danced behind his eyes. A heavy weight dropped atop Gabriel as Royle pinned him to the floor so he couldn't cast any magic.

"He's here!" Royle screamed. "Gabriel Capello!"

"Shut up!" Gabriel hissed, desperately trying to free himself.

"Security!" Royle bellowed, his voice nearly louder than the alarm.

Gabriel struggled against his grasp but to no avail. Royle might have been shorter than Gabriel, but he was much broader and heavier and easily kept him pinned to the spot.

Over Royle's shoulder Gabriel saw that the illusion was still standing there, in the corner of the room. Just waiting for Gabriel to give it an order.

He'd barely been able to cast any magic without movement—rarely any Incarnate could. It was a connection that was developed with years of practice, the movements unique to each person. But Gabriel had found that a connection with an illusion was far easier to maintain since they already shared a bond.

Don't just stand there, he thought, willing it into motion. *Help me!*

Clumsily, the illusion stumbled toward them, standing over Royle's shoulder.

"Perhaps I'll break something of yours before they get here." Royle pressed his knee into his chest and he felt bones threaten to crack.

Help me! Gabriel screamed within his mind. *Do something— anything.*

The illusion stared at him blankly.

Darkness bled into the edges of Gabriel's vision, and as he met the illusion's eyes, he spoke in a hoarse voice. "Break him."

The command was enough. With a frightening strength, the illusion wrenched Royle backward, hands seizing either side of his head before snapping his neck in a single, clean motion.

A chill swept through Gabriel, feeling the ghost of broken bones beneath his own fingers. He watched Royle's body collapse to the floor, finally silent. In the aftermath, Gabriel took a moment to reconcile with what he'd just done.

He didn't feel anything for Royle, damn the useless fucker, but rather it was the sudden resurgence of death by his own hands that troubled him.

Death was no stranger to Gabriel; they were old companions. They'd met when he had been far younger than he ever should have been to commit such acts. But Grislow had demanded it of him in exchange for his own survival, so common were acts of violence that they became expected. It was something which he thought he'd long since left behind when he'd gone to Verchiél to take up a noble life—a better life.

Gabriel clenched his hands into tight fists, trying to will away the feel of bones breaking and looked up at the illusion. "Thanks."

The illusion stared blankly at him, awaiting another order.

Gabriel sighed. "I'm just talking to myself, aren't I?" He snapped his fingers and it vanished back into the shadows.

That was foolish—no, irredeemably idiotic. Ada had told him not to leave a trace of himself and not only had he set off an alarm—he looked down to Royle's fallen form—he'd left evidence.

He should have picked nervous Theodora or timid Norbert. Neither of which would have fought back when threatened. Instead he'd chosen the one person who'd made the most noise. Royle's last act—Gabriel's ears pricked at the sound of footsteps sprinting down the hall, raised voices shouting orders—was making sure he was caught.

Gabriel braced himself as the heavy oaken doors burst open and grey uniformed guards poured inside, their faces turning from expressions of shock and confusion to horror as they saw Royle on the floor, piecing together what had happened.

Pistols were raised toward him, swords drawn, but before any could attack, Gabriel pulled his mask from his face, making sure they saw his eyes.

Exactly as he'd hoped, everyone froze. A few even backed away in fear. Gabriel kept his hands raised in a gesture of surrender and spoke in the calmest voice he could manage. "I'd like to speak to the council."

At the prospect of Grislow's natural history, Zoe had expected displays of taxidermy animals and paintings depicting how they appeared in reality. Stiff. Dusty. Boring.

Instead she felt as if she'd stepped into another world.

The hall was a massive, less man-made structure than a forest that had inexplicably sprouted in their midst. An intricate iron-fenced path cut directly through its middle, providing a fragile barrier from the animals that roamed freely through the environment.

Birds squawked and monkeys chattered as they leapt from branch to branch. Alligators lounged lazily in the fountain waters, barely visible among the green and grey foliage. Snakes coiled around tree branches or warmed themselves upon the heated rocks. Butterflies of every conceivable pattern and colour flew in and out of the fresh flowers.

Ada strolled forward at a leisurely pace, observing everything with a critical eye, every so often nodding approvingly to herself or shaking her head in distaste.

"Do you like this?" Zoe edged away from a large bobcat that watched them with interest from a nearby rock. "Nature?"

"I like the idea of it. The natural world is so straightforward. If a wolf is hungry it hunts and kills without a second

thought. What is needed is taken. A world existing in exact decisions."

They stopped in front of a small waterfall , the spray from
the water creating a mist that collected upon her skin.

Ada faced her. "But nothing in life is so simple. Specifically why I've gone through the trouble of dragging us out here to
have a private chat."

"Should I feel honoured?"

"The honour is only mine, dear Sun." Ada rested her hand
atop Zoe's. "We're a lot alike. You and I."

Zoe pulled her hand away. "I fail to see that."

Ada noticed the shift in Zoe's voice and took a step back.
"We're both women with an interest in business."

"I'm interested in honest work," Zoe countered, her tone
sharper than she'd anticipated. All the years she'd spent with her
father, the work they'd put into making sure their clients were
never charged a single cent more than they'd arranged, she'd taken
pride in it all. But in the end, they had wound up with less than
nothing while people like Ada flourished. The wrongness of it left
a bitter taste in her mouth.

Ada smiled. "Those of us who haven't been blessed by the
heavens rarely have the privilege of not getting our hands dirty.
But I'm no monster in disguise. I understand your animosity toward me comes from the fact that you don't fully understand what
I do."

"I already know you deal in secrets. Hardly business so
much as gossip mongering and blackmail."

Ada leaned back, her face thoughtful. "Did you see the
people here tonight? All the nobles and royalty, the business giants
and the wealthy and influential."

"What about them?"

"I deal in a great many things, including truth. It's information— valuable at that. Why shouldn't I use it?"

"And just what sort of truths have you gathered?"

Ada's easy smile faded, and her mismatched eyes hardened. "I know the business they conduct in back rooms and the family secrets that are hushed for generations. I know who they like to crawl into bed with, along with their deepest desires and most ridiculous fantasies but more importantly—" She leaned forward. "Is it so wrong? To discover truths that have been concealed by lies?"

"Maybe not," Zoe found herself agreeing. "But isn't it wrong to use those same truths as leverage against them?"

"It's human nature to seek advantage. You came here tonight with an old friend and perhaps made a new one as well."

"Just because I'm listening doesn't make us friends."

"Business partners?" Ada's lip twitched. "You wish to make a deal with the council, but what would you say if I could offer you one instead? In addition to an alliance, you also have some qualms with the fact that I bought your old family business from Alessi."

"How do you know—"

Ada gestured to the chamber around them.

"Right…" Zoe said quietly. "Walls have ears."

"Walls? No. Many talented individuals at my disposal? Yes."

Zoe paused, momentarily at a loss. She had envisioned this meeting going many different ways, but certainly not in the path of an alliance.

Ada spoke in her silence. "You think I'm lying?"

"No. I think you're being honest. It's what you want that concerns me."

"You think I'm going to ask for something outlandish?"

"Undoubtedly. But explain why I should ally with you instead of the council?"

"Because they don't understand how precariously a life without second chances needs to be lived."

She paused, her father's words echoing back to her. *The things you truly wanted in life never came for free.* They especially wouldn't from a person like Ada.

"What's the deal?" Zoe asked.

Ada's smile faltered. "There was an incident—years ago now—where I found myself alone and so very close to dying. The work I do can provide endless opportunities. But with those opportunities often comes risks. Sadly I can't control the outcome of every imaginable situation. But, I do like to mitigate loss. I choose everything in life based upon what will allow myself and those around me the longest, most lucrative existences possible."

"What does any of this have to do with me?"

"You see, dear Sun, I've been told that the magic of Incarnate Suns—particularly your set of gifts—extends well into the skills of healing." Her eyes widened. "Imagine, to heal even the most fatal of wounds"—she snapped her fingers—"like that! I've never been one for reverence, but I can see why the people of Verchiél would hold you in such high esteem."

"I can't make you immortal, if that's what you were hoping."

Much to Zoe's surprise Ada threw her head back in unrestrained laughter.

Ada grinned. "If you could, I would have contacted you a long time ago."

"So you want me to join the Hound's Teeth?"

"Of course not," Ada said. "I don't have a recruitment agenda. Rather, if you agree, consider the release of your friend from obligations to me an incentive. The true deal is that you'll work with me, with my people— and no one else. I don't need any of my competition coming to you after they've been injured. You'd be in the employ of the Hound's Teeth alone."

"I'd have to heal people everyday?"

"Bruises and cuts can heal on their own. You would only be summoned in the most dire of circumstances, when not even the most skilled physicians could offer help. The remainder of the time you'd be free to do whatever you please, however you please."

Zoe met Ada's gaze, suddenly feeling bold. "How do I know someone else won't give me a better deal? There are plenty of gangs in Grislow."

Ada smirked, clearly pleased. "I doubt they could manage such a feat. But to ease your mind…" Ada pulled out an envelope from her jacket, offering it to Zoe. "How does this sound?"

Tentatively, Zoe opened the envelope, her heart pounding as she slid the paper out and stared at the amount of money written upon it.

Her hands trembled. "This is…"

"Alessi's official release of debt from their business," Ada said. "Plus some to show we're serious about welcoming you."

Zoe traced her fingers along the numbers written in Ada's scrawling hand.

Ada continued speaking. "You'd have nothing less than the finest of living arrangements of your choosing. Along with an account in your name in which you'd receive a more than handsome sum of money for your continued presence."

All ideas of the council began to fade entirely from her

mind. Wasn't this exactly what she'd come here for? To find aid? Ada's offer would be more than enough to cover the costs for Alessi; she could buy back the business for herself.

Zoe looked up at Ada with a smile, finding it was returned in kind.

"I don't know what to say," Zoe admitted.

"A simple yes would suffice. But feel free to get creative."

Something cold settled in Zoe, her excitement vanishing just as quickly as it came. "But if I took this deal, I'd need to stay here. In Grislow."

"Naturally," Ada replied. "Heaven forbid if I'm ever stabbed or shot to pieces. I'd expect you to arrive within moments, not weeks or months later."

"But…" Zoe looked down at the cheque in her hands. "I had plans," Zoe found herself admitting, though she had a feeling Ada already knew.

She fell quiet, gripping the envelope tightly in her fingers.

"You can still have a hand in the business," Ada assured her. "You'll simply have to hire others to do the voyages for you. I'm certain we can make something truly special of it here."

Zoe didn't doubt it. Trading businesses thrived in Heathland, the most concentrated centre of commerce in the Isles. With Ada's support she was certain it would be a lucrative venture. It was a perfect deal; Alessi could move on debt free and she would live in comfort for the rest of her days.

But still she hesitated. Gabriel's bitter sentiments echoed in her mind. She didn't need validation, she could make her own decisions. But that still left her with the realisation, the decision Alessi made, to sell their debt, and more vitally their business, to Ada was an awful one to consider. But it had still been their decision. Theirs, not hers. As much as she cared for them, how was it fair to spend the rest of her life making up for that decision?

She had no interest in directing from afar, only witnessing the results as stagnant figures on paperwork. She wanted to take those voyages herself. To immerse herself and travel as broadly and often as she could possibly imagine.

"This is a generous offer." With hesitant, pained movements, she slid the paper back into the envelope, offering it to Ada. "But I don't think I'm the right person for the job."

Ada let out a quiet sigh before she took the envelope back. "I'm very sorry to hear that."

So am I, Zoe thought as she watched the envelope disappear into Ada's jacket.

Ada met her gaze. "I respect your decision, but sometimes the very best thing we can do is run toward what frightens us."

"You think I'm making the wrong choice?"

"No. But personally, I've always gone where the money is."

Suddenly a distant alarm sounded out.

"What's that?" Zoe asked.

"Probably some fool who was caught where they shouldn't have been."

Ada brushed her coat off briskly. "If you change your mind, meet me on the conservatory rooftop in…" She checked her timepiece. "Six minute's time."

"Why the roof?"

"It has a stunning view of the city, and it's easier to avoid gossiping socialites. My own people included."

Ada snapped the time piece shut and gestured for Zoe to follow, and they quickly cut their way back across the path they'd come until they reached the front door, which Ada heaved open for her.

As Zoe passed through the door, Ada whispered, "Watch yourself, little Sun."

"Thanks for the walk," Zoe managed.

Ada gave a slight inclination of her head in acknowledgement before she swept down the staircase, her eyes already focused back upon the crowd below.

As Zoe made her own way down the stairway, the noise of the party filled her ears and she couldn't help but feel uncertain whether she'd walked away with an ally or another enemy.

Navigating the chaos was a chore, the crowd sparser than outside but still packed. After the third time she'd investigated the grand foyer, she finally spotted Alessi, in jovial conversation with a group of guests as they clinked wine-glasses together.

She muttered her apologies as she cut through the crowd, making her way toward them.

Alessi looked up at the sight of her, a relieved smile spreading across their face. "Zoe, you've finally made it!" They took her aside, speaking in a more hushed tone. "Vard didn't give you any trouble, did she?"

A twinge of guilt rose in Zoe's gut as she recalled Ada's offer, but she pushed it away, managing a small smile. "No more than she gave you."

Alessi shuddered. "Poor thing, grab a drink and let's do our best not to think about it for the rest of the night."

"Actually," Zoe said, "have you found any of the councillors?"

Alessi nodded ahead to a crowded section of the conservatory. Sure enough Zoe recognized the hunched and greying form of

Councillor Carrington.

"I've kept an eye out for him, though he's been surrounded by people all night. It'll be difficult to get close without anyone else watching."

Zoe drew in a breath, stepping forward. "Then I'd better be quick."

"Wait, Zoe—" Alessi grabbed her arm, their face anxious. "Maybe you shouldn't go. I don't want you to wind up in trouble."

Zoe paused. Should she tell them about Ada's offer? She imagined the relief they'd feel knowing they didn't have to worry about being beholden to Ada anymore. But she had her own cost to pay. Could she really stay here? Spend the rest of her life stuck in one place? Would that truly be better than staying back at the palace in Verchiél?

She looked up at the conservatory clock. Six minutes, Ada had told her. She still had enough time to decide what she was going to do.

She squeezed their arm back. "I'm doing this for myself too." She looked back at Carrington. If she could convince him to help gain her throne back then she could pay off Alessi's debt to Ada and leave the palace. It was risky, but she needed to try. "I just need to know."

She followed the councillor and his party at a distance, but Alessi was right, and it was next to impossible to get close to him when he wasn't surrounded by dozens of people wanting to speak with him.

She followed at a cautious distance, only trailing close enough to keep track of him, and finally when he excused himself from the crowd, she made her move.

She slipped in the door behind him and in a moment of

branzenss, broke off a fragment of the nearest animal skeleton next to her and slid it between the door handles, blocking it shut.

"Councillor Carrington," she called out.

He paused, his shoulders tensing before he turned to her with a look of disbelief.

"Zoe Okoro?"

Zoe spoke quickly. "I have a lot to say to you and I don't have long to say it. How dare you break your promise. You not only broke trust with myself and Gabriel, but with Verchiél itself when we needed your aid the most. What do you have to say to that?"

He was silent for a long moment, his jaw gaping open and closed before he spoke."What…are you talking about?'"

She huffed, irritation coursing through her. "You allied with Niklas Osenson after our countries were supposed to make a deal of peace. I hardly see how you could have forgotten."

He shook his head, his eyes confused. "I'm sorry, but I haven't the slightest clue what you're referring to."

The area felt so quiet compared to the party raging on in the main hall. She intently studied his face, determined to pick apart any attempt to sway her from calling his bluff, but there were no lies there, only someone who was just as confused as she was.

"What do you mean?" she demanded. "We've sent messages and diplomats for months now— some of your fellow councillors were at the winter solstice. Are you telling me you haven't heard a single word from us concerning an alliance?"

Carrington nodded, face grave. "Yes, I'd thought that after the passing of Enzo and Aria, you and your counterpart wanted to cut ties." He looked thoughtful before frowning deeply. "Didn't you receive any of my correspondence? I wrote to you both quite frequently. I'll admit, I was rather upset when I didn't receive an invitation to the solstice celebrations."

Zoe's mind raced with this new information. A few missed letters wouldn't have raised any suspicion, but to go for months on end without receiving word? Even Gabriel wasn't that stubborn. If their correspondences were being tampered with from both sides then there was another person behind this, changing everything before she'd even realised it was beginning.

"So you never aided King Asbjorn's son?" Zoe asked.

"Son?" Carrington frowned. "His son is dead."

"It's…" Zoe said weakly, "a very long story."

She felt a small flicker of hope rise. "But this means we can still fix things. I'm here now, as well as Gabriel."

Carrington looked around the room, concerned, as if expecting Gabriel to leap out from a hiding spot and scare him.

"Well, not 'here' specifically," Zoe amended. "But we're in Heathland now, you can still ally with us."

Carrington shook his head. "I'm afraid I can't. I've kept a peaceful stance with Bjordal for as long as I could. But between Verchiél's silence and Heathland crying out for new leadership, and now that Bjordal is threatening to march on Verchiél, I've already made a deal with Prince Hakon, King Asbjorn's adopted heir."

"But—"

The door handle rattled behind them, followed by the sound of muffled voices arguing about how best to open it. *Shit.* Her time was up.

Carrington bristled at the sight of the blocked door. "Did you lock me in?"

She spoke quickly. "I understand your predicament, but

there's clearly more here going on than either of us understand."

A thud came from the door. Clearly one of the guards was throwing their weight against it.

"Miss Okoro," Carrington explained patiently, "it isn't a matter of my personal decision. The entire council has already voted and the deal is all ready to go through in a few days' time."

"Yes, but—"

The door burst open and several of the Grey Guard came rushing inside, weapons drawn, looking from Zoe and Carrington with uncertainty.

"Stand back!" one ordered.

Zoe held up her hands, her mind whirling furiously. She could run and escape! But she'd never been much of an athlete... Fight her way out? No, she didn't have any magic right now and the last thing that would help her case was to start a fistfight.

The guards surrounded her from all sides.

Shit.

A million words were on Zoe's lips but before she could decide on any of them, Carringtonn spoke up.

"Stand down, gentlemen," Carrington said, walking between them. "We were merely having a civil conversation."

The guards didn't look convinced, but at Carrington's continued stare they lowered their weapons.

Zoe allowed herself to relax a little, hopeful that she'd be able to get out of this situation after all when Carrington nodded to the guards. One reached for her wrist and she yanked her arm away, defensive. "What do you think you're doing?"

"I'm terribly sorry, Miss Okoro," Carrington explained. "But part of Prince Hakon's request was to apprehend any and all Incarnate to be found within Heathland's borders."

"You said you were making a diplomatic deal." Zoe struggled against the guard's grasp. "Not capturing Incarnate."

"You've seen them," Carrington hissed, a note of panic entering his voice. "The public who put more faith in filth such as Vard rather than their own elected government? This deal with Bjordal will not only stabilise the council's power, it will increase it over the conlords and criminals. I can't let any opportunity slip me by."

Zoe was dragged out of the room in the grasp of both guards, guests whispering and staring with curiosity in their wake. Anxiety and fear churned through Zoe's body in waves. What had she done? How was she supposed to get back to Alessi, let alone help them? She would have even taken Ada Vard's help at this point. She would be waiting for her up on the roof in only a few minutes. Would she wait for her even after the time limit expired? Or would she shrug it off and leave?

But Zoe wasn't entirely alone in this bleak city. Silje would never allow it. She'd be furious if she knew what was happening, right along with Gabriel. She'd be out of here by the morning at the very least, then she could find Ada and ask if her offer still stood.

She repressed a groan as she imagined the smug look on Gabriel's face when she told him they were going with his original plan to work with Ada.

The thought entirely vanished as the door opened and was met by the sight of Gabriel, handcuffed to a chair with an armed guard stationed on either side of him.

"Zoe?" A wide smile spread across his face. "Now this is a surprise indeed."

21

GABRIEL

After being promptly manhandled by the guards, which, despite the murder, was honestly rude. Gabriel had been led to a spare room, where the canister had immediately been taken from him. Unfair considering it had barely been in his possession for a few minutes. Then he was promptly handcuffed to a chair, but not even in a fun way, before finally being told to wait. But as he was met with Zoe's shocked eyes, he realised that perhaps the night would become more unexpected yet.

"Okay, first of all—" Gabriel looked at Zoe, eyeing up her suit. "You look amazing. Second, I really hate to say it, but this is bad timing for me."

"Bad timing for you?" Zoe hissed as she was led to a chair beside him. "You're the one who's handcuffed—and why are you even here in the first place?"

"I want to tell you, but I have a feeling you won't like anything I have to say. So you see my dilemma?"

"Wonderful, Gabe." Zoe let out a long breath, raising her eyes to the ceiling. "Just wonderful."

Past Zoe, Gabriel's eyes landed on Councillor Carrington in all his frail glory entering the room, followed promptly by another pair of guards. He looked far smaller than Gabriel recalled. A mere wisp of a man in a grey suit, his family coat of arms pinned to his tie.

"Councillor Carrington," Zoe immediately spoke up. "You don't have the legal right to hold us here. I had an official invitation."

"Yes," Gabriel quickly lied. "We both did."

Carrington waved his hands for order at the sudden influx of voices. "I'm a bit more concerned about the murder that has just taken place under my roof!"

The room went silent.

Zoe's eyes burned upon him and Gabriel determinedly avoided her stare.

Carrington turned to Gabriel with a grave look in his eyes. "Would you care to explain why you've broken into my conservatory?"

"I didn't break in," Gabriel corrected him. "I walked in."

Fell in, he almost said. But from the vein bulging in Carrington's forehead, he guessed that the man wasn't in the mood for jokes.

"Without invitation," Carrington said. "And then proceeded to use one of my trusted councillors to break into my personal safe?"

"I only wanted to see what was inside."

"And finally proceeded…to murder him."

"In my defence, he tried to kill me first."

A quiet murmuring came from his right and he realised it was Zoe, cursing under her breath.

"Is that so?" Carrington held his hand out and Gabriel watched as one of the Grey Guards handed him the canister, which Carrington looked at gravely before he met Gabriel's eyes, his voice cold. "And why would you want these documents badly enough to risk yourself for them?"

"I would also like to know," Zoe said with a pointed look thrown his way.

"Reading material?" Gabriel answered lamely.

"Do not lie to me." Carrington's eyes sparked with anger. "You were upstairs stealing from my personal offices and I want to know why."

All eyes in the room were upon him but what could he possibly say? The truth was out of the question. *Oh, nothing much. I just popped by to rob you of some secret documents, all the while delivering them to your sworn enemy solely for my personal gain. Excellent party, by the way, though the refreshments were a tad bland.*

"Look," Gabriel explained. "We can spend all night pointing fingers, but it's obvious now that someone has been playing us from the very beginning and we still don't know who they are."

"We already know that answer." Carrington's voice rose. "The same person who's behind every foul thing in my city. That cursed mutt—"

"Might I advise you not to say that around her?" Gabriel suggested. "She really doesn't like it."

Carrington's eyes snapped to Gabriel's, his thin fingers tightening around the canister. "And what would you know," he said quietly, "about Ada Vard?"

"Not much," Gabriel dismissed him. "Other than the fact that your fellow councillors were working for her."

Carrington bristled. "They would never do such a thing."

"Are you sure?" Gabriel asked. "You haven't had anything strange happen within the last few months that would point to interference?"

Zoe shifted uncomfortably. Carrington paused, thoughtful before he asked, "Who told you this?"

"Royle. Right before his…untimely passing," Gabriel said carefully. "It's not Vard— well, not entirely. Someone from Bjordal hired her. Someone who wanted the information for themselves."

Carrington shook his head. "Don't be ridiculous. Heathland has outstanding relations with Bjordal. I'll be signing a peace treaty in a few days' time."

"Just ask Theodora or Norbert. They'll be able to tell you."

"They've retired for the night."

"How convenient," Gabriel muttered. How was he ever going to convince this man? His eyes settled on Zoe and relief swept through him. Zoe would surely believe him—

"Councillor Carrington?" Zoe spoke. "Are you sure it's Ada?"

That idea immediately cracked and shattered and Gabriel was left blinking dumbly. There was only one possibility—Ada had already gotten to Zoe and offered some sort of deal. It had to be good if Zoe was defending her.

Carrington was silent for a long moment before he finally nodded to the guards. "Bring me Norbert and Theodora. Tell them it's urgent."

A pair of guards saluted before briskly exiting the room.

"If this is all true," Carrington said, "if an unknown Bjordal party has been hiring Vard for such tasks, then it's treason." His eyes shone. "That's finally enough to hold against her in a proper court."

"Well, I for one am ecstatic that we could help you come to this conclusion." Gabriel held his cuffed hands up. "Now if you'll kindly remove these, we'll be on our merry way—"

"Despite recent events," Carrington continued like the slam of a door to a face. "The treaty will go through with Bjordal in a few days' time. If they discover I'm harbouring either of you—or fulfil the Verchiél contract—they'll call everything off."

"We're Verchiél citizens," Gabriel protested. "You can't just send us to Bjordal without a fair trial."

"There won't be a fair trial," Zoe pointed out, her eyes still locked on Carrington. "The man in charge of Verchiél is against us too."

Gabriel opened and closed his mouth, desperate to find some argument that would magically sort everything out. All he managed was: "Fuck."

"Sir?" One of the guards approached Carrington, giving a short salute before whispering to him. Carrington went through a variety of emotions before his face turned cold.

"I see…" He turned to face the group. "Mark my words there will be consequences tonight, but I've yet to decide a final course of action."

Carrington exited the room, the canister still clutched tightly in his hands, followed by a pair of guards. The door shut and locked behind them.

Gabriel immediately turned to Zoe. "What did Vard offer you?"

"What did she offer you?"

He fidgeted with the cuffs at his wrists. "We can argue later. We need to get out of here."

Bjordal steel. Carrington was right, Heathland had to be on Bjordal's good side if they were trading their precious supply of steel.

Gabriel's ears pricked with the sound of a lock turning in

the door, and both he and Zoe whipped around to watch as a figure entered the room. Gabriel was prepared to talk or fight his way out of this until he recognized them.

"What the fuck, Zoe!" Alessi straightened, keys in hand, when their brown eyes settled on Gabriel with surprise. "Gabriel?"

Gabriel smiled, memories flooding of when they'd first met how they hadn't been able to take their eyes from each other. How despite Zoe's warnings they'd entered into a courtship as short as it was tumultuous. It hadn't been a stable time for either of them, but it had been fucking fun. Even now a surge of fondness swept through Gabriel at the sight of Alessi.

"What a lovely surprise to see you here, Lesi."

Alessi didn't look nearly as impressed when they addressed Zoe. "Why is he here?"

"He murdered somebody and got caught," Zoe said, leaning forward as Alessi unlocked her Bjordal steel cuffs.

"Allegedly," Gabriel added.

Alessi considered Gabriel with a look of exhausted disappointment, which he knew all too well. "Still causing trouble are we, Freckles?"

"Depends." Gabriel grinned. "Are you looking for some?"

"As much as I'd love to untangle the threads of your failed relationship," Zoe said with no small amount of sarcasm, "we really are on a time limit."

Alessi unlocked Gabriel's cuffs. "I'd ask why you're both locked up here but I already have a pretty good idea that you're both in trouble."

"Carrington is making a deal with Bjordal, he said they'd look more favourably upon the council if they caught any Incarnate in their borders," Zoe explained.

Alessi ushered Zoe toward the door. "Then you need to leave."

"Wait!" Zoe twisted in their grasp. "What about the guards?"

"I've taken care of the pair by the door, I can't make any promises about the rest of them."

"How?" Gabriel asked, for as athletic as Alessi was, Gabriel knew that they couldn't throw a punch to save their life.

Alessi looked annoyed that he'd asked but answered honestly. "Vard's reach goes a lot further than many know about, that's all you need to know."

"Of course it does. Is everything and everyone in this cursed city connected to Vard in some shady way?" Gabriel said.

Alessi gave him an all-too-knowing grin. "And you weren't?"

Gabriel tried his damnedest to ignore the indignant heat that crept up his neck, recalling how many of his exploits he'd once proudly told Alessi about, before he'd grown wise enough to manage his loose lips during pillow talk.

"Never mind," Gabriel dismissed them. "What about you?"

"I'll be fine," they said.

"No," Zoe protested, clinging tighter to Alessi as if she was fearful they'd disappear. "I was going to talk to the council, to find a solution to regain my throne so I can take care of the debt with Ada. I want to help you—"

"Zoe." They caught her hands, speaking seriously. "The best way you can help me right now is to get out of here. If they catch you again, it's going to be so much worse."

Zoe looked as if she wanted to argue, to solve the problem with the right combination of words, but Alessi held her gaze and eventually she nodded, the fight draining out of her.

"Promise I'll see you again?"

Alessi managed a grin. "You'd be hard-pressed to be rid of me now."

Zoe's eyes shone with unshed tears before she threw her arms around Alessi, holding them close.

It was moments like this that starkly reminded Gabriel that no matter how long he and Zoe had known each other, she still had parts of her old life that not only had been good, but existed entirely outside of him.

A part of him wondered if that's why he'd been so enamoured with Alessi in the first place. If he'd been searching for the same level of comfort and familiarity Zoe found in them.

But what Zoe and Alessi had was unbreakable. Even time hadn't corroded it. Even when he and Alessi had been together, their bond hadn't run nearly so deep.

Gabriel looked away, wanting to give them a moment of privacy. After another moment, Zoe placed a hand on Gabriel's arm. "Let's go."

Gabriel froze. The canister.

"Wait!" Gabriel said, retracing his steps back down the hall. "I need to grab something."

Zoe huffed, following closely on his heels. "What could possibly be so important? If Carrington sees us out he's going to shut down the entire conservatory."

"Trust me," he reassured her, "he won't even notice we're here. This is going to help us in a big way."

They ran along the hall silently, but both slowed in their steps at the sight of the closed office door. Gabriel jiggled the handle with no luck, and in frustration, threw his shoulder against the door, pain wracking his arm as the panel barely budged.

"What are you doing?" Zoe asked, dismayed. "He'll hear us—"

Suddenly the sounds of a struggle came from inside the office: Muffled voices. Shattered glass. A scream of fright that faded into a gasp of pain.

Gabriel and Zoe exchanged a fearful look. Neither hesitated as they threw their full weight against the doors. It took several shoves, but between the two of them, the heavy oaken panels finally crashed open, the sound of another distant alarm sounding out.

They fell into the room just in time to see a masked guard plunge a knife deep into Carrington's throat.

"Hey!" Gabriel screamed.

The guard's head whipped up at his shout, but before he could so much as cross the room, they were gone again, slipping soundlessly out the broken window.

Gabriel bolted across the room, leaning out of the window. His eyes swept down to the grounds of hedge mazes below then to the ledges around him. But there was nobody there.

He picked up the knife from the floor; it had been snapped in half during the fight, made from a single piece of cruelly curved metal. He flicked the blood from its surface, and it made a soft chiming noise. On a sudden impulse, he placed it in his pocket.

"Gabe!" Zoe shouted. "Help me."

He turned and saw Zoe trying with little success to staunch the flow of bleeding from the knife wound, while Carrington lay eerily still. Gabriel realised that she was still trying to heal Carrington, hands clutching at his neck, sweat gathered on her brow as she whispered beneath her breath.

"Hey, hey—" He grabbed her now bloodied forearms.

"Zoe!"

She was in shock, her eyes wide, her entire body shaking.

"He's dead," Gabriel said. "You can't help him anymore."

Her voice was strained and quiet. "He was supposed to help us."

"I know," he said, unable to offer her any form of reassurance at that moment.

He thought of Ada on the roof. He fumbled for his timepiece—two minutes.

He got to his feet and walked back to the safe and breathed a sigh of relief as he noticed it was still cracked open. He retrieved the canister, hoping Ada wouldn't mind a few bloody fingerprints.

Zoe was still curled up on the floor, her eyes faraway.

"Zo?" He placed his hand on her shoulder and she jumped. "We need to leave."

"But...we had so many plans and now..."

"It'll be fine," he reassured her. "Ada can still help us."

"That's what worries me." She looked at him. "Do you really think we can trust her?"

"I don't know if you've seen either of us, but it looks like we just committed a bloody murder." He offered a hand. "We need to leave. Alessi is still waiting for us."

At the mention of Alessi her eyes focused. She nodded and wiped at her face, taking his hand as he helped her get back to her feet.

As the alarm finally faded, the sound of many shouting voices echoed from the halls. A quick peek into the hallway and Gabriel was promptly met by the sight of dozens of guards rushing toward the door.

Gabriel snapped the door shut, and, unsure how to work the

intricate lock, wedged a chair beneath the handles, then turned to Zoe. "So you remember how you said we'd get caught if we came back this way?"

"Yes," Zoe replied with an edge to her voice.

"We've been caught."

She shook her head and began searching around the office. "There's got to be another way out."

Gabriel looked along with her, but there were no additional doorways. They had one exit that was currently surrounded by guards and a broken window that led to a drop that was many dozens of feet high. Even if he used his magic, they wouldn't be able to survive such a fall.

Just when he was about to give up the search, Zoe gave a cry.

"Gabe! There's a rope over here."

Gabriel stood beside Zoe at the broken window. Sure enough a rope had been attached to the side of the building, anchored somewhere high above. He gave it a tug, but it was sturdy.

At least they knew how the killer had gotten away.

Gabriel gathered Zoe up in his arms and summoning his magic they vanished from the ledge, reappearing he thrust a hand forward and caught the rope, thirty feet above the ledge they'd previously stood upon. His arm buckled with the sudden weight and Zoe screamed as she clung tighter to the rope.

A crash resounded from below and he looked down, seeing multiple guards had finally broken through the doors of the office and now stood at the broken window, watching in disbelief as they climbed high above.

One grabbed the rope and moved as if to start climbing, but Gabriel swiftly drew the broken knife from his pocket and with some difficulty sawed away the length of rope below him, watching it fall away until it was left limp in the guard's hands.

"You should have left it," Zoe said. "Now they're going to try to catch us at a window."

"Then let's stop climbing, shall we?"

"Where?"

Muscles burning with pain, they climbed onto the ledge, both out of breath as they leaned back against the glass. Gabriel looked up. It was still another fifty feet at least to the top. Had the killer climbed all the way to the roof? Or had they found another way through?

He jumped as a furious banging echoed from the glass, driving away his thoughts. Alessi stared back at them from inside.

"Break the window!" Gabriel shouted.

"Don't break the window," Zoe protested. "It'll set off another—"

Alessi hurled a chair and the window shattered. Gabriel ducked as glass shards flew everywhere.

Just as Zoe had warned, another high-pitched alarm sounded out, filling the night with a horrible screeching that echoed out over the lawns below.

Alessi leaned out of the broken window. "What the fuck are you two doing out here?"

"Long story," Gabriel shouted over the blaring of the alarm, helping Zoe balance as she took Alessi's hand, and they helped her around the broken glass and into the room.

Alessi held out a hand to help Gabriel but paused, mid-stride, eyes widening in horror. "Gabe?" Alessi's face blanched, a queasy look on their face as their lips curled at the sight of blood. "What the fuck happened?"

"Carrington was murdered. Need to run," Gabriel said as he jumped down into the room, rushing ahead of the group, trying to make sense of the ink map on his forearm that was now so smudged it was entirely illegible.

"Wait, wait—" Two pairs of footsteps rushed alongside him. "That's Carrington's blood?" Alessi asked. "Who killed him?"

The weight of the silver knife in his pocket. The nagging feeling that he was forgetting something important.

He shook his head. "I can't remember."

Alessi frowned. "What do you mean you can't remember?"

In the distance Gabriel caught the sound of the city clock tower ringing. They were running out of time. Gabriel ripped his timepiece out.

One minute.

"We need to go. Lesi, can you get out by yourself?"

They looked mildly offended. "Can you?"

"Fair point." He turned to Zoe. "We don't have time to argue. Please just trust me on this."

Her eyes flicked from his face to Alessi's, and much to his relief, she nodded. "Let's hurry."

Gabriel turned to Alessi. "I don't suppose you have any heartfelt words of farewell for me?"

"Not particularly," Alessi said.

"Admit it," Gabriel said. "You missed me."

"I missed parts of you."

Gabriel bit his lip. "You don't need to if you see me again…"

"Time limit, remember?" Zoe said loudly, hand already on the door handle. Clearly her annoyance at their involvement with each other hadn't lessened in the years since they'd first courted.

Alessi nodded. "Zoe, stay safe, and Gabriel—" They kissed him before breaking away all too quickly and cuffing the back of his head. "Don't be an ass."

Gabriel beamed. "Speaking of parts of me that you missed—"

"Time to go!" Zoe seized Gabriel's arm and pulled him along. He caught one final glimpse of Alessi as they slipped back downstairs into the crowd of guests.

Zoe pushed him ahead. "Go!"

They sprinted up the final flights of stairs, the pounding of many footsteps growing fainter behind them. He chanced a look at his timepiece and nearly tripped.

Ten seconds.

Muscles aching and out of breath, he forced himself forward, throwing himself against the doors and shoving them open.

The cold air struck him as the wind blew strongly along the rooftops. The city's clock tower chimed loudly in the distance, also marking the end of his allotted time.

He laughed, letting out a whoop. They'd made it, and with documents in hand. The night certainly hadn't gone… as planned, but he'd succeeded in what Ada had set out for him. He'd finally have an ally strong enough to help him take back Verchiél.

"Gabriel?" Zoe said, turning in a slow circle as she surveyed the area. "Are you sure this is the right place?"

"I'll admit, I didn't think either of you would make it up here in one piece." Ada approached from the shadows, changed out of her silk waistcoat and now dressed smartly in crisp black. Her slicked-back hair was tousled by the wind. Her mismatched eyes roved over them with interest, lingering upon the dark stains of blood on their clothes. "Mostly in one piece…"

Another figure strode toward them and Gabriel recognized Tari. She had changed out of her silver dress and swan feather cape, owl nowhere in sight, and instead wore a simple jacket and trousers. She stopped twenty paces away, her eyes sweeping over them before she nodded. "Didn't believe you when you said she'd come, Vard."

Ada's gaze went to Zoe. "I'm especially delighted to see you, Daughter of the Sun. What decision have you made?"

"Decision?" Gabriel asked.

"Don't interrupt us." Ada's tone was sharp. "She's speaking."

Zoe met Ada's eyes. "I want a contract drawn up. A legitimate one."

Ada smiled. "Gladly."

"What contract?" Gabriel asked.

Zoe drew in a breath, an anxious expression growing across her face that he instantly recognized whenever she had something she wanted to hide from him.

"Oh, dear," Ada said at the prolonged silence. "I never meant to be the cause of any quarrels between you two," she said in a tone that suggested that had been entirely her intention.

"I'm not going back to Verchiél," Zoe blurted out.

Silence fell between them again.

"I'm releasing Alessi from their debt and getting my family's business—my business back. To do that, I need to live in Heathland."

"But you don't want to stay here of all places, do you?" he asked, incredulous. "You told me for years that you wanted to go— well, everywhere. How is staying here any better than going back to Verchiél?"

"I need to change something. I can't go back to the way things were."

Ada checked her time-piece impatiently. "A touching picture of sentiment but we're on a schedule." She addressed Zoe, "You'd best make your goodbyes now."

Zoe turned to him. "Gabe." But nothing else came from her mouth as she continued to stare at him in silence. He had a million questions he wanted to ask her: Why would she have chosen to stay with Ada instead of him? How was he supposed to return to Verchiél without her? But most of all why hadn't she told him the truth in the first place?

At their continued silence Tari eventually placed a hand on Zoe's shoulder, murmuring soft words he couldn't quite hear before she went to stand with the rest of the Hound's Teeth. Zoe looked over her shoulder.

He felt as if something had torn and shredded, felt the empty space beside him and suddenly felt so alone as he was met with Ada's steely gaze.

Ada held out her hand to him expectantly, but Royle's words still echoed in his mind. *She hired us once too.*

"I have a question." Gabriel weighed the canister in his hand. "About these documents—"

Ada's smile tightened. "I'll answer whatever you like, when you keep your end of the bargain."

"But I need to understand—"

Ada's face twitched, the easy-going demeanour vanishing. "The only thing you need to understand is that we're making an exchange. You don't need to think, you need to do as you're told." Ada raised her hand slowly and suddenly many figures from the shadows began to stir.

Ten, twenty, thirty—

The Hound's Teeth.

He smiled, his voice tight. "Quite the entourage you've gathered."

"Theatrics make the mundanity of life a little more bearable. But they're not here for a show, they're making sure business goes as planned." Her eyes snapped to his hand. "You were about to pass me that canister."

A screech pierced the night sky and a blur of feathers and talons dove at him, snatching the canister out of his hand. Gabriel flinched, watching Thaddeus land gracefully on Ada's arm, where she took the canister from his talons.

"Thank you, Thaddeus." Ada gave his feathers a ruffle before he flew back to Tari's shoulder. "Tell me, Gabriel, is it embarrassing to know that even a bird has better manners than you?"

"Fucking owl," Gabriel muttered, clutching his bleeding hand to his chest.

Ada uncapped the lid, reading swiftly through the documents before her eyes flicked back to him and he was shocked to hear the genuine impressed note in her voice.

"Well done." She pulled a match from her pocket, which she swiftly struck. Gabriel watched, stunned as she held the flame to the papers, the creamy pages catching fire.

"What do you think you're doing?" he asked.

"Already told you." She flicked the last of the ash from her fingertips. "None of your concern."

"So that's it?"

"You've completed your end of the bargain within the allotted time with a single casualty. I'd call that satisfactory at the least."

Despite himself a smile spread across his lips. He'd done it. He was finally going to get out of this cursed city. He could go home. He would have his old life back.

"Oh," Ada said. "And I nearly forgot. Ivy?"

The towering woman approached and clapped a new set of Bjordal steel bracers over Gabriel's wrists, dragging him along.

Panic surged through him as he shouted back to Ada, "Hey! What do you think you're doing?"

"Sorry, I thought it was obvious." Ada explained. "I'm capturing you for a reward."

"You can't do that," he said. "A deal's a deal. Besides who will ever work with you again once word gets out that you can't be trusted on your promises?"

"When it comes to Incarnate, this is an exception rather than the rule. I'm certain everyone else will be positively jealous that they didn't think of it first. And after you snuck in here to take revenge on the very man who denied you aid?" She shook her head. "The authorities will be delighted to have the true culprit in custody."

Realisation swept through him. "You...you had Carrington murdered."

Ada shrugged. "I was never here tonight, none of us were. The right people will agree with me. I've already made sure of that. Besides, I have a contract. That much money can't be overlooked, and if I don't turn you in, someone else will. Why shouldn't that person be me?"

"So, you just got us to do your dirty work, had us incriminated, and then decided to capture us for a reward." He was thoughtful. "That's actually quite clever."

"Delighted to know you approve." Ada nodded to Ivy.

"Keep those bracers on him. I don't want him trying anything—"

"Stop!" Zoe stepped between them, her mind clearly whirling quickly before she spoke to Ada. "You can't take him. Why can't you just hire him too?"

"He's a liability I'm not willing to take on," Ada said. "Even if you'd give up your ridiculous fantasies of being a prince, I know you'd never lift a finger if it didn't directly benefit yourself."

"Either you let him go"—Zoe stepped away from Ada to stand beside him—"or keep your end of the deal."

"You're giving up a chance for a new life"—Ada gestured to Gabriel in disbelief—"for that?"

"No. I'm choosing what's right. You were the one who told me to run toward what frightens me. Besides—" She met his eyes. "I know he'd do the same for me."

For one of the first and only times in Gabriel's life, he was speechless. To know that their friendship had weathered so much and yet still endured in their own strange way, it was a comfort he couldn't quite describe.

When he managed to find his voice again, he was quiet. "Zoe, I—"

"You're still a twat," she reassured him. "In case you were wondering."

"Fair enough," he said.

Ada, much like Gabriel, also seemed to be struggling with a moment of speechlessness, opening and closing her mouth as if about to argue before she shook her head tiredly. "I'm regretful to hear that but if neither of you can be swayed." She nodded to Ivy and Tari. "Take them both."

Tari grabbed Zoe and dragged her along. She panicked and instinctively struggled against her grasp but Tari held firm.

"Taimak mu, jowan!" Zoe said in Uzoman, hoping that Tari would give some sympathy, but Tari gave her only a look of pity, answering in Heathall. "Don't make this any harder than it needs to be."

Apparently nothing got in the way of business in Grislow. Tari was right and there was nothing they could do; there were dozens of them and the Bjordal steel bracers were still snug around Gabriel's wrists.

That meant they were both powerless.

Shit.

"Hang on—" Gabriel fidgeted in Ivy's grasp, managing to slip away long enough to free the knife from his jacket pocket. "The contract is only if we're delivered alive." He held the knife to his own chest. "And unharmed."

"Gabe!" Zoe muttered furiously. "What are you doing?"

"Improvising."

Ada looked bored. "You're as predictable as you are vain, I know you'd never so much as put a scratch on yourself."

"Wouldn't I?" Gabriel challenged. "Just what will you tell a very angry king when he finds out I've been brutally mutilated at your cruel hands?"

"I'll tell him you're an idiot."

"I'll tell you he's an idiot," Zoe added.

"You do realise"—Ada flicked her wrist and a sharp blade appeared from her sleeve—"that there's a whole lot of technicality within the definition of *unharmed*. I'm certain a few cuts and bruises to bring in two unruly individuals isn't going to be a deal breaker."

The other women backed away from Ada, giving her space as she advanced toward them. Her brows drawn so low Zoe couldn't see the mismatched colours of her eyes anymore as they both were dark. And Zoe knew at that moment she wasn't a mutt. She was a wolf, leading her pack. And she'd fight to the death before she let them go.

Ada flicked her wrist and another sharp blade appeared from her sleeve, but before she could lunge forward, a figure moved from the shadows, their sudden appearance so unexpected that nobody had time to properly react. A masked guard— the same masked guard from the councillor's office. They seized Ada from behind, and with immense strength pulled her away.

Safe, a voice assured her. *You're safe.*

Ada snarled, caught off guard by the sudden intrusion, and stabbed the knife deep into the guard's thigh.

The guard gave a horrible shriek and swiftly knocked Ada back onto the roof. Ada wiped at her split lip. When her eyes landed on the guard a tense silence stretched across the roof, her voice barely a whisper. "You—" Ada hauled the guard to their feet. "You're the most ignorant bitch I've ever met. You told me that you didn't know where they were."

Ada ripped the mask from the guard's face and Zoe took a

step back, a chill sweeping through her.

"Silje?"

Silje tilted her head back, her face and pale hair stained with blood, smiling breathlessly at Ada. "You fight better than you fuck—"

Ada slapped Silje across the face, hard. Silje gasped, her eyes bright with excitement before she slapped Ada in return.

Shouts of protest rose from the gathered members but Ada held them back. Threats and curses hurled like knives as the Hound's Teeth watched on, furious.

"Do you like it when you get to play rough?" Silje stood deliberately in Ada's space. "I'll let you do it again, but only if you ask me nicely."

Ada shushed her, teeth gritted. "We have guests."

Silje looked from Ada, and a smile blossomed across her lips, her voice sweet. "Hello, my loves."

Ada looked down at Silje, something like pity in her eyes. "Oh, you poor thing. Do you think that they love you? That anybody does?"

Silje's smile faded, her eyes narrowed.

"That's what I thought," Ada said. "You're a being of singular purpose."

"Silje?" Zoe asked. "What is she talking about?"

Ada's eyes didn't leave Silje's. "Didn't she tell you the kind of person she is?"

"An Incarnate?" Gabriel asked.

Ada's head snapped up. "What?"

Silje met their eyes and shook her head quickly.

"An Incarnate…" Ada rested a hand under Silje's chin, tilting her face to hers. "There's a lot of things you've been hiding from me." Ada scrutinised Silje's pale eyes closely. "Moon or Sun?" Silje didn't answer, her eyes narrowed in a terrible glare. Ada shrugged at her silence. "It doesn't matter. In any case, you'll all be travelling as a merry little trio to Bjordal."

"Bjordal?" Gabriel asked. "What contract are you fulfilling?"

"My contract comes from the father, not the son. King Asbjorn and his heir have taken a great interest in Incarnate as of late."

At the mention of Asbjorn, something dark flitted across Silje's face. Though it didn't extract any emotion from her so much as remove it. Her eyes grew distant, her mouth setting into a grim line.

"Verchiél is unstable," Ada continued. "Everyone knows it. Bjordal might be stuck in their ways but they've been more reliable than the southern kingdom ever has."

"That wasn't a part of our deal," Silje said, voice cold.

"What deal?" Zoe asked, her eyes on Silje. "You told us you were offering aid as an Incarnate. Not making back alley deals with conlords."

"Neither of you connected the dots?" Ada asked, disbelieving. "You've been seeking aid from the same person who usurped you. In addition to committing various acts of political ruination for coin, she likes to play games," Ada said. "Don't you?"

"You hired me," Silje said.

"Rest assured it was a mistake I won't repeat."

"You were the Bjordal woman?" Gabriel asked.

"Tell them." Ada shoved Silje toward them. "Since you love the sound of your own voice so much."

Silje looked between the two of them, opening her mouth as if to speak before she turned back to Ada. "I haven't been very honest with you."

"That's putting it lightly."

Silje limped forward, holding her injured leg gingerly. "I'll tell the truth, but I wonder, do you know what kind of Incarnate I am?"

Ada shrugged. "Does it matter?"

"No. But you still want to know because you can't help yourself. You always need to be the smartest person in the room."

Ada crossed her arms before she answered simply. "Moon. You live only to bring death. Not to mention"—Ada nodded in Gabriel's direction—"there's another here who shares in your taste for being a sneaky fuck."

"Hey!" Gabriel shouted. "You're calling me a sneaky fuck? You sneaky fu—"

Zoe shushed him, eyes only on Silje.

"Well?" Ada asked, impatient. "Was I right?"

"My poor dear." Silje took the last step forward, the first rays of morning light rose in the sky and Silje smiled, her eyes filled with gold. "You never did listen to me."

Ada, realising her mistake, flipped a knife in her hand but before she could lunge out, Silje seized Ada's arm and twisted it violently. Ada screamed and Zoe winced at the loud crack that resounded.

Silje forced Ada to the roof, digging her knee into her back.

Members rushed into motion, weapons drawn but above it all, Silje's voice settled heavy over the air like a blanket.

"Stop."

The area was still, everyone held in place by Silje's magic.

"That's better, isn't it?" Silje picked up a discarded pistol and tossed it to Zoe, who caught it with fumbling fingers, the metal cold and heavy in her hands.

"Do it." Silje nodded to the pistol in Zoe's grasp. "Finish her."

"You're not going to kill me yourself?" Ada spoke between ragged breaths. "Lazy."

Zoe backed away, holding the pistol in a shaking grasp, unsure who to aim at anymore.

"Zoe?" Silje asked. "What are you waiting for?"

Ada's eyes, hazy with pain, met Zoe's. "Kill me and you'll never leave this city alive—"

Silje shushed her, putting more pressure on her arm, which made her hiss before falling silent.

"I think I might need a little help with this, as you can see I'm terribly outnumbered," Silje said, looking across the frozen members of the gang with idle interest before she called out, "Tari? Ivy? Would you mind keeping Ada in line for me?"

As Silje spoke, Tari's and Ivy's expressions went oddly blank and Ada's face went from amusement to shock as the two women seized her, restraining her.

"Tari? Ivy? What the fuck are you doing?" Ada's gaze narrowed on Silje. "What did you do to them?"

"Asked very nicely. Something you should try more often." Silje smiled. "But let's not rush things, we have so much to catch up on." Silje cupped Ada's cheek. "I'm going to miss this when you're gone—" Silje gasped and pulled her hand back, blood welling up where Ada had bitten her.

Ada spat blood. "Get fucked."

"Funny." Silje flexed her hand. "She told me the exact same thing."

"What are you talking about?"

"You have a friend in Verchiél who misses you so much." Silje snorted with laughter. "It's rather funny. She actually thinks that she killed you and has been moping around ever since. Can you believe it?"

"Silje," Ada growled. "What are you talking about?"

"I'll tell you if you promise not to bite."

Ada glared before she finally gave a curt nod. Silje leaned forward and whispered into Ada's ear. Ada's confusion faded, and her hazy eyes widened, staring at Silje as if she'd just uttered an omen.

Silje nodded at Ada's expression. "Funny, right?"

A strained note entered Ada's voice. "Dabria?"

"I could have told you sooner, if you'd bothered to ask." Silje clapped her hands cheerfully and rose to her feet. "But sadly we're running out of time, and as you like to say we're on a schedule."

"Wait—where is she?!" Ada screamed, her voice cracking.

Silje ignored Ada as she approached Zoe, her face gentle. "Go ahead."

Zoe shook her head, her voice strained. "No."

Silje tilted her head to the side, her brows furrowing. "You can't or you won't?"

Zoe looked back to Ada, who still struggled against the grasp of her own gang. Even if she'd purposefully made that predatory deal with Alessi, that still wasn't something worthy of death.

Zoe pushed the pistol away. "This isn't right."

Silje frowned as if trying to work out a problem. "Why?"

Suddenly a sharp pain burst in the back of her mind, a pressure unlike anything she'd ever experienced before. Then—

Nothing but an eerie calm.

"You can do it." Silje offered the pistol again. "Just take it."

Horror swept through Zoe as her hand reached forward of its own accord, taking the pistol from Silje.

"Much better," Silje said. "Stand here."

Zoe's voice was muffled in her throat as she strained against the weight of her magic. She stood where Silje indicated, raising the pistol toward Ada.

"Zoe!" Ada shouted. "Fight it! Is this really the best you can do?"

Her insults were thrown with a venom clearly meant to incite her into a rage, to try to get her to fight back. But the weight of Silje's magic felt less like a blanket to be thrown off than an entire ocean crushing down on her back. Drowning her.

She gritted her teeth, her entire body shaking from the effort of resistance, the pistol held in an unsteady aim.

"No, no," Silje chided. "You're doing it all wrong." She wrapped her arms around Zoe, her steady hands covering hers as she guided the pistol toward Ada. "You see?" Silje's breath was warm against her neck as she rested her chin on Zoe's shoulder. "Right through the heart."

With Silje's presence rose an assuredness— a calm that reassured her. Everything else fell away, and she focused solely on the task set out for her.

Her steady hands aimed the pistol and she felt that a part of herself, however small, still wanted to please Silje. That frightened her most of all.

Silje's lips brushed her ear and all went silent except for her voice.

"Shoot her."

Zoe closed her eyes, shutting everything and everyone out

until the only thing that remained was the golden glow of the magic tethering her to Silje. It had been there since the moment they'd met, why hadn't she seen it long before now? Wrapped around her, threads crisscrossing in chaotic ways, but the more she focused, the easier it became to pick away at. One thread and the whole thing would unravel. She focused on every sense of that golden thread and this time, she unravelled the whole thing.

"No," Zoe said.

With a cry, Zoe shoved Silje's magic away. It was a brief respite; Silje's arms spasmed and she stumbled backward with a gasp, her magic vanishing. The shot that would have struck Ada's heart grazed her shoulder.

Ada let out a pained yelp, everyone collapsing as Silje's control left them. Zoe was the only person who remained standing. Her entire being was overwhelmed with golden magic, her arms shaking from the effort of contorting her magic to a new shape.

"Stop it!" Zoe shouted at Silje. Her voice echoed with the same force, the same commanding energy that Silje had spoken with only moments before. Its power twisted through her body, weighing heavily in her bones.

Silje's eyes were fully golden, but rather than anger, her expression was ecstatic as she beamed at Zoe. "You can do it too?"

She moved forward as if to embrace her but Zoe backed away sharply. "Don't come any closer."

"My love—"

Sparks and a wave of heat gusted across the rooftop, leaving her skin burning. "Don't call me that!"

Amid the roar of blood in her ears, Zoe caught the shout of a familiar voice.

"Zo!" Gabriel shouted. Now free to move, he sprinted toward her and outstretched a hand.

It took her golden eyes a moment to focus on him, before she understood what he was doing. She fled from Silje as she leapt forward, her hand clasping his as he focused on their shared magic and the rooftop began to fade before his eyes.

Silje, mimicking Zoe's movements, seized his other arm. He tried to shake her away, but her grip was too tight, her nails digging into his skin.

The rooftop faded around Zoe and she caught the sight of Ada behind them, a grim smile adorning her lips as she watched them disappear. As the Hound's Teeth faded from view, they were replaced by the oncoming street below them.

Gabriel's screams and Silje's laughter rang in her ears as she refocused the unstable magic and all three reappeared on the cobblestone street below the conservatory.

Silje let out a shriek of delight, a wide smile across her face, her hair messed and blown about by the wind.

"That was fantastic!" Silje looked up at the conservatory, her eyes entirely gold in her excitement. "I didn't know you could do that."

Silje looked back to them, her smile fading. "What's wrong?"

Zoe was out of breath, the air around her still sparked and hummed.

"Zo?" Gabriel placed a hand on her shoulder. "You okay?"

"Yeah," Zoe muttered, her eyes not leaving Silje.

"Good," he assured her before turning back to Silje. "Who are you?"

"What are you talking about?" Silje asked. "You know who I am—"

"No. I don't think we do." Zoe reached for Gabriel's hand, and he took it, helping her to her feet. Silje's eyes flicked to their clasped hands, and her face twitched with a dark expression before her smile tightened.

"Fine. What do you want to know?"

"You and Ada?" Gabriel asked.

"We're business partners—well…" Silje bit her lip as she stifled a giggle. "A little more than that for a time, but that's private business."

"You killed him," Zoe said quietly.

"Who?"

"Councillor Carrington!" Gabriel shouted, dismayed. "Are you telling me you've killed others tonight?"

Silje's brows scrunched up in deep thought. "It was a rather busy night." She brushed ash out of her hair. "But it doesn't matter now. We're all fine."

Zoe felt the tension in Gabriel's grip as he backed away from Silje. She looked around the street, wondering how quickly they could run—let alone where they'd go in the first place. They'd placed so much trust in this woman, and relied on her promises. Now that all of it had been ripped away, she wasn't quite sure who they could turn to anymore.

"Gabriel? Zoe?" Silje followed, her voice confused. "Where are you going?"

"Away from you," Zoe said.

"Why!?" she screamed. A gust of wind blew through the street, Zoe's skin burning with heat. The glass in the street lamps overhead shattered, and Zoe threw up an arm to cover her head.

Silje's golden eyes blazed. There wasn't a single hint of the softness she'd shown either of them as the scent of ash rose in the air, the tang of metal in the back of Zoe's throat.

"Sleep and forget."

And so she did.

Zoe awoke slowly, tucked under quilts and furs. So soft, comfortable.

Safe, the voice said, *you are safe, sleep—*

She sat up, heart racing. This was her cabin on the Prakt.

Her chest of clothes was still set at the foot of her cot, the polished set of drawers adorned with a vase of flowers and many silver platters of pastries and fresh fruits. But something cold and heavy was snug around her wrists and she recognized the Bjordal steel bracers.

She struggled with them uselessly, unable to feel the golden pull of her magic even as the sun shone through the porthole.

"Sleep well?"

Zoe whipped around. Silje sat in a plush chair, regarding her fondly, and gestured to the platters of food. "I made you breakfast."

Zoe stumbled to her feet, unsteady.

"Take these off."

"Are you going to leave me?"

Zoe laughed, a dry and humourless sound. "The better question is how you think I could stay after what I've seen." Zoe recalled the final moments before she'd lost consciousness, how desperate Silje had been to make her forget. "I'm never going to forget what you've done."

"But my dear Sun," Silje said, rising to her feet. "Don't you see? You're supposed to be with me—" She leaned closer and Zoe instinctively took a step back. "You and Gabriel."

"Where's Gabriel?"

"He's still sleeping," Silje explained. "You might remember, but I'm going to make him forget and then we can all go back to being happy again."

"You can't keep us here," Zoe protested.

"That's why we're on our way to Bjordal."

Zoe tensed. "Bjordal?"

Silje nodded excitedly. "I'll finally get to show you my home"—she turned toward the door—"I have unfinished business there."

Zoe followed close on her heels, anger spurring her on. "The crew won't allow it, once they hear me."

Silje smiled pitifully. "Oh my dear, who do you think they answer to?"

A chill swept through Zoe.

"But until then," Silje said in her silence, "stay put, my love. We'll be in Bjordal in no time."

The door shut behind her, the lock letting out a hollow click in her wake.

With Silje gone all the tension suddenly flooded out of Zoe, and she leaned against the door, taking stock of where she stood.

Kidnapped by a madwoman, her best friend brainwashed, and headed to a country which was infamously deadly for Incarnate.

Alessi would surely come for her if they knew where she was. She needed to warn Gabriel, but if she was locked in here until they docked, she wouldn't get to him before Silje did.

But if she was the only one who remembered the truth, she

had to try. Zoe stumbled back to her bed, and curling up and listening to the rocking waves outside, she planned.

23

GABRIEL

Gabriel cracked his eyes open. The air was frigid and he lay in a cot, tucked under piles of blankets and fur. Memories slowly resurfaced: the confrontation with Ada, Carrington's murder, and a pair of golden eyes looming above him—

"Silje?"

She sat beside the bed, bundled in furs with her long hair pulled back, her arms crossed tightly as she regarded him with a cold stare.

"Silje—" He smiled and reached for her hand, but she pulled it out of his grasp, her eyes narrowing in anger.

"Are you...all right?" Gabriel asked.

"Am I all right?" Her voice was sharp. "Are you serious?"

"My dear, I'm sorry," he said, genuine confusion descending over him. "Have I done something to offend you?"

Silje's frown softened. "You're not feeling unsettled?"

"I feel like I was hit by a train."

"But you're not...upset?"

"Why would I be upset?"

A smile found its way across her face and she threw her arms around him, hugging him tightly.

He laughed, patting her back. "What's this for?"

Her voice was muffled against his shoulder. "It's good to

see you normal again."

"Wasn't I normal before?"

"No." She curled up against his side, resting her head contently on his shoulder. "Not at all."

As his senses focused, he noticed that this wasn't the manor in Heathland—this room was moving. Nausea began to creep over him as he felt the motion of the ship, heard the distant sound of gulls and water crashing against the hull. This was his cabin on the *Prakt*.

"Calm down," Silje soothed as she placed her hands on his shoulders. "You've been on this ship before."

"That doesn't mean I want to repeat the experience. Where are we going? I thought we were staying in Grislow."

"There's been a change of plans, we're going to Bjordal."

Wait, what?

"Bjordal?" Gabriel laughed. "Are you out of your mind?"

"We need to regroup and what better place to do that than my home?"

"That's all well and good if your home didn't want to kill people like us."

Silje frowned. "I wouldn't take us there unless I knew how to keep us safe."

"Right…" Gabriel said, faltering under her stare. "What day is it?"

"The fifteenth day of the Month of Frost."

Fifteenth. That couldn't be right, the gala had been on the twelfth. How could he have been asleep for three days?

"You had a very nasty fall," Silje said. "Don't you remember?"

He thought back to the gala, his mind hazy as he recalled

rushing up to the rooftop. Blurry shapes swept through his mind, too distorted to recognize. The triumph as he'd presented Ada with the papers before she'd set them alight. The betrayal and fear as he and Zoe ran across the rooftop—wait, Zoe!

"Is Zoe safe?" He sat up straighter. "And Alessi? And what about—"

"My Moon." Silje took his hand in both of hers, drawing in a deep breath. "Zoe stayed in Heathland."

Gabriel was silent. He wanted to laugh and rebuke such an absurd statement, but Silje's face retained an air of sombreness.

"She took the deal she'd made with Ada," Silje continued to explain. "She won't be coming back."

"But that's not like her," Gabriel protested. "She wouldn't have just left without telling me."

"I'm sorry, my Moon." Silje squeezed his hand. "She's gone."

Zoe left him?

He couldn't speak. His throat was constricted.

"It's all right, my Moon," Silje soothed and kissed his hair. "I'm still here. We'll take back Verchiél, I promise."

He looked at her anew. Zoe had left. But perhaps he didn't need to be entirely alone. He and Silje would return to Verchiél and he wouldn't be the only Incarnate there, he'd have a friend and more. He pictured her dressed in the gold of an Incarnate Sun. What it would be like to wake up beside her every day? They'd make a fine pair. They'd rule over not just Verchiél, but the entirety of the Isles. Between him and Silje he had no doubt that they couldn't achieve it. As an Incarnate she'd be accepted by Verchiél. Nobody had to know what she'd done. Perhaps his life had been torn apart all so it could be built back stronger and better than before, so she could be there.

"Verchiél has a need for a queen."

"Gabriel Capello," Silje laughed. "Are you proposing?"

"It's a logical match. We're both Incarnate, both children of royal houses."

She was more than an ideal match, she was the other half of him, sharp and unforgiving, and he loved her for it.

"A queen?" Silje spoke slowly.

"Yes," Gabriel said. "What do you—"

A brisk knocking at the cabin door interrupted them.

"Silje?"

One of the crew, his voice threaded with worry. "The waters are getting rougher." Gabriel sat up straighter at that. "The captain has fears that we should stop at the nearest port, are you sure we should continue—"

"Busy!" Silje snapped.

"But…" Gabriel added, "there's not going to be a storm, is there?"

"Of course not." Silje tried to soothe him but he couldn't relax with the man's words still in his mind and the sound of the waves growing outside the cabin.

Silje sighed, sensing he wasn't going to believe her. "I'll talk to the captain. Happy?"

"I'll be happy once we're off this damned death trap."

Silje got to her feet, pressing a kiss to his cheek with the motion. Gabriel watched the door close behind her and flopped back onto the cot, trying his damnedest to ignore the sway of the ship around him.

Silje might have been here with him, but Zoe had left. Without even saying a proper goodbye. It didn't make any sense, they'd been best friends since childhood. What could possibly compel her to suddenly make such a rash decision?

Gabriel watched the sun sink lower beyond the growing clouds and found himself impatient. Where was Silje? She was only supposed to be gone for a moment, and right now he wanted some damned attention.

With some protest from his stiff limbs, he got to his feet and threw on his coat from where it hung from the back of a chair. With the sudden motion, something metallic clattered to the floor.

He bent down to pick up what had fallen. A broken knife, made from a single piece of metal and shockingly light. Its jagged edges were stained with what he recognized as dried blood.

A chill swept through him. Had he hurt somebody? No, that didn't feel right. He'd never owned a knife like this. He turned it over in his fingers, and wracked his mind for an answer. Something important, his instinct told him. It was something—

The ship suddenly rocked with the force of a larger wave, and he nearly dropped the knife in shock. Fuck this. He swiftly pocketed the broken knife and left his room.

The cold sunk into Gabriel's bones as soon as he emerged on deck, and his breath plumed in the frigid air. In the waves he caught the sight of tusked whales gliding along the ship, their smooth and speckled skin tinged blue underneath the dark waters.

He'd never been this far north before. He noticed the speed at which the ship cut through the choppy waters. A wave of nausea threatened to rise as another wave crashed against the ship and he drew in a deep breath. The sky had darkened, and though it was evening, he could have sworn it was the middle of the night. The distant rumble of thunder echoed and the waves crashed higher against the ship, the salty spray ice cold against his face.

He shivered and retreated from the railing, walking below deck, his feet leading him to Silje's door.

"Silje?"

Silence greeted him.

"Silje," he repeated. "It's Gabriel. Can I come in?"

He knocked again and the door creaked open with the motion and he realised with some surprise that it had been left unlocked. He paused, casting a glance over his shoulder before he slipped inside the cabin.

As his eyes adjusted to the dim light, his jaw dropped. Behind the unassuming door, the spacious cabin was overflowing with luxuries.

Heavy oaken wardrobes which had been left open contained soft wool coats, suits or flimsy wisps of dresses, each article in every imaginable colour and pattern. Multicoloured bottles of perfume lined the window ledges and caught the weak light from the increasingly dark day outside.

With light footfalls, he approached a large canopy bed topped with many layers of silk throws and fur blankets. He ran his hand along a pile of silk robes, and another wave rocked against the ship and he grabbed a bed post to steady himself, fighting back nausea as he forced himself to focus.

At the back of the cabin, his gaze settled on a vanity, the surface cluttered with all manner of cosmetics and jewellery. He approached and opened a drawer at random.

Inside, along with a few stray cosmetics, was a cluttered assortment of knives, cases of bullets and the pistol he'd seen Silje carrying the night at the manor, as well as possibly the oddest object, a lock of auburn hair. The hue was familiar, it almost looked like—

Pain wracked his skull and another headache threatened to grow. He took a few deep breaths, forcing himself to set the lock of hair down and turn his eyes back to the vanity.

He opened another drawer, then another, rifling through each with haste. His hands moved with an urgency of their own.

He moved to the large wardrobes around him, throwing the doors open. More clothes— no, not clothes, uniforms. Servant, cathedral caretaker, even a row of Bjordal folk masks. Among the oddities, he instantly recognized the black and gold of a Verchiél palace guard.

A soft chiming noise sounded out and he froze. Opening the wardrobe, he saw the black gown Silje had worn the night of the gala along with the cape of silver feathers.
He moved to grab the cape, but let out a hiss of pain and drew his hand back. His fingers were bleeding.

Carefully, he held up one of the silver feathers, running his finger along the edge and watching as a thin line of red welled up.

He reached into his pocket and withdrew what he had thought was a broken knife and held it up to the silver feathers. A chill ran through him as he realised they were the same. He forced himself to think past the pain. Remember. Why couldn't he just remember—

"Enjoying yourself?"

Silje watched him from the doorway, an expression he couldn't quite place on her face, but her knuckles were stark white against her crossed arms.

Excuses were on his lips even as he looked around the ransacked cabin. In his haste he hadn't realised what a mess he'd been making.

With a loud snap the door shut and Silje strode into the

cabin. "Might I ask what you're doing rifling through my personal belongings?"

"Would you believe I was looking for a drink to celebrate our engagement?"

"I believe you could come up with a better lie." She crossed the room and opened a dark wood cabinet. "But if you want a drink, I'll play along."

She settled herself into one of the chairs and nodded to a seat across from her. "Sit."
Despite her calmness, he immediately recognized it as an order, not a request, and sat without protest.

"You travel well," he began carefully, watching her fill two glasses with an amber coloured liquid. "Something for every occasion?"

"I never go without, if I can help it."

He managed a smile, clinking glasses. He drank deeply, grateful for the moment to have a distraction.

Silje made no move to drink, swirling her own drink around in her glass.

"It occurs to me," Gabriel began. "that I haven't asked much about my wife-to-be."

"What is there to know?"

"To start, having grown up in Bjordal as an Incarnate, you must have quite a few stories."

"Many. None of which bear re-telling if you're looking for something lighthearted."

"I'm not interested in lighthearted. I'm interested in memorable."

"What are you suggesting?"

"Just making conversation. I'd like to know more about my

benefactor."

Her eyes narrowed, voice turning icy. "I'm not a benefactor."

"Then what are you?" he asked.

She tilted her head to the side, expression softening. "A friend."

Gabriel was shocked to hear the uncertainty in her usually forceful voice, as if fearful he'd contradict her.

"Yes," he agreed, "and since we're friends, I'd like you to answer a question honestly. About these recollections I've been having, it feels almost like memories."

Her fingers tightened around her glass. "What kind of memories?"

"That's just the thing, I can hardly remember what I've been doing these past few weeks, not to mention the constant headaches. I think there's something wrong with me—"

Silje snorted, biting her lip as she held back laughter.

"Would you enlighten me," he said, irritated, "as to what you find so humorous?"

She rested her hand on his knee, voice patient. "You came here with this story because you wanted a bit of extra attention, didn't you?"

He straightened, indignant. "I don't need to beg for anyone's attention."

"So you agree that you made everything up?"

"I don't know, it's just…"

"There's no shame in wanting my attention." She took the glass from his hand. "After all, we never got to have our wine the other night, did we?"

He watched as she drained the remainder of his glass in a

single swig, her eyes not leaving his.

"The whiskey was fine enough."

"But don't you want more than just a drink?" She leaned so close that he caught the heady scent of whiskey on her lips. "Don't worry," she added. "I always want more." He imagined pressing his lips to the crook of her neck, sweeping his hands along the curve of her hips. The forgetful haze which had plagued him for so long cleared from his mind and he saw she waited for his answer. "Would you like that too?"

"Yes."

As soon as the word left him, Silje seized the back of his neck, crashing her mouth to his.

Gabriel returned the kiss earnestly. Silje wasn't light and gentle in her affections, there was a hunger to her touch. The magic between them crackled and sparked beneath his skin, recognizing one another. Equal parts frigid and scorching.

She slipped onto his lap, running her hand through his hair, and pulled his head back, baring his throat to her lips and teeth. A moan rose deep in his chest, and he wrapped a shaking hand around her waist. Gold behind his eyes. Fire on his skin. The presence of her magic was so strong he felt drunk.

He swept a hand from her hip, along the curve of her thigh, and suddenly she winced, drawing in a pained breath.

"Silje?" He took his hand away, concerned. "What's wrong?"

"Nothing."

But he saw the way she held herself gingerly. Through the fabric of her trousers he caught the trickle of blood.

"But your leg…it's bleeding."

"It's an old wound," she dismissed him.

"You're an Incarnate Sun. Why haven't you healed your-self?"

"I can't unless—" She fell silent, suddenly realising she'd said something she hadn't meant to.

Confusion rose with her words. Not all Incarnate Suns excelled in the magic of healing, but even the least skilled could still manage mending something as simple as a cut.

"What do you mean you can't?" he pressed. "That doesn't make any sense—"

"It doesn't matter." She moved to kiss him again, but he turned his face away and pushed her off of his lap.

"You can touch me," he said, "when you tell me the truth."

"What truth?"

"Any truth."

"You think I'm a liar?"

"I think you're not telling me something and I don't know why."

She looked as if she was about to argue, but he quickly intercepted the shift of conversation. "Didn't you say we were friends? Friends tell each other secrets, why won't you trust me with yours?"

Her face softened at his words. "I can tell you?"

"Yes," he said, relief spreading as they were finally getting somewhere. "My dear, you can tell me whatever you wish."

She moved to the divan at the end of her bed, patting the space beside her. He sat down, genuinely curious.

She exhaled a long breath before she spoke. "I have a secret I've wanted to tell you since we first met. But it's been difficult to figure out the right time." Silje fidgeted anxiously with her hands before she looked up at him, a nervous smile on her face. "It's rather embarrassing."

"You can trust me," he said, genuinely meaning it.

She gestured for him to lean down and she cupped a hand around her mouth, whispering in his ear, "Sleep and forge—"

Another wave slammed against the ship, and the entire world tilted.

He screamed as they fell to the floor. Furniture in the room slid from their places as the floor swept upward. Wardrobe doors fell open, spilling their contents across the floor.

"Silje!" He seized her hand and pulled her close, covering her body with his.

At that moment he didn't know which way was up or down. Everything felt like it was thrown out of control of both gravity and his own sense of direction.

He wrapped himself tighter around Silje, burying his face against her shoulder in an attempt to avoid the falling furniture and shards of broken glass that were swept about the room by the rolling waves.

This close to him he sensed her magic just beneath his fingertips. *It's here. I only need to reach out a little further.* He forced himself to ignore the chaos, and seized her magic, and in a rush of pain, everything he'd forgotten came rushing back to him.

How every time he and Zoe were so close to remembering the truth, Silje had guided them in exactly the direction she'd wanted. The ways in which she'd influenced them were both terrifying and incredible. Getting them to make useless plans for alliances, or in more subtle ways, making them irritable around each other, instead encouraging them to seek her out at every turn.

Then, a clearer memory, but it wasn't his own, it was Silje's.

The summer heat sweltered throughout the Verchiél palace, and Silje checked her reflection in a mirror, her eyes neither gold nor pale blue, but a dark amber like honey. Her wig of chestnut curls was tucked into a simple bun, and she was dressed in the black and gold uniform of a servant. She approached Enzo and Aria, bowing her head meekly as she served two glasses of tea.

It should have been harder, she thought in disappointment, *to kill a king and queen.*

Silje excused herself and walked back toward the stairway when a shout of laughter echoed through the halls and she slowed in her steps. Gabriel watched through Silje's eyes as he and Zoe laughed together in the courtyard.

Silje clutched the tray to herself with a white-knuckled grasp. An order had been given and a promise broken. Lives had been spared and lives had been exchanged but she had been told to take two and so she had.

Poison meant for a Sun and Moon would instead take their king and queen.

Father was going to be furious when he found out. Then she'd truly have nowhere left to turn. She stifled a giggle at the thought of him red-faced and angry. A thousand times she'd seen him in a temper, but it never ceased to amuse her. A pity she wouldn't see it in person, not that it mattered anymore. She had better things owed to her.

Her eyes lingered upon Zoe and Gabriel. The temptation to approach was excruciating. She wanted their attention. Their company. Their love. All for her.

Only for her.

And why wouldn't they choose her? After everything she'd done for them? She'd saved them. Spared them when others in her position wouldn't have batted an eye.

They were hers.

But she needed them to trust her first. See her and know her. As impatient as she was, at least it would make a fine challenge. One she would easily win.

Soon, she comforted herself. *They'll know you soon.*

She left the palace. Nobody paid the slightest bit of attention to a lone servant, even as a triumphant smile curved her lips.

They'll love you soon.

In the dim ship cabin, Gabriel and Silje gasped and broke apart.

Silje scrambled out of his arms, her golden eyes flashing brightly. Gabriel was out of breath, a raging headache tearing through his skull as he stared up at Silje with wide eyes.

"You…" He spoke between breaths. "You killed them, you started all of this. Everything we've been through, everything that's happened—" He forced himself to his feet, not taking his eyes from her. "It's all your fault."

Silje hadn't uttered a word, her gaze distant. He expected her to argue, to shout, to start a fight. But to his shock, she was silent.

"Why…why didn't you just ask for help?" he asked. "Enzo and Aria would have let you stay with us."

She shook her head. "No, I couldn't leave Niklas behind. If we'd come to Verchiél for aid as Incarnate publicly, we would have been turned away. A Bjordal citizen is one thing, but a Bjordal Incarnate can't defect to the power of another nation, exiled or not. It would have started a war."

"How do you and Niklas know each other?"

She paused, and a small smile rose on her face. "He's my

brother."

Shock coursed through Gabriel. He had a difficult time picturing the tall, flame haired Niklas beside Silje, who was so petite and pale she was nearly invisible. At this shocked look Silje added, "Half siblings technically. Though Asbjorn is the headache we both share."

"You and Niklas planned everything?"

"I was ordered to take two lives and so I did, just not the ones I was supposed to."

"King Asbjorn?" Gabriel asked, surprised. "Daughter or not, why would he work with another Incarnate? Let alone allow you to live when he knew what you were?"

"I was useful to him." She picked up a knife from the cluttered mess upon the floor. "What use is a hand without a blade? Or reach without control? I did what the king as a public figure could not."

Gabriel watched Silje flip the knife through her fingers so quickly it looked like a blur of liquid silver.

"Did Niklas kill for him too?"

Silje's hand abruptly stopped, catching the knife, and she let out a hearty laugh. "Hardly. Asbjorn always did his best to keep Niklas in the guise of a perfect little prince," she said with a slight sneer. "He even trained him as a Bjornvangar. Secretly being an Incarnate is one thing, but being an Incarnate who freely kills at the behest of the king? The people would have Asbjorn's head and strike the Osenson name from the face of the earth."

"But Asbjorn lets you do those things?"

"As the bastard daughter, I'm the exception." She offered the hilt of the knife to him. "Honestly, I just wanted a better life. For myself and Niklas"

Gabriel took the knife, speaking slowly. "Then why are we going to Bjordal?

A smile grew across Silje's face, and Gabriel realised that this was exactly what she'd been waiting to tell him.

"Niklas has Verchiél," Silje explained. "Heathland is unstabilized and once I take Bjordal, there won't be anyone left to stop us from ruling." She cupped his face in her hands, her pale eyes shining wildly. "We'll own the entirety of the Isles, all between Incarnate. Together!" She threw her arms around him, hugging him tightly.

He stood still. He didn't know what to do. In that moment she felt so impossibly small as she clung tightly to him.

"Silje?"

She looked up at the sound of her name, her face hopeful. But behind it, he heard her voice, again, stronger and more insistent than ever before.

Trust me. A Sun and Moon, we're the same. You need me. You can't live without me—

Slowly, he cupped her face. "You're right." With his other hand he gripped the knife. He leaned down to whisper in her ear. "We are the same."

He jabbed forward, but before the blade could meet flesh, his muscles seized and Silje's voice cut through his mind.

Don't move.

"Trying to trick me?" There was an unmistakable note of fondness in her voice. "Clever. But the point of any game isn't to know your opponent's next move." She grabbed the silver serpent around his forearm and pulled out the hidden flexible blade, before settling it against his throat. "It's to anticipate it."

They stood so close, eyes locked, his nose nearly touched

hers. His blade at her sternum and hers at his throat.

"We don't have to stay in Bjordal," she said. "After I finally take my throne, we can go wherever we wish. Haven't you been happy with me?"

"Only because you were fucking controlling me!"

"My poor Moon. Don't you see? With my power you could be happy all the time. You'd never have to feel anger or sadness ever again."

Despite the absurdity of the idea, it still made him pause and consider.

What if he could forget his past in Heathland? Or the terror of what it felt like to drown?

Even the small and petty things that still flitted unwelcome in his mind from time to time could be cut away: regrets over paths not taken or heartbreaks over old lovers. With Silje's power, he could even forget that Zoe abandoned him—

"You know, don't you?" Silje said. "How powerful my gifts are. I could take it all away, you'd just be…free. I can make you perfect."

Gabriel managed a smile of his own.

"You could do that?"

Her smile was radiant. "Do you want to see?"

"I think"—he leaned forward—"I'd prefer to feel it."

He knew damn well that Silje wasn't going to take no for an answer, which was fine by him. It was nearly night; all he had to do was stall for time. After all, psychotic plans aside—

She shoved him down onto the bed and kissed him deeply.

There were worse ways to spend his time.

She pinned his arms above his head. "You'll marry me?"

"Of course," he assured her.

She dragged her lips along his neck, her voice raw. "You'll love me?"

"I already do."

He'd already played such games countless times. It was all a matter of telling his chosen party what they wanted to hear, and what Silje wanted was love.

She let go of his arms to unbutton his shirt with a swiftness that impressed even him.

"What else will you give me?" she asked.

"Everything. I'll do anything for you."

Her fingers stopped before the last button, and she sat up, considering him. "Anything?"

"Anything," he echoed.

She pulled out a knife from heavens knew where and he laughed. "Don't threaten me with a good time, darling. I do love it when someone makes me scream."

Silje didn't laugh. "Do you know how many people have begged for their lives from me?"

"Probably a lot," he said, watching the steel dance between her clever fingers.

She nodded. "And do you know how I can always tell when they're trying to outsmart me?"

She didn't wait for an answer as she traced the edge of the knife from his stomach up his chest, the steel cold against his skin. "They're always so…" She brought the knife to rest at his throat. "Desperate."

He was silent, unsure how to respond, the only sounds in the cabin the crashing of waves from outside.

"I think you're desperate, Gabriel."

"I don't know what you mean."

"You do." With her other hand she brushed her fingers through his hair. "You play nice and pretend to give me what I ask for just until the sun conveniently sets and you then have enough magic to fight me because you're not strong enough to do it your-self."

She grabbed a fistful of his hair and wrenched his head back, the knife flush against his throat. "There's a reason why I'm still alive, and it's not because I'm fool enough to fall for every idiot who throws themselves at me."

"Silje." He grabbed her wrist, lowering the knife. "I love you."

For a moment he thought she wouldn't react, her eyes like ice, but eventually her gaze faltered and her lip wobbled a fraction. It was such a lonely expression that he nearly pitied her.

"Promise?"

He cupped her cheek. "I swear it."

She placed a hand over his, steady and sure, and smiled before she plunged the knife into his chest.

A scream erupted from him as pain shocked every nerve and fibre of his body.

"What the fuck—"

"Did you know if I take the knife out—" She spoke in a tone close to bored. "You'll bleed out in a matter of moments?"

"No, don't—"

She wrenched the knife out, earning another scream from him. He couldn't breathe, he couldn't move without needles of pain stabbing through every part of him. He writhed in pain and landed on the hard floor, reminded vividly of bleeding out in the palace.

"The only way you'll survive is if I heal you." She knelt

beside him. "And we both know the sun is setting."

"Silje," he begged, "please…"

"Tell me, Gabriel." She didn't move, watching him unblinkingly. "Do you love me now?"

He couldn't speak, all he knew was pain. His vision was rimmed with darkness and he began to fade. As the last rays of sun sank and Gabriel struggled to draw in a weak breath, Silje finally clasped her hand over the wound. Heat scorched from her touch; his skin was on fire. Another scream was torn from his raw throat, but when she took her hand away, the wound was gone, the only evidence that it had been there was the dried blood on his skin.

His limbs went limp, heart beating wildly in his newly healed chest.

Silje considered her bloodied hand with distaste before she licked the blood and inky black magic off her thumb. "Salty."

He breathed deeply, looking up at her. "Fuck you."

"Remember? I did tell you that I love an enemy at my feet."

Gabriel struggled to his feet as quickly as his body would allow. Even with the return of his magic he was still so weak from the brief moment of Bjordal steel inside his chest.

She offered her arm and he didn't protest, leaning against her as he walked.

"You're going to stay put in your cabin until you remember your manners."

Fuck that. He wasn't going to be locked up.

As they reached the last stair before the deck he tripped her. She was thrown off balance and it was enough to make a run for it. Except there was one problem—where was there to run to on a ship?

Gabriel climbed up on the railing.

Silje followed him at a leisurely pace, watching him with amusement. "My Moon? Where do you think you're going?"

"You want me to stay?" Gabriel shouted over the waves, the sea spray cold against his back. "I'll throw myself off."

"You hate the water."

Silje didn't seem bothered by his threat, so confident was she in his fear that she was certain there was no other alternative. It was almost certainly death, but this way, it was going to be on his terms.

"Silje," Gabriel said. "I hate you more."

He took the last step and let himself drop. Silje screamed behind him.

It felt like it lasted an eternity, just like when he was a child, but now there was no blindfold and he could see everything. See the waves crashing high around him. The dark sky that lit up with lightning beyond the clouds. A pair of beautiful golden eyes as she watched him fall.

He hit the water hard, the impact nearly knocking him unconscious. The sky was swallowed up by black waters above him, around him—everywhere. He floundered in the water, a horrible cold enveloping him, chilling him instantly to the bone.

The surface couldn't have been more than ten feet away, but in that moment felt so impossibly far. Pressure constricted and pain burnt in his lungs. He closed his eyes, fear overwhelming him, and felt himself sink. Another wave pushed him forward and he felt himself being pulled along by the current.

He kicked and thrashed and barely managed to breach the rolling waves, gasping for breath. Blinking salt water from his eyes, he spotted the ship, already so far away.

He screamed but his voice was swallowed up easily by the

raging storm.

He spotted a solitary figure standing at the back of the ship. Silje. Still as stone and perched at the back of the railing, her eyes trained on him. She didn't move, didn't speak. Her face impassive as she watched him in silence until he could no longer make out her pale form, like a ghost fading into the darkness.

Gabriel screamed as the water tossed him about like a rag doll. As soon as he sank below the water he was back there again—

Rough hands dragged him through the streets before shoving him over the barrier. Canvas scratched his skin as he thrashed and struggled out of the sack. The filth of the river filled his lungs as he'd sunk.

He breached the surface again, drawing in another heaving breath, every fibre of him wanting to scream in fear but unable to spare the breath.

So useless.

He was supposed to be a saint— a god. But when he was in the water he was useless, nothing more than a frightened child once more.

He blinked the salt out of his eyes, and in the distance, he saw it.

Land.

It was too far. He'd drown before he reached it.

He stretched out his arm, coldness surging as he managed to summon what little magic he had in that moment.

He surged forward for a moment before crashing back into the water, exhaustion spreading through him.

No, no, no—

He tried again. His chest ached from where Silje had stabbed him, the cold reaching far into his bones, and Niklas' words echoed through his mind.

You use your magic like a crutch.

He threw his head back and screamed, his throat tearing with the volume. But there was no one to hear him out here, it was just him and the dark waters again.

But when hope was gone, the one thing he always had left to cling to—

Spite.

Spite to stay fucking alive because he needed better than this.

His body screamed in protest as he forced his limbs to move, a single stroke forward—

Another wave crashed into him, sending him beneath the surface. He thrashed violently before he breached the surface once more, drawing in a heaving breath and, with it, a growl escaped him.

He made himself move, one stroke, two, three—

Wave after wave continued to crash in the storm and he was buffeted around the water, but he didn't stop to think, let alone to feel. He knew once he did, he wouldn't be able to start again.

It took a lifetime.

When his foot finally touched the sandy bottom of the shallows, he staggered forward, his limbs unused to the solid ground after so long struggling to keep himself afloat.

With much difficulty he dragged his exhausted body onto the shoreline, and whatever strength he'd managed to summon for the swim vanished and he collapsed. Darkness overtook him and his eyes drifted closed; he was desperate to remember anything other than the endless cold and Silje's golden eyes.

PART THREE
BJORDAL

Strength to those who seize it

24

DABRIA

"Desperation," Ada had once told Dabria, "is a beast of endless hunger. You feed it, but it doesn't feed you."

At the time she had still been in Grislow, in her old gang's club in the basement. Given the task of watering down crates of wine.

Grunt work. Dabria had complained, but arrived exactly on time. Knowing the mundane nature of the task would assure she and Ada would be left well enough alone for an afternoon.

"I still don't get how no one knows the difference." Dabria grimaced and watched the wine shift from the colour of dark blood to a watery red. "Tastes like horse piss once it's been mixed with the river water."

"If people are drunk enough they can't tell their heads from their asses and that's all the better for us," Ada replied cheerfully, her slender hands sorting through the bottles with practised ease. "When someone gets sick, we'll break out the good bottles again."

She winked and grinned wickedly, which caused a fluttering to rise in Dabria's stomach, making her smile along with her. *Get away with murder with a smile like that,* as the old man liked to say, slapping Ada across the shoulder with a laugh. He had a soft spot for her, but Dabria knew better. Ada was simply tolerating him. Planning for the day when she'd finally take his place as a boss.

Dabria desperately wanted to fit into this life too, but it never worked quite the way she planned. She hated the crowded club, was too impatient to gather information and not large enough to be a bruiser. Maybe she'd just become Ada's second in time. The less she had to worry about finding her place in this dump the better.

"What's the point?" Dabria re-corked the watered-down bottle and reached for the next. "Getting so wasted you don't know your own name. It's embarrassing."

Ada laughed. "Bria, my sweet, it's an escape.

All we need to do is keep the people too distracted with what we're giving them so they don't stop and wonder why they aren't getting ahead. Which keeps our pockets full and our futures bright."

Dabria's eyes dropped to the row of bottles in front of her. "What happens when we're desperate? When the beast knocks at our door?"

Ada uncorked a bottle of good wine and took a swig before offering it to Dabria.

"We feed it."

Dabria spun Niklas' silver ring around her thumb. The skin beneath was long since raw, but the pain was a welcome distraction from the scene before her.

Verchiél's coronation chamber was full to the point of bursting. The sun had set but the heat of the day lingered stubbornly, and despite the open doorways sweat ran down Dabria's back until she felt the fabric soak through. She shifted uncomfortably in the rigid jacket, tugging at the clasp of the silk half cape. She didn't know why she'd been required to dress in something so useless. Her guard uniform would have been more than acceptable in her opinion. But no one paid her the slightest glance, everyone's attention focused on the figure in the centre of the room.

Niklas stood still as ever, his face a mask of perfect calmness. She barely recognized him in the finery. His beard was properly trimmed and his red hair fell to his shoulders in soft waves, even brighter against the jet-black of his clothes. He'd been given garments befitting an Incarnate Moon of Verchiél. Dressed wholly in black and silver.

With many rows of people above him, however, it felt more like a trial than a coronation. Dabria stood at the edge of the room on the ground floor, far away enough not to be scrutinised but close enough to mark her association with Niklas.

Official Lyon, the head of the noble council overseeing the coronation, finally motioned for silence, addressing Niklas solemnly. "Niklas Aleksander Osenson, you're the only Incarnate currently remaining in Verchiél, is this correct?"

Niklas inclined his head. "To my knowledge."

Official Lyon held his gaze steady. "I will be candid. Despite the nature of your blessing, you've put this country in a very precarious position. The protests and political instability has only been the start. Though they've been momentarily quelled, many among us still question when will they end?"

Niklas' gaze faltered, his eyes darted to his feet.

Dabria scowled. They'd practised this; he had to hold it together in front of a crowd. With a few people he was a condescending asshole, but a confident one. In front of a large group, however, he collapsed in on himself. The silence stretched on, and some people in the crowd began to whisper discontentedly among themselves. Dabria ground her teeth.

"Prince Osenson?" Official Lyon asked. "Did you hear me?"

Niklas didn't reply, instead he looked back to Dabria as if waiting for her to offer an answer.

Idiot.

Keep talking, she mouthed.

"Prince Niklas?"

He looked up at Official Lyon.

"Do you have anything more to add in your defence to these claims?" she asked.

"No."

"Would you care to elaborate?" Official Lyon pressed.

"I…" He drew in a breath, no doubt trying to find the right words that he thought would make everyone happy when another of the officials snorted loudly.

"He knows he's on thin ice, that's why he's hesitating."

Official Lyon looked at the man tiredly. "Official André, please keep your personal comments to yourself."

Niklas spoke up. "My father disinherited and exiled me, I hold no power nor influence in Bjordal."

"And what's to stop you from gaining power once you've secured Verchiél as a prize for your father?" André countered.

Niklas was silent. Whether he was shocked that the man had guessed his true intentions or was thinking up what to say next, Dabria wasn't sure, but this time she didn't give him the chance to stand in awkward silence and quickly spoke up.

"Excuse me, but technically none of that's true."

All eyes in the room shifted from Niklas to her and she

froze. Dabria had never hated attention, but the sudden influx of hundreds of stares upon her was enough to make her heart race. So distracted that she hadn't realised that Official Lyon had been speaking.

"—would you explain what you mean, Captain Kimura?"

Dabria cleared her throat and spoke loud enough for her voice to carry. "Niklas has been disowned and publicly exiled by Bjordal's crown, he's technically not even a Bjordal citizen anymore." Niklas' black eyes were inscrutable, but at that moment Dabria had a feeling that he was watching her closely. "He's also one of the only people left in Verchiél who is actually qualified to rule a state, not to mention he's an Incarnate to boot. I'm no politician, but you'd be foolish not to take what he offers."

The other official, André apparently, snorted. "First Bjordal? Now Sakai? Verchiél isn't yet so small that we can't have our own people govern ourselves."

Dabria frowned. "I'm from Grislow."

This just made André laugh. "Heathland too? Heavens, we've really lost our way. In my time—"

Many voices rose and the entire chamber now openly broke into arguments. People yelled among one another while Official Lyon shouted for order with little effect.

Dabria barely resisted screaming alongside them. This was exactly why she didn't want to participate in any of this ridiculous shit. "Politician" was just a nice title for petty and psychotic individuals arguing over the best way to commodify and control people's lives. It frustrated her to no end. Just put a sword in her hand and let her solve her problems that way. She'd soon carve her way to a solution.

A sudden chill swept past her and she shivered. Beside

her, Niklas stood deathly still and silent, but she noticed the water pitcher nearest to her was slowly freezing over, until the entire thing was encased in solid ice.

"Niklas?" Dabria said.

He didn't respond, his pitch-black eyes unreadable though the unnatural cold continued to grow more severe until the pitcher cracked and splintered, shattering into many pieces, though no one other than herself seemed to notice or care as they continued to shout and fight among themselves, one particularly bold scribe going so far as to fling a book at André's face, pages flying everywhere in the process.

"Niklas." Dabria sidled closer, placing a hand on his arm and instantly recoiling back. He was as frigid as ice, frost collected on his dark clothes until it shone like stars.

"Hey, Niklas," Dabria hissed, "I know you're stressed but you really need to cut that shit out. You're going to scare people."

He met her gaze, speaking calmly. "I know."

He raised his arms and the lights in the chamber flickered. Some people began to take notice and fell silent, watching Niklas.

André still shouted loudly, his face red from the effort. "These northern bastards aren't ruling us again. I've voted against it once and I'll do so again—"

Niklas swept his arms down and all of the lights went out, gaslights bursting and candle flames blown out by the frigid chill of some unnatural wind that made the hair on Dabria's arms stand up.

A single light remained above. In the near darkness, all eyes went to Niklas, who stood calm and composed beside her.

He spoke softly. "The Treasure of the Isles, and yet you can't even decide who to lead you?"

"Prince Niklas." Official Lyon was the first to speak when she managed to find her voice. "What is the meaning of this?"

"Meaning?" He spoke calmly. "I've renounced my titles and offered to serve and still it's not enough. I cannot control my birthplace any more than I can control being Incarnate. You'll crown me or no one else."

This sent another wave of discontent through the chamber, people murmuring among themselves and watching Niklas closely.

André bristled. "Is this a threat?"

"An order." Niklas held his hand aloft. "Something you should be better acquainted with."

Niklas snapped his fingers and several figures sprang into being, similar in stature to Niklas though without proper form, made of darkness and ice in equal measure. Something reminiscent of Gabriel's magic, and it occurred to Dabria that Niklas was copying what he'd seen the damned princeling do.

They surrounded the gathered officials, and the air was charged. Once Official Lyon had picked her jaw up off the floor she sputtered. "What is the meaning of this?"

"You've never dealt with a Bjordal Incarnate before, have you?" Niklas watched her calmly. "Not that you'd ever had the chance to in the first place."

Niklas shot his hand forward and one of the shadowy figures responded, seizing André by the throat, hoisting him into the air. André gasped for breath, his face tinged with scarlet as he struggled against the unyielding grip of the magical figure restraining him.

"You were supposed to help us years ago. Bjordal Incarnate fought alongside Verchiél, against our own people for the hope of safety," Niklas said. "Instead you turned your backs on us and signed a treaty for peace with Bjordal at the cost of our own salvation. And you have the audacity to call yourselves the city of the Incarnate?" Niklas' lip curled. "Your city is built on the bones and blood of my kind."

Some of the other officials tried to pry the figure's grasp away from André, but to no avail. Whatever this thing was made of was stronger than any human.

Dabria tugged on the back of Niklas' jacket and whispered furiously, "Hey, I know I said you need to be more forceful and scary but I don't really know if this is the best way."

Niklas paused for a brief moment, considering her. "It's the only way."

He turned back to the chamber, announcing, "A final chance, to concede and crown me as you originally promised. What do you say?"

André, whose face was now tinged with purple, spat, "Go to hell."

Niklas clenched his outstretched hand into a fist and the figure mimicked his movements, crushing André's throat with a sickening crack that echoed throughout the chamber.

Someone screamed, and a collective shock passed through those gathered. Dabria included.

Oh fuck.

When she'd talked Niklas into this, she'd thought that he'd be calm and collected. Able to sway the people to their cause with some fancy bullshit royal words he always liked to use. She supposed that he had, in his own way, but the memory of Alfio bleeding out across the floor flashed in her mind and she recalled her wish to Niklas, to see him as the man she'd met on the night of the solstice.

Niklas turned to her now, a look of expectant hope on his face, and Dabria's stomach dropped when she realised—

He was looking for her approval. Even now, he couldn't act without the order of another. She'd simply taken the place of Silje.

At Dabria's continued silence, Niklas frowned and turned back to the chamber. Dabria noticed something different present in the people gathered.

Fear.

Niklas considered the chamber calmly. "Does anyone else object?"

The chamber was silent in response. The remaining officials still eyed the shadow figures with anxiety, too afraid to move lest they go the way of André.

Eventually Official Lyon found her voice, addressing the nearest servant in a whisper.

"Do as he says."

Dabria watched as the servant brought forward a circlet of silver with trembling hands. It was a wreath of twisting silver, a half moon at its centre. A crown for an Incarnate—no.

A crown for a king.

"Niklas Osenson," Official Lyon announced. "Moon of Verchiél."

Normally there would be cheers and celebration at the crowning of a new Incarnate. Instead there was only silence and fear.

Ada had only been partially right. Dabria hadn't fed the hunger.

She was the hunger.

25

NIKLAS

Niklas considered the table set before him. The tea he'd requested had been delivered with an unsettling swiftness. None of the usual colourful tins of sweet tea, but rather a simple pouch of Bjordal herbs. It was something which had clearly been scrounged up from some dusty corner of the kitchens out of desperation, but he hadn't even had a chance to thank the servant who delivered it as they swiftly fled from the room, no doubt fearing he'd be displeased.

Everyone hurried past Niklas now, nobles and servants alike. The news of the coronation had spread like wildfire and now none stopped to bother him. He supposed it came with the new territory. Beside the tea set was a letter stamped with a royal blue wax seal, a canine tooth at its centre. A letter for Dabria. Sent from Grislow. He'd read it, knowing full well she'd be livid if he had, but wanting to know who could possibly reach them. He couldn't risk her seeing it yet; she'd stood beside him during the coronation, he needed her here beside him. Not halfway across the Isles.

He opened the pouch of tea. The scent of juniper and pine wafted through the air and he inhaled deeply, the scent a comforting reminder that he was now one step closer to going home. He reached for the teapot, but the water froze over as soon as his fingers brushed it, the porcelain cracking until the entire thing shattered. The unnatural chill he'd displayed in the coronation chamber followed him, frost encasing the area around him, shadows trailing him wherever he walked. It was something he resisted, wanting to remain as human as possible, even during the night. Now as he considered the shards in silence, he leaned into the numbness.

A loud knocking at the door startled him out of his stupor, and he slipped the letter back underneath the pile of papers, hiding it.

"I'm busy," Niklas said.

"You were the one who told me to knock," Dabria replied, voice bitter. She didn't wait to be invited inside and instead entered the office, agitated and pacing. "What the fuck did I just witness back there?"

"My coronation," he replied simply.

Her frown deepened. "You know that's not what I mean, smart-ass. What the fuck were you thinking. You murdered a man in cold blood."

Niklas had needed to prove that he was serious. He'd deliberately picked André, contentious even among the most rigid of the officials as well as the oldest of the group. Another twinge of guilt rose in his gut at the memory, but he pushed it away. What was one life in comparison to what he was working toward?

"When I am received by Asbjorn, not only will I have Verchiél under my control, but I'll be able to negotiate, to change Bjordal and make it a safer place for Incarnate."

And myself, he thought.

Dabria's frown softened, though she didn't appear any more relieved by his words as she bit her lip in thought.

"Niklas… I need to tell you something."

"Can it not wait?" He moved back to the desk. Someone else could clear up the mess. "I intend to clear the protests away at the front gates—"

"I lied to you," Dabria blurted out. "About your father. He's not going to take you back. Silje just told me to say all that shit to make you think that you needed to be on the defensive."

Anger, slow and simmering.

"You wanted me to be like this," Niklas said, "so did Silje and my father and every single person who brought me here. Now you're telling me it was all for nothing?"

Ice gathered in erratic patterns at his feet, crunching beneath the soles of his shoes as he paced.

"I killed a member of the council in front of an entire court."

"I never told you to kill him," Dabria said.

Foolish. Even the last person he had left to place his trust in had manipulated him.

"I've been too lenient," Niklas decided. "Even now you've never listened, there's an order you need to learn again, even from the moment I first met you."

His eyes narrowed on her, his voice low. "Bow."

"Fuck you"—Dabria's lips curled back—"bitch."

He shot his hand forward, ice and darkness springing to life. Dabria drew her sword, anticipating his movement and cut through the first figure that materialised before her.

He shot out another hand, magic sweeping across her but she just did the same thing. Too wise to his movements.

She laughed. "Can't even kill me right. Silje was right, you are weak—"

He growled and swept his hands downward, slick ice coated the floor and Dabria slipped. Unbalanced enough that when he summoned the ice and darkness to his hands again, she was unable to dodge when his magic swept across her in a blinding rage.

She gasped, sinking to the floor, a slash of blood present across her shoulder where she'd taken the brunt of the attack.

Horror dawned over him as he realised what he was doing—what he'd almost done.

"Dabria!" He dropped to the floor, helping her sit up with delicate hands, wishing not for the first time in his life that he had been gifted the powers of an Incarnate Sun rather than a Moon. "Are you all right?"

"Fuck!" Dabria winced. "No thanks to you, you dick."

"Dabria, I'm sorry." Niklas said. "This is all my fault."

"Niklas." She placed a hand on his head and he flinched. "Would you just look at me?"

Slowly, he met her eyes. He was surprised not to see the usual fiery determination there, but a fatigue he felt deep in his bones. She was tired. They both were.

"Listen," Dabria said, "I mean, I didn't exactly help, did I? Silje told me to say that stuff to you. She was convinced that it would help, but it just made a bigger mess of things. I like it when you think before you act and drink shitty tea to be polite, it's way fucking better than whatever that was, what you were like at the winter solstice." She went quiet for a moment before she shook her head. "Fuck that shit."

Shakily she rose to her feet, and held her hand out.

"Get your royal ass up,"

He didn't rise. "How can I?"

"You know"—Dabria's lips twitched— "if I liked men I'd say that I enjoy seeing you on your knees, but this is all starting to be rather pitiful."

Her humour, as crude as it was, he recognized as an olive

branch.

He took her offered hand, standing up.

"You were doing the right thing before," Dabria said. "You know, I've never given a shit what people think of me. I think you should try it sometime."

Niklas smiled sadly. "You're a better captain than I deserve."

"And you were a better Incarnate—well, without all the killing," Dabria amended. "You listened to people. Not like the others, one was too nervous to do anything and the other was always dicking off somewhere. It would be a nice change to have more like you."

He considered at that moment one of the things he'd forgotten to tell her.

He crossed back to the desk and picked up the letter, offering it to Dabria. "This is yours. From Grislow."

Dabria's face shifted. "Where did you—"

"I feared you'd leave if you read it, but it's yours to do with as you please."

Dabria took the letter with trembling hands, her eyes swiftly reading through its contents, though he knew there was only a short message there.

She met his eyes, a vulnerability in her expression that he'd never seen before.

"Thank you," Dabria said.

"Don't thank me, it was yours to begin with."

"Dabria, I—"

She waved him away. "Don't. I'm not good with goodbyes. If you're going to do some weird magic shit just do it already."

He smiled tiredly. "Stay safe."

She flipped him off in response, the letter still clutched tightly in her other hand.

Niklas stood there, watching the space where Dabria had just been.

If she could face her past, then surely he could face his own. Niklas crossed to the desk, where he took the lock of pale hair out of the desk drawer.

Silje. He couldn't put her off any longer. He was going to face her. Not only was he going to give up what she'd spent so long trying to gain, he wouldn't answer to her anymore.

He drew the Bjordal steel knife across his palm, magic bleeding along the wound, and clutched the lock of hair tightly in his hand, closing his eyes.

He concentrated, feeling his magic seek across hundreds of miles of darkness before he caught the strands of Silje's golden magic. So far away this time...much further than he'd anticipated—

For the first time in years, Niklas stepped into Bjordal.

26

GABRIEL

Gabriel's eyes shot open and he immediately emptied his stomach.

Nothing but salt water—*disgusting*. His throat ached with thirst. He shivered and wiped his mouth, lips cracked from the dryness, forcing himself to his feet. His clothes were entirely soaked through and his feet were bare. He hadn't bothered to tie the laces of his boots, a fortunate thing as they would have only weighed him down in the storm.

He stood upon a massive beach of black sand. Further inland were sheer and towering cliffs that felt as if they reached the very heavens. Hundreds of gulls cried overhead, flying in and out of the mists.

He glared at the ocean. "Fuck you!"

As if in response, the waves crashed roughly against the shore and he hastily retreated. He resolved never to set foot inside another body of water unless it was a shallow, steaming bath. *Exactly what I need right now.* A freezing wind tore across the beach and he shivered again. A cough wracked deep in his chest and he spat up more sea water and a horrid amount of phlegm along with it.

He caught his breath and tried to remember what had happened. His mind was a jumble of confusing memories. Confronting Silje, jumping from the ship—

"Silje!" A scream was wrenched from him. "I'm not dying until you see my fucking face!" He screamed until his throat was hoarse and he was bent double coughing, his chest aching.

He forced himself to his feet, feeling a new resolve solidify. He was going to escape this miserable place and go back to Verchiél. But before any of that, he was going to find Silje—

And he was going to kill her.

He turned away from the ocean to face the cliffs. There was no way he could climb. They were hundreds of feet high, and he couldn't even see the peaks, obscured in thick mists. He looked along the beach and noticed a smaller cluster of hills that sloped gently upward. He set off, desperately hoping that Bjordal's legends of beasts and monsters the size of mountains were simply legends.

The hills, as it turned out, concealed a trail that led inland. Wedged between the massive cliffs and poorly used to the point of non-existence. But enough of a guide that he soon left the black sands and noisy gulls behind.

He marched continually upward, the path so narrow at some points that he needed to shuffle sideways to squeeze himself through. The climb wasn't a long one, but it was difficult. There was a wet, rattling noise inside his lungs that grew worse with each breath. Every step was painful to his bare feet, cold and raw from walking across the sharp rocks.

Along with it, the earth felt unsettled beneath him. He wondered if Bjordal was prone to natural disasters. It would be just his luck to be marooned and then caught in an earthquake.

He forced himself upward to the crest of the path and

emerged from the cliffs and drew in a breath at the sight below. In the valley, slopes of volcanic ash and sparse shrubs stretched out for miles, their dry stalks rattling as the wind blew through them, eventually meeting a canopy of ancient forests, with towering mountain ranges piercing the sky in the distance.

Gabriel's hope sank. There wasn't the slightest sign of any civilization. Bjordal, the largest country in the Isles, and also the least populated.

He couldn't stop shivering; he had never been so cold in his entire life. His skin was equal parts frigid and burning. He fought with the urge to simply lie down and go to sleep, he was so tired. He didn't know anything about wilderness survival. *How does one even light a fire without matches?* People were so much easier to deal with. All he had to do was smile and simper and flirt and he was brought whatever he liked whenever he liked it. But nature didn't care if he was hungry or cold. There were no bargains to be made. Only a challenge that he had no resources or knowledge to face.

He had to keep moving. Surely there would be some remote village or perhaps even a hunter's cabin he could loot. He'd kill for a pair of warm boots.

A scattering of dirt fell loose from the cliff. He cursed and brushed dust from his shoulders, looking around for the cause of a disturbance but found nothing in sight.

But if he found someone out here and played his cards right, perhaps he'd even be able spin a tragic story of abandonment and gain sympathy with some of the Bjordal citizens.

He looked too southern to pass as fully Bjordal, not sharing in the commonly pale blond or auburn-haired complexions. But perhaps he could pass as being from one of the southernmost cities near the Heathland border, after all he did speak the language fluently.

But if I'm going to find any help—He watched the afternoon sun sink lower in the sky. He needed to find it soon.

He moved to step forward but paused when he felt the earth tremble beneath him, the small fragments of stone around him shaking. He hastily picked his way down the hillside, his limbs stiff and painful. He didn't know what was happening, but if there was going to be an earthquake, he didn't want to be caught anywhere near the cliffs.

That was when he heard the first horn.

Gabriel froze, listening intently. The shaking had only grown worse and he felt it as a constant rhythm beneath his feet. Along with it a loud rumbling stretched out for minutes. The sound echoed loudly in the valley below.

He drew in another breath, blood rushing in his ears and watched as riders—dozens, perhaps hundreds—emerged from the mountain pass.

Each rode upon a sturdy grey horse; their dappled flanks shone like polished silver, their manes cut with intricate patterns. Hunting hounds yapped and barked as they ran alongside. The riders carried long, gleaming spears, rifles slung across their backs. The foremost bore flags, and Gabriel recognized the Osenson family crest of a white bear upon a scarlet backdrop.

He watched with an awe that quickly vanished when he remembered that here in Bjordal, he would be considered as good a game as any creature.

He ducked behind a boulder, a fleeting feeling of understanding sweeping through him as he imagined Niklas and Silje doing this for an entire decade. But he refused to feel pity for the man who had usurped him and the woman who'd just tried to murder him.

He held his breath and waited. The hunting party had nearly passed when another fit of coughing wracked him and he was presented with a problem.

When the night came he wouldn't have any supplies to keep himself safe or warm. He didn't have the slightest idea where the nearest civilization was, and if he didn't freeze to death, he would probably be eaten by some wild creature.

He coughed again, the pain deep. If he didn't make a choice now then he'd never get the chance to find Silje, let alone go back home to Verchiél.

"Damnit, Silje." Gabriel peeked over the top of the boulder. "I hope you're fucking happy."

Against all better judgement, he rose to his feet and ran down the hill toward the hunting party, waving his arms and shouting at the top of his lungs.

At first he thought they weren't going to hear him. Riders continued to gallop past, paying him no mind. But when he drew closer some slowed in the procession, shocked at his sudden appearance before another series of horns rang out.

At once, the party changed direction. The ground trembled beneath Gabriel's bare feet and he watched, horrified, as hundreds of riders circled him from every side.

Shouting rang through the air, words becoming indistinguishable in the sea of voices. The horses stretched powerful flanks and tossed their heads, clearly irritated at the sudden change of direction. The musky stench of their wet fur was strong.

Through it all, he made sure to keep his hands raised in a gesture of surrender. After some shouting the crowd finally parted, a semblance of order restored as a single rider forced his way to the front of the group. A pale, broad-shouldered man with thick chestnut hair and a beard. Gabriel surmised he must be in charge since he wore the largest coat, decorated with a ridiculous amount of military medals for a hunting party.

Gabriel might be a lone Incarnate in Bjordal, but he was still an unknown one. He couldn't let them know what he was, let alone that he was from Verchiél. He was going to be just another Bjordal citizen, someone who could pass by without second thought. Above all, he had to be perfectly forgettable.

Showtime.

Gabriel stumbled forward, speaking Bjordal, his accent flawless. "Takke Birgen, du'erst herr."

"This is private land," the man replied curtly, his eyes cold. "Only the royal hunt is permitted to pass."

"Beklag." Gabriel bowed low, making the sign of Birgen in the air. "But I was marooned along the coast."

Murmurs rose and many of the soldiers now eyed him with outright suspicion rather than confusion. This made Gabriel wonder if he'd said the wrong thing.

The man considered him with renewed interest. "What is your name?"

"Isak, sir. Isak Valla," Gabriel said. "But who do I have the honour of speaking with?"

The man's nose scrunched as if he'd asked an extremely stupid question. "Hakon Vollon, heir of House Osenson."

Gabriel froze. This wasn't just any soldier, this was the man who had replaced Niklas as the prince of Bjordal. The one who'd initiated a contract for his and Zoe's capture.

"Prince Hakon, it's a true honour." Gabriel bowed again,

keeping his face low, and hoped in his dishevelled state that Hakon wouldn't be able to recognize him. "Forgive me for not recognizing you immediately. It has been a rather long day."

Relief swept through Gabriel when Hakon dismissed him. "You certainly look like it. Tell me, what were you doing out in those waters?"

"I'm a hunter," Gabriel lied. "My family sent me from Torvald to trade furs in the capital."

Hakon raised a brow. "You're pretty scrawny for a hunter."

"Small game," Gabriel assured him. "But I would ask to be brought back to any town or city along your path. So I can start making my way home."

Hakon turned to one of the men beside him and they spoke in low voices, only pausing every so often to shoot Gabriel a scrutinising look.

Gabriel shivered; the cold had numbed his feet and he noted with alarm that there was a blue tinge to his skin. He coughed again, crossing his arms tightly to try to retain some semblance of warmth.

Through the sea of scarlet coats, Gabriel noticed that only three of the men wore black. Each ranged nearly a decade in age, though most appeared battle worn in some way.

Bjornvangar.

Gabriel shrank back from the black-clad trio. The motion caught the eye of the youngest of the group, a man in his twenties. Clearly their newest recruit as he had a face still free of scars and weathering, his long blond hair tied back neatly at his neck. He noticed Gabriel's lingering stare and glared in response.

Gabriel flinched when a spare coat was thrown at him, bright crimson, the material rough but warm and lined with thick fur. He pulled it on gratefully, burying his face in the fur.

"You will accompany us back to Ulvested," Hakon announced. "And stand before King Asbjorn to answer for yourself."

Something cold settled in Gabriel's stomach. Being accompanied by a near army of soldiers was one thing, being forced to speak with their king, a man famously known for his hatred of Incarnate, was another.

"I'm honoured," Gabriel said. "But surely someone as dishevelled as myself shouldn't be placed before the king." Another cough wracked him and he emphasised it for good measure. "What a disgrace I would be."

"Make no mistake," Hakon said. "Being in the presence of the king is an honour, and not one you are worthy of. Rather you've broken the law by trespassing upon royal lands. As such you are required to answer for your crimes."

Gabriel bit back a screech of frustration, forcing himself to take a measured breath. *It's fine. I can still work my way out of this.* He'd play along and accompany them into the city where there were more places to hide, then he'd slip away the first chance he got. *Easy.*

"How generous," Gabriel said with as much cheer as he could muster and reached for the reins the nearest soldier held. "Do I get a horse too?"

The soldier yanked the reins from his hand and barked into the crowd.

"Edvin!"

The crowd shifted and the young blond man approached cautiously on horseback.

The soldier nodded to Gabriel. "The trespasser rides with you."

Gabriel edged away, dread coursing through him that out of the entire party, he'd been placed with one of the Bjornvangar.

Edvin didn't seem to like the idea either as he scowled and opened his mouth to protest, but the lingering eyes of Hakon appeared to drive away these thoughts. Edvin snapped his mouth shut and gave a silent nod.

The soldier rode ahead, pausing only long enough to mutter to Edvin. "Perhaps he could teach you a thing or two about hunting. Maybe you'd even manage to snare a rabbit."

Edvin's face flushed and his eyes fell to the ground. He waited until the men rode further away before he kicked his horse forward and reluctantly offered Gabriel a hand. "Opp!"

Gabriel looked at the large horse with fear. Yet another thing far out of his area of expertise. "Yes, but *how* do I get up?"

Edvin muttered something low under his breath before he got down from the horse, holding his hands out as he helped Gabriel up into the saddle.

Laughter rose as nearby soldiers watched him scramble into the seat of the saddle. Gabriel might have been embarrassed had he not been entirely focused on not falling onto his face.

"It's very high up here," Gabriel laughed nervously. "Be careful not to drop me."

"I won't drop you," Edvin snapped, seating himself behind Gabriel before he snatched the reins out of his hands.

The other two Bjornvangar moved forward, one paused to smirk at Edvin.

"Have fun, little bear."

Laughter echoed among them and Gabriel watched them ride further ahead, feeling the tension in Edvin's body as he steered them to the very back of the hunting party.

Gabriel waited until they were far enough away from the rest of the group before he spoke to Edvin. "Why don't we get to ride with them? Aren't you all Bjornvangar? And why did they call you a little bear?"

"Do you always ask so many questions?" Edvin growled.

"You don't know this yet since we've only met," Gabriel explained, "but I *really* love the sound of my own voice."

"If I answer, will you shut up?"

"I'll listen, is that a start?"

Edvin was silent for a long moment before he spoke in a quiet voice. "This was my first hunt as a Bjornvangar. As is custom, the king chose our quarry and I was to take down the beast."

"What creature did he choose?" At Edvin's silence, Gabriel added with a grin, "Not a rabbit I suppose?"

"Elk," Edvin answered curtly.

"An impressive choice," Gabriel said. "So why is the mighty Bjorvangar so moody?"

"Made a new friend, Edvin?"

A pair of scarlet-clad soldiers slowed their horses to ride alongside them. Edvin tensed, discomfort radiating through him.

"No," Edvin replied, stone-faced.

"That's a shame," the other man said with a smirk. "You could use at least one."

This sent a ripple of laughter between the pair, and Gabriel heard Edvin's jaw grinding.

"My good gentlemen," Gabriel said. "My travelling companion here was just telling me about your thrilling tales from the hunt."

"It's none of his concern," Edvin quickly answered.

"Don't be such a miserable lump, Edvin," the first man

said.

"It's a damned good story," the other added.

"What happened?" Gabriel asked, ignoring Edvin's scowl.

The two men shared a smirk before the first spoke. "I said, why's he the one who gets to hunt this year? I realise it's tradition and all, but he's the worst out of the whole group—"

The other nudged him. "Get to the point."

"Right, anyways," the man continued. "Twenty feet away. Right in front of him. The biggest elk I've ever seen, like old Skagen himself had walked back on the earth. It practically served itself up on a dinner plate and he still missed his shot."

"You're right. That is embarrassing." Gabriel looked at Edvin. "I've had a horrible day but I'm still glad I'm not you."

At this the men guffawed with laughter, many heads turned at the source of the noise. Edvin's face burned scarlet. "Always a pleasure, but if you'll excuse us—" Edvin kicked the horse ahead and moved to the outer edges of the group.

Edvin waited until they were out of earshot before he hissed at Gabriel. "If you don't keep quiet I'm going to drop you. It's bad enough that I'm stuck at the back of the hunt, watching you like a lost child, without you humiliating me."

"You say that like it's a bad thing. I'll have you know that I'm rather interesting to watch." Edvin was silent, though his pale eyes seethed with anger. "Let's talk about something happier," Gabriel said, attempting to change the subject. "Do you have anyone special in your life?"

"Bjorvangar aren't allowed to take partners until their tenth year of service," Edvin replied in a practised voice.

"What year are you in?"

"My first."

Gabriel gagged. "What's the point of living? You have nine years of misery ahead of you."

"It's an honour to serve my country and king."

"You don't sound enthusiastic."

Edvin looked past Gabriel to Hakon at the front of the group before answering in a quiet voice, "We've spoken enough."

Gabriel was about to protest but another series of horns rose through the air and the riders all picked up speed. Edvin grunted and kicked his horse into a canter, which made Gabriel lurch, seizing the horse's mane and hoping dearly that Edvin would keep his word that he wouldn't fall.

The ashy slopes soon gave way to an ancient forest.

To Gabriel, it felt like another world. Here the trees were so tall that he had to tilt his head back to peer up into the snowy canopy, and wide enough for dozens of people to fit across their trunks.

A pathway had already been carved through the snow. No doubt the trail they'd forged when they first set out.

Every so often a horse would kick up a patch of ground and he was struck by the scent of greenery and damp earth as they rode beneath the massive evergreen trees.

Edvin slowed the horse as the party came to a momentary halt, only long enough for Hakon to leave a twisting wreath of ash and juniper branches at the start of the forest.

"An offering," Edvin explained to Gabriel, "for safe passage."

Out of each of the three countries, Bjordal still held nature and everything in it in a much higher regard than Verchiél and especially industrialised Heathland. Even though Birgen was now the only accepted god, old traditions remained rooted firmly.

Between the fresh air and the sturdy weight of Edvin's arm wrapped around him after he'd nearly fallen during a downhill passage, Gabriel started to drift off. Falling in and out of a fitful sleep before the loud call of another horn made his eyes shoot open.

He startled awake but Edvin caught him, an edge of irritation to his voice. "Told you I wouldn't drop you."

They weren't in the wilderness anymore. They now stood at the gates to a massive snow covered city. Ulvested. Capital of Bjordal and home of the royal family.

The city was composed of many wooden and stone buildings painted in colours of blue, red and yellow. Everything was covered in a thick layer of snow, and though all of the windows were illuminated with gold, Ulvested gave off the distinct impression of an illustration from a children's storybook.

The day had grown cloudy and dark and Gabriel hadn't expected anyone to be outside in the cold. But at the sight of the procession, citizens rushed to the edges of the road to watch them pass with wide smiles and cheers. Some tossed sprigs of fresh-cut pine and holly along their path, the air filled with the scent of sap and greenery.

Most were focused on Hakon and the Bjorvangar at the front of the group, but a few eyes lingered upon Gabriel, staring at his bare feet and borrowed coat with strange looks.

Despite himself, Gabriel smiled and waved before Edvin swiftly slapped his hand, voice stern. "It's a ceremony. Not a parade."

"Those sound like the same thing to me."

"There's no ceremony without cause."

"Because you ruined the ceremonial hunt?"

"There's still time to drop you."

As they rode on, the scent of ash stung Gabriel's nose and they passed the smouldering wreckage of a burnt house. Many people went to and from the still-smoking ruins, clearing the mess. Gabriel recognized a pastor of the Church of Birgen making prayers over the ruined structure while the people watched on.

Gabriel nodded to the symbols painted upon the charred wood. "What are those?"

Edvin gave him a strange look. "Don't they have heksun in Torvald?"

Heksun. Cultists.

To some, heksun meant the recluse covens in the furthest reaches of the wilds whose supposed deeds of blood rituals and sacrifices sounded more like wild gossip than anything. But mostly it meant practitioners of the old gods, Bjordal's oldest religion.

"I thought heksun were all hiding in the wilds?" Gabriel said.

"Normally, yes. But they've grown bold in the past few years. Coming into larger towns and cities, and now this—" He nodded to the piles of burning wood. "They claim the king corrupts this country. That by exiling his son, he's committed heresy against the old gods."

Gabriel watched as the smoke rose high in the grey sky. "Why don't they just paint over them? It seems like such a waste."

"Birgen demands purification. To cover up corruption is to only assure its continued rot. But to burn it away entirely is to ensure that something new can take its place."

"What about the people whose homes have been vandalised?"

Edvin shrugged. "They rebuild."

"What do you believe?"

"Does it matter?"

"It should."

Edvin looked at him strangely before growing silent, tugging irritably at the collar of his coat. Suddenly men shouted out orders and some rode ahead of the hunting party. Gabriel looked ahead and drew in a breath, understanding why.

Castle Osenson towered high on the cliff, above the city and surrounding pine forests. It was a structure of weathered grey and green stone, and it was clear to Gabriel that it had grown old long before the Verchiél palace had ever been built. The area immediately grew darker as they passed under the entry gate, through the thick stone walls. Gabriel's awe quickly fell away when he heard the sound of the large gates closing behind them

The hunting party finally came to a halt at the castle entrance. Soldiers began to dismount and castle servants immediately bustled into action to greet them.

"Wait here," Edvin ordered as he dismounted. "I need to find out what I'm supposed to do with you."

"Would you find me a pair of boots while you're at it?" Gabriel asked. "I think some of my toes fell off during the ride."

Edvin grunted and walked into the crowd. Gabriel watched until Edvin was out of sight before he slid off the back of the horse. This was his chance. He could sneak away with the rest of the crowd and leave through one of the many castle gates. Long before Hakon ever saw him.

He limped forward, struggling to walk on frozen feet and muscles stiff from many hours of sitting in a saddle.

"And where do you think you're going?" A sturdy hand

clamped upon his shoulder and he was pulled backward. Gabriel looked into the faces of the other two Bjornvangar, hunting hounds at their sides.

"Just stretching my legs," Gabriel said.

"Interesting," The second man stepped forward. "Considering that you have an entire yard to walk around."

"Too crowded for me," Gabriel assured him, trying to edge away.

One of the hounds let out a low growl at his presence, hackles rising, and Gabriel swiftly backed away. The hunting hounds, much like the horses, were an uncanny silver. The wretched creatures were much larger than a regular dog, and Gabriel got the feeling that they wouldn't mind taking a bite out of him as much as any game they regularly stalked. He'd never much cared for animals, especially not when they were large enough to maul him.

"Sva! Haelen," the man said, tugging sharply on the dog's leash. "Odd," he looked at the hound quizzically. "She's never done that with anyone before."

"She must know I'm a cat person," Gabriel said dryly. Doing his damnedest to stay as far away as humanly possible without trying to appear like he was actively running away.

Over their shoulders, Gabriel watched Edvin approach. In the presence of the other Bjornvangar, Edvin slowed, looking like one of the hounds about to be beaten.

The eldest turned to Edvin. "Why didn't you bring him with you?"

"We caught him wandering toward the gates," the other added, not giving Edvin time to respond.

"Give me your hands," the eldest ordered Gabriel.

Before Gabriel could protest, a pair of heavy bracers was

clamped over his wrists.

The man slipped the key into his coat before shrugging at Gabriel's expression. "Hakon's orders."

Gabriel hummed thoughtfully, trying to keep the note of panic out of his voice. "I don't love these. They make me feel, dare I say it? Like a prisoner."

"You are a prisoner."

The Bjornvangar immediately stood at attention as Hakon approached. "Until King Asbjorn has decided otherwise." Now that he was on foot, Gabriel was alarmed to see that he was one of the tallest men present, though unlike Niklas' lean form Hakon was all stocky muscle.

Hakon's stare was icy. "I understand that there's been word of a heksa trespassing into Bjordal."

At that a silence descended over the yard. Men muttered among themselves, some backing away while others rested their hands on their weapons, even Edvin stared at Gabriel with renewed interest.

"Heksa?" Gabriel gave a hearty laugh more out of nerves than anything else. "Prince Hakon, surely there must be some mistake."

"You've been caught—"

"Rescued?" Gabriel chanced.

"Trespassing on royal lands under suspicious circumstances," Hakon finished gruffly. "Forbidden to all without direct permission from the Osenson family, and as such you will provide answers for your actions as well as provide proof of your humanity."

A quiet voice broke the tension between them.

"Mon prins?" Edvin spoke up. "Perhaps he doesn't need to

wear those while he's under our watch?"

"Are you questioning my decisions?"

"No," Edvin said quickly. "But—"

Hakon struck Edvin across the face, the force of the impact knocking him to the ground.
The entire yard went silent. People determinedly avoided the scene as they rushed back to their duties.

Edvin clutched a hand to his face, his bottom lip split and bleeding. Hakon knelt before Edvin. "You've already ruined the hunt, now you speak where you shouldn't." He seized the front of Edvin's coat. "Do I need to have another chat with your father?"

Edvin bowed his head. "Apologies, mon prins."

"Good. Then take care to remain quiet." Hakon brushed the dirt off his coat. "And orderly."

Hakon stormed away, barking orders with renewed force, the two Bjornvangar following him with their hounds in tow.

Gabriel moved forward to help, but Edvin shook his head, getting to his feet on his own. "Don't. He'll be angrier if he sees."

"What an ass," Gabriel said.

Edvin wiped his bleeding lip. "He's not usually this bad. But ever since he heard the news of the eksil's reappearance, he's been insufferable."

Gabriel didn't need to ask to know who the eksil was; the most notable exile of all was Niklas.

"Why?" Gabriel asked with some surprise. "If he's an Incarnate then he can't take his father's throne regardless."

Edvin frowned, taking his hand away from his bleeding lip. "Incarnate?"

Gabriel cursed himself. He'd grown so used to the term that he'd never given it a second thought. In Bjordal there was no such thing as Incarnate. There were only heksa. Cursed ones.

Gabriel tried to keep the strain from his voice. "Yes. That's what I meant. But I'd just heard the news from a Grislow customer not long ago. It must have stuck in my mind."

Edvin gave him a strange look, appearing as if he was about to say more but was interrupted by the shout of another soldier. Edvin immediately stood at attention.

"Time for the audience." The man nodded to Gabriel. "Bring that one while you're at it."

Gabriel's chilled skin burnt painfully when he entered the warm interior of the castle. He'd been given a fresh change of clothes and leather boots two sizes too big, before being forced to drink a hot concoction with the consistency of sap and taste of something long since past fermentation. He might have thrown it up had it not been stuck in his throat. It calmed his cough, and the heavy feeling in his chest settled to a more manageable amount.

Tension grew as a group of soldiers in crimson flanked him from every side. Passing through the halls, Gabriel noted the layout; it was clear how the castle had evolved over generations. Wood replaced by stone, that in time had been overlaid with a more delicate touch of gold and brass decor, which couldn't entirely hide the roughened nature of the structure.

Aged wooden carvings remained upon doorways and pillars in intricate, swirling designs of animals and forests, while fine oil paintings in gilt frames graced the cold stone walls. The majority of which were royal hunts and vast landscapes, but one larger canvas caught his eye: A woman dressed in a royal blue and silver bunad. Her amber eyes were soft and her thick honey-blond hair was piled in braids across her head. Her hand was offered to a young boy who stood at her side. Clearly her son, as he shared all her features, except for a head of bright auburn hair.

Gabriel paused, staring up at the sullen expression on the child's face before a hand shoved him sharply in the back, forcing him forward.

The procession entered and a great din rose from those already gathered. It was a sprawling chamber filled with nobles and servants alike who were all gathered around the figure seated on the throne.

Asbjorn Osenson. Looking at Niklas' father was like staring at a distorted reflection, familiar but at the same time entirely different. He was a tall and sturdy man in his late fifties. His hair and well-trimmed beard a greying auburn, his eyes the palest blue. The chamber hushed as Hakon strode toward Asbjorn, pausing only to bow before he approached the throne.

"Mon kogen, this year's hunt has been a failure. Bjornvangar Edvin Sørensen was unable to bring down his quarry."

A murmur went through the crowd. Gabriel caught the snatches of shared sentiments, people muttering about bad omens and the Bjornvangar. growing weak.

Much to his credit, Edvin held the king's gaze steady as he approached. He bowed low, though Gabriel saw how his face was tinged with scarlet. "Beklag, mon kogen."

Asbjorn considered Edvin before he spoke thoughtfully. "We will see that your training regimen is increased. In the meantime your duties will be revoked to that of an initiate. Your family will hear of your actions. Particularly your father."

Edvin bowed lower, the hand upon his chest shaking. "Ja,

mon kogen."

"After which you will be required to miss the feasts you failed to provide for." Asbjorn waved a hand sharply, sparing no words for the dismissal.

The motion was enough to make Edvin retreat swiftly back to his spot with the two Bjornvangar. Discontent whispers and even some open curses were thrown his way.

Asbjorn addressed Hakon. "What else have you brought that's caused so much upheaval? I haven't heard so many whispers in quite a time."

Hakon gestured for the soldiers to bring Gabriel forward, but Gabriel swiftly stepped out of their grasp and approached the dais. He bowed to Asbjorn exactly as he'd seen Hakon do, with his left hand over his chest, and spoke the formal greeting in a flawless Bjordal accent.

"Mon kogen, er en heurne."

Hakon inhaled sharply at the interruption, but Asbjorn eyed Gabriel's battered appearance and borrowed soldier's coat before he addressed Hakon with some irritation. "You've brought me a vagrant?"

"Our hunting party found him in the middle of Svartik. In the furthest reaches of royal territory near the coast," Hakon said.

A flicker of interest appeared across Asbjorn's face before he asked Gabriel: "Where do you hail from?"

"Torvald," Gabriel answered. "My family owns a tannery and I was sent to trade furs."

"Where are your furs?" Asbjorn asked.

"I lost them."

"You lost what you were sent to trade?"

"After my boat was wrecked along the beach," Gabriel lied

quickly, "my cargo was swept away by the sea."

Hakon stepped forward, speaking loudly enough that the entire room could hear. "And yet no one with a sane mind would venture out into those waters in the midst of winter."

"In all fairness, your majesty," Gabriel countered, "I never claimed anything about being sane."

A few snatches of laughter echoed throughout the chamber, only causing Hakon's frown to deepen, but Asbjorn looked thoughtful. "What is your name?"

"Isak, mon kogen. Isak Valla."

"Isak," Asbjorn explained patiently, "are you aware of the severity of trespassing on royal lands?"

Past the window the sun was sinking fast. He needed to play his cards carefully; time wasn't on his side.

"It was born out of dire need," Gabriel reassured him. "I never would have trespassed if I had no other choice."

Asbjorn nodded. "A fair answer."

Hope surged through Gabriel's chest, and he bowed low, trying not to let the excitement trickle into his voice. "I thank you for such fair counsel. However I would now ask to part from your generous company—"

"A moment." Asbjorn held up a hand. "Isak? Are you aware of the individuals in the Isles who exist as heksa?"

Like your son? Gabriel wanted to say but bit his tongue, instead replying in a grave voice, "I am aware of the state of unnaturalness in which they exist."

"Then you must also be aware," Asbjorn continued, "that there's a search happening within the Isles for someone of your exact description."

Gabriel felt the weight of hundreds of eyes on him.

"Search?" he asked dumbly.

Hakon snapped his fingers and a servant brought forward a thick roll of paper that Hakon snatched up, reading importantly. "A nationwide search has been issued for the capture of two Verchiél fugitives. One bearing the description of a man: aged twenty-six, with pale, freckled skin and black hair."

Gabriel laughed. "I didn't take you for a man of humour. But this must surely be some sort of joke?"

Hakon turned the paper in his hands, revealing startlingly accurate sketches of both his and Zoe's faces.

Gabriel turned toward Asbjorn imploringly, feeling desperation take hold over him. Though he knew he'd find no mercy from the man who'd turned his own son away for the same reason. "I'll gladly answer for whatever crimes I've committed while trespassing. But I've no idea what Prince Hakon speaks of. I'm a Bjordal citizen—"

The whispering grew louder, and Gabriel felt walls closing in around him. Playing dumb was getting him nowhere. He needed to change his tactic. Outrage would have to do.

"I understand the pressures of your search." Gabriel's voice rose until it carried across the chamber. "But being forced to stand here as a citizen of this country and defend myself as you accuse me of treason?"

"We don't need to accuse you of anything," Hakon said. "You'll tell us everything we need to know soon enough."

Gabriel looked up; past the thick glass of the high windows, the sun was low and the final rays of deep golden light were fading fast.

"If it pleases you," Gabriel said with much difficulty, "I'll gladly stay longer. Though I'm afraid you'll find nothing more at the end of this search than disappointment. I would hate to be the cause of any further wasted time for the royal family."

Asbjorn spoke. "If my son has made a mistake in his judgement, we'll gladly pardon you for the inconvenience caused by this display. However the sun sets as we speak, it's of no wasted time to us."

Gabriel looked between them, seeing the patient interest in Asbjorn's eyes and the fervour in Hakon's. It was like Edvin had said, this adopted prince was desperate to prove himself. What better way than to capture an Incarnate trespassing through their lands?

Here he was in the very heart of Bjordal, about to reveal himself in front of the king and his court. As the final rays of sunlight vanished behind the forested mountains, Gabriel did the only thing he could think of.

He closed his eyes.

Muttering spread throughout the room. Some people laughed. One of the guards shouted for silence but through it all, Asbjorn's voice rose, a tension evident where it hadn't existed before.

"Why are your eyes closed?"

"Ah, you see I was, er…" Gabriel spoke clumsily, words escaping him in a panic. "I was nearly blinded by the snow and I'm still feeling the effects—"

A sudden, sharp whack to Gabriel's ribs startled him and his eyes shot open.

Someone shouted. Collective shock passed through the chamber, nobility and servants alike, before it settled into a horrible tension. Whispers were exchanged, some in anger and others with fear, one even went so far as to spit on the floor, disgust clear on their face.

Even the soldier who had just struck Gabriel took a cautious step back.

Hakon was the only one who smiled, triumphant as he leapt down from the dais. "I told you all and I was right!" He barked out orders to the gathered soldiers who drew their weapons, surrounding Gabriel in a tight circle from every side.

Gabriel backed away from Hakon, but not before he managed to seize the lapel of his coat, dragging him forward. "A snake in the midst of us this entire time. Arrest him."

"Just wait a damned minute! You were just about to pardon me and now you're locking me up?"

"You've lied to not only a prince but a king"—Hakon gestured with disgust to Gabriel's eyes—"and concealed the nature of what you truly are."

"You know what?" Gabriel said. "Niklas was much politer than you. And that's really saying something considering that he usurped me."

At the mention of Niklas, Hakon's eyes blazed anew with anger. "How dare you speak that traitor's name in this place—"

"Niklas, Niklas, Niklas!" Gabriel shouted. "He's not even in Bjordal anymore but he still managed to become a real prince, didn't he?"

The words stung Gabriel as well, but witnessing the look of rage they incited in Hakon was well worth the effort. Hakon moved to strike him but Asbjorn rose to his feet and silence immediately fell throughout the room.

The old king hadn't taken his eyes from Gabriel, his voice when he next spoke so quiet that Gabriel nearly missed it.

"Niklas?"

Gabriel realised it wasn't a statement. It was a question.

Gabriel shoved Hakon away and addressed Asbjorn. "Niklas Osenson usurped myself and the Sun of Verchiél. We were forced to flee the country for our lives. Please," Gabriel pleaded. "You can't lock me away. I have information you need to hear."

"Why are we listening to more of his lies?" Hakon drew a sword from his belt and people screamed. "Let's cut the head from this snake and be done with it."

"Hakon," Asbjorn said in a weary voice. "Stand down."

Reluctantly Hakon sheathed the sword, looking like a child who had just been denied a great treat.

Asbjorn nodded to Gabriel. "Speak, heksa."

"There's an assassination plot against you led by one of your own citizens."

Hakon scoffed. "The king is an important man. Do you expect us to believe every little—"

"Orchestrated by a woman of the name Silje Osenson," Gabriel said. "Your daughter."

Many people whispered anew, casting incredulous to disbelieving looks between Asbjorn and Gabriel. Hakon was among them as he openly laughed. "What did I tell you? There's no truth in this creature. Our king has no daughter."

But Gabriel focused only on Asbjorn. For the first time during their entire conversation, Gabriel saw a true reaction from Asbjorn: his eyes widened, knuckles whitening.

"Leave him," Asbjorn said.

The soldiers halted in their restraint of Gabriel, looking at Asbjorn with shock. "Mon kogen?"

"Leave him!" Asbjorn boomed.

As if scalded, they unhanded Gabriel, confused looks

thrown his way. Hakon wasn't the only person who looked at Asbjorn with disbelief. "You're letting him speak?"

Asbjorn ignored Hakon and declared to the room, "Everyone but Prince Hakon and the heksa, *out*. I wish to have a private audience."

A mixture of relieved and disappointed murmurs came from the gathered crowd. Nobles glad to leave as the chamber doors opened, guards curious while they watched Asbjorn. Only once the doors shut and they were left with the three of them did Asbjorn continue.

"Where is she?"

Anger sparked once more as his last memories of Silje ran through his mind. "The last time I saw her she was trying to kill me after I proposed to her so I jumped into a storming ocean instead. Why do you think I was stranded?"

Hakon laughed. "She must have really hated you to not only refuse a proposal, but also want you dead because of it."

"She wasn't trying to kill me because of the proposal, you ignorant twat!" Gabriel snapped.

Asbjorn's eyes narrowed. "How did you know each other?"

"What I'm far more interested in," Gabriel said, "is how you and Silje know each other."

"She is a minor noble in Bjordal's court."

"That's not what she told me," Gabriel said. "She said that she's your daughter and that for years you've been using her for political sabotage and assassinations for Bjordal, or more specifically your personal gain."

Hakon gave a hearty laugh. "What a ridiculous story."

"She even told me." Gabriel continued, "that you sent her to murder me and my co-ruler."

Asbjorn stepped forward, rising to his full height, and Gabriel backed away, startled to see that he was taller even than Niklas.

"Whatever she's told you is a lie." He leaned forward, his voice dangerous. "Silje is a liability. There are reasons why I keep her in my sight."

"Are those reasons why she was in Verchiél as well?"

"Hakon." Asbjorn didn't take his eyes from Gabriel. "Please escort our prisoner to his cell."

Hakon moved forward but Gabriel stepped out of his grasp, playing his last card. "I can help you find her."

"Don't listen to the heksa," Hakon said. "I can have an entire squadron of my men sent out within the hour. We'll scour the city."

"We're the same. Incarnate…heksa," Gabriel corrected him. "We have a connection, a bond if you will."

Hakon muttered something under his breath in disgust but Asbjorn was silent for the longest time yet, his eyes not leaving Gabriel's before he spoke slowly.

"Did she accept this…proposal?"

"Of course," Gabriel said, defensive. "Anybody would be foolish not to—"

"So you mean something to her." Asbjorn spoke more to himself than to Gabriel or Hakon. "Something which she didn't want anybody else to have."

"Er, I suppose," Gabriel said, unnerved by the sudden intensity with which Asbjorn was considering him. "She loves attention, but more importantly she loves to show off. Throw an event big enough and I'm certain she'll come to you. You won't need to waste any time searching and you can find her on your own turf."

Asbjorn nodded. "What event would you suggest?"

"Well, I for one would love some sort of party. If you give me the chance I'm certain I can throw something exceptional. It'll make up for the fact that this year's hunt has gone awry."

Hakon scowled. "We're not wasting our resources on such foolish things, especially not letting a heksa plan it."

"Please," Gabriel said. "You wouldn't know good taste if it was shoved up your ass. Just look at you—" Gabriel gestured to his medals. "Do you wear so many of those ridiculous things to warn people you're coming?"

Hakon reached for the hilt of his knife before Asbjorn clapped his hands, demanding their attention.

"If she realises you're still alive"—Asbjorn looked at him closely—"she'll come back and find you."

"Now the way you're saying that makes me think that you're going to use me as bait."

"That's a good idea," Hakon agreed

"Now, you think it's a good idea?" Gabriel snapped. "When it involves my bodily harm?"

"An event large enough that even she will not be able to resist it?" Asbjorn said. "I do believe that we can make up for the failure of the hunt yet. Our men abandoned the hunt in the noble pursuit of capture of a foreign heksa spy instead." Asbjorn's eyes alighted upon him. "Gabriel Capello, you will be executed by firing squad on the eighteenth day of Frost."

A numbness spread through Gabriel. That was only three days from now. "Why would I help you if you're just going to kill me regardless?"

"Or I could kill you now?"

He'd spent too long, clawed his way out of too many near

misses and horrible places to die now. He couldn't give up before he'd exhausted every other possibility. He was desperate and they knew he was going to cling onto any deal he got just to see another day.

"I'll take your deal," Gabriel spoke through gritted teeth.

Asbjorn nodded to Hakon. "Send for some of the guards to take our prisoner to a cell until further notice. The people of Bjordal have not seen the execution of a heksa for quite some time. I'm certain it will encourage them for the times to come."

As the guards were summoned to drag him from the throne room with rough hands, Gabriel glanced back over his shoulder.

Hakon still glared, obviously disappointed that he hadn't gotten the chance to kill him right then and there. But Gabriel ignored him, instead focusing on Asbjorn, whose familiar pale eyes held him with an unnerving intensity.

He was going to escape this place or die trying.

27

ZOE

Tromvik was Bjordal's largest port. Racks of dried fish lined the dockyard market while a massive whale carcass was harvested by the docks. Hundreds of gulls flew overhead, screeching and diving to snatch up what scraps they could.

Crews of Bjordal and Sakai worked alongside each other. The nations always had a closeness that Verchiél had lacked, partially from a location standpoint, but also for many generations now, crews of whalers and fishers had worked together, sharing their knowledge and lessening the dangers of their trade on the open waters.

Since this was a larger port city with many travellers, Zoe found that she didn't stand out as much with her deep brown skin among the pale Bjordal. Though she still drew curious glances when people overheard her speaking Verchiél with Silje. As curious as Zoe was about the sights around her, she didn't have the chance to explore as all her attention was currently on the woman before her.

Zoe and Silje sat at a small wooden table at a cramped inn, both at a stalemate. After Silje unlocked her from her cabin, Zoe hadn't screamed or fought as she'd wanted to. Instead she walked out as calmly as she could manage, knowing full well that between her lack of knowledge of Bjordal, and needing to hide her golden eyes, she was going to need Silje's help.

Not that she wanted it.

Silje smiled and in an attempt to break the tension, or because she genuinely thought it was an appropriate point of conversation, said:

"My dear, what's wrong? You've barely touched your Rømmegrøt."

Zoe frowned, pushing her plate away. "I'm not eating anything you're giving me."

Silje clucked her tongue, growing annoyed. "You need to trust me."

Zoe picked up the butter knife closest to her, the weight reassuring in her hand. "You murdered my adoptive parents, kidnapped me and Gabriel, not to mention you've been erasing our memories. Have I left anything out?"

Silje considered this. "I went to a casino and played Malizia instead of speaking to the council."

Zoe glared. "Not making this any better."

Silje reached across the table as if to take her hand, but Zoe only pulled away and gripped the butter knife harder.

Silje laughed. "My darling, do you honestly think that's a weapon?"

"Do you think it won't hurt if I stab you in the eye?"

Silje smiled and rested her head on her hands. "You're adorable."

Zoe fumed, about to argue, when the server brought several plates of food to their table. Zoe recognized a loaf of dark bread, dried fish and, surprisingly enough, waffles.

Zoe's stomach lurched at the sight of it; she couldn't remember the last time she'd eaten. Silje had left an abundance of food in her cabin, but Zoe hadn't eaten a single bite, not trusting her not to have tampered with it in some way.

Silje, sensing her hunger, stated, "It's not poison. I promise."

When Zoe still didn't touch the meal, Silje plucked up a waffle and took a hearty bite, raising her brow as if to make a point.

Zoe took one, famished. The buttery dough melted in her mouth, crystals of sugar providing a blissful sweetness.

They ate in silence for a time. Only once the platter was nearly empty and Zoe's stomach strained did she meet Silje's eyes again, noticing her watching her closely.

"I don't understand it," Silje said.

"Understand what?" Zoe asked.

Silje frowned, confused. "Why leave when you can stay here?"

"What's here for me?"

"Me," Silje said simply.

"Gabriel doesn't belong to you, neither do I," Zoe said.

Silje rolled her eyes. "It's not a matter of belonging, it's a matter of existing. We've always been connected, whether you knew it or not." Silje touched her hand and even then, Zoe's skin pricked with golden warmth. "You can feel it too, I know you can."

Zoe didn't have time to unpack all this. She pulled her hand away, even as the magic that existed beneath her skin ached for Silje's touch.

"It's not that simple," Zoe said.

There was something like pain, or loneliness in Silje's face, but before Zoe could say anything more the front door burst open, a cold wind sweeping through the establishment.

More than one patron's gaze was drawn to the group that entered. Several men dressed in bright scarlet, and Zoe recognized the sigil of the Osenson bear emblazoned on their arms. Soldiers.

"Look at me," Silje whispered, and Zoe didn't need to be told twice, hastily ducking her head, pulling the brim of her hat lower over her eyes even though they were currently their usual dark brown. The result of Silje's illusion cast over them both.

Silje continued speaking calmly and happily to Zoe, though now she spoke in Bjordal. Zoe didn't fully understand what she was saying, but she didn't need to. It was meant to be camouflage, nothing more.

Zoe kept her eyes focused on Silje, nodding along with her words as if she was listening intently. Zoe had nearly thought they were in the clear as the soldiers took seats at a table across the establishment, but as they passed by one man caught sight of them and hesitated, saying something to the others before he approached the table.

Silje's eyes flicked from Zoe to the intruder, though she smiled sweetly. Zoe immediately recognized the threat of aggression beneath the mask.

"God morgen," Silje said.

The man's eyes raked over Silje before settling on Zoe. "Heard around the docks that there was a Verchiél here." The man looked at her with some interest. "You're a long way from home."

"Ja…" Zoe managed.

The man's expression was stony. "I have a few questions for you—"

Zoe's heart hammered in her chest but Silje spoke up before the man could get another word in. "Dear sir, would you kindly do us a favour?" Silje smiled sweetly, her voice magically echoing. "And fuck off."

Zoe tensed, on the edge of flight, but the man only smiled dumbly, and nodded along with Silje's words. "Yes... I will fuck off."

Dreamy smile still plastered on his face, he left obediently. As soon as he was out of earshot Zoe whispered,

"Hurry, we need to leave. Now."

Silje was unbothered. "A little advice from someone who has been avoiding idiots like him for a decade? Don't run, it'll only make things worse. We're going to sit here and finish our meal because we're not doing anything wrong, right?"

As much as Zoe wanted to disagree, this was once again one of the reasons why she'd agreed to stick with Silje in the first place. She needed her for the time being. Zoe reluctantly sat down, perched on the edge of her seat.

The men laughed and talked merrily with one another, one of the establishment workers swiftly clearing a table for them while another brought drinks. It was clear that they expected to be waited on, but also they didn't seem to be causing any trouble as they chatted earnestly among themselves.

Zoe relaxed a fraction, content to let them mind their own business on the other end of the floor.

"We need to start searching for Gabriel," Zoe said.

"My Sun," Silje explained patiently. "He was the one who threw himself off, even if he survived—"

"He did," Zoe said, adamant. "I know Gabe."

Mercifully Silje didn't protest and instead leaned forward, listening. "Then what do you suggest?"

Zoe was shocked by Silje's sudden willingness to compromise, but instead of questioning it Zoe spoke. "I don't know...we can check along the coast. I'm sure he probably hasn't gotten too far if he's on foot, we'll probably need a horse if we're going to travel that far and…Silje? Are you listening—"

Silje didn't respond as she continued to listen in on the group of soldiers conversing behind them. Zoe's Bjordal was a bit rusty, but she picked out enough words to piece together what one of the men was saying.

"…he was lost…looked southern…talked too much…"

Silje slowly rose to her feet and Zoe watched in horror as she walked directly toward them.

"Silje?" Zoe hissed. "What are you doing—"

"Kind gentlemen," Silje said, resting her hand on the back of the nearest man's chair. "It sounds like you have quite a story, would you tell us more?"

Zoe hastily got to her feet, tempted to simply bolt out of the premises before any of the soldiers caught onto them, but each of the men smiled, their expressions dulled with the same dreamlike contentment any victim of Silje's magic experienced.

"Yes, I was just telling them." The first man gestured broadly to the others sitting with him. "We caught an odd prisoner on our last patrol."

Silje and Zoe exchanged a glance, Zoe's heart beating with this newfound information.

"A prisoner?" Silje pressed. "Where from?"

The man frowned as if struggling to recall details. "Couldn't tell. Maybe Heathland. He had a southern accent."

"And what's so special about him to garner the king's interest?" Zoe asked, carefully applying some of her own magic.

Silje frowned at her intrusion, but the man looked delighted that she'd spoken, answering eagerly. "He thinks he's a heksa."

Zoe met Silje's eyes then, wide with discovery.

"Thank you, gentlemen, that will be all." She placed a hand on Zoe's shoulder, steering her away. "But wait…" The man reached out as if to grab her. "Don't you want to stay—"

Silje snapped her fingers sharply and the three men instantly fell into a stupor, collapsing onto the table or, in one case, right onto the floor. One of the serving girls approached with another pitcher of ale, eyeing the unconscious men with confusion.

"Exhausted," Silje explained. "Poor lambs."

The girl merely placed the pitcher onto the table before retreating back into the kitchens.

Silje hastily led Zoe out of the inn, the frigid winter air hitting her face, a shock after the warm interior of the inn, and turned to her with a wide smile.

"You're right, he's here and we know where. All we need to do is break him out."

"Excuse me, we?" Zoe shoved Silje away. "It's your fault that he jumped off the ship in the first place!"

"Don't be stupid! You can't go by yourself. You don't even speak Bjordal."

"Watch me." Zoe stormed off.

"My dear," Silje said patiently. "The capital is the other way."

Zoe's face burnt but she still faced Silje, indignant.

Silje, sensing she was fighting a losing argument, amended.

"Zoe, I can help you. I know where to go and who to talk to. I grew up there, remember?"

"I don't trust you."

"You don't have to trust in me, but you need to trust that we both want the same thing."

Zoe softened at her words. As much as she hated to admit it, Silje was right. They needed each other to make this work.

"Fine," Zoe conceded. "We help each other just this once, okay?

Silje smiled, her eyes flickering with gold as she took Zoe's hand and led her around a narrow, snow-covered alleyway.

"Uh, Silje?" Zoe pulled her hand away, not trusting herself to be left alone with her. "What are we doing?"

"Transversing. I was going to teach you eventually, but I suppose plans change." From her pockets Silje pulled out a small Bjordal steel knife and what looked like the fragments of some ancient bones.

"Give me your hand."

Zoe curled her hands into fists. "Why?"

Silje spread her own hand flat out and cut her palm, liquid gold bled across her skin.

"Bjordal steel," she explained. "A regular blade won't work."

Silje held her hand aloft, clearly waiting for Zoe to follow suit, but Zoe hesitated. She'd never used this type of magic before. What if she somehow ended up permanently bound to Silje? Unable to follow her own will?

Silje added at her hesitation, "Every moment you hesitate is a moment he's alone. The sooner we get there, the better."

Against her better judgement Zoe took the blade from Silje. With a single slash she drew it across her palm, barely registering the pain as she watched the golden magic pool in her palm.

"What now?" Zoe asked.

Silje clasped her hand in hers, the pain stinging but overshadowed by the heat of their combined magic.

"Focus," Silje commanded, "and when you sense it, reach toward it."

Zoe closed her eyes, not quite sure if this was supposed to be part of it, but it helped her concentrate. She closed out the snowy alleyway from her sight as she focused on her breathing and the electric feeling of her and Silje's shared magic.

Snow melted from an awning, dripping against her cheek. Silje squeezed her injured hand tightly, the pain grounding her. "Silje, I can't—"

"Focus." Silje pressed closer, her breath warm against her cheek. "You'll see."

Zoe didn't want to add that with Silje's close proximity it made concentrating more difficult, and instead focused on counting her breaths.

It came slowly, less of a grand realisation and more of a thread to follow. A single golden thread that wound itself from where they stood far into the distance, where Silje had pointed to the direction of the capital.

"There," Silje said. "Reach out and grab it."

Zoe reached out, fumbling for a moment with the thread, seemingly as fine as spider silk before it solidified in her hand, grounding her, moving her.

Zoe's stomach lurched as Silje wrapped her arm around her, pushing them both toward the golden light that enveloped and blinded Zoe with every step. It felt impossible at first, like wading through wet sand, but eventually her feet became used to the rhythm of it, less of a dance and more of a steady and sure gait. She wasn't sure how long they stayed like that—it might have been minutes or seconds—but eventually the feeling of resistance vanished, Zoe's knees buckled beneath her, and she collapsed into the snow.

    Zoe's eyes flew open; she drew in a deep breath of the frigid air and expected to see the snow-covered alleyway she and Silje had been crouching in but instead was startled to see that they stood in an old pine forest.

    "Don't worry," Silje assured her, "it gets easier."

    Zoe whipped around and saw Silje looking into the distance. She followed her gaze and was met with the sight of a massive stone castle.

    Silje smiled at her stunned look. "Welcome to Castle Osenson."

28

GABRIEL

Gabriel sat upon the cold floor of his cell, passing the uneventful hours by scribbling away in a book of Birgen which he'd been given for his sole reading material.

Over a course of three days the holy tome had accumulated a new collection of drawings, which, in his opinion, vastly improved the original content of the book: Hakon with a grotesque face, Hakon being executed, and perhaps the gem of the collection, Hakon being trampled by a herd of elk. He was so consumed with his work that he didn't notice another person approaching the cell.

"Did you know that you could be horsewhipped if someone saw you drawing in a holy tome?"

Edvin looked through the bars, regarding the drawings with amusement.

"Art is subjective," Gabriel countered and flipped to a fresh page, beginning a new sketch. Silence hung heavy in the air and the only sound was the scratching of pencil against paper.

"I brought you fresh water." Edvin slipped a metal cup through the bars.

Gabriel swatted it away, the metal clattering loudly across the stone floor. He ignored Edvin's shocked stare and went back to scribbling.

"It wasn't poisoned," Edvin said.

"Poison I can handle. Pity is another thing."

"You think I pity you?"

"Why else are you here? For the sparkling conversations? Or the smell? Your king's hospitality is so poor that not only have I faced the humiliation of pissing in a bucket, but I haven't been able to bathe since I've arrived."

"I can't say that any of his other prisoners have received better treatment."

"Lucky me." Gabriel scratched out another drawing. "So, I have a question about this execution deal. Do I get a last wish? If so, I would love a bottle of wine and someone beautiful to drink it with. Preferably two people, but I don't want to seem greedy here."

"I can get you a bottle of wine and sit with you while you drink. But I can't guarantee it'll be good."

"The wine or the company?"

"Either."

Gabriel looked up at Edvin, but there wasn't the same skittish fear that he saw upon everyone else's faces.

"Why?" Gabriel asked.

"I'm just trying to help."

"Bullshit."

The candle flames in the cell wavered as if caught in a breeze, but the steel bars held fast and his magic was smothered, leaving only an aching hollowness in its wake.

Edvin shifted uncomfortably.

"You're one of the people who put me in this cell." Gabriel rose to his feet and gripped the bars. "I'm one of the very beings your country loathes. You've taken an oath to murder people like me and yet here you are, trying to get me a drink? What"—Gabriel's lips curled into a snarl—"do you want!"

"Can we talk somewhere else?" Edvin held up a ring of keys.

Gabriel lunged but Edvin held them out of his grasp.

"Give me the fucking keys!" Gabriel hissed.

"I need to talk to you."

"Then start talking."

"Privately," Edvin said. "I don't want any of the other Bjornvangar coming to check on you. You have to trust that I'm not going to hurt you."

"Then give me the keys."

"Are you going to escape?"

"No, I'm going to have a tea party with Hakon—of course I'm going to escape!"

Edvin let out a growl of frustration. "Trust me. Just for tonight, okay?"

"What do I get out of this?"

"In addition to your request? A possibility to get out of your execution."

Gabriel narrowed his eyes, fully suspicious. "Why are you helping me?"

"Do you want the offer or not?" Edvin snapped.

Gabirel weighed his options. For his last night on earth he could remain stubbornly in a cold cell and continue to scribble increasingly unflattering drawings of Hakon, or he could get buzzed on what would most likely be vinegar for wine and stare longingly at Edvin from across the room.

"I'll come on one condition."

"What's that?"

"I want a bath."

"Fine."

Edvin approached the cell door and took out a pair of steel handcuffs. Sensing Gabriel was about to protest, he shrugged by way of apology. "Orders."

"Please," Gabriel scoffed, holding out his wrists, which Edvin cuffed through the bars of the cell. "You couldn't begin to imagine the things I can do in handcuffs."

"Just in case you get any ideas," Edvin added, "the guard watch has been tripled since you've arrived."

"All this for little old me?" The door creaked open. "You shouldn't have."

Edvin held the door open. Gabriel's first instinct was to bolt, but Edvin watched him closely, hand resting on the sword at his side. He had one chance to get out of here and he wasn't going to waste it.

He walked forward, muscles stiff from sitting for so long. The old boots he'd been given were ill fitting and slid around with every step he took. The hallways were empty with the late hour and the few servants they passed quickly skittered out of the way once they saw Gabriel.

"You Bjordal sure know how to make a person feel welcome," Gabriel muttered.

"Ignore them," Edvin said. "They're on edge with the feast celebrations."

Gabriel didn't miss how Edvin's voice tightened. As they ascended up another floor, Gabriel's heart sank as he caught the sight of the broad-shouldered frame of Hakon marching down the hallway.

Edvin immediately stood straighter, tension radiating in his body, appearing for all the world like he wanted to hide, but Hakon caught sight of them.

"Bjornvanger," Hakon addressed Edvin, his eyes lingering on Gabriel with distaste. "I see you're taking the dog for a walk."

Impulsively, Gabriel held out the ruined book to Hakon. "I made these for you," Gabriel placed a hand on his shoulder and leaned forward, his voice husky. "I put something extra special on the last page."

Hakon shoved the book back into Gabriel's hands, disgusted. "I don't want anything tainted by you!"

"You look well," Edvin said, clearly trying to change the subject.

And Gabriel had to admit he did. Dressed in crimson and gold formal wear, the colours of House Osenson. But there was an awkwardness to the amount of overdecoration, which made it feel as if the clothes wore Hakon rather than the other way around. He carried a walking stick that was clearly just for show with its overly gilded decorations.

Hakon stood taller, smugness radiating from him. "As heir of House Osenson I've been invited to attend the feast gathering in my father's stead."

Gabriel squinted at one of the gold lapel pins upon his red jacket. "Is that a weasel?"

Hakon bristled. "It's an ermine! The sigil of House Vollon."

"If you're such a special son then why aren't you wearing the Osenson crest?"

"I haven't been crowned yet, have I?"

"That's an awfully nice way of saying you're not a real prince."

Hakon's eyes blazed with anger, and he raised the walking stick to strike. But Edvin stepped in front of Gabriel.

Hakon lowered his hand, his voice dangerous. "Watch

yourself, some might question where your loyalties lie."

Edvin held a hand to his chest. "Only with my rightful ruler."

Hakon held Edvin's gaze before he shoved past, clipping Edvin's shoulder roughly with the motion.

"Bye!" Gabriel called after him in a cheery voice, waving enthusiastically.

Edvin grabbed his arm, pulling him along the hall. "Will you be serious for a moment? You were moments away from having your skull caved in."

"I'm going to die tomorrow, if I can't get properly drunk or fucked then I'm going to be as annoying as possible."

They arrived in a hall larger than many of the others, though the decorations were minimal and the doors fewer. Edvin opened one of the worn wooden doors and gestured for Gabriel to walk ahead. He entered cautiously; it was a spacious living area in traditional Bjordal style, built with dark wood and worn down over time and the many different Bjornvangar who had inhabited it over generations.

"This is nice," Gabriel said, turning in a circle. "I thought you were demoted."

Edvin's ears flushed with the comment, and he mumbled. "My father has—they haven't decided where to move me yet."

Edvin ushered Gabriel to a small but well-kept bathing area. An old tub sat in the corner of the tiled room, with brass taps rusted with age but still gilded with a sense of finery long since past.

Edvin motioned for him to enter. "I'll be outside."

Gabriel held his cuffed hands out. "And just how am I supposed to bathe in these?"

Edvin unlocked the latch connecting them. The bracers remained tight on his wrists but his arms were free to move.

"Don't want to help?" Gabriel asked. "I'll let you wash my back." He bit his bottom lip. "Maybe a bit more than that if you'd like…"

"Just hurry up!" Edvin snapped, slamming the door shut behind him.

Gabriel had to admit, for as shitty as things were, making Edvin blush was an enjoyable pastime.

Gabriel stripped off his filthy clothes, tossing them into a heap across the chamber for good measure. With some alarm he saw that his bones jutted sharply against his skin from the recent lack of food and his skin bore many bruises in hues of sickly green or mottled purple. No doubt from the fight with Silje. He hadn't looked this poorly since he'd first left Grislow.

He twisted one of the brass taps and waited for the clawfoot tub to fill. The water was steaming and he slipped into it before it had the chance to cool. Though the temperature scalded his skin he let out a content sigh, taking the liberty to scrub himself nearly raw with a coarse bar of soap.

Glumly he considered that this was the best thing that had happened to him in the entire time he'd been here. A small grace of kindness amid so many horrid events. But it raised another pressing question—what did Edvin want from him?

It had to be political. The way he was skirting around made it obvious he was hiding something. Not to mention that there was nothing else he could gain from him. But he'd promised a possible way out of his execution. Would Edvin keep his word? He was Bjornvangar after all, even a demoted one wasn't an ally to readily consider.

Gabriel tried to slip the bracer off his wet arm and hissed with frustration as the motion resulted only in the bones of his hand nearly being crushed. With frustration he rummaged through his pile of filthy clothes before he caught a glint of gold, snatching it up. He examined Hakon's gold lapel pin. He'd managed to steal one of the plainer ones when he'd distracted him with the book. No doubt he'd notice if something as valuable as his family crest went missing. Gabriel traced his fingers along one of the bracers, feeling the nearly invisible seam. He fidgeted with the pin, and began the tedious process of prying it open.

It was a shame that Edvin was so averse to any attempts of seduction. It was delightfully adorable, but sadly little use to his current predicament other than to provide a bit of amusement. If this were Verchiél or Heathland he would have already fucked his way out of his problems.

After the third time the pin got stuck, Gabriel huffed with irritation and let himself sink under the water, closing his eyes and holding his breath. Thoughts, darker and quieter, rose in his mind. Would he escape this place? And if so, could he still find Silje?

Suddenly he was back in the ocean, beneath the crashing waves, watching as her golden eyes faded above him.

Sinking down in the dark and cold...

His chest constricted and he threw his arms out and wrenched himself out of the water, drawing in a shuddering gasp.

A loud banging came from the door.

"I'm fine!" Gabriel coughed, crawling out of the bathtub.

"You don't need to shout." Edvin's voice was muffled through the door. "You just sounded like you were drowning. Are you done yet?"

"I don't have anything to wear—"

The door cracked open just enough for a pile of clothes to be thrown unceremoniously onto the floor.

Gabriel held up the clothes in disappointment. "I don't suppose you have anything in silk?"

"Would you prefer to wear nothing?"

"Don't tempt me." Gabriel pulled the wool sweater over his head.

As the clothes were all Edvin's size, they fit poorly. The sweater was so large Gabriel had to roll up the sleeves twice, while the pants were both baggy and rested above his ankles. The fabrics were all coarse wool or starched linen, but as promised they were clean and dry.

Edvin nodded in approval as Gabriel entered the living area. "Much better."

Gabriel scratched his arm. "This sweater itches."

Edvin gestured to a chair by the fire. "Sit."

Gabriel fidgeted with his sleeve, taking a seat across from Edvin. The table had been set with not only a bottle of wine, but also a selection of food: a hearty-looking stew, dried fish and a fresh loaf of dark bread.

Edvin shrugged at his questioning look. "From the kitchens. I may not have been invited to join the feast but that doesn't mean either of us should go hungry."

Gabriel took a tentative bite of the dark bread. It was dense with molasses and filled with nuts and seeds, nothing like the fluffy, spiced breads of Verchiél, but at that moment it was the best thing he'd ever tasted.

Gabriel scarfed the remainder of the food down, not bothering with his usual table manners with the vicious return of his appetite. Edvin sat quietly, looking into the fire, though his tension was betrayed by the glances he snuck from the corner of his eye.

Only once his plate was cleaned of every crumb and a hint of nausea stuck him with his suddenly full stomach did he stop.

Edvin looked at him seriously, his voice to the point. "We need to talk, it's a delicate matter."

Gabriel laughed, sitting back and fidgeting with the bracer. "If you wanted some alone time with me all you had to do was ask. Though I appreciate the effort you've gone through to get us here."

"This isn't a date."

"It's not? And here I was hoping for a good-night kiss."

"I'm serious."

"So am I."

Edvin frowned. "What will it take for you to trust me?"

"Take off these bracers."

"I'm sorry, I can't."

"That's all right." Gabriel shrugged. "I'll do it myself."

A click sounded out and Edvin's face fell. One of the bracers fell from Gabriel's wrists and hit the floor with an audible thud.

While Gabriel had been in the bath, the heat of the water had expanded the metal enough for him to slip the pin into the nearly invisible seam. It hadn't been much, but it was enough.

Edvin was knocked to the floor and freezing shadows swarmed him, but they flickered in and out of existence, thanks to the singular bracer that remained on his other wrist, and struggled to take form without the full weight of Gabriel's magic behind them.

Gabriel snatched a knife from Edvin's belt and held it against his throat, but Edvin seized Gabriel's wrist in a crushing grip.

"Stop!"

Edvin's forehead smacked into Gabriel's and pain exploded through his skull. The single moment was enough for Edvin to pin Gabriel beneath him, poising two Bjordal steel knives in an arc above his throat.

"One move and you're dead."

An illusion, half-formed and weak, appeared above Edvin. It seized him from behind, hands prepared to snap a neck.

"Same for you."

"Call it off," Edvin ordered.

"No."

Gabriel felt the ghost of Edvin's heartbeat through the illusion's fingers.

"I told you to trust me."

"I don't."

"You should."

The knives pressed closer against his neck and in response the illusion tightened its hold.

"Then tell me what you want," Gabriel growled.

"I want to kill Hakon!"

Both fell still, breathing unsteady.

Gabriel's frown deepened. "You're full of shit."

"Do you think I'd go through all this trouble if I was lying?"

Gabriel considered it. He didn't trust Edvin, but he'd still been the only one here who talked to him like a person. If Edvin had wanted to murder him, he would have done it back in the cell, and if he wanted to hurt him, he would have let Hakon strike him in the hallway.

"If I let you up," Edvin said calmly, "will you listen to what I have to say?"

If anything, this was more time for him to break out of this other bracer.

"You have as long as the wine lasts," Gabriel relented.

Cautiously, Edvin took away the knives and with the motion the illusion faded back to shadows. He offered Gabriel a hand up, but Gabriel ignored the gesture and instead got to his feet on his own, dusting himself off.

"Where's my drink?"

Edvin gestured to a side table where a bottle of wine and a glass sat. Gabriel plucked up the drink and took a sip. *A fine vintage, something the noble guests would have been served.*

Sated, he took a seat across from Edvin. "Start talking, Bjornvangar."

"In the short time you've been here you must have noticed, Bjordal isn't as unified as the king likes to think."

"That's putting it lightly."

"Many of us hate Hakon. He tears this country apart, all to cling to outdated traditions and displays of power. But nobody will do anything about it. They complain but continue to live the same way. It's infuriating."

"What does any of this have to do with me?"

Edvin seemed to be waiting for this moment. "I want you to kill Hakon."

Gabriel took a deep sip of wine and was silent for a long moment before he said thoughtfully: "Do you have another bottle? I'm not drunk enough for this conversation."

"It's a good idea," Edvin countered and gestured to his bare wrist. "You broke out of that easily enough. You attacked me and nearly succeeded—"

"I'd go so far as to say that I would have triumphed over

you had it not been for your ghastly little tricks."

"But you've killed before, have you not?"

For a stark moment he was back in Grislow in the dead of night, as his old boss gave him a new job, another fool who needed to be taught a lesson, always one more life to ruin.

It had started with simple tasks: observe and report, stealing if the mark had anything worth taking. But as he grew older his work became more violent: staging "accidents" for the people they no longer needed or coercing information out of reluctant individuals, because magic cut deeper and crueller than any blade could.

He had been less a servant or even an attack dog who was sent after people who were foolish enough not to honour their contracts. He had been an ill omen. Everyone knew to listen or they'd have a shadow slipping past their front door.

Gabriel wasn't above such actions, he was simply above taking those orders from anybody else ever again.

"Why can't you do this since you've clearly been planning for so long?" Gabriel asked, a bite to his tone.

"Because you have what none of us do." Edvin's eyes met his and Gabriel knew what he was looking at.

"So you want to unify your country by having the scary heksa murder your royal prince? How could you possibly think this would make people look favourably upon me? Or Verchiél for that matter?"

"There are more people who look favourably upon Verchiél and Incarnate than you might think."

"Do enlighten me, because I haven't met any of them."

"The king's court isn't a good example. It's full of superstitious elites who leverage fear to control the masses. Or pay lip service to the church to stay close to the king's side."

"Even if your plan would work and I could help you"—Gabriel gestured to his eyes—"I'm an Incarnate Moon. The execution is set for the middle of the day and I'd have no magic."

"I understand that heksa—Incarnate," Edvin corrected himself, "have a short amount of time during their opposing times of the day in which their magic lingers. As such we're going to move you in the morning rather than the afternoon. Once the crowd sees you present, the event will commence regardless of Hakon's original plans."

"That's a very narrow window of time."

"It's better than nothing."

Gabriel huffed."If you're so desperate to be rid of him then take this damned bracer off and let me kill him tonight."

"Too coincidental. The other Bjornvangar know I'm on duty. If anyone sees you loose, they're going to put two and two together."

"Well, that's all well and fine for you. But it doesn't change the fact that you're still leading me into a potential execution. I could die a thousand different ways before I ever reach Hakon."

"If we're going to do this," Edvin said, "I need to know that you trust me and I can trust you."

"If you knew better, you'd realise that you shouldn't trust me at all."

"You don't need to trust me unconditionally. You only need to trust me once."

Gabriel tapped his fingers against the arm of the chair, irritated. "So once you get rid of Hakon and force Asbjorn to abdicate, who's going to lead Bjordal?"

"We have another who will take the mantle of leadership."

"Who is he?"

"*She,*" Edvin corrected him, "has been working with us from the beginning. In fact you've already met her."

Gabriel smiled slowly. Of course Silje would have people working for her from the inside, why hadn't he thought of it before? After all, if Edvin was helping her, then not only would he have a chance to escape and see her again.

He'd finally be able to kill her.

"Silje is…an interesting choice to say the least," Gabriel said carefully.

"She wants what's best for the future of Bjordal and the Isles."

"I'm sure Asbjorn thinks the same of Hakon."

Edvin sighed. "There's nothing I can say that will convince you. But what I can tell you is that you'd be hard-pressed to find worse than Hakon."

Gabriel couldn't disagree with that.

"So once Hakon is dead and your new queen sits on the throne, what will become of me? I expect rewards for my aid. Financial, political, perhaps a statue in my honour."

"I cannot speak for her, but I'm certain she'd make a fair deal with you."

Or try to erase his memory or kill him, neither was particularly enticing. Precisely why he had to kill her first.

"You're going to force me regardless," Gabriel said.

"I can't force you to do anything. But I know you want him dead as much as I do. Even if you made it back to Verchiél tonight, if you leave Bjordal like this, it will only grow worse."

"Burn the rot away?"

"Exactly."

Edvin's hand strayed instinctually to his neck as Gabriel

had seen him do so many times before, but this time he wasn't wearing his thick coat, and he noticed what Edvin clutched at was a small pendant: an elk. The old god of the woods—Skagen.

Gabriel curled his lip, fascinated. "The elk you missed with your arrow?"

"It's a sin to kill an avatar of your god."

"Did you know you could be horsewhipped if someone saw you wearing the idol of an old god?"

"With the coup, the Church of Birgen will finally be excommunicated from Bjordal. As it should have been years ago," Edvin explained.

"Political coups and religious reforms? You're a much more intriguing individual than the miserable beauty I originally mistook you for."

Edvin gave a rare smile and Gabriel continued speaking, encouraged. "You've answered why you want Hakon gone. But you still didn't tell me why you don't hate me for being a heksa."

The smile faded as quickly as it came. "I knew someone once…who was a heksa."

"Who?

"My brother." Edvin was silent for a long moment before he spoke quietly. "He changed young. The king's men came for him and dragged him out of the house, screaming. I never saw him again after that." Edvin's voice faltered. "I know it sounds mad, but I still hear his voice sometimes…"

"How did you end up here?" Gabriel asked, genuinely curious.

"My father sent me. He wanted to salvage our family name. A son in the Bjornvangar would do just that. He paid for King Asbjorn to take me into the guard."

"So you want out?"

"I've wanted to leave since the moment I arrived." Edvin's fist clenched, a feverish light in his eyes. "My brother, he'd hate me if he saw me here. Wearing the same uniform as the men who took him…"

Gabriel spoke carefully in the tense silence that followed. "Well, if your plan will work then we'll both leave this place tomorrow. What could be better than that?"

Edvin looked up, his face hopeful. "You'll help?"

He'd be able to escape and take his revenge. He'd be a fool not to.

"Just promise that you'll do everything in your power to keep me alive."

Edvin knelt before Gabriel and took his hand in both of his, giving it a tight squeeze. "On his death, I swear it."

"And would you look at that?" Gabriel placed the empty glass back down. "My drink's done."

"Sva," Edvin cursed, getting to his feet. "Let's get you back before anyone notices how long you've been gone."

Gabriel looked to the bed in the corner of the room, piled with many layers of thick quilts and fur. Exhaustion suddenly swept over him and he moved toward it.

"I'm going to sleep—"

Edvin grabbed his arm and redirected him toward the door. "No you're not. If anyone sees you walking out of my room in the morning, we'll have a different problem on our hands."

Gabriel cursed Bjordal's rigidness; he would kill for a night in a proper bed. Especially with a warm body beside him.

Gabriel nudged Edvin. "Are you just afraid that you won't be able to resist me?"

"Yes," Edvin said dryly. "Terrified."

"You know," Gabriel said, watching Edvin neatly fold up a blanket, "you're a lot more tolerable when you don't take yourself so seriously."

Edvin shoved the blanket into his arms. "And you are when you're quiet."

Edvin escorted Gabriel back along the hallways; given the late night hour they met no one along their way. Dread crept into Gabriel at the sight of the cell, but Edvin's voice softened when he unlocked the door. "One more night."

"Easy for you to say when you're not the one who has to sleep here." Gabriel hugged the blanket tightly to himself and walked inside the cell. Edvin closed the door behind him.

"What now?" Gabriel asked.

"You rest." Edvin locked the door. "I plan."

"Edvin—" Gabriel caught his arm through the bars. Edvin startled at his touch but didn't pull away. Gabriel blanked, for once struggling to articulate his words. "Thanks."

Edvin gave a bitter laugh. "Don't thank me until we're out of this mess."

Gabriel listened as Edvin's footfalls faded back upstairs. He wrapped the blanket tightly around himself and curled up in the corner of his cell to get what sleep he could before the morning came.

29

DABRIA

Dabria cursed her every life decision.

She clutched the letter in hand. It was a single page, written in a hasty, aggressive scrawl that she recognized instantly though the message's contents contained only two words:

Return immediately.

A part of her had always known how easy it would be to find Ada, that's why she had never tried. Because then she'd have to face her again and own up to the fact that she'd made a choice to abandon her to keep herself safe instead.

Before Ada rose to the station she now occupied, there had been only the two of them. Favourites of their old boss, which of course meant that every other member viewed them as competition to be snuffed out.

It had started with small things: insults spat with bitter words or threats muttered when they turned their backs. As time passed, skirmishes became all too common, then outright brawls which left both parties bloodied and bruised. It had become a habit for Dabria to constantly watch from the corner of her eye, and keep a knife under her pillow at night.

One last job, Ada had promised. Make their fortune, then they'd finally leave Grislow for good. But Dabria had known better. With Ada, there was no such thing as one last anything;

she was embedded, as much a part of Grislow as the ancient stone and brick that cursed city was built upon. Ada never would have left; uprooting her would have killed her the same way as tearing a plant from the earth. But for Dabria, she had grown tired of the constant empty promises as months bled into years spent in that grey, unforgiving place. Ada wouldn't leave.

But Dabria would.

Dabria had snuck from their makeshift bed, a pile of blankets in the attic in the middle of the night. She'd caught the first ship south she could find.

She knew that leaving Ada would have put her in danger. Everyone knew their faces, and even their own gang was no longer a safe place for them.

And yet Dabria had still chosen herself anyways. What had bothered Dabria most wasn't the hollow lies Ada had told her to buy more time, it was inaction. Sometimes staying was worse than running.

She traced the letters with her fingers, imagining Ada's own hand had touched the paper not so long ago. It wasn't signed with a name, only a single *A*, Pretentious and to the point. As always.

She let out a muffled screech and buried her face in her arms on the desk. Why was it when she had something to lose she was always presented with a crossroads?

Alfio would tell her to follow her heart or some sentimental bullshit like that. Niklas would tell her to be practical and assess the situation for advantages. But Dabria? What would she do?

A knock at the door interrupted her thoughts, but she didn't move and she snapped, "Go away!"

"I think you'll find time for me."

Dabria tensed. She didn't trust herself to move let alone

speak. She knew that voice.

"You didn't send your response—" Footsteps, confident and calculated, entered the room. "I had assumed you were employing your usual stubborn tactics and were trying to avoid me, but much to my surprise I arrived at a most curious turn of events. Finding you, of all people, in service to the most powerful people in Verchiél."

The footsteps came to a halt beside her. Dabria's heart was beating so fast she felt light-headed but still she refused to look up.

"Dabria."

Dabria flinched when a slender hand rested on the back of her neck.

"Look at me."

Slowly Dabria raised her head and met Ada's mismatched eyes.

She looked nothing like Dabria remembered, which she now realised was a ridiculous notion. The scrawny girl with a terrible haircut had been replaced with a sleek woman in an expensive suit. Subtle, but Dabria knew it was the kind of shit that would convey power. A detail that wasn't lost on Dabria, though the entire charade was damped slightly by the fact that her left arm hung clumsily in a sling.

Ada smiled. "Hello, Bria."

Dabria screamed and threw a heavy punch.

Perhaps life as a conlord had hardened Ada to shock or she had somehow expected this all along, because she swiftly backed away, even with her broken arm, managing to dodge Dabria's many repeated attempts to hit and kick and claw whatever part of her she could reach.

Ada seized Dabria by her lapel, and despite being a scrawny bitch, shoved her against the wall. The only words that made it out of Dabria's mouth were—

"Fuck you!"

Ada spoke, out of breath. "Blunt and unrefined as always. You haven't changed a bit."

"Neither have you, you bitch."

Ada laughed, her voice deep and scratchy and an ache went through Dabria at the sound of it.

"If I release you, are you going to behave yourself?"

Dabria glowered. "Why don't you let go and find out?"

Ada slowly released her. Dabria shrugged her off, glaring daggers.

Ada smirked in response.

"I have an offer for you."

"That's what you have to say?" Dabria paced, too jumpy to sit still. "We haven't seen each other in what? Eight, nine years?"

"Ten," Ada said precisely.

"How did you even find me? It was Silje, wasn't it?"

"Ah, I was going to ask how you know that little witch."

"Answer my question first."

Ada pulled out a chair and seated herself across from Dabria. "You weren't exactly difficult to track down with your history with the law. Not to mention the news of your recent involvement with Verchiél's newest Incarnate." Ada gestured to her. "Congratulations on the coronation. If it's any consolation, a single casualty to usher in a new dynasty is quite impressive."

"So you heard?"

"Of course. Heathland is circling like a vulture while Bjordal threatens war. It's a dreadful time, but it's also profitable."

Dabria's stomach sank. "That's why you're here? You just

want to use me?"

"Oh, Bria, if I wanted to use you, then you wouldn't even know. I want to make a deal."

"What kind of deal?"

"The kind where your life changes." Ada sat forward. "Tell me, what do you think of Niklas?"

Dabria was put off by the sudden change of subject but answered truthfully. "He's miserable, but you can reason with him. Why? Do you have some sort of deal with him?"

"I've only had the pleasure of doing business with his sister."

"What a bitch."

Ada rubbed her shoulder. "Quite. My last grand plan didn't turn out to be as grand as I'd hoped."

"I take it this has something to do with your broken arm?"

Ada's lips tightened before she asked, "What would you say to being my second in command?"

Dabria laughed. "You had me real good there, for a second I thought you really came all the way here to give me a shitty offer."

Ada didn't smile. "Many would jump at the chance."

"The chance to what? Follow you around at all hours of the day or night and put up with your mood swings?" Dabria moved to walk past her. "No thanks, I've done that before—"

Ada gripped her arm, nails biting into her skin. "You're running."

Dabria snatched her arm away, skin still prickling at her touch.

"I'm not running."

"You can't sit still, even now."

Dabria drew in a sharp breath. "I'm not going back to Grislow."

Ada laughed without any humour. "And what's for you here? A failing ruler and a population ready to spill blood the first chance they get? If an Incarnate isn't safe in Verchiél, then what makes you think that you will be?"

Ada had a point, but Dabria would never admit it. She couldn't go back. Her life was here now. She'd made that choice; to go back now would admit defeat and only show Ada that she'd been wrong in the first place. That her abandonment had all been for nothing.

Dabria drew in a steadying breath and met Ada's mismatched eyes. "I'm staying here."

Ada held her stare. "I don't believe you."

Dabria's fingernails bit into her palms, frustration spurring her on. "I never asked to go back."

"Then why did you look for me?" Ada asked. "Morbid curiosity? Or the unspoken truth, that you want change but as always are too stubborn to admit it to anybody but yourself?"

This bitch.

"You want to make a deal?" Dabria stormed around the desk and seated herself in the old leather chair, facing Ada as if they were holding a business meeting. She placed her shaking hands palms down on the desk and met Ada's eyes.

"We split everything. Fifty-fifty."

"Now you're the one making shitty offers."

"You wouldn't be here unless it was on the table."

"You assume too much."

"Do I? Then don't assume I won't break your other damned arm for coming here."

Ada only rolled her eyes. "Do you know what happens to people who threaten me, Dabria?"

"Let me guess, you kill them?"

"Sometimes. I prefer to take every bit of hope and joy from their life until there's nothing left."

"Well, your job is already done on that front."

They glared at each other, each unwilling to stand down. How many times had they done this? More than she could count and yet they always came back. Constant and inextricable. As predictable as planets in orbit around one another.

Eventually Ada looked away first as she rose to her feet without a word.

"Where are you going?" Dabria asked.

"Grislow. I've been away long enough."

"That's it?"

Ada raised a brow. "What's it?"

"You're just leaving again?"

"If I recall correctly"—Ada said—"you were the one who left."

Dabria rose to her feet and followed Ada. "Then why did you even come back?"

"Curiosity, if you will."

Dabria reached out and slammed the door shut before she could walk out.

"You want me to come with you."

Dabria took a step forward, deliberately into her space. Ada didn't budge, staring right back. It was an old game they played, to see how far they could push each other without backing down. After so long apart, neither would sway so easily.

"You could never resist gloating when you had the chance."

She stood close enough that Dabria caught the scent of her. *Fuck.* Why did she smell so nice? Clean with the hint of something expensive and smoky, the kind of fancy shit she used to steal when she was still wearing second-hand suit jackets from the older boys in the gang.

"I'm giving you a choice, Dabria," Ada explained. "You can stay here and live out whatever meagre plans you have for yourself, or you can come back."

In one swift motion Ada opened the door and slipped out. Dabria was out of breath as if she'd just sprinted, and she watched Ada walk down the hall. Dabria was frozen to the spot; she didn't know what to do, let alone trust herself to move.

Niklas said he'd given her back a choice, but what was her choice? Stay and guide Verchiél through a revolution? Or go back to her?

At that moment Dabria decided that she wasn't going to choose based on sentimentality or even tactical advantages.

"Ada!" Dabria shouted.

Ada paused, turning to look at her.

"You'd better have one of those fancy fucking suits in my size, because I won't be wearing my guard uniform."

Instead Dabria did what she always did best—

Ada smiled.

Find a new path forward.

"Welcome back, Dabria."

30

GABRIEL

Gabriel was startled awake as someone hit the metal bars of the cell repeatedly, the sound reverberating loudly off the stone walls.

"Vakne opp!"

He grimaced and stretched his jaw, his face aching from where he'd fallen asleep against the bars. From the small grate at the top of his cell he could see the dawn. Three men stood before the cell—a red-clad soldier, the eldest Bjornvangar and Edvin.

Edvin unlocked the cell door and Gabriel gave him a tired smile.

"Good morning, Bjornvangar."

Edvin's eyes were cold as he snapped, "Stad ned, heksa!"

He hauled Gabriel roughly to his feet and shoved him face first against the bars. Another pair of Bjordal steel handcuffs were locked tightly upon his wrists and a fear swept through Gabriel. This was just an act, wasn't it? Edvin handed Gabriel off to the other Bjornvangar and they forced him out of the cell. Or had he been wrong in his judgments last night?

No one spoke as they forced him to march. This time they didn't lead him through the upper halls, but rather a long stone tunnel hewn through an oldest portion of the castle. The temperature dropped considerably and damp collected on the stone walls, causing Gabriel to cough again. Despite the horrid medicine he'd been forced to drink every day, the sickness in his chest felt heavier after days in a cell.

With each step Gabriel's uncertainty grew and his feet began to drag, causing the elder Bjornvangar to curse and shove Gabriel forward none too gently. Were they taking him somewhere where they could kill him in private? He tried to catch Edvin's eye, a challenge as he walked at the back of the group, but if he noticed the effort, he was clearly ignoring it.

After what felt like an age of walking, they reached an old wooden door which the Bjornvangar shoved open with a grunt. The morning light was a shock to Gabriel's eyes after walking through the dimly lit tunnel.

The elder Bjornvangar and soldier shoved him forward but this time they walked in front of him, leaving Edvin to flank his right side. The snow crunched beneath Gabriel's old boots and he took in the landscape. His breath plumed in the cold air and he caught the sight of what looked like an encampment in the distance. Dread crept through him at the sight of it, and he slowed in his steps. With the motion Edvin bumped into him, and Gabriel felt something slip into his hand. He chanced a look at his palm and saw the little wooden pendant of Skagen.

Edvin kept his eyes ahead but whispered, "For luck."

Relief spread through Gabriel and he tried not to smile.

"I don't suppose I'm going to kill Hakon with this?"

"Don't be absurd. I've hidden a pistol at the base of the pyre."

"Pyre?!"

Edvin shushed him. "No one's going to burn you. It's for ceremonial purposes."

"That's a relief, the way you said that made it sound like—

"

"You will face a firing squad."

"You really know how to inspire confidence in a person, you know that, right?"

Gabriel looked at the backs of the two men ahead of them. "Who can I trust?"

Edvin nodded to the man in red. "Tarik is one of our own. But don't trust any of the Bjornvangar. We've planned a distraction for the beginning of the execution. Once it starts, get out of view of any of the Bjornvangar as quickly as possible and get to Hakon."

"But how will I know once it happens?"

"Trust me," Edvin assured him. "You'll know."

As the encampment neared, Gabriel began to pick out the sounds of activity. People rising with the morning sun, gathering wood for the fires or chatting among themselves. Young children screeched as they wove their way between the rows of tents. The scents of food being roasted on open fires made Gabriel's stomach growl.

If he hadn't known better, he would have thought that a grand festival was set to take place rather than an execution. But perhaps to these people the death of an Incarnate was worth celebrating.

Past the tents Gabriel caught the sight of the pyre, stacked high with wood and situated far closer to the podium than he would have preferred.

As their party made their way closer, people began to notice. Their eyes lingered over the presence of the Bjornvangar with confusion before they caught sight of Gabriel and understanding swept across their faces. After the incident in the throne room Gabriel had expected shouts and jeering, for people to look upon him with hatred and anger.

Instead a hush came over the crowd and people stared at him with wide eyes. People stopped in their activities and watched in silence as they passed. That unnerved Gabriel more than anything. He looked to Edvin, wanting some sort of reassurance. But he kept his eyes straight ahead to where Asbjorn stood.

Asbjorn towered taller than any gathered in the crowd. Dressed in the Osenson house colours of gold and crimson, with a mantle of thick bear fur. Gabriel craned his neck, knowing wherever Asbjorn was Hakon wasn't to be found far. But when Gabriel searched the crowd he was nowhere to be seen.

Edvin noticed it too as he grew tenser and began to chew his bottom lip in a way that Gabriel didn't entirely hate watching. He muttered quietly though Gabriel was unsure whether he was addressing him or speaking aloud to himself.

"He must be in the crowd somewhere."

As their party approached Asbjorn, a sequence of emotions so swift passed across the king's face that Gabriel barely caught them: shock, confusion, anger, before settling back into a composed mask.

"Bjornvangar. Anders. Guardsman Tarik." He scarcely glanced at Edvin, not bothering to address him. Gabriel couldn't quite work out whether or not Edvin preferred the insult or the lack of attention. Either way his jaw clenched so tightly Gabriel heard his teeth grind together.

"Mon kogen," the elder Bjornvangar. addressed Asbjorn. "We've brought the heksa as Prince Hakon requested."

"I was not aware of this development," Asbjorn said.

Tarik stepped forward and handed an envelope to Asbjorn, who snatched the paper out of his hands, breaking the seal in a swift motion. He skimmed over the content with distaste.

"Mon kogen?" Edvin bowed low, a thread of anxiety evident in his voice. "Where is Prince Hakon?"

"You tell me," Asbjorn snapped. "I haven't seen him since the feast celebrations last night."

Gabriel and Edvin exchanged a worried look.

"Shall I send someone to fetch him?" Edvin asked.

Asbjorn waved his hand impatiently. "Leave it be. The fool probably had too much to drink again. If he can't make an effort to make public appearances, let alone correspond through anything other than a letter, then he will suffer the consequences."

Gabriel was shocked to hear Asbjorn speak of Hakon in such a manner. There was a bitterness to his voice that hadn't been present upon their first meeting, but the king was in a foul mood.

Asbjorn narrowed his gaze on Gabriel. "You'd better hope you were right about her."

Gabriel didn't know what he was right about anymore. All he knew was that he wanted to get out of here alive.

Asbjorn looked into the crowd. "Regardless, today will be a spectacle whether she shows herself or not."

Asbjorn stormed off, barking orders at any nearby guards who happened to be unlucky enough to be in his line of sight along the way.

"What now?" Gabriel whispered to Edvin.

"We continue with the plan. When the distraction happens, you'll need to be ready to move." Edvin nodded ahead of them. "You see those trees in the distance? Run to the forest in the east. We can regroup afterward."

Gabriel, who didn't have the heart to tell Edvin he'd run the first chance he got and never return, smiled.

Edvin led Gabriel to the makeshift stage and the crowd caught wind of what was happening. People shifted and whispered, buzzing and agitated, and Gabriel, who had always loved being at the centre of attention, suddenly felt all too exposed. Absurdly he considered that it felt like a play about to begin. He might have enjoyed the crowd and attention had they not been eagerly awaiting his imminent demise.

A wooden post had been driven into the ground right against the stage. Edvin backed him toward it and tied his hands behind him with a sturdy length of rope.

"Stay smart." Edvin gave his shoulder a squeeze. "Stay alive."

Edvin left the stage and Gabriel felt a new sort of anxiety claw its way up his throat, almost making him call out to Edvin. But that wouldn't do in the least, a prisoner would never call their captor back to them. Instead Gabriel looked out into the crowd, which was his next mistake.

Hundreds of pairs of eyes stared back at him. Evidently word had gotten out about his capture as among the Bjordal there were also some Sakai and Uzoman spectators. Whether they had mistaken this for a festival or came out of morbid curiosity he wasn't sure. But the temptation to call out for someone to help him was excruciating.

Stay alive. Stay smart, he repeated to himself. *Stay alive. Stay—*

"My people!"

Asbjorn had risen from his seat and addressed the crowd. Even at his age the king still cut an imposing figure. Gabriel could only have imagined what a terror he had been in his youth.

"Our usual celebrations have not taken place."

In what was a dramatic display even Gabriel couldn't deny, Asbjorn pointed his large hand back to him. "The capture of a heksa trespassing upon royal lands."

Though Gabriel had been in full view the entire time, people now crowded closer, as if they could catch a glimpse of something new. More murmurs passed through the crowd.

Asbjorn waited a pause before he continued speaking in a heavy tone.

"My son has deemed this man to be dangerous and unhinged—"

Rather uncalled for considering how politely I'm standing here.

"—of fiendish and unsound mind—"

Or rather fiendishly good-looking.

"—a creature driven solely by crude impulses and desire—"

Okay now he's just being rude.

"The only punishment fitting is death."

Gabriel's stomach dropped; the ropes at his wrists suddenly felt much too tight.

"Despite Prince Hakon's absence, we will commence regardless."

Gabriel's eyes searched the crowd desperately for any sign of Silje. He spotted a few figures with white-blond hair, a young man, an elderly woman, a child. But none were her.

Gabriel pulled at his bindings, the ropes biting into his wrists. *Where is she?* He was so concentrated he didn't realise he was being spoken to.

"Hva?" Gabriel asked.

Asbjorn replied irritably. "You may give your last words if

you wish to speak them."

He caught Edvin's eyes, looking for any measure of guidance, and he mouthed one word to him.

Stall.

There had been few times in Gabriel's life when he doubted himself, but in that moment the severity of his situation came crashing down upon him like a crushing wave.

What if the distraction didn't work? What if a stray bullet caught him?

What if he died?

He would bleed out in the snow and there were so many things he'd never be able to enjoy again. He'd never get to attend another party or share kisses with beautiful strangers. Never see Zoe and Alessi again. He'd never get to go home.

He would have given anything in that moment to be back in Verchiél. To feel the sun warm his skin and sit in the shaded alcove of the palace, where the very worst thing he ever had to suffer was a hangover.

Where the language wasn't his first, but he made every effort to assure himself that Verchiél blood flowed through his veins as much as any of the other citizens. It was his home. The only place where he'd ever been accepted—no, celebrated and rewarded for who he was.

If he were stronger he would have broken free of his bindings and fought his way out. If he were smarter he would have found a clever way to escape long before this display.

He recalled what Ada had told him. *The streets might have raised you, but you've forgotten all of the lessons you've learned.*

Yes, he was a lying bastard who'd grown too comfortable and couldn't throw a punch to save his life. Perhaps he wasn't good at much, but this? He knew this. He was an actor and this was his stage. He would give a final performance like no other.

Gabriel closed his eyes and tilted his head back as if feeling the morning sun upon his face before he spoke out in a mournful tone.

"I regret the actions that have led me to you all this day. I regret my mistakes and sins and selfishness. But most of all—" He let his words ring out across the clearing, watching as the people leaned forward to catch what he would say next.

His lips curled into a wicked smile.

"I regret the terrible curse which will befall each and every single one of you on this day."

A hush fell upon the crowd.

He hadn't used the usual Bjordal word for curse, *forbanne*, but rather *heksun*, the kind of curse which could never be revoked or undone, something so old and dark even the whispered word of it was never permitted to leave someone's lips. Something only a heksa could do.

Utter horseshit. If Gabriel had ever had so much power he certainly wouldn't have been languishing away in a cell for days. But Bjordal was a country and a people steeped in superstition. The thing about that was that it worked both ways.

The sudden quiet was unnerving in a crowd so large. Gabriel chanced a look toward Edvin, who inclined his head in a motion Gabriel took for encouragement as he continued to speak.

"Your lands will be desolate, your harvests barren, your people will grow sickly and wither and die one by one like crops in a drought—" In the distance a child began to wail, which encouraged Gabriel as he appreciated the dramatic effect. "Your children and your children's children and probably their children too will be shackled with the burden I give them today. Mark my words: strike me down and you will all suffer."

As the dire proclamation ended, the only sounds were the wind across the snowy landscape and the distant creaking of the old forests.

Then one by one, people began to raise their voices. Old and young alike as arguments and screams broke out.

"Let him go, you fools!"

"Are you kidding? Shoot him now!"

"Please, don't hurt him!"

It was chaos, and through it all, Gabriel held Asbjorn's gaze steady. The old king sat perfectly still, hunched upon the wooden throne with his head in his hand. His pale eyes watched him closely, but what he was thinking, Gabriel couldn't discern.

Eventually Asbjorn stood and the crowd fell into a shaky silence.

"Proceed, Bjornvangar.."

Screams echoed out and the guards had to form a wall before the stage to prevent people from rushing forward.

The men raised their pistols.

"EDVIN!" Gabriel screamed just as the world burst into flames.

31

GABRIEL

The world was burning.

Gabriel awoke on the snow-packed ground, a dull thrum echoing through his skull.

The fire from the explosion had spread from the pyre and now steadily ate away at the stage he'd stood upon only moments before. The heat seared his skin and he hissed in pain as he crawled forward for a few feet before collapsing, pressing his face against the cold ground.

He moved to get to his feet, but his entire body screamed in protest. There were nothing more than a few bloody cuts along his arms and legs, the impact that had knocked him momentarily unconscious left his limbs shaky and weak.

It didn't help his progress as people shouted and pushed their way through the crowd, while others lay wounded or crumpled in the snow. Children cried. Unease swept through Gabriel. When he agreed to this he hadn't been aware civilians would be involved. Let alone that there would be a huge fucking explosion that nearly immolated him. Surely this had to have been a miscalculation. The same man who had given him a spare blanket couldn't have done all this.

Suddenly pain exploded through his side as a heavy boot struck his ribs. He yelped and was met with the sight of the elder

Bjornvangar., blade raised. Instinctively Gabriel raised his hands to shield himself, but the blow never came as another blade sliced through the man's chest.

Gabriel flinched as warm blood rained upon him. Edvin stood behind the Bjornvangar., wrenching the blade out of his back, letting the man fall to the ground.

Edvin wasted no time and grabbed Gabriel's arm, hauling him to his feet.

"You never told about a huge fucking explosion!" Gabriel managed, still wavering unsteadily.

"Sometimes change requires more than a nudge." Edvin had clearly been caught in the blast as an angry red burn now scorched up his neck and across his jaw. Before Gabriel could re-act, he shoved a pistol into his arms. "Perhaps we'll meet again."

"Wait!" Gabriel grabbed Edvin's arm. "What about Ha-kon?"

"The plan has changed—" Edvin pulled his arm out of his grasp. "We need to get out of here. Especially you."

Gabriel followed him, yelling over the chaos, "You can't just leave me here. You're supposed to help. What happens if I get caught?"

"Sva—" Edvin rounded on him. "You want safety? Leave. You already have everything you need."

"Why can't you come with me?"

"Because there's still much I need to finish, for Bjordal."

"How fucking noble," Gabriel said bitterly. "If you're say-ing goodbye at least give me a proper kiss."

Edvin hesitated before he reached forward and grasped the back of Gabriel's neck, pulling him closer to press his lips against his forehead.

He pulled away, eyes sorrowful. "Farewell, heksa."

Gabriel watched as Edvin vanished back into the crowd. The wind shifted and the fire swept across the stage, encompassing it completely. Heat seared across his skin and he ducked low, covering his head.

"Holy fuck, Edvin."

Ash fell like snow and Gabriel pulled his sweater up to cover his mouth and nose. He needed to leave. The sickness in his chest hadn't fully healed and he couldn't risk falling ill again.

East. Edvin had told him to go to the forest in the east. At this point, Gabriel wasn't feeling particularly inclined to trust anything else Edvin had planned, but the possibility of a safe space outweighed his hesitation.

He was bustled about in the screaming crowd, and he pushed his way past.

"Let me through!" Gabriel snapped.

He used the last dregs of his magic and shadows swept around him, his voice rising on the wind. "Get out of my way!"

Finally people noticed, swiftly backing away from the shadows with fear. As recognition grew they steered far out of his path.

"Heksun!"

A chill swept through him when he recalled his words: *Your lands will be desolate.*

Fire burned.

Your people will fall one by one.

Figures lay crumpled in the snow.

You will become nothing more than dust.

Whispered curses followed his progress but no one dared to stop him. The last of the shadows faded away and the moment of strength he'd felt quickly fled. As the path ahead cleared he saw her. He froze, a chill sweeping across his skin.

Like a droplet of blood in the snow, she wore the scarlet uniform of a castle servant, her pale hair tucked into braids across her head.

"SILJE!"

Her pale eyes met him and she halted in her steps. Both stood, shocked, staring at each other across the snowy field.

That was until her lips curled into a smile and she began to laugh. Red flickered in his vision, and he drew the pistol, which she matched eagerly, raising her own in tandem.

"My Moon," Silje called out. "What a lovely surprise. Did you come all this way just to see me?"

"I'll fucking kill you!" he screamed.

"Oh, you poor thing." She pursed her lips. "You have it bad. But I'm afraid I have to go, I have some urgent business to attend to."

Gabriel blocked her path, pistol clutched tightly in his grasp.

"Get out of my way," she growled.

"No."

"Gabriel," she warned, her voice low. *"Move."*

"You're not going anywhere."

Her pale eyes sparked with gold. Fear coursed through him at the familiar pull of her magic, but she didn't give him any orders yet. He held his ground.

"Poor Gabriel." Silje walked closer. "You still can't leave me alone, do you know why?" She didn't wait for him to answer as she leaned into the barrel of the pistol. "Because we're exactly the same—"

He pulled the trigger.

Silje smiled as the pistol clicked hollowly in his hand. "Did you think Edvin would trust you enough to give you a loaded pistol?"

Gabriel snarled and threw the pistol into the snow in frustration but before he could turn to fight, another explosion sounded out and he was knocked to the ground.

Where is she? She can't have escaped yet—

He looked back up to Silje, and to his shock, she lowered the pistol. She pressed a finger to her lips and disappeared back into the crowd.

He sprinted after her, taking no care as he knocked people out of the way. He'd hadn't dragged himself through all this hell only for her to escape again.

He caught snatches of laughter as she wove her way gracefully through the crowd, at times purposely lagging behind as if she was enjoying the chase. She was just out of his reach, taunting him, so close—

He leapt forward, fingertips brushing the back of her coat, but they closed around nothing but air. Hands seized him from behind and he was being pulled backward, the entire world tilting around him.

He landed hard on the snow-packed ground, Zoe's face looming above him.

"Gabriel! What the fuck?"

He should have been shocked at her sudden appearance, stopped and wondered why she was here of all places instead of Heathland. But at that moment he was solely focused on one thing.

Killing Silje.

He was on his feet again, trying to spot Silje in the crowd, but the area was now a sea of scarlet uniforms. She was gone.

He screamed in frustration and moved to sprint before Zoe caught him around his middle, halting him.

"Let me go," Gabriel snarled. "She was right here!"

"In case you haven't noticed," Zoe said, struggling to hold Gabriel back. "We don't want to be near her."

Gabriel thrashed against Zoe's grasp. "I'm going to kill her!" He didn't care what she thought, what anyone thought. He was going to take his revenge or die trying.

Suddenly a voice cut through his thoughts, clear and commanding.

Stop.

The fight vanished from him, his limbs went limp and a primal fear ran through him, the commanding magic so painfully familiar, but this time, it was Zoe.

"What the fuck are you doing?" Gabriel spoke between breaths, unable to hide the tremor in his voice. "How?"

"I'm sorry, I learned it from her. I know you're upset but we don't have time to argue, we need to leave now."

He looked back toward the castle. Silje was inside, if he could just get to her—

"Gabe."

He looked back at Zoe.

"Let her go."

"I can't." His voice was raw, pleading. "And neither should you."

"We can go home—" She knelt beside him, forcing him to meet her golden eyes. "To Verchiél."

Home. He could still go home…

His resolve wavered for a moment before being crushed by

his anger. As long as Silje was free, he, as well as Zoe, would be in danger. He needed to see this through.

"You can go," Gabriel said. "But I'm not leaving until I face her. She took everything, I need to do this."

The fight in Zoe's eyes dimmed before she snapped her fingers and the feeling returned to his limbs.

He drew in a shuddering breath, exhausted before he accepted Zoe's offered hand, and rose shakily to his feet. "Don't *ever* do that to me again."

Zoe nodded awkwardly, but so relieved was he in her presence that he couldn't help but break into a smile and throw his arms around her. She returned the hug, burying her face into his shoulder.

"I missed you so much, honeybee."

She clung to him tightly, as if she didn't want to let go. He let her, relishing the contact of another person that wasn't painful for once.

"I'm coming with you." Zoe looked past his shoulder to the castle. "How are we going to get inside?"

Gabriel smiled. "Lucky for us, I just so happen to know another way in."

32

ASBJORN

Asbjorn Osenson, King of Bjordal, protector of the realm of the Northern Isles and holy anointed son of the Church of Birgen was panicking.

He gave a nod to the soldiers stationed before the throne room, and only once he heard the satisfying sound of the heavy panels shutting behind him did he finally let out a breath and close his eyes.

The Verchiél heksa had escaped. Half of the royal estate had been destroyed and the entire capital was in complete chaos. A waste of resources—*a waste of power*. People wouldn't just whisper now, they would shout at his negligence. Demand action, which he was more than willing to give. He'd rally his men and have a party sent out to search for the heksa. But leaving himself in such a vulnerable position wasn't something he had initially prepared for.

He rested a hand at his waist, assured that the heavy weight of the pistol still remained. He took another deep breath and opened his eyes.

Silje was the real problem.

He hadn't seen the slightest trace of her during the entire event. Not that that meant anything. She knew better than any how to remain unseen. She'd show herself when she was ready.

He walked along the chamber, ascending the dais to his
throne. When the crown had been placed on his head he vowed to
keep the way of Birgen as his father had done and his before him.
A long line, unbroken and upheld by tradition. A short time ago
he had been a prince, then a father, finally a leader of his people,
untarnished like so many before him.

Now what was he?

He ran his hand along the worn wooden arm just as a cheerful voice cut through the silence.

"It feels good to be alone, doesn't it?"

He turned around, but the chamber was empty.

"But that's not true," the voice continued. "You're never
alone. Not when you have me."

"Show yourself," he ordered. "Then we will speak—"

He moved to sit on the throne but passed through it, nearly
falling to the floor. He stumbled and cursed, blinking rapidly. His
vision shifted and cleared until he saw that the throne was twenty
feet away and he still stood at the bottom of the dais.

Wild laughter echoed across the chamber, hitting his ears
harshly, and his shock was replaced by anger. He rose to his full
height and boomed out in a commanding voice, "What is our first
rule? Never use magic—"

"Against me," she finished in a gruff mimicry of his voice.

His eyes finally found the source of the voice and where the
throne had previously been empty sat a pale young woman dressed
in servant's scarlet.

Silje beamed as his eyes landed on her. "Hello, Father."

Despite everything, a surge of fondness still swept through
him at the sight of his daughter. The result of an affair in a northern
village during a military campaign. He and Karina had learned to

love each other in their own ways, but they'd only been wed for political alliance. He'd never loved another like Vanja. There had been a vicious spark in her that had caught his interest. Years later a young girl with his eyes had shown up at the castle gates in the middle of the night. He could have cast her away—*should have*—but he saw too much of himself in her, and when her eyes turned to gold in the morning light he knew, above all, that she was his greatest secret.

"You're not to call me that in public," he replied curtly.

She gestured to the empty chamber around them.

"There were guards," he added.

"Yes. There *were* guards."

"I cannot say I am surprised."

"You did teach me well."

"A little too well." He counted his steps up the dais before he drew the pistol.

Silje didn't move. Her eyes flicked from the pistol to his face, unimpressed. "You're not going to shoot me."

"I will."

"You won't."

"Don't tell me what I—"

She flicked her wrist lazily and his hand burnt as if he'd stuck it into an open flame. He hissed in pain and immediately dropped it.

He flexed his hand, struggling to contain the anger in his voice. "You forget your place."

"What are you talking about?" She leaned back comfortably on the throne. "I'm exactly where I'm meant to be."

"I have half a mind to drag you outside and the people will still have their execution."

"We both know you won't do that. Because then you'll need to tell everyone the truth. That for years you've used your own daughter to assassinate your enemies?" She clasped her face and gasped theatrically. "What a scandal!"

From day one she'd been a troublesome child. Prone to boredom and quick to anger. For her everything was a game to win. He placed a wooden stick in her hand and she dropped it for a sword. He taught her how to twist an arm and she bent it until she broke bone. The more he pushed, the harder she pushed back. She never hesitated. Never regretted. She was everything Niklas was not. Bitterly Asbjorn mused that she had been cursed for that exact reason: one more thing for Birgen to take from him.

"I gave you a path," Asbjorn said. "But I never forced your hand."

"You never gave me other options either."

"What else would you have preferred?"

Her nose scrunched up in thought. "Perhaps I wanted to open a bakery and sell little cakes."

Asbjorn sighed deeply. "Do you even understand what you've done? First Verchiél and Heathland, now Bjordal? You've plunged the entirety of the Isles into disarray."

"Whenever something bad happens, why do you always blame me?"

"Then I take it you had nothing to do with Councillor Carrington's recent assassination? I heard the poor man was stabbed through the throat with a knife."

She leaned forward, a thread of excitement in her voice. "I had a cape made of knives. You should have seen it."

"He was off limits."

"Well, now he's permanently off limits to everyone. I had

a job to do and a lifestyle to support. You'll just need to ally with someone else."

Asbjorn's voice darkened. "You don't work for yourself. You work for me. Just as you were supposed to be rid of the Verchiél heksa."

Silje shrugged. "I liked my idea better."

"You don't need to have ideas. You need to do as you're told. Too many times you've directly disobeyed my orders. Sneaking them into my city—my country."

"It's mine too." She glared. "But you always forget that."

Hers too? He bit back a laugh.

"If you hadn't had my protection you would have been killed in your mother's village. Dragged away in the night or swarmed in a furious mob."

"I would have survived just fine without a stubborn old man telling me what to do."

"Enough of this foolishness," He snapped his fingers briskly. "Up."

"No."

"Get up." His teeth clenched.

"Nope," she said, popping her lips with the word. "I'm Osenson. It's my right to sit here."

"Silje, you're—"

"A bastard." They both spoke at the same time.

"Yes. I know." She waved her hand, dismissing the argument. "But your whoring wasn't my fault. Now, listen—" She spoke as if explaining something very simple to him. "You're old and going to die soon so you need an heir." She pointed to herself. "That's me."

"I'm not so aged as to be on my deathbed."

"Really?" she asked with some surprise. "You have a lot of wrinkles."

"Not to mention," he said, ignoring her, "that I already have an heir."

The humiliation of choosing another to take Niklas' place was nearly too much to bear. Hakon certainly wasn't what he had originally planned. But he made an adequate replacement given the circumstances.

Silje hummed thoughtfully, tapping her fingers against the throne. "Well, I'm very happy for you. In fact, I came all the way here to give you a special present."

She pulled out a silk parcel from her coat and offered it to him. At his hesitation, she shook it. "Don't you want it?"

He took the package and something shifted inside. Carefully, he unwrapped the parcel. Silje clapped her hands and fidgeted with excitement, watching him.

Within the folds of silk was a length of metal, filthy with dried blood. Wiping the grime away, he recognized it as a lapel pin, with a golden ermine in its centre.

Asbjorn turned the pin over in his fingers. "I see you've met Hakon."

"Briefly." She stifled a fit of giggles. "He was a crier."

His temper snapped and he clamped his hand over her throat, lifting her easily from the throne. For the first time during their entire exchange, there was panic in her eyes.

"Do you understand how close you are to exposing me?" he growled, tightening his grip. "Niklas might have tolerated your outbursts, but you don't play games with me—"

Her pale eyes blazed golden and pain exploded through his arm as if his skin was aflame. He dropped her and backed away swiftly, watching with fear as the traces of gold faded from his hand. Revulsion coursed through him and he tightened his shaking hand into a fist. "You listen to me."

Silje coughed, steadying herself. "I'll do what I like."

They glared at each other, her eyes flickering from pale blue to gold in anger. He forced himself to draw in a deep breath; he needed a calmer approach with her temper. Their temper.

"Silje." He knelt before her. "You are my daughter, my greatest pride." He forced himself to meet her eyes. Past the gold he could see their pale blue colour—his eyes. But covered, tainted by a sickness that would never leave her, that could never be cured or cut out. The curse would follow her to the grave. Even now he could smell the taint in the air around her. Ash and metal. Omens of death and corruption.

He shook his head. "But you will never rule Bjordal."

Her face fell, the gold in her eyes dimming. "But…you promised. You said you'd choose me instead of Niklas." She rose to her feet, a thread of panic in her voice. "And Hakon is gone. You *have* to choose me. There's no one else left."

"Silje—"

"Choose me!" she screeched.

He forced himself to remain calm even as the air around them grew hot, the scent of ash rising. "You're staying here." He looked to the corner of the room, to the hidden guards who awaited his orders, but Silje's eyes were still focused on him. He needed to keep her attention on him.

"Are you going to cooperate?" Asbjorn asked, deliberately speaking in a tone he knew would irritate her. "Or are you going to make a spectacle of yourself as usual?"

She drew a pistol from her coat.

He laughed tiredly. "You won't shoot me."

"I will."

"No." He stepped away, nodding to an approaching guard behind Silje. "You won't."

She stepped forward just as the steel bracer clamped over her wrist.

Two fully armed soldiers blocked her from either side, weapons raised, another with the set of Bjordal steel bracers.

Silje drew in a sharp breath through her nose before meeting his gaze. "There were no guards."

"Yes," he said. "There *were* no guards."

He nodded to the bracer upon her wrist. "From now on those will remain on at all times. You've been sloppy for too long. No more running off and playing games, but don't worry"—he added at her shocked expression. "You won't be alone for long. I've sent some of my men to retrieve Niklas and dispose of the two heksa when they inevitably return."

Silje's eyes flashed. "You or your men won't lay a fucking finger on them."

Asbjorn paused at that. "You don't actually care about them, do you?"

"They're my friends."

"Friends…" He spoke slowly. "Who abandoned and disavowed you?"

She flinched as if she'd been struck. "They're just confused."

He drew in another measured breath. "Regardless of the other heksa, you and Niklas will remain in Bjordal under close supervision. We'll pretend this whole ordeal with Verchiél never happened."

"Liar," Silje hissed. "He'll die here. If it's not you who does it, it'll be one of the soldiers."

"That's not your concern."

"He's my brother. It's entirely my concern."

"It would be a far kinder thing," Asbjorn explained, "to remove yourself from his life."

"I saved him—"

"You ruined him!" Asbjorn boomed. "He was already weak, but once you'd filled his head with your 'Incarnate' nonsense he never listened to me again. Teaching him that he is anything more than a curse. He's been the only person in your life to stay because he's too weak-willed to say no. If you didn't have that you would be entirely alone."

Asbjorn expected her to fly into a rage, but her eyes dimmed, and something he could have mistaken for sorrow crept through her as she spoke bitterly. "And what about me? You're just going to lock me up again? Only the bastard daughter. Not even worth letting anyone remember that I exist?"

"I'll do what I see fit for the best interest of Bjordal." He nodded to the guards. "Escort her to a holding cell until further notice. I want two armed guards, minimum, stationed by her at all times. No exceptions."

"That's okay." Silje stood eerily still as the bracers were fitted snugly upon her wrists, as well as an additional collar fashioned from the same steel. A tad excessive, but he wasn't going to let her escape again, or worse, use her magic. "I don't need magic."

He waited, bracing for some shift of the air or pain to explode through his body. But nothing happened. The steel bracers held fast.

"Do you think you'll be able to do anything?" Asbjorn

asked.

"No." Silje looked to the guard beside her. "But he can."

Silje snapped her fingers and the guard bearing the pistol shot the other, not waiting for the body to drop to the floor before the gun was aimed at Asbjorn.

Silje's lip curled. "I know you too." She looked thoughtful. "Don't shoot him yet, Edvin. He has to say he's sorry first."

"Edvin?"

Asbjorn stared at the youth with thinly veiled shock. Admittedly he had never suspected a thing from him only because he had always been a weak recruit. He had only taken him in as a favour to his father, who funded the coffers of Bjordal's military. Evidently this carelessness had been misguided on his part.

The boy bowed his head low. "Apologies, mon kogen."

Silje nodded to Edvin. "Consider your oaths paid. You're free to leave the service of the Bjornvangar."

"Mon prinsvenne." Edvin placed a hand over his chest and bowed in the fashion one would to royalty. The gesture made Asbjorn's jaw clench.

Asbjorn turned to Silje, disbelieving. "Prinsvenne?"

"I'm a royal daughter of House Osenson. Why shouldn't I be referred to as such?"

"You're not a legitimate child."

"That argument is getting so old. Just like you. We both know the real reason why you won't let me."

"The people will never allow it."

Silje gestured to Edvin. "What about him? What about all the other soldiers and citizens who helped me stand before you right now? They want change as much as I do."

Asbjorn glared at Edvin. "You've helped to doom your own

country."

Edvin spoke politely. "The only person who's doomed any-thing is yourself, mon kogen."

She lowered the pistol and smiled thoughtfully. "Do you remember that game we used to play? When you'd make me count and I had to find you? Let's play one last time."

"I'm not playing any games."

"Don't worry. I'll give you a head start."

"Silje—"

"One."

Edvin unlocked the bracers and collar, and already the air hissed and crackled.

"Two."

Her gaze snapped to him, her eyes now fully golden.

"Three—"

The collar fell to the floor with a heavy thud and she smiled.

"Run."

Perhaps another would have run. But not him.

He lunged forward, and with a heavy swing knocked the pistol out of her grasp, it clattered across the chamber. She didn't slow in her movements as she unsheathed a knife from her boot and slashed across his chest, the thick fur he wore taking the brunt of it, but he still stumbled backward.

He had taught her everything he knew about fighting, but that was more than a decade past. Now it was painfully obvious that he was an old man who was too slow.

She paced around him leisurely. "I was going to let you choose how you wanted to die, but since you've made every other decision in my life—" She flipped the knife to her other hand.

"Why not let me make yours?"

She threw the knife, and he dodged just in time as the blade struck the wall behind him, plaster and dust rising with the impact. He picked up the first thing he could find, a candelabra, and swung it with all the force he could muster. It made contact, striking her hard across the face and knocking her to the floor.

Silje let out a scream of rage and clutched a hand to her bloodied face. "A candelabra?! What the fuck is wrong with you—" She pulled another knife from her jacket, but this time he didn't wait to face her.

He sprinted from the chamber, and Silje's screams echoed loudly behind him.

He needed to get out of here. He'd regroup and plan with whichever men were left who hadn't turned traitor. Once they succeeded, he'd finally have Niklas under his watch. As he should have for the past decade. Without Silje guiding Niklas, his men would have no difficulty taking him into their custody. Then soon into his.

At least he knew Silje wouldn't leave Bjordal if he was still living. Better to keep her close, even if she was going to throw a tantrum while doing so. A weariness settled over him with the thought. *Why couldn't I have had children who just did as they were told?*

People shouted and gasped as they watched their king sprint past, confused words thrown his way before a pistol shot rang through the air, striking the wall beside him.

Screams resounded but he didn't slow his pace. He rushed through the hallways, out onto the front steps of the castle.

"Mon kogen?" asked a guard. "Is everything—"

Another shot sounded out. Silje marched resolutely down

the steps, blood streaming down her face from where he'd struck her, the pistol raised.

At the sight of her, the guard unsheathed his sword, raising it as he stepped in front of Asbjorn. "Stand away from your king—"

Silje let off a shot, striking the guard between the eyes.

He toppled to the ground and she stepped over him, her golden gaze not leaving Asbjorn.

"Name me heir!"

"Go ahead." Asbjorn gestured to the crowd. "The world watches you."

His worst fear. But this could still work in his favour. She'd finally see that he'd been right all along. These people would never accept her.

She took in the crowd, her anger fading as she smiled sweetly. "It's such a pleasure to see you all here." She turned to Asbjorn. "On such a special day too."

"Who are you?" One of the guards spoke up, weapon still raised.

Silje announced proudly. "Silje Osenson, daughter of Asbjorn Osenson and heir to the Kingdom of Bjordal."

Voices erupted in shock. A pair of guards moved forward to seize her, but she held up a hand and they froze in their tracks.

"Is it true?" someone asked. "Lady Karina had a daughter?"

Better they hear it from him than Silje.

"She is not Karina's," he announced.

This sent a new wave of shock throughout the crowd. People pressed forward to catch a glimpse of her. Silje, if anything, was incredibly pleased by the extra attention. She held her bloody head high as she smiled sweetly for everyone.

One of the noblemen scowled. "You're nothing but a bastard—"

"I'm a prinsvenne." Silje's smile tightened. "Isn't that right?"

The man's scowl faded and a hollow expression entered his eyes, his lips turning up into a smile. "Yes, of course, Prinsvenne Silje. How could I ever have forgotten?"

"Silje," Asbjorn warned.

"You love me." She turned her eyes to the crowd. "You all love me. I'm your princess."

Voices rose from the crowd. All merging into a single chant that sent a chill through him.

"Princess Silje!"

Gold began to pool at the corners of her eyes like tears. Revulsion coursed through him but none of the people noticed as they watched on, entranced.

"Beloved by my people. Wouldn't I make a better queen than a princess? In fact—" Silje looked back to Asbjorn, tears of gold streaming down her cheeks. "Wouldn't I make a better queen than he would a king?"

"Queen Silje! Kill him!" the crowd shouted.

She let off a shot and he grunted as it struck his shoulder. She never missed a mark; this was her way of letting him know she was going to make him hurt first.

Her lips curled back. "Kneel for your queen."

"Silje," he ordered, "stand down—"

Another shot and his knee shattered. He gasped and buckled to the ground where she kicked him over, pressing her heel into his chest so he wheezed.

He looked up at her. Even now he saw the young girl he'd

spoiled when he pretended not to notice how she snuck extra sweets or wandered the castle late at night. A seed of violence had always been there. But he'd nurtured it into something he could no longer control, less like a weed than an overgrown forest.

Silje dug her heel into his throat and Asbjorn coughed weakly. "You won't…"

Silje raised the pistol. "I will."

Asbjorn saw the anger in his daughter's eyes. His eyes. Their eyes, then—

Nothing.

33

NIKLAS

Niklas held a hand to his forehead, the sharp thrum of a headache starting.

He hadn't been to Castle Osenson, let alone Bjordal, in a decade, but as soon as he'd stepped out of the shadows he'd recognized the castle. It was all painfully familiar from the halls he and Silje had endlessly sprinted up and down as children to the courtyard where he'd walked with his betrothed under the pale moonlight. The balancing stone still remained in the courtyard pool, though now buried under a layer of snow and ice.

When he had used Silje's lock of hair to transverse, he hadn't expected to be brought here. He walked cautiously down the halls, suspicion increasing with every step he took in which he saw no other person. Even at such an early hour there should have been servants or even the usual military officials going to and from a meeting with Asbjorn. But the entire area was empty of anyone save himself.

At a familiar painting, Niklas' steps slowed and he stared at his own face, preserved at the age of ten. It had taken many sessions, hours upon hours of standing in stiff silks while his mother chided him for fidgeting.

Her amber eyes—his eyes—stared back at him with a dreamlike haziness which she'd never had in real life. Her gaze had always been sharp and discerning. Able to tell when he'd done something wrong or pinpoint the exact reason why he was upset.

He was shocked that his father hadn't taken it down or had it destroyed in his absence. Perhaps there was a trace of sentimentality left in him. Or maybe he'd simply forgotten it was here. Either way, it left a weight in his chest that didn't quite fade even once he turned away from it.

Silje couldn't be far, and knowing her, she would go where Asbjorn was. Past the hall, the doors of the throne room were already ajar. He took a deep breath, focusing. A moment passed before he sensed her presence, golden and sharp as it always was. He paused before the doors, pressing a hand to the weathered wood.

"Niklas?" Silje's voice called out.

Silje creaked the doors open, her golden eyes looking at him in surprise before she burst into a radiant smile.

"Niklas," she said. "You're here!"

Silje threw her arms around Niklas and hugged him tightly. Niklas grimaced and patted her awkwardly on the back before pulling away to look at her. She'd been in a fight. Recently too. There was a spatter of blood across her cheek and a feral shine to her eyes that hadn't quite faded yet.

"What have you done?" he asked. "Where is everybody?"

She practically bounced on her toes as she stifled a fit of laughter. "I have a surprise for you, but you can't peek."

"Silje, we need to talk—"

"Just wait." She grabbed his arm and pulled him along. "You're going to love it."

With much difficulty due to their height differences she covered his eyes with her hands and led him into the chamber. He couldn't hear anything over the echo of their footsteps and Silje's muffled laughter. Once they had walked for a distance Silje took her hands away. "Ta-da!"

The chamber had been decorated for the traditional feast of Midnventer, which was to take place over several days. The area had already been set with long wooden tables laden with dishes of every kind, centrepieces of fresh-cut pine and juniper decorated each, leaving a scent of greenery in the air. But among all the finery, Niklas' eyes fell upon who sat at the head of the table, beaten and bloodied but holding his gaze with an intensity even now he faltered under.

Asbjorn regarded his son with shock and disbelief in equal measure, his voice quiet when he spoke. "Niklas?"

As a child, Niklas had never seen any semblance of himself in Asbjorn, but in that moment he was struck by their similarities. The same deep frown and red hair, but now Asbjorn's was threaded with grey, his tall figure drooped with not only age but also pain.

"Silje..." Niklas backed toward the door. "What's going on?"

"Isn't this fun?" Silje took a seat, placing a pistol on the table. "One big family reunion."

Much to his credit, Asbjorn appeared merely annoyed rather than angry. "Would you tell your sister to put that thing away and return to her senses?"

"Where's Hakon?" Niklas asked, eyeing the corners of the room, half expecting him to leap out at any moment.

"Dead," Silje said cheerfully. "Father's been awfully put out by it though, perhaps he'll be more agreeable now that you're here."

"If I'm not happy to have you for company, why would I be about him?" Asbjorn snapped, sitting up and wincing with the motion. At that moment Niklas realised both of Asbjorn's legs were bent at odd angles from the knee down. A twinge of panic swept through Niklas as he now knew where the blood on Silje's face had come from.

Niklas turned to Silje. "You hurt him."

"Yeah? That's the whole point," Silje reached for one of the nearest platters and plucked up a pepper cookie. "He can't run if his legs are broken."

Asbjorn scoffed. "You should have broken my jaw, it would have saved me the trouble of having to speak to you."

Silje took a large bite out of the cookie, speaking through a mouthful of crumbs. "There's still time, old man."

Niklas had truly forgotten how alike they were. Although Asbjorn had a great deal of bravado, he was clearly in pain, but he'd never admit it.

Niklas moved forward to help Asbjorn. "Then at least let me—"

"I don't need your help!" Asbjorn boomed.

The words felt like a slap, and even now Niklas struggled to meet his eyes, frozen in place by an old fear of stirring his anger.

Silje merely rolled her eyes at the outburst, reaching for more food. "And he calls me a bastard."

Niklas struggled to breathe evenly. "You're a stubborn fool."

"Do forgive me for not accepting help from a heksa," he spat the word as if it were something bitter in his mouth.

Niklas clenched his fists, his fingernails biting deeply into his palms. "This has been happening long since before I changed. You always hated me."

A tense silence spread. Silje lowered the pheasant leg she'd been in the process of tearing into and spoke only loud enough for Niklas to hear. "Okay, this is getting kind of personal, even for me."

Niklas ignored her and held Asbjorn's gaze steady, a challenge, but Asbjorn wasn't prepared to argue as Niklas had suspected, instead he just looked tired.

"I never hated you, Niklas."

"You did and you still do. You never wanted me, I was always a disappointment—"

"You reminded me too much of her," Asbjorn cut across.

Niklas fell silent. He knew instantly who Asbjorn meant, specifically because he'd never been allowed to speak of his mother to him. Even now Asbjorn spoke slowly, the words leaving him with a hesitance.

"Karina was…you were always so conscious of the world around you. Thoughtful, calm. But also too hesitant to show force, let alone use it. The other leaders worried, they spoke to me first, then behind my back, of the strength you lacked to lead. Your mother thought it would be a welcome change, but Bjordal doesn't change, not easily, and certainly not with the lifetime of a single king."

"So you used me being a heksa as an excuse to get rid of me?"

"Do you think me of so weak of mind as to care what they think? No. I was fearful of what they'd do, especially when I was no longer there to protect you—"

"You exiled me!" Niklas' voice rose. "Your men hunted me, even now I can't walk freely in my own country. When have I ever had your protection?"

Anger entered Asbjorn's voice. "Why do you think I spent

so long training you? Giving you the most difficult tasks for the least amount of praise? I had to prepare you for what Bjordal needed. Not what she or I wanted."

Niklas wanted to scream. He bit the inside of his cheek, tasting blood. He had thought that in all the years that had passed he'd finally have the upper hand on Asbjorn, that he'd be unaffected and unbothered by what had happened in the past. But in that moment he was a youth once more, struggling and failing to be taken seriously.

"You could have taught me how to hide it," Niklas said bitterly. "Like you did for Silje."

"As a bastard, Silje was the exception," Asbjorn said.

Silje clucked her tongue in annoyance. "I'm starting to think that's his favourite word."

Asbjorn continued speaking. "You are a heksa and the son of a king, safety was never going to be an option for you. Even now…" His voice trailed off, though whether it was from the pain of reminiscence or the pride of not wishing to speak, Niklas couldn't tell. "First she passed before her time, then you were changed. It was like losing her all over again. Except you were still here, and I still could catch glimpses of her when that horrible taint had lessened its hold during the day."

"I'm still your son."

Whatever moment of vulnerability that there was vanished, and his pale eyes hardened like steel. "My son died that day, you're just what's left."

Niklas could have snapped. He could have taken him into his hands and broken every bone, torn each muscle. It would have been too easy. He could finally be the powerful and vicious leader Asbjorn had wanted all along.

But everything he'd done wrong in Verchiél was still fresh in his mind. He'd already learned the hard way where violence got you—surrounded on every side by enemies. He needed to handle this calmly to ensure no further blood was shed.

Niklas took a deep breath, infusing his voice with every bit of the cold detachment Asbjorn had ever given him. "Then I have nothing left to say to you."

Silje rose from her seat and placed a hand on his arm as if to comfort him, but Niklas flinched away. He could barely stand the sight of either of them.

"You see?" Silje said. "He never loved you. He never loved us." She picked up the pistol and offered it to Niklas.

Niklas backed away. "No."

Asbjorn laughed weakly. "I told you he'd be too weak."

"Niklas," Silje said, her voice tense. "He exiled you, disinherited you for Hakon. He was the one who let his soldiers torture you, he's been the cause of every horrible thing in our lives and you'd spare him now?"

Niklas looked back at Asbjorn. He realised it was the same way Asbjorn had originally looked at him with pity. "I don't want to be like him." He looked at Silje. "Or like you."

Asbjorn spoke thoughtfully. "Perhaps the boy has grown a spine after all."

Silje let out a pistol shot into the table, wood splintering with the impact. Her eyes flickered from pale blue to gold in anger. "I'm so sick and tired of everyone not listening! First them and now you?"

She paced, the irritable movements reminding Niklas of a wild animal about to pounce. "I did so much for you, I gave you every opportunity I could and now you'd just give in?" She raised the pistol to Asbjorn. "I won't let you ruin this."

Niklas screamed. "Silje, no—"

He lunged to knock the pistol out of her grasp, but she anticipated his movements. Her eyes flashed for a brief moment with gold, and her voice pierced through his mind.

Move!

His traitorous body caused him to swerve to the side, buckling under the weight of her magic. It was brief, but the distraction was enough. She let out a shot, and the bullet pierced right between Asbjorn's eyes as he slumped back into his chair.

Niklas' heart beat wildly in his chest, his limbs unmoving as he stared at the man who had caused much sorrow in his life. A king no longer, but still crowned in blood.

What had they done?

Slowly Silje lowered the pistol and cocked her head to the side to consider the mess with mild interest. "Odd, I thought it would feel different."

"Wh-what have you done?!" Niklas shouted when he finally found his voice.

"Bjordal is ours, brother." Silje smiled and reached for the wine. "Have a glass, let's celebrate."

Niklas knew that Silje had been hiding more from him than he'd originally known, but this was something else entirely.

"Why would you do any of this?" Niklas asked. "I thought we were going to stay in Verchiél."

Silje poured the wine. "Don't you see? I have Bjordal, you have Verchiél, there's still the matter of Heathland… Perhaps I'll give that one to Zoe, she'd like it better than Gabriel would—"

Niklas knocked the glass out of her hand and it shattered against the floor.

"I'm going to pretend," Silje said dangerously, "that I dropped that."

"Was this your plan the entire time?" Niklas demanded.

Silje considered him for a moment before she placed the wine bottle down.

"What are Incarnate in any of these nations? Servants, pawns, playthings to be traded and bartered or monsters to be put out of their misery. But now? We're free to do anything we like.

"Asbjorn used me like he used you. Zoe and Gabriel didn't know it but they were being used too. Why settle for such a fate when we can achieve so much more together?"

Niklas reached for the ancient fingerbones in his jacket. "I'm leaving. This is madness and I won't be caught here with our father's blood on our hands."

Stop.

Gold edged in at the corners of his vision as Silje's voice rose in his mind. "What did I tell you? You're not leaving. No one is."

The sun shone through the castle windows and he felt the last of his magic leave him for the day. Panic set in. He was back in the heart of Bjordal with no magic.

"Now." Silje seated herself on the throne, golden eyes blazing in the sunlight. "Let's begin, shall we, brother?"

34

GABRIEL

"So where's the throne room?" Zoe asked.

Gabriel considered the many ancient and twisting hallways of Castle Osenson. "It's, uh...around here. We just need to take a right up at this bear carving..." He frowned. "Or was it the wolf?"

"You're lost," Zoe said.

"Look," Gabriel explained, "I was the one who was locked in a fucking cell. I think I'm doing a pretty good job of remembering, all things considered."

"You don't need to snap at me," Zoe said, a touch of hurt in her voice.

Gabriel paused, guilt twisting in his gut. He needed to remind himself that Zoe was here because she'd chosen to come back and help him.

"I thought you left," Gabriel admitted. "Back on the ship, when I woke up, Silje told me that you'd taken Ada's deal and stayed in Grislow."

"Well, there's your first problem, never believe anything Silje says."

"But you did take her deal."

Zoe fidgeted with her hands, one of her anxious tics. "Gabriel—"

"Why didn't you tell me you wanted to leave?"

"Because I didn't think you'd take it well, and to my credit you didn't."

"Sorry to be upset that my co-ruler decided to leave me."

She gestured to him in frustration. "Well, what did you think would happen?"

"Well, to start, we'd stay in Verchiél and live grand lives of luxury and comfort, beloved by all. I'd live to a hundred and you to a hundred and one so you can throw me the grandest funeral ever seen and tears would be shed for ages to come." He shrugged. "It all sounds pretty stupid now."

"Gabe," Zoe said. "We've always been two very different people who want different things."

"Yes, but that's exactly the problem," Gabriel said. "Once you leave you'll realise how sick of me you are, and I'll never see you again. I know it's selfish wanting you to stay, but I don't quite know what I'd do without you. You're kind of my best friend."

Gabriel couldn't bring himself to meet her eyes after such an admittance. He'd spoken with Zoe about everything from plans of petty revenge for his rivals to deep declarations of passion for lovers. But for some odd reason the hardest thing to do was to speak honestly about their own friendship.

He tensed when Zoe began to laugh, but there was no judgement in her eyes, only incredulity. "Just because I want to leave doesn't mean we still can't be friends."

Despite himself, hope was threaded in his voice. "You'd come back to see me?"

"Gabe, look—" She placed her hands on his shoulders, forcing him to meet her eyes. "You can be a selfish ass who spends way too much time lazing about and flirting for your own good, not to mention that you don't know the first thing about impulse control—"

"Is this really necessary? Asbjorn already gave me quite the roasting earlier."

"Yes, because my point is," Zoe cut across him, "despite everything, you have been and will always be my best friend too." Zoe scrunched up her face in thought. "Well, my second best friend after Alessi."

"I fucking knew it."

She gave his shoulder a reassuring squeeze. "I won't be gone forever. I'll come back to visit. I promise."

"You'd better, what would I tell everyone during the summer solstice with no Incarnate Sun?"

She smiled, and unable to further articulate the relief he felt, he continued their trudge through the castle halls. Zoe fell into a familiar step with him, eyeing the looming carvings of Bjordal predators with unease.

"What are we going to do when we find Silje?" she asked.

"Simple. Get in. Kill her. Get out again."

"We can't kill her."

"Why not?"

Zoe gave him that look which told him he'd said the wrong thing; it was an expression he was well acquainted with. "We need to talk to Silje."

"Ah, yes, because that's always worked in our favour before."

"I agree that a fight is probably inevitable," Zoe said carefully, "but let's agree to at least reason with her first, okay?"

Gabriel bit the inside of his cheek in frustration. He wanted nothing more than to storm into the throne room and finish his fight with Silje once and for all. But if he had to play nice and pretend to listen so he could make Zoe happy, he'd do it.

Then he'd kill Silje.

"Fine," Gabriel relented. "But first sign of trouble and I'm going to fight Silje."

Zoe appeared more confused. "With what? You don't have any magic."

"I can handle myself."

Zoe looked at him with something unfortunately close to pity. "She's an Incarnate Sun and a trained assassin."

"Well, all the more reason for us to stick together," Gabriel said.

Luckily it didn't take much longer before they passed through a more familiar set of hallways. The memory of being escorted through this area by Asbjorn's soldiers was still fresh in Gabriel's mind.

"Ah! You see?" Gabriel said, excitement coursing through him as he quickened his steps. "It's right up here past Niklas' creepy childhood painting."

"Past what?' Zoe hissed, running after him as quietly as she could.

The doors of the throne room were already ajar, though the area was terribly silent beyond. He placed his hands on the worn wood, standing still and listening, but he heard nothing. He cast Zoe a look and she watched him closely, her golden eyes bright in the dim gloom of the hallways.

He moved to walk forward when Zoe caught his arm, halting him.

"Just…" Zoe struggled for words before she said. "Don't do something stupid."

Despite himself, he grinned. "A tall order, but I'll try my

best."

Zoe looked as if she wanted to say something more but Gabriel was already pushing the doors open, unable to wait another second longer. He knew Silje was here; there was nowhere else that she could possibly be. When he fully opened the doors, however, he didn't expect to see this.

The chamber had been lavishly set, clearly for a feast. Perhaps even a celebration of his supposed demise, but there were only three people in the room. Gabriel instantly recognized the crumpled form of Asbjorn seated at the head of one of the long tables, what used to be his face now a horrid mess of blood and gore. Zoe drew in a sharp breath at the sight and sidled closer to Gabriel. But apart from the deceased king, there were two figures. His stomach clenched when his eyes landed on Silje's pale form seated comfortably upon the wooden throne. But curiously enough, beside her stood Niklas.

"What the fuck?" Gabriel yelled.

Both siblings whipped around at his voice, which echoed around the chamber, taking in the sight of them with mixed expressions. Shock and fear from Niklas, and something eerily close to joy for Silje.

"You see, Niklas?" Silje smiled. "I told you they'd come."

Silje stood up and walked down the dais, as if she were a benevolent ruler awaiting her guests. "My Sun and Moon, I'm so happy that you're here,"

"Oh, I'm going to deal with you in a minute," Gabriel said to Silje. "But first of all, how the fuck is he here?" Gabriel said, pointing to Niklas.

"Transversal magic," Zoe said softly. "You need a piece of another Incarnate mixed with your own magic to reach where they are."

Gabriel blinked, taking in this newfound information. So not only were there types of magic he didn't know about, but he also could have travelled back to Verchiél in the blink of an eye this entire fucking time?

He whirled to face Zoe. "You're telling me this now?"

"Silje just taught me today, how do you think we got here so fast?" Zoe said.

"Add that to the list of lies she told us." Gabriel turned to Silje, already feeling his temper rise.

"So ungrateful." Silje clucked her tongue. "I would have taught you in time, when you were ready."

"Ready my ass." He started forward and Zoe grabbed the back of his shirt, holding him back. "You just didn't want to teach us in case we left you."

Silje gave him a scathing look. "And to think, I so readily accepted a proposal from someone with such little impulse control."

"Proposal?" Niklas and Zoe spoke at the same time, looks of dismay clear across both of their faces. Zoe released her hold on him enough that Gabriel slipped free and stood before Silje, who looked, if anything, delighted by his anger and eagerly stood toe to toe with him.

"The only reason why I haven't killed you yet is because I promised Zoe to talk first," Gabriel growled.

"Oh? And here I thought you came all this way to beg me to take you back."

"The only place I'll be taking you is into a fucking fight—"

This time it was Niklas who pulled Silje back.

"Sva! Enough. You're like children."

"She was the one who started it all to begin with!" Gabriel hissed, trying and failing to get closer to Silje now that Niklas stood between them.

"There doesn't need to be further bloodshed," Niklas said in a calm tone, which only further set Gabriel on edge. "You came here to talk, yes?"

"Yes!" Zoe blurted out before Gabirel could interject with anything more.

"Then," Niklas said, shooting a look of warning at Silje, "let us talk."

Some semblance of order was shakily formed as the four Incarnate faced one another, Niklas and Silje on one side, Gabriel with Zoe on the other.

Though Zoe had assured Gabriel that she wanted to talk, she made no move to do so just yet and looked between Niklas and Silje anxiously. Whether she was stalling for time or collecting her thoughts, Gabriel had no idea. But the momentary silence was enough that Gabirel heard Niklas whisper in Bjordal to Silje.

"Seriously? You accepted a proposal from him? A slug has more backbone—"

Silje cuffed Niklas on the back of the head, speaking in rapid Bjordal. Gabriel was taken aback. This was entirely different from how he'd seen either of them act and he was starkly reminded that, enemies or not, they were still siblings and treated each other as such.

"So, er…" Zoe began, casting the still quietly bickering siblings a glance. "I want to discuss what comes next."

"Yes, I agree," Gabriel seconded. "Also I can speak Bjordal."

"Yes," Niklas said, "I'm aware." A trace of the same smug

self-assured figure he'd met on the night of the solstice shone through.

Gabriel fumed, but before he could retort, Zoe spoke. "We want to make an offer of peace."

Niklas' brows rose and Silje looked caught off guard as well.

"You do?" Silje asked.

"We do?" Gabriel echoed.

"There's been enough fighting and death already," Zoe said. "For as different as we all are I believe there's more that connects us than separates us, and as such I see no reason why we can't work together to achieve a peaceful outcome."

Niklas eagerly nodded along with Zoe's words but Silje merely looked impatient.

"Lovingly sentimental as always, my dear Sun. But what exactly does your peace entail?"

"Well," Zoe said, "when we return to Verchiél, you need to come with us. To stand trial."

Silje tilted her head to the side. "What for?"

"Oh, I don't know," Gabriel said, "maybe the fact that you murdered our former Incarnate, orchestrated a coup and kidnapped Zoe and me all so you could have a bit of fun."

"I did you both a favour," Silje said, a touch of anger re-entering her voice. "You wanted power, so I gave it to you."

"Do enlighten me as to what you call power," Gabriel snapped. "Because I don't consider being brainwashed very empowering—"

Silje's pale eyes flickered with gold and the area grew hotter. A gust of her magic swept past him, searing his skin.

"You wouldn't understand on your own, that's why I had to

help you."

"Silje, please understand," Zoe pleaded. "You committed regicide in two countries—"

"Three," Niklas corrected her, his voice quiet.

A beat of silence passed through them, Asbjorn's body a heavy presence in the room. Gabriel couldn't say he was surprised. Silje didn't strike him as the sort of person who was picky about who she wouldn't kill. Although he couldn't help but wonder what Bjordal's late king would think if he knew there were four Incarnate in the heart of his castle, two being his children, all arguing with each other. He'd probably die all over again from the blasphemy of it all.

Silje shrugged. "Technically Heathland wasn't regicide."

Zoe's voice wavered but she continued speaking. "Given what we know, if we're to seriously broker peace, then you'll both need to stand trial for what you've done."

Silje laughed. "Why? They're already dead. What difference does it make? As if there could ever be a fair trial for any Bjordal in Verchiél—"

Niklas spoke up. "As much as I disagree with my sister, I too cannot help but share her skepticism of any fair trial on Verchiél soil. There was already much political unrest simply from my presence as a ruler, I cannot imagine the treatment a prisoner would receive."

"Then what would you suggest?" Zoe asked, obviously relieved to have someone else to talk to who wasn't actively making threats or denying their involvement in regicide.

"Let us disappear," Niklas said. "You'll never hear from us again."

"Well, that's all well and good for you two," Gabriel said.

"But what will we tell Verchiél?"

"Whatever you wish," Niklas said. "Dead, missing, exiled. What does it matter so long as you have back what's rightfully yours?"

Irritation flared through Gabriel as he looked at Niklas incredulously. "Don't you get it? Nothing and no one is ever going to be the same in Verchiél, in the Isles again and it's entirely the fault of you and your fucked-up family."

"Gabriel," Zoe said, her tone a warning, but Niklas sighed and shook his head.

"He's right, and though it doesn't begin to make amends, I want to help find a solution."

"A solution for what?" Silje asked. "You're all talking like there's something to be fixed, but there isn't, we're exactly where we're supposed to be."

When no one spoke, she looked between the three of them, incredulous. "Don't any of you understand?"

"Understand what exactly?" Gabriel asked.

Silje frowned as if he'd asked a very stupid question. "The heavens didn't bless us. We are the bastardised saints they propped up. They sought to create their own gods. Instead they created us. Why shouldn't we take what we want? We've been used for our entire lives, now it's our turn instead."

"As much as I adore revenge fantasies," Gabriel said, "I'd much rather use that odd travel magic and go back to Verchiél. I've spent more than enough time here freezing my ass off and nearly being killed by Bjordal fanatics."

"You aren't leaving," Silje said simply. "None of you are."

"Silje," Niklas interjected. "They make a fair offer, better than many would give. It would be unwise to oppose."

"No more!" she shouted. "Either you stand with me or you're against me."

Niklas moved forward, but instead of preparing to fight, he stood with Gabriel and Zoe.

Silje's face fell. "Niklas?"

He shook his head, standing firm. "I won't help you. Not again."

"I gave you everything!" she screamed. "All of you." Heat radiated from her in waves, and though they were in Bjordal in the midst of winter, Gabriel felt as if it were a hot summer day. "Ungrateful, short-sighted—" Silje's eyes blazed fully golden. "You don't deserve the gifts you were given, and you'll not use them against me."

"Silje." Zoe raised her hands. "We don't have to fight—"

"Speak for yourself," Gabriel muttered.

"Stand down, Silje," Niklas said.

Silje was silent for a moment, her golden eyes inscrutable before she spoke.

"Niklas?" Her voice echoed, inescapable. "Won't you help me?"

Niklas must have known what was coming as he started to flinch away, his face pained and muscles spasming. He was fighting against some unseen force, which all too swiftly won when all the tension left his body and his face went oddly blank, his amber eyes filled entirely with a gold that mirrored Silje's own.

Zoe held her hand toward Niklas, trying to reverse the hold of Silje's magic as she'd done in Grislow, but to no avail. A wave of heat lashed out at them and Zoe drew her hand back, her eyes watering with pain.

"What did you do to him?" Zoe asked.

"Reminded him of where his priorities lie," Silje said. "Now, which to choose…" Silje's fingers danced between the two of them before ultimately pointing to Gabriel.

"I think you and Niklas have some catching up to do, don't you?" Silje smiled. "Break him for me would you, brother?"

Niklas lunged and Gabriel narrowly jumped out of the way. Magic or not, Niklas was deadly enough from size and physical strength alone.

"Fight it!" Gabriel screamed.

Niklas seized Gabriel by the throat, hoisting him into the air as if he weighed nothing, Gabriel sputtered, struggling to breathe. Golden magic licked from Niklas' palms, scorching Gabriel's skin before he was thrown against a wall. The impact shocked his body, pain radiating through his limbs as he collapsed to the floor.

"Fuck—" Gabriel coughed, struggling to stand. "That's not how I like to be choked!"

In a twisted imitation of Gabriel's own magic, Niklas disappeared in the blink of an eye before he reappeared in a blinding flash of golden light and loomed over him. He'd picked up one of the many heavy iron candelabras which decorated the chamber and raised it to strike. Gabriel swiftly rolled out of the way, stone and plaster cracking under the heavy impact.

He couldn't fight Niklas hand to hand; he'd never been a good brawler. Even when his opponent didn't share the same height and weight as a tree. He didn't have his magic and Zoe was too busy concentrating on fighting Silje to share any. In lieu of any better ideas, he needed to do what he always did best—

Fucking cheat.

What had Niklas told him that night of the duel? He used his magic like a crutch? When Niklas had been in control of himself, he had used his magic sparingly, mindful when to pick and choose for the best advantages. Under Silje's control he was a tempest of magic. It was horrible to fight, but it was also easy to predict.

Niklas blinked in and out of view, golden magic swirling in his wake as he followed Gabriel's retreating form across the chamber. Niklas shot his hand forward, golden light shooting from his hands, which left black scorch marks across the floor.

Gabriel continued to dodge and weave from side to side, purposefully lagging behind at times as if he was growing tired.

Niklas pressed closer, disappearing then reappearing before Gabriel. He was close enough now that he'd be unable to course correct. As Niklas disappeared in a wave of golden light once more, Gabriel pivoted from where he'd originally been moving and dodged to the side, seizing the candelabra nearest to him and gripping it with all the force he could muster.

Niklas reappeared exactly where he needed him and Gabriel swung the candelabra. It made contact, striking Niklas across the back of his head and knocking him down. He collapsed, unmoving. His red hair was stained with blood.

Gabriel caught his breath and shrugged at Niklas' fallen form. "Nothing personal—oh wait, actually it is."

Another scream sounded out, and his attention was drawn back to Zoe and Silje, who duelled viciously in the centre of the chamber.

Golden magic moved so quickly it gave it the appearance of lightning, crackling through the air as Silje and Zoe fought, any pretence of peace vanished. They were fighting for blood.

Gabriel scoured the area around him for a weapon. Surely he could find something better than another fucking candelabra.

He caught sight of the oily barrel of a pistol, discarded on one of the long tables. He picked it up, checking to see that it was still loaded. His eyes next landed on Asbjorn. The unfortunate king was still dressed in the finery and bear fur mantle from earlier, but Gabriel remembered that all the Bjordal military carried issued steel by their sides.

Gabriel swept his mantle aside and sure enough there was a Bjordal steel sword still sheathed at his side. Gabriel snatched the sword up and shrugged by way of apology. "I need it more than you do."

Another scream echoed across the chamber, followed by a loud crackling and clap of magic. The area had grown stifling with heat, and both women circled each other, exhaustion creeping in as they each healed their respective wounds.

Gabriel watched as Silje's face flickered with pain, as gold glowed along her arm, veins swirling until her skin knitted back together seamlessly, healing perfectly. She picked up her blade again, shifting it restlessly from hand to hand, moving with renewed energy. It was no good, they'd only continue to heal themselves whenever they both became hurt; they were evenly matched with the same powers.

But unlike Zoe, Silje was completely alone. She'd used Niklas for so long that there was nothing left for him to give.

He met Zoe's gaze and gave her a nod, which she returned. Enzo and Aria had once told them that the sun and moon were opposites, but they were equals as well, constant companions, always keeping each other in balance.

"SILJE!" Gabriel bellowed.

Silje hesitated, and when her golden eyes met his, her lips curled into a smile.

He raised the pistol and let out a shot and she disappeared, reappearing in a flash of golden light about ten feet ahead just as Niklas had done. He didn't hesitate, letting out shot after shot. She continued to disappear then reappear, dodging each and every single one. Only once the pistol was left clicking hollowly in his hand did she reappear only inches away from him, a wide smile on her face.

"Boo!" She laughed, knocking him backward.

From his side he drew the knife he'd picked up, slashing it across her arm. Silje let out a gasp of pain and disappeared again, reappearing fifteen feet away as she clutched her forearm which now bled gold.

Zoe squared off, facing her from the opposite side. Silje was trapped between them.

"You…" Silje spoke between breaths. "We had everything. It would have been perfect."

"Perfect for you. Not so much for the rest of us. You really should have taken Zoe's offer," Gabriel countered.

"Why?" Silje laughed. "So I can fade into obscurity and you can abandon me?"

Silje was a blur as she lunged forward, sword drawn. Gabriel tossed his own sword up in the air, where Zoe caught it. He dropped immediately to the ground, barely in time as he managed to slide under Silje's oncoming swing, the air shifted over the back of his neck, ruffling his hair as her sword passed over him. Zoe met Silje's blade with a collision that made his teeth clench.

Zoe's golden eyes found him and she reached out a hand toward him. He didn't need words. He already knew.

Gabriel seized Zoe's hand and she pulled him along through a flash of golden light. A brighter mirror of what they'd done during the duel. They reappeared and Zoe spun him so that he landed behind Silje, who barely managed to counter the sudden onslaught as their blades met.

He didn't slow his movements as he slashed out at Silje, only further spurred on by her sudden proximity. He tossed the blade up, caught it with his other hand and lunged out from a different angle.

Silje met every single blow with a parry. She had a skill he couldn't deny, but she'd already been fighting with Zoe for much longer before he arrived, and she was growing tired.

Fed up with his antics, Silje lunged toward him viciously.

He brought his sword up just in time to cover himself as Silje brought her knife down upon him. The screeching of metal on metal made him cringe, but he held steady, shoving her away.

They circled her now; the acrid scent of golden magic was strong in the air, his mouth tasted of ash.

"You'll die before you leave."

Silje lunged, blade drawn, and Gabriel pushed Zoe out of the way, prepared to meet Silje head-on.

"Gabriel!" Zoe screamed, though her voice was a distant echo in his ears.

But if he did one thing right in his fucking life it would be this.

The blow never came. Gabriel's ears were ringing, though the room had grown deathly silent.

He looked up.

Silje's entire body spasmed. A blade had been plunged through her chest from behind.

Behind Silje, Niklas gripped a Bjordal steel blade tightly, his face bunched with pain as he held it locked in place.

Silje's face still bore an expression of shock as she turned to look at her brother.

"Niklas?"

His mouth moved but Gabriel couldn't hear what he said. Silje's face contorted with rage and she dove for Niklas, plunging her own knife into his side and slicing her hand in an arc across his face. He gasped, his face streaked with blood and gold.

Silje collapsed, scrabbling desperately with the blade still lodged in her chest, but she'd landed on her back, only pushing it further through her. Blood and golden magic wept from her like a river.

"Zoe…" Gabriel crawled over to her where she lay on the floor, winded. "Are you all right?"

"Yeah." Zoe caught her breath. "You?"

His gaze was drawn back to Silje, who lay sprawled across the floor. Her breaths grew weaker, shallow, and she looked between the two of them desperately, her golden eyes dimming.

"Neither of you?"

Zoe shook her head, backing away. But Gabriel remained rooted to the spot, unable to tear his gaze away.

She looked so pitiful, her lovely limbs contorted in painful ways, covered in her own blood. This had been what he wanted, but why did it feel…wrong.

Gabriel knelt beside her. "I can take the blade out, you'll be able to heal yourself."

Silje frowned, though it was an expression born of confusion rather than anger.

"Why? So I can rot in a cell?"

"You'd have your life."

"Gabriel." She smiled through blood-flecked lips. "I hate

you more."

A weak laugh escaped her and she spat up more blood along with it before she went eerily still, her golden eyes fading back to pale blue. She lay across the floor, pale hair spattered with bright crimson, her limbs twisted at odd angles.

Gabriel rose to his feet. A bitterness had settled in him that didn't fade as he tore his eyes away from her broken form.

Zoe considered Silje in silence, her golden eyes wide. "I really thought she'd change her mind."

"I think she made up her mind a long time ago," Gabriel said.

A pained groan caught their attention, and he looked up to see Niklas stirring where he'd fallen.

Oh right.

Zoe rushed to Niklas' side, instantly feeling at his wrist for a pulse, her golden eyes widening in shock.

"He's still breathing!"

Gabriel snorted. "Of course he is."

Zoe shot him a withering glare before she rummaged frantically in Niklas' pockets, eventually coming up with what looked like several ancient knuckle bones.

Gabriel's nose wrinkled. "That's disgusting."

"This is our ticket home," Zoe said, grabbing a small knife from her side, and before Gabriel could protest or even comprehend her actions, she slashed it across her hand, golden magic pooling in her palm.

"Take my hand," Zoe ordered.

Gabriel stared at her with apprehension. "What? Why?"

"Just do it!" Zoe snapped.

As he took Zoe's offered hand, he caught one last glimpse

of Silje, her pale eyes still wide as if she were watching them. As Zoe's magic took hold, the chill of the throne room vanished and Gabriel felt oddly weightless, able to see nothing more than the brightest gold.

35

ZOE

When Zoe's feet touched the floor of the crypt in Verchiél, she crouched over Niklas, the heat of her golden magic already at her fingertips as she assessed him.

She tore away the shredded remnants of his jacket and was startled to see that nearly every inch of his skin was covered in scars. Some were only random slashes while others were too methodical to simply be accidental. She ignored the old wounds and instead focused on the damage Silje had done. The wound was not unlike where Gabriel's had been but deeper and more jagged, bleeding with the remnants of Silje's golden magic as well as his own blood.

She pressed her hands to the wound, willing her magic to heal. The bleeding slowed, but didn't stop, his skin slowly stitching itself back together. As soon as she took her hands away, the wound reopened and bled with the same golden magic, as if she'd never healed it at all.

"Help me," Zoe said.

Despite the fact that a man was bleeding out in her arms, Gabriel looked unfazed.

"Why in the ever loving fuck would we do that?"

"Because he helped us."

"So? He also caused all our problems in the first place. He

deserves what he's gotten."

Zoe resisted the urge to snap at Gabriel; it would only make her case worse. She had to try an approach he would understand: revenge.

"If he dies here then there's not going to be any chance for him to atone for what he's done," Zoe said. "Not to mention the bargaining chip we'll have with Bjordal if he's still alive. I'm sure their new successor won't be happy to learn that Asbjorn's son still lives and is allied with their enemy."

Gabriel paused then, reconsidering Niklas with renewed interest. "I suppose it would be a waste of a perfectly beautiful man, wouldn't it?"

"Gabriel," Zoe said, gritting her teeth. The effort of keeping Niklas alive was straining her. She felt for his heartbeat; there was the barest flutter of a pulse and then nothing.

Gabriel, perhaps more out of stubbornness than anything, took another painstaking moment to consider Niklas before he offered his hands to Zoe, which she grasped with a tight grip. Focusing deep within as she drew Gabriel's own magic to her.

It was slow, the effort of using both her and Gabriel's magic. Familiar golden warmth and a deep chill all at once. Eventually the damage of the golden magic retreated, seeping entirely out of the wound as muscle and skin began to knit itself back together.

The deeper she focused, the more she caught flashes of an unfamiliar life:

A blonde girl and a boy with flaming red hair laughing and playing in the snow

An withdrawn adolescent in the midst of military training

A screaming man pinned against a table while a knife carved dedicated marks into his skin and magic bled from him—

Finally Niklas gasped, drawing in a heaving lungful of air. His amber eyes were bloodshot and looked around wildly before he slumped back to the floor. His entire body was rigid with pain.

Zoe sat back, catching her breath, exhausted. Gabriel didn't appear to be any better off, and she had a feeling that he'd seen what she had from the unsettled look on his face.

"Niklas?" Zoe bent down and took Niklas' large hand in hers, grimacing when she noticed the bright gold veins which stretched under his skin. "Silje did a lot of damage."

"If he's made it this far, he'll live," Gabriel said.

Zoe gently let go of his hand and reconsidered Gabriel. Gabriel who she'd travelled to the other end of the Isles with and back, and who, despite everything, was still here.

"I suppose you're pleased with yourself?" Gabriel said.

Zoe threw her arms tightly around Gabriel. He tensed in surprise, but after a moment hugged her right back, both quiet and shivering on the ground.

"You okay?" she asked.

"Oh, simply peachy, darling. How about you?"

She laughed. "I…don't know."

After another moment in which Zoe more than suspected Gabriel was merely tolerating the hug for her, he helped her to her feet.

They were back, but they'd both made it clear that they didn't want the same things. She wasn't going to lie anymore. Apparently neither was Gabriel when they both spoke at the exact same time.

"I'm leaving," Zoe said.

"I'm staying," Gabriel said.

36

ZOE

Verchiél's Incarnate had officially returned, and in the following weeks people rejoiced at the good fortune of having their Sun and Moon back, throwing festivities in homes or the streets that lasted for all hours of the day or night. But along with merriment and relief there was something else in the city and its people that hadn't been there before.

Discontent.

Whispers turned to outright talk and then shouting. That Incarnate were nothing more than outdated figureheads. Magic was no longer a wholly blessed thing but rather something which could be used and abused by human greed. It had always been, but not always regarded so.

The celestial pair remained in the palace, the walls no longer felt constricting like a cage but instead protective as a barrier against the unrest outside. The palace itself had been cleaned and repaired, the marble scrubbed of blood and any evidence that there had been any violence there in the first place, but both their heads remained free of silver and gold crowns as debates continued over the legitimacy of Incarnate.

Gabriel simmered with a quiet anger, ready to brim over at any moment, but there was a quiet sort of satisfaction in Zoe at the change. For once she wasn't constantly watched and scrutinised in her every action, rather left to her own devices. It made what Zoe had to do all the easier.

The Crimson Bat was dead during the day. The only people milling about were staff who restocked the supplies of alcohol or cleaned the areas which would no doubt become filthy once more by the end of the night. Technically it didn't open until sunset, but the owner gave her a knowing look, gesturing to the back of the establishment.

Zoe walked inside, worn velvet muffling her footsteps as she neared the only occupied table. Tari and Ada sat beside each other, a bottle of half-drunk wine shared between them. If Zoe didn't know better, she'd think they were only having a pleasant afternoon drink together.

"Ha!" Tari smiled as Zoe approached. "Told you she'd show, Vard. You owe me a fiver."

Ada shot Tari an irritated glance but tossed her a coin, which Tari caught with graceful fingers.

"Where's Thaddeus?" Zoe asked.

"Back in Grislow," Tari said. "Apparently it's considered odd to carry an owl around with you."

"Have a seat, lovely." Ada pushed out a chair with her foot, the arm Silje had broken now resting in a sling. "What have you called us here for? I assume it's not because you missed us."

Zoe sat on the edge of her seat, hands clasped tightly in her lap.

There was nothing for it.

"You owe me," Zoe said.

Ada's brows rose. "A bold way to start, but I do love that in a woman."

"I saved your life," Zoe said. "As well as the countless lives of your members at the conservatory."

"I mean, she's not wrong," Tari murmured, earning another irritated glance from Ada.

"I didn't recall officially enlisting you for your efforts," Ada countered, rubbing irritably at her shoulder. "Not to mention that you already turned down the one offer I did give you."

Zoe held out her hand, nodding to Ada's wounded arm. "I can heal that for you."

"You'll understand why I'm a little hesitant to have another Incarnate Sun touch me," Ada said.

"I understand, but I can also fix what Silje broke," Zoe offered.

Ada considered her. "What do you want in return?"

"Simply for you to hear my offer," Zoe replied calmly.

Ada and Tari exchanged another glance, though it was clear there was some sort of wordless exchange happening. Eventually Ada sighed and offered her broken arm.

With delicate fingers, Zoe took Ada's arm in her grasp, careful as she worked, all too aware of not only Ada's eyes upon her but Tari's as well.

"I want to discuss the debt you bought from my friend," Zoe began. "You clearly bought the business because you saw a potential to gain not only a substantial amount of growth from a business venture, but a front for something much more profitable as well."

Ada laughed, wincing when Zoe moved her hand to her shoulder, golden magic wrapping around her. "If this is going to be another moral lecture, it's falling on deaf ears."

"Actually, I want to make you an offer."

Ada considered her with renewed interest. "All right,

shoot."

"You forgive the debt on Alessi's behalf," Zoe said, quickly adding at Ada's shocked expression, "and I want a share of the business in my name."

Zoe focused her golden magic, the last of the broken bones and torn muscles swiftly healing under her grasp, and with a twist of her wrist, any trace of Ada's injury was gone.

Ada stiffened at the shift and felt her shoulder. She stretched and bent her arm, an expression of caution swiftly turning to delight as she ripped the sling off. "Months of healing done in a few seconds. Are you certain you won't reconsider my offer?"

"I'd rather you consider mine," Zoe said.

Ada sighed. "You still haven't answered my question, what do I get out of this deal?"

"A privateer."

Ada raised a brow. "A fancy title for a smuggler."

"Yes, which is precisely what you need right now."

Ada said nothing, clearly waiting for Zoe to explain herself.

"You've placed a new candidate in Carrington's old position," Zoe explained, "one which you chose specifically because you can control them. You're a councillor in everything but name now."

Tari shook her head fondly. "Look at your influence, Vard, the innocent little swan has been corrupted."

"A little bit of corruption is just fine by me," Zoe said. "Once you release Alessi from their contract, you'll need someone else to run the business for you, to make sure that illegal trade isn't happening and people aren't making off with the council's, or rather, your profits."

"And who would take this role?" Ada asked.

"Myself, of course," Zoe said.

Ada laughed, her eyes crinkling with amusement. "You're right, Tari, she has been corrupted."

"I'm serious," Zoe said, a touch of warmth flushed in her cheeks at their amused expressions.

"Don't take it personally," Tari said. "You just don't really have what it takes to be a smuggler."

"Hence privateer and not pirate," Zoe emphasised. "If you secure official working orders for myself and the business, then it's all perfectly legal. A smuggler needs to be discreet, a privateer acting on the authority of Grislow's council however? That's a different matter entirely."

Ada and Tari exchanged another look, though this time there was an excitement palpable to it.

"So you want me to forgive the debt and give you a stake in the business?" Ada said. "It's still steep price for me to pay. How long did you have in mind exactly?"

"Give me a year," Zoe said.

Ada considered her closely. "Three months."

"Six," Zoe says. "I won't take anything less."

Ada's mismatched eyes considered her closely. "And if you don't earn out?"

Here it is, all or nothing.

"Then I'll accept your original offer and work for you and the Hound's Teeth as an Incarnate Sun." Zoe gestured to her arm. "That should be sufficient proof of my skills, though I can fix your nose if you'd like?"

Tari's eyes widened at the bold words, wine-glass still raised to her lips mid-sip. Though Ada's broken nose it wasn't hard to miss. Ada smiled politely, though there was a touch of irritation to her voice. "I like it just fine this way."

Zoe didn't press the subject and instead returned to her previous point. "That's my final offer, take it or leave it."

Ada was silent for the longest time yet. Zoe wasn't sure if she was actually considering her offer seriously or if she was just stalling long enough for a dramatic pause, perhaps both. But after some hushed whispers exchanged between Ada and Tari, Ada finally turned to Zoe, an amused smile on her face.

"Very well." Ada shook her hand. "Pleased to officially make your acquaintance, Privateer Okoro."

37

GABRIEL

Gabriel sat attentively upon the silver throne, adorned in the finery of an Incarnate Moon, all black and silver. The silks felt like a blessing after the hand-me-down clothes he'd practically lived in.

Though it was the middle of the night, the chamber was packed with people; Verchiél elite, dignitaries and even some regular citizens alike had gathered to hear his first announcement since returning. He didn't intend to deprive them of a grand show.

Gabriel smiled, spreading his arms wide.

"Verchiél thanks you for your presence on this day, from both the Sun and the Moon."

The golden throne sat empty beside him, untouched since the night of the solstice when Zoe had graced it.

"I'm sure you're all wondering why I've summoned you here today," he continued.

"Son of the Moon." Official Lyon spoke up. "There have been wild rumours—"

"You'll need to be a tad more specific, my dear, I'm afraid I have a good dozen rumours circulating about myself at any given time."

The usual polite laughter sounded out, but it set Gabriel on edge. He noted the people who it came from.

"Where is the Daughter of the Sun?" Official Lyon asked.

"Lady Zoe Okoro, our beloved Sun, has made the decision to take a sabbatical, if you will."

Discontent murmurs spread throughout the room at this declaration, entirely expected and exactly what he had prepared for.

"But Verchiél has never stood for so long without both celestial halves," Official Lyon said. "There needs to be a balance set to rebuild our nation."

Evidently Niklas' solo rule had left a sour taste in their mouths, and they weren't keen to trust another Incarnate Moon left to his own devices.

"Rest assured that your Moon will provide for you," Gabriel said.

The answer clearly wasn't what they wanted to hear as more murmurs spread, but another voice spoke up.

"Are we going to war with Bjordal?"

"On the contrary," Gabriel soothed. "We're going to broker peace with Bjordal."

"How will you do that?" another voice asked.

Gabriel's lip twitched. "I have my means."

More discontent murmurs with his words, though another voice piped up.

"What about Heathland?"

"We're entering a new era," Gabriel explained. "We're going to open trade with Heathland to create a new industry in Verchiél, one of commerce and, more importantly, entertainment. Starting today, every gambling and entertainment establishment are considered fully legal and protected under Verchiél's laws."

Titters at this, while some looked openly relieved or even excited.

"But, Son of the Moon," another person said, "we're not like Grislow, we don't have the money to compete with a nation like Heathland."

"Ah, I'm so glad you brought that up," Gabriel said. "Because that brings me to my next point."

The room quieted one more, in anticipation of his next words, and Gabriel relished in the attention before announcing:

"Our noble council is hereby dissolved."

A heaviness was suddenly present in the room as the weight of Gabriel's proclamation set in.

"I beg your pardon?" one noble asked.

"You've all been dismissed," Gabriel explained.

Another laughed anxiously. "But there's been a noble council alongside Incarnate for generations now, it was decided when the monarchy was abolished for the rule of Incarnate."

"Yes, well, now I'm abolishing the nobility as well," Gabriel explained. "You'll be stripped of titles and holdings, everything will go toward rebuilding and improving your city and to support your Incarnate."

Discontent murmurs set in again, eyes cast toward him with equal measures of disbelief or outright hostility.

"You can't do this," another said.

"Can't I?" Gabriel asked. "Not a single one of you lifted your fingers to help myself or the Sun of Verchiél. If you can't be trusted in our worst hour then why would I keep you around now?"

"But our houses have stood for generations," Official Lyon protested.

"And yet now they fall," Gabriel said.

Another protested, "We've already had the last Incarnate come in here and ruin everything." He started forward. "I won't have you do the same—"

Gabriel snapped his fingers and shadows sprang to life, surrounding the gathered members.

"You mistake my words for a request rather than what they are—an order." He leaned forward. "I've done the courtesy of informing you all face to face, but I'm afraid the time for polite debates has passed."

The shadows pressed closer, the room darkening.

"I am the one you pray to at night," Gabriel said. "The only person in this entire city who can do what nobody else can. I'm more than a king or a saint, or saviour, I'm your Incarnate and you'll obey me or suffer the consequences."

After the initial shock wore off, one by one people filed out of the chamber, no longer the expressions of anger or impatience on their faces but something much more familiar to Gabriel.

Fear.

He could work with that.

Official Lyon lingered only long enough to cast him one last look.

"You're playing a very dangerous game, Son of the Moon."

"I don't play any other kind," Gabriel replied.

He seated himself back on the silver throne, reaching for a glass of wine.

The news would spread like wildfire, and by morning the entire city, maybe even the whole country, would know. Let them be discontent. He was ready for anyone who would dare oppose him again.

He looked to the sliver of the moon through the tall windows.

His fingers brushed against the cold metal of the ring in his pocket.

He had his own problems to deal with.

38

NIKLAS

Niklas watched the thin crescent of the moon in silence, the night air still tainted with a winter chill. There was a particular sort of silence in the gardens that might have been peaceful, had it not been for the absence of any living creatures except for the second Incarnate Moon who approached with confident steps.

"Beautiful night," Gabriel called out. "Wouldn't you agree?"

"Am I to be burdened with your presence so frequently?" Niklas asked, not bothering to disguise the contempt that dripped from his voice.

You know." Gabriel walked around the bench, gravel crunching beneath his feet. "Some have given me jewels to spare even moments of my time. You should consider yourself fortunate."

Niklas fidgeted with the heavy Bjordal steel bracers at his wrists. He'd woken up with them on and he knew better than to ask for their removal. Though Gabriel was nothing but smiles and charm, Niklas understood that he was his prisoner, not his guest.

"Fortunate that I have survived long enough to become your prisoner?" Niklas met Gabriel's eyes, always unsettled to see the same black mirrored back at him. "Or fortunate that you've come to remind me personally?"

Though the same magic flowed through their veins, something about Gabriel bothered Niklas. It wasn't the magic itself, even now the cold of it was familiar to him. Rather it was a moral corruption of his character which was only made worse by the unnatural power that coursed through him. He played a charming act, but there was a cunning, a darkness deep inside him that made Niklas' skin crawl.

Lokan, Bjordal called them. The spirits of tricksters. Sent to torment those deserving of punishment. Apparently Gabriel was his.

Gabriel gave him another shallow smile. "Both."

Niklas' lip curled. "That I doubt."

"But I should be delighted to be in such renowned company as well." Gabriel gestured to him. "The Prince of Bjordal himself."

Wind picked up from the waters and Niklas shivered, pulling his coat tighter around himself. After the last fight, Niklas found that there was a weariness in him which hadn't quite faded, not even at night when he was supposed to be at his strongest.

"I'm no prince," Niklas said.

"Then do you have stunning revelations you brought back from the other side?"

"Only that I am tired," Niklas said quietly.

Niklas tensed as Gabriel sat beside him, crossing his legs neatly. "You should know that none of us have found Dabria. I've had people scouting, but there's been no sight of her."

Relief spread through him with this news. At least one of them was free of this wretched place.

"If she doesn't wish to be found, then there's nothing you can do."

"You two seemed close."

"I trusted her."

"Like you trusted Silje?"

Gabriel held out the silver ring. Niklas tensed at the sight of it before he took the ring from his palm. He still remembered the day when he and Silje had received them as children. She had been so…happy. One of the few times in his life when he recalled ever seeing genuine emotion from her.

"You mourn her?" Gabriel asked with some surprise.

"She was my sister. How can I not?"

"You were the one who killed her."

Niklas squeezed his eyes shut, trying to suppress the memories of what it felt like to slice a blade through her back. Like a coward who couldn't look her in the eye while he did it.

"Look on the positive side," Gabriel added. "There's going to be a brand-new Incarnate to take under our wings."

"You're searching for them?" Niklas asked, desperate for anything to distract himself from the memory of his sister's bloody corpse.

"Naturally," Gabriel said. "I like to keep my problems where I can control them. Why do you think you're here?"

Niklas glared, a quiet anger simmering in him. "You can't keep me here."

"Can't I? You helped Silje murder our former Incarnate, not to mention usurping and nearly killing us in the process." Gabriel leaned forward, and Niklas instinctively flinched away at the close proximity. "I think I can do whatever I like with you."

Gabriel snapped his fingers and an illusion appeared before Niklas, lunging for him.

Niklas instinctively shot both hands forward. But when nothing happened and the moment passed with Gabriel and the illusion watching, Niklas' eyes widened in realisation of his mistake as he looked at the Bjordal steel bracers fastened snugly at his wrists. Trying to summon a power that was no longer fully under his control.

"Oh, dear." Gabriel tapped his lips, amused. "That's a nasty little habit we're going to need to break you of."

Niklas crossed his arms tightly. "What does it matter when I can do nothing?"

"You see, my dear prince." Gabriel snapped his fingers and the illusion faded. "We've been given an opportunity to move things to our advantage."

"*Your* advantage."

"If you are in my favour then you also benefit from my advantage."

"Why would I care for your favour?"

Gabriel looked back toward the guards. "Do you see them? They all see the man who ruined their city and wonder why he still lives. In the time since we took you in, I've prevented three separate attempts on your life, all from within the palace."

Niklas' frown deepened. If Gabriel wanted to keep him alive, that meant he was going to use him.

"Do you want my thanks?" Niklas asked dryly.

"Well, it certainly wouldn't hurt to dust off your manners every now and again. But don't you see how generous the Moon of Verchiél is? I will keep you safe in exchange for a favour."

"What kind of favour?"

"You're the last of the Osenson bloodline and the firstborn son of Bjordal's late king and queen. What's to stop you from marching back home and taking your father's throne for yourself?"

"You want me to take my father's place?" Niklas asked,

unable to keep the skepticism from his voice.

"I'd love it." Gabriel smiled. "In fact I've already made arrangements to escort you back to Bjordal."

Niklas was fully suspicious now. Kindness simply for the sake of it wasn't to be found here. Especially not from this wretched creature.

"How is any of this a favour to you?"

"You should know better than any that Verchiél and Bjordal have never gotten along. War and then a shaky peace before we all grew paranoid or angry and threw another war over who said what. But the way I see it, why continue to fight when we've been given a chance for peace?"

"You want peace?"

"I want advantage," Gabriel said. "Niklas Osenson, in exchange for your life, your words, your actions, every waking moment as king will be dedicated to Verchiél."

"Not Verchiél," Niklas said. *"You."*

Gabriel touched the silver circlet in his hair. "We're one and the same now, are we not?"

"No," Niklas snapped. "I already made that mistake for one person. I won't do it again."

Gabriel was clearly irritated, but he managed another smile and a polite laugh. "I'm afraid you think I'm asking you for your permission, but this is an order, not a request."

"You have no right."

"Neither did you when you took away my life. I nearly died a thousand times over thanks to you and your sister. Think of this as recompense. You stayed here because you felt you owed a debt for your actions, correct?"

"Yes."

"But you don't want to stay in Verchiél, do you?"

"No."

"You want to go home to Bjordal."

Bjordal. Even at the opposite end of the Isles, his home brought a great melancholy to him. His people could never fully accept him for what he was, but still, they deserved better than anything people like Hakon could offer them...

"Not as your puppet," Niklas said.

"Why not? How could I ever waste such a valuable asset?"

Something in Niklas snapped. Before Gabriel could react, Niklas pinned him against the bench, his hand tight around his throat. For the first time since the winter solstice, a flash of genuine fear and uncertainty passed across Gabriel's face. *Good*, Niklas thought. *Let him remember that even a chained hound can still bite.*

The guards at the entrance jumped to attention, swords and pistols raised, but Gabriel held up a hand, forcing them to halt as he focused on Niklas.

"I'm *not*"—Niklas' lips curled back—"an asset."

"Debatable," Gabriel said as calmly as he could manage, though Niklas felt the panicked flutter of his pulse beneath his hand. "But if you kill me now, you'll never get out of here alive. Your entire family is dead. You have nowhere left to go. You need me."

The anger which had spurred him now flickered out until all that was left was a familiar, cold realisation: he was alone.

Slowly, Niklas' hands fell away from Gabriel's throat, and he sat himself on the very edge of the bench, as far away from Gabriel as he could manage. "I'm Incarnate," Niklas said, voice cracking. "Bjordal will never accept me."

"All the more reason why you need me," Gabriel repeated. "Who else is going to watch out for you? Or truly understand what you are?"

"You would do the same as Silje, but for another throne?" Niklas asked.

"Don't compare madmen to tyrants. I think you'll find we couldn't be more different."

"What's the difference?"

"The difference is that I want you by my side rather than at my feet."

Niklas ran a finger along one of the Bjordal steel cuffs. "If I were truly at your side, I wouldn't be your prisoner."

"A precautionary measure. I can't just instate a king without knowing whether he intends to go to war with me once I leave him there."

"And if I refuse?"

"If you refuse then I'm going to give Verchiél's people what they want. You will be swiftly executed for a multitude of crimes, being a usurper in a coup among them, and what a travesty it would be to waste that beautiful face of yours."

Niklas laughed without any humour. "Do I have a choice either way?"

"No, but I do love the guise of politeness. Makes my manners appear sparkling." Gabriel offered his hand once more. "Niklas, do we have a deal?"

Niklas tried to keep his face blank, determined not to give Gabriel the satisfaction of seeing his discomfort. But he felt it, in the way his jaw clenched and his muscles tensed to the point of tearing. It was obvious and Gabriel was enjoying this in the same way a cat enjoyed playing with prey before devouring it.

As much as he loathed to admit it, for as different as they were, Gabriel was still the only other person here who understood what he was. Some part of Niklas found a sliver of comfort in the fact that perhaps he wasn't entirely alone.

Slowly, reluctantly, Niklas reached forward and took Gabriel's hand.

Niklas crushed Gabriel's slender hand so tightly that his bones ground together. But if the insufferable boy felt any pain, he hid it well. Instead he offered a sharp smile, his black eyes shining with thinly veiled delight.

"Yes," Niklas agreed. "We have a deal."

If you enjoyed this book please leave an honest review where you purchased it to help new readers discover it.

ACKNOWLEDGEMENTS

This book would still be a collection of unorganized files on my computer had it not been for the help of so many people. Three in particular started out as critique partners and became dear friends.

To Rutendo, my very first critique partner, fellow writer and trusted friend. I never would have gotten past the first draft phase without your consistent kindness and encouragement.

To Victoria, whose intelligence and razor-sharp wit made me determined to not only finish this story, but make it as good as it could be.

To Helen, whose patience, willingness to work through 8 hour time zone differences, and literary knowledge helped me shape this story into the book you hold in your hands now.

A huge thank you to my editor Beth Attwood. Bless you for fixing my numerous grammatical mistakes and making this story legible.

Finally a very special thank you to Hester van Leusen, who was generous enough to lend their incredible artistic talent to this book, and bring the characters to life in a way that words alone couldn't quite achieve.

ABOUT THE AUTHOR

S.A. Christianson is a resident of British Columbia, Canada. When she's not writing about her many fictional characters, she works full time as a game developer. *An Incarnation of Shadow and Light* is her debut novel.

Made in the USA
Coppell, TX
12 February 2023

12672499R00282